Daughter of Dragons

Kathleen H. Nelson

www.dragonmoonpress.com

DEDICATION

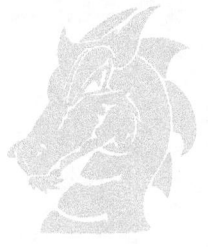

this book is dedicated to:

My father, Jerome Hall,

who always said I was a storyteller,

and who was a bit of a storyteller himself;

My mother, Frances Punska Hall,

who taught me better ways than quitting;

And,

My beloved husband, Lester David Nelson,

who has held my hand for seventeen years,

but never held me back.

PROLOGUE

The cavern floor was a sprawling tangle of necks and tails and distended bellies: eleven drowsing dragonets and their mountainous dam in post-feeding repose. The she-dragon regarded this latest brood of hers through hooded eyes, slyly spying on their dreams, then abruptly broadcast a thought.

"Attend me."

Eleven triangular heads popped up, all swivelled in her direction. Instant curiosity fired the sleepy glaze in their eyes to a high and expectant gloss. Seeing this, she rumbled her approval and then projected another thought.

"Listen carefully and remember well, for what you are about to receive is a piece of your past…"

Sunset had come and gone, signalling the end of another spring day for the villagers who dwelt on the edge of Farwild Forest. Now, in the waning moments of twilight, a procession of shadowy, slouch-shouldered figures trudged homeward. Most were farmers who reeked of sweat and freshly turned dirt, but there were a few woodsmen with axes and a swineherd as well. One by one, these shadows disappeared into squat wooden huts whose doors shuddered as they were barred for the night.

A stranger watched these tired goings-on from his hiding place in the woods. He had been watching for hours, watching and waiting for the sun to go down. He didn't like crouching in the bushes like a sack of flea-bait, but there was a great prize at stake tonight.

And he'd suffered worse indignities in his life.

As if in response to that thought, his right leg began to throb—a pain as bitter as it was familiar. He reached down and began to rub the blighted limb: first the foot that looked more like a five-toed club, then the ill-formed calf. Oh, how he hated this affliction! There was no respite from it, no relief; and together with his hideously cleft lip and two-coloured eyes, it rendered him a target for other people's abuse. He scowled, fending off a flurry of remembered blows, then consoled himself with a long-cherished pledge: some day, he was going to be the one swinging the stick.

The strip of rutted earth that served as the village's road was deserted now. He hauled himself onto his feet with his crutch, wincing as blood coursed sharp and hot back into his bad leg, then hobbled out of hiding. As soon as the pain died down again, he conjured an illusion of emptiness and set himself within it. A faint psychic chirring accompanied the spell, but he didn't care. Nobody in the immediate vicinity had the power to hear it. Of that, he was quite sure.

He followed a residual trail of his own magic to a shack on the village's outskirts. To his delight, the door was not latched. He grinned at the owner's unwitting hospitality and then prowled into the gloom beyond the threshold. Almost as an afterthought, he exerted his Will. The door closed with a soft creak, then barred itself. A fire flared to life in the hearth. Its dull yellow light exposed two rooms: a tiny cell that stank of rancid furs and a full chamber pot; and a larger common area that boasted a grimy wooden table and two sagging plank benches. Obscure symbols adorned the rough-hewn walls. Fetishes dangled from the rafters alongside braids of drying herbs. The cripple sneered at these trappings of witchcraft. They were useless, an impotent facade. Their fool of a maker should have spent his time and energy on a sturdy warding spell instead. The fool in question was sprawled face-down on the dirt floor in front of the hearth. His limbs were stiff; his skin was blue. This came as no surprise to the cripple, for he'd slain the man with magic earlier on in the day. It had been a blissfully easy kill—caught unwarded and unprepared, the warlock had succumbed to the deadly spell almost immediately. He flipped the corpse onto its back, meaning to rifle through its pockets, then tensed as its hands flopped into view. One of them was clenched around a thick ivory horn whose carvings were both intricate and obscene. Although this was the first time the cripple had ever seen it, recognition blazed through him like a wildfire. That was the talisman for which he had come a-hunting!

And this idiot had been trying to wield it like a magic wand!

He sneered at the idea. The talisman possessed power in plenty, true, but none that a mortal man might use. In the warlock's hands, it would've been no more than another gaudy prop.

But at least he didn't have to ransack the place now.

As he wrested the horn from the dead man's grip, the air in the shack began to buzz with a power not his own. Quicker than thought, he raised the shields of his Will. In the next instant, the corpse sat up and loosed a hair-raising psychic scream.

"'Ware the rogue sorcerer!" it cried. "As he has slain me, so shall he slay you! With my death, I curse him! Curse him! Curse him! May his living heart be torn from his chest and eaten before his eyes!"

Then the body collapsed back onto the floor and did not move again.

The cripple was livid. For a long moment, he could only glower at the corpse and fume. Who would have guessed that a peasant-witch would be capable of channelling the power of his own death into a post-mortem spell? The curse itself did not cause him any real distress—that had been nothing but pure bluster. But the warning that had accompanied it was irksome to an extreme. He had no clue as to how far it might travel, or how many ears it might reach before it finally dissipated. If the wrong person heard it—

He dismissed the thought with a scowl. He'd worry about that if and when it ever became a problem. Right now, he had still had work to do.

So he shrugged off his shabby wool cloak and then opened a series of inner pockets which yielded to no one's touch but his own. From these, he withdrew two golden fists, life-like down to the long, opposing thumbnails; and a pair of obsidian spurs that were cruelly curved like dew-claws. They had been shaped by the same power that had shaped the ivory horn. It had taken him almost seven years to find them all.

The sinister-handed fist had come to him first. He had stolen it from a merchant's stall with the hope of selling it to another of the fat fools. While searching for a suitable mark, though, his mind had begun to whirl—an awful spinning that had robbed him of balance and sight. Fearing plague, he had staggered into an alley to hide from those who might jump to the same conclusion and kill him for it. As he languished beneath a garbage heap, the gyre had spun itself into a voice both seductive and foul.

"Do not part with the fist," it had commanded.

Believing himself delirious, he had resisted such a notion. He needed food, warm clothes, a safe place to sleep. The gold in that fist would buy him those things, and perhaps a few coins for his pocket, too.

"The gold in your hand is nothing compared to the powers you harbour within you," the voice had said then. "Accept Me as your Mistress, and I will show you how to use those powers to get all you want from this world."

He had laughed at that. Him? Powerful? This wasn't delirium, it was outright insanity!

"I will forgive your insolence just this once, for you are ignorant. But henceforth, do not presume to question My word on anything."

Something dark and swift and sharp as a scorpion's sting had struck at the core of his mind then. At that moment, his perceptions had shifted, and he'd gotten his first glimpse of his own fell potential. And oh, what an intoxicating glimpse it had been! He would've sworn allegiance to anyone—or any thing!—who offered to show him more.

"So be it," his new Mistress had intoned. "From now on, you shall be My highest servant. If you serve Me faithfully and well, you shall have power beyond a beggar's dreams. But if you fail or forswear Me, you shall suffer as no mortal has ever suffered before."

The threat had not daunted him. His only thought had been for what he must do in order to reap his reward.

"Find the rest of My talismans," She had told him then. "The first is in your hands already. The whereabouts of the second has been placed in your head. When it is safely in your custody, use your newfound knowledge to summon Me again. At that time, I will give you further instructions. Hunt in secret; no one must know what you are seeking or why. Most importantly, no one must know Whom you serve. Go now, and do My bidding."

With that, the voice had withdrawn. Shortly thereafter, he had started his quest for the talismans. His journey had taken him all across the continent: from the desert plains of the southlands to the gulf of the fresh water sea; to steamy Cos province and now to the edge of Farwild Forest. In each instance, he'd tracked down a single talisman, never knowing what it was until he saw it. And in each instance, he had found it in the possession of a person who practiced some style of magic.

He knew very well that this was no coincidence. One of the fundamental dictates of sorcery was that power attracted power. At times, this inevitability lent a certain amount of convenience to his quest. But at others, he thought, turning to scowl at the warlock's body again, it was an outright pain in the ass.

Then he swept the grudge from his mind. There was still much to do before the night was over, and no one to do it but him.

His first task was to ward the shack—not a complicated procedure, but taxing in terms of time and energy. And while he begrudged both expenditures, he dared not stint on either, for without wards, he would become conspicuous to any and all who could hear the resonations of his magic. And the sorcery which he meant to perform tonight was especially loud. So he swallowed his reluctance without another thought and began to construct the barriers that would insulate him from the rest of the world.

When he was done, he returned to the table and sat down. He was hungry now as well as tired, but aside from a plate of souring milk that the dead man had left by the hearth, there was nothing in sight to eat—not even the resident mouser. Just as well, he told himself. Cat meat gave him gas.

After an all-too-brief rest, he retrieved a chunk of charcoal bone from the inner lining of his cloak and moved from the table to an uncluttered section of the room. There, he sketched a hexagram onto the hard dirt floor and enclosed it within a circle. Next he placed the talismans within the diagram: the horn at the lowest point, flanked by the spurs, and then the two fists. The crowning point remained vacant. Finished with the preliminaries, he then drew himself to his full height in front of the diagram and began to chant: hard, arcane words that caught at his mouth like fishing hooks. He did not falter at the pain; it was part of the mantra, both a token sacrifice and a focus.

As he chanted, an eddy appeared within the circle; a cloud of charcoal dust lent it texture and mass. Encouraged by his litany, it then spiraled into a ceiling-high funnel, spinning so fast as to seem motionless. At the core of this maelstrom, two eyes winked into view—red pupil-less slits which flashed like flowing lava. Brimming with excitement, he forced the last of the incantation from his now bloody mouth.

For a long moment, a ghastly silence prevailed. Then a maw fringed with dagger-like teeth chasmed into being. The wind which gusted forth from it smelled as foul as a thousand sun-ripened corpses.

"I expected you sooner than this, Malcolm Blackheart," his Mistress intoned, although Her mouth did not pattern the words. "Did you encounter difficulties along the way?"

"None at all, my Queen," he said, purposely foregoing any mention the warlock's death-spell. It had been nothing more than a trifling annoyance, too insignificant to recount. Besides, it had not delayed his quest in any way. "If I am slow in realizing Your expectations, it is because my powers are still limited."

"Some limits cannot be overcome," She told him, a reply steeped in supernatural indifference.

"Quite true," he countered unctuously. "But they can, at times, be circumvented."

"Say how."

"A host of your demons at my beck and call would give me a mobility that I could never hope to achieve on my own," he replied, trying to sound blasé about this nearest and dearest dream of his. "They'd also serve as extra eyes and ears."

"A curious notion," She said. "I will consider it. Now let us address the next leg of your quest. It will take you in pursuit of the last and greatest of My talismans."

"I am Yours to command, Mistress," he replied, although his heart was still set on the subject of demons. "Where must I go?"

Her unblinking gaze turned suddenly remote. At the same time, Her cyclone lost a measure of velocity. These changes didn't alarm him. From past experience, He knew that She was straddling another dimension in an attempt to divine his next destination.

"How strange," She murmured, when She returned from this excursion. "I saw a man-city ringed by tall white walls. I saw you stealing down its littered streets, hunting a being possessed of powers similar to your own. But beyond that, I saw little else—the augury was overshadowed by confusion and strife."

Spooked by the uncertainty which he heard in Her tone, he hastened to reassure her. "I know the city of which You speak, Great One. It is called Compara. To those who dwell within its wall, confusion and strife are common maladies—maladies which could aid a clever man."

Sly amusement crept into her laval eyes. "A man such as yourself?"

"None other," he replied. "Have no doubt, Great One. I will find the talisman for You."

"That would not be your only task, Blackheart."

"As well I know, Great One," he boasted. "Once I have the talisman, I must bring You back from exile. That will be a prodigious feat of sorcery, but—"

Her eyes flashed, a warning that raised the hackles on his neck. Before he could brace himself for the onslaught of Her displeasure, though, the blood in his veins turned into liquid fire. For one excruciating moment, pain defined the whole of his existence. Then it abruptly disappeared again.

"Never interrupt Me again, mortal," She commanded, as he gagged for breath, "for what you know is no more or less than what I choose to tell you. Yes, as you pointed out, you will have to work high sorcery to forge a bridge between these two planes. But—" She spat the word out like a gob of phlegm. "But before you do that, you must first find a body for Me to occupy. It must be a living body; one which possesses powers that are at least the equivalent of your own. I do not care what it looks like so long as it is healthy and not too old."

"I know you could retrieve the talisman for Me, Malcolm Blackheart. But are you clever enough to procure the body I need as well?"

"I believe so, Great One," he replied, the very essence of humility now.

"One without the other will not do," She cautioned. "If you fail to provide Me with a suitable vessel, I will have no recourse but to claim yours. Knowing that, do you still wish to go to Compara?"

He nodded. The promise of power was worth any risk.

"So be it then. You shall go." A familiar touch snaked into his mind, then deftly withdrew again. "I have given you knowledge that might prove useful to you. Use it wisely, and as ever, be discreet. No one must learn of our plans."

"I will do as you say," he swore. Then, emboldened by Her generosity, he dared to importune Her again. "Great One! There is one thing more!" Her glare raised an uncomfortable itch along the base of his throat. He suppressed the urge to scratch it. "Will you give me the demons?"

"You shall have them. But not now," She added, upending the smile that had started to take hold of his mouth. "Dawn will be here soon. You must leave this place before someone comes calling on yonder carrion."

"Go to Compara. Find yourself a stronghold and ward it with all your skill. Then summon Me again and I shall grant your desire."

"I shall leave immediately, Great One," he replied, all eagerness and unction again. Such a deferment spoiled his hopes for an easy trip to Compara, but that was no setback, only a minor disappointment. "Many thanks for—"

Her eyes snapped shut. Her maw disappeared as well. An instant later, the cyclone redoubled its furious dance. Yet even as it accelerated, its extremities unravelled, stripping the funnel to its core of swirling charcoal dust. A moment later, the dust spiralled to a lazy stop and then flurried to the floor.

In the preternatural silence that followed, he smiled. Despite his hunger and fatigue, despite the unrelenting ache in his leg, he was as happy as he had ever been in his life. Still smiling, he fetched his cloak and stowed the talismans in their secret compartments. Then he recast his illusion of emptiness and headed for the door. He did not bother to wipe away his handiwork: anyone who saw it would credit the dead man with its making.

At his touch, the door unbarred itself, then swung open. He stepped into the night, then took a series of deep breaths to purge The Dark One's lingering stench from his nostrils.

At that moment, a small, four-legged shadow slunk out of the house and raced away without drawing his notice.

CHAPTER 1

As Lathwi padded down the cool stone passageway, echoes of her calloused footfalls scampered off in both directions. She walked with purpose, but not haste; and while the ochre gleam of rock light limned her path, she could have as easily found her way in pitch darkness. She was heading toward her mother's favourite chamber—a chamber which few others were privileged to visit. Lathwi had spent the better part of her short life in there.

The entrance to that chamber loomed to her right. Even though she had no doubt that Taziem had heard her coming long before now, she cleared her throat just the same, for it was never smart to surprise a full-grown dragon. Especially when that dragon was ensconced in a den full of diamonds.

Her mother's nest was resplendent, a veritable glacier of blue-white stones. A single glimpse of it inspired envy and awe in equal measure. Yet it was nothing but a trifling heap of pebbles compared to the black-scaled dragon who was lounging in its midst. She was magnificent: twice as tall as Lathwi at the shoulder, nearly ten times as long from head to tail, yet sleek and streamlined, an aeronautical wonder. The great membranous wings which carried her through the sky were folded now, all but invisible against the span of her sinuous back; and her whip-like tail was daintily coiled around her. Both sets of eyelids were closed.

As Lathwi waited to be received by the she-dragon, she projected a self-thought at her. On one level, it was merely a reiteration of her arrival; on another, it poked sly fun at her mother by insinuating that her senses were not as keen as they used to be. Lathwi took great pride and delight in her skills with dragon-speech. To her, well-wrought images were as pleasing as diamonds.

Although Taziem's eyes were shut and she had not yet deigned to acknowledge Lathwi's presence, she was not asleep. Indeed, she was busily contemplating Lathwi's last thought—the latest illustration of her bizarre imagination. To most dragons, nothing was more pleasing than diamonds. Even she, The Learned One, an advocate of logic and intellect, admired them to an extreme. And it would never have occurred to her to compare the star-like stones with something as dissimilar as dragon-speech. Yet now that she considered the notion, she saw how such a comparison might be drawn: both possessed a multi-faceted beauty which ranged from subtle to raw, both contained images for others to contemplate. The tip of her tail twitched approvingly. Clever Lathwi.

Her eyelids opened to slits, affording her a covert view of her unlikely daughter. She was a runt, magnitudes smaller and weaker than any dragon. She was also wingless, tailless and nearly neckless; dull of tooth and nail; and appallingly tender-skinned. The supple shell of scales which she wore to preserve herself against the casual violence of other dragons had originally belonged to a tanglemate who had lost its life to a fall. The claws she carried with her were cast-offs as well.

Lathwi, The Soft One. It was an appropriate Name.

A memory flooded her awareness. In it, she was sunning herself in a meadow far from her usual hunting grounds. Her belly was swollen to monstrous proportions by a mad feeding binge and the clutch of unborn dragonets which had prompted such gluttony. Tomorrow she would have to return to her nest and stay there until she gave birth. She rumbled to herself, deploring that last and most tedious phase of pregnancy, then abruptly dismissed it from her thoughts. She did not intend to let tomorrow's woes spoil today's last snooze in the sun.

Her eyelids closed—the transparent inners first, then the scaled outers. Yet even as she began to drowse, a faint, arrhythmic thrashing dragged her back to awareness. The sound was not alarming, so she did not shift out of her comfortable pose, but she did continue to listen. The noise drew closer, then closer still. The sour stench of a red-blooded animal's sweat invaded her nose. This smell continued to foul the air long after the thrashing retreated. Curious, she raised her outer lids a notch and surreptitiously scanned the area. To her vast surprise, she found a human youngling staring at her from less than a dragon's length away.

Her curiosity flared like an itch in need of scratching. Never one to deny such impulses, she proceeded to study the creature.

Its eyes were its most remarkable feature. They were a glorious shade of blue, the colour of a cloudless summer sky; a dragon could almost take wing within them. But apart from those intriguing orbs, there was not much to see. It was a scrawny thing with a black mane and pale flesh. Its forearms were caught behind its back, seemingly entangled around a fat length of wood. A ring of wilted flowers hung from its neck.

Taziem was quick to grasp the youngling's significance: it was meant for her. She snorted, venting her scorn. What purpose was such a gift supposed to serve? She had already slaked her pre-birthing hunger, and so had no need for more food. And even if it had been otherwise, so scant a morsel would not have satisfied the least twinges of that boundless appetite. She eyed the youngling again, no longer bothering to disguise her scrutiny. In response, it gurgled something unintelligible and then displayed its flat white teeth.

The gesture intrigued Taziem. She had no doubt that the youngling was frightened, for its fear was as pungent as its sweat. Yet few of any race, her own included, had dared to meet her gaze so boldly. Prompted by this contradiction, she delved through her memory for more information on humans. One of her tanglemates maintained that they were dumber than cattle; her chosen, Bij, despised them as thieves. But that was all hearsay. The only things she knew for certain about humans were that they were a noisy bunch, and not very tasty.

Such ignorance was intolerable! She was Taziem, The Learned One; it was her lot in life to know more than other dragons. She decided then and there to bring the youngling back to her nest and study it during the last stages of her pregnancy. If it proved to be an enlightening subject, she would let it go just before the birth. Otherwise, she would feed it to her newborns.

Eager to begin her research, she lurched to her feet and overtook the youngling. It was then that she discovered that its arms were not entangled behind its back, but deliberately bound. She hissed, wholly insulted by the implications. Did those who had left it for her really think that she could not have caught it otherwise? She hissed again, half-inclined to go and teach the fools a much-needed lesson, but then decided to save it for another day. Right now, she had the youngling to consider.

With a delicate swipe of her claws, she freed its arms. It yowled as the log thudded to the ground, but made no move to escape. Taziem hugged its feather-light body to her great chest, then unfurled her wings and invoked the secret Name of Wind. Aided by an obliging breeze, she then vaulted into the sky. Pride coursed through her veins like fire as she soared beyond the meadow and toward the distant jut of her mountain. She was Taziem, a dragon in flight—for the moment, nothing else mattered or sufficed. She celebrated that fact with an aerial dance, then bugled her joy to the world.

At that, the youngling loosed a squeal that defied its small size. Although she was sure that it was merely venting its fright, Taziem swung her long neck around to investigate. What she saw then amazed her. Its mouth was stretched into a toothy grin, its blue eyes were focussed on some faraway point in the sky. As she watched, it squealed again—a sound of pleasure rather than fear.

So, she thought, the youngling liked to fly. Therefore, it had more intelligence than a cow. The distinction pleased and encouraged her. At this rate, she would know all there was to know about humans before the sun went down.

A whisper of movement in the chamber drew Taziem out of the memory. She returned to her covert scrutiny of Lathwi, who was still waiting to be acknowledged. She could not be faulted for her patience, the she-dragon granted. Or for her cleverness. Many a dragon had survived fortune's whims with no more than those two traits in their favour. But Lathwi had an extra advantage: Lathwi was smart. It was hard to believe that such a runt could possess so voracious an intellect, but the evidence was irrefutable. Long after her tanglemates had lost their appetites for learning and gone in search of other diversions, she was still living in Taziem's caves and coming to her for morsels of lore. Curious as to how much she could retain, Taziem had let her stay.

Until now.

"*Lathwi.*" The image which accompanied the thought was deliberately harsh: soft and pink like prey. "*Why are you here?*"

Lathwi's eyes narrowed. Her mother was not in the habit of questioning the obvious. Therefore, something strange was afoot.

"*I am here for knowledge,*" she replied warily.

"Know this then. It is time for you to leave."

Too shocked for subtle speech, she blurted, "Why? I have not yet learned all there is to learn."

Taziem snorted. "That is certain. Not even I can lay claim to such an accomplishment, and I have been studying for centuries. But that is irrelevant. Tomorrow you must take your leave of my caves and go in search of your own fortune."

"*Why?*" Lathwi asked again.

A view of her teeth and claws was the only explanation that Taziem would have bothered to give to anyone else. But she had often times made exceptions for Lathwi because she was wingless and weak. Today she would do so again.

"I am almost ready to mate again," she said, flashing her an image of two dragons entwined in mid-flight. "Bij is on his way. If he finds you here, he will eat you."

"I will stay away while he is here," she said, twitching her shoulders up and then down to show her unconcern. "When he leaves, I will come back. It will be like the last time. Remember?"

Taziem rumbled to herself. Impertinent sprat. Despite her age, her memory was superb. And she remembered the last time all too well.

Shortly after they arrived at Taziem's nest, Taziem made a most astonishing discovery: the youngling could mind-speak! Its imagery was crude, true, but still the ability was there. This wholly unexpected sign of higher intelligence fanned her interest in humans into an academic frenzy.

The youngling, too, became excited. Using gestures and a sort of infantile dragon patois, it told her that its own kind communicated strictly with their mouths; and that they did not like or want it near them simply because it was able to hear thoughts other than its own. It went on to tell her that it liked it here in these caves; that it thought Taziem was a marvellous creature; and that it was not an it at all, but a female who had been born that way.

So the hours began to pass, one right after the other; and for Taziem at least, it was a time of perfect bliss. For not only did the youngling gladly answer her every question, she strove to please in other areas as well. She scratched itches that Taziem could not easily reach; rubbed the kinks from idle-sore muscles; applied her body's own diffuse heat to joints that a gravid circulation had left swollen and cold. Taziem quickly grew fond of such pampering. Indeed, it was that fondness which persuaded her to let Lathwi stay and help as she claimed she could when the birthing finally began.

How convenient it would be to have to that kind of help again! How absolutely luxurious.

"No," she replied firmly, addressing herself as well as Lathwi. "If you came too early, Bij might still be here or I might be in the throes of the pre-birthing hunger. In either event, you would most likely wind up as dragon meat."

"What if I came later—perhaps after the birth?"

"No. If you are not here when the dragonets are born, then they will not recognize you later on. And if they do not recognize you, they will try to eat you."

"And if I came after the hunger but before the birth?"

Taziem rumbled a warning. "Lathwi, you are stretching my patience toward its limit today. Perhaps you were meant to see the lining of a dragon's belly after all."

Lathwi exposed her throat, inviting the she-dragon's teeth. "It would be a privilege, Mother. That is far from the worst fortune that could befall me."

The image-thought was laced through and through with sincerity; all camouflage for a single strand of laughter. A perfect response, Taziem mused to herself. Too perfect. Her study had taken a slow and unintentional turn over the years. As a result, the only thing still human about Lathwi was her feeble form.

"Get your stumpy neck out of my face," Taziem rumbled irritably. "You are not worth the trouble that it would take to swallow you."

"Then may I know why I cannot come after the hunger and before the birth?"

"Because bonds formed at birth last a lifetime," she replied, a grudging tribute to her fosterling's persistence. "Members of the same tangle know each other by their secret Names. In times of need, they can Call upon those Names for aid."

"I would welcome another set of tanglemates."

"So would any reasonable dragon. But why should you have an advantage that the rest of us do not?"

"Ah, I see now." A flush raced across the plains of her dragon-scarred cheeks—a display of distress that she could neither hide nor control. *"Then I can never return."*

"Your logic is sloppy." The thought was quilled with scorn. "Bij and his offspring will go their own ways in due time. You may return then if it pleases you."

"Time." She curled her lip at the concept. "Only a hungry dragon counts the hours. How will I know when you are finally free to teach me again?"

"I will Call you," she said, working the last half of the reassurance around a massive yawn.

Lathwi barely noticed the she-dragon's chasming jaws or the oddly delicate curl of her snake-ish tongue. Her thoughts were hollow, and all for herself. *"What shall I do between now and then?"*

"That," Taziem replied, yawning again, "is none of my concern, so long as you do it far from here."

She shifted onto her belly, then deliberately closed her eyes. Lathwi stared at her for a moment longer, then turned to leave the chamber. Quite by accident, a displaced diamond lodged between her toes. Instead of shaking it loose as she had done so many times in the past, she clenched her toes and continued on to the outer caves without so much as a hitch in her stride. There, she stopped to examine her prize. It was not a diamond at all, she discovered then, but only a reddish stone. Although it did not appeal to her, she popped it into her mouth anyway, because a thing that had belonged to Taziem qualified as a thing worth keeping.

Then she went outside and retired to her favourite sunlit rock. Almost as an afterthought, she Voiced a Name.

The narrow landing that prefixed Taziem's caves spanned sharply into view. The bronze dragon circled the spot twice, then touched down upon its smooth rock surface and furled his wings. Before he could announce his presence, a shadow came bounding down the mountain's side and toward him.

Delight took wing within him. Lathwi! Out of all his tanglemates, he liked her best. He extended his neck as she drew near, and then gently touched noses with her. Her scent was pungent and dry like a dragon's, yet sweetly spiced with animal musk and red blood. It thrilled him for reasons which he did not bother to define.

A thought danced into his head. *"Shoq! You came!"*

"You Called," he replied.

As always, her size surprised him. How could she be so small? When he pictured her in his mind, she was almost as big as Taziem.

"Are you never going to grow?" he asked.

"I do not believe so." She rolled her shoulders to show her unconcern, then stepped back to get a better look at him. A moment later, her strange blue eyes flared with approval. *"I am glad to see that you are not suffering from the same affliction. If you continue to grow at this rate, you will be the*

rival of any sire in less than a century."

"*It is true,*" came his thought, all puffed with pride. "*I am large for my age.*" He swatted her with his forearm, a playful cuff which tumbled her to the ground. "*Perhaps that is because I am so quick: a quick dragon gets all it wants to eat.*"

"*Perhaps.*" With cat-like dignity, she picked herself up. "*Or perhaps it is because you are nothing but a giant bladder of gas.*" She punched his sensitive nose then. His surprised hiss prompted her to add, "*A bladder that leaks.*"

He roared with appreciation. As small as she was, she was still every inch a dragon.

"*Shhh, you will wake Taziem,*" she cautioned. "*If she finds me here, she will eat me.*" He glanced furtively toward the mouth of the cave, then arched his neck into an unspoken query.

In response, she said, "*She wishes me gone.*"

"*Ah.*" He did not ask why; it was none of his concern. "*Then we had best be off.*"

He spread his forearms, exposing the junctures between limb and body. These were a young dragon's soft spots, for the scales here were slow to mesh. She toyed with the idea of tickling those spots, but decided to postpone the attack until such time as she could enjoy his bellows of protest without fear of waking Taziem. Then, because she could not avoid the moment any longer, she backed into her tanglemate's embrace. As his forearms closed around her, she turned her eyes away from the mouth of her mother's caves.

"*Go,*" she told him.

He coiled into a crouch. His wings unfurled with a leathery snap. With a powerful thrust of his hind legs, he catapulted them into the sky. Then a slipstream of cold mountain air whisked them away from Taziem's fang-like spire and toward the shaggy-pined slopes of lesser peaks. Lathwi watched the world pass beneath her with disbelieving eyes.

"Where do you want to go?" Shoq asked.

"I do not know," she replied. "Could we just fly for a while?"

In response, he aligned himself with an outgoing wind.

The mountains subsided, giving way to scruffy foothills; as the day passed, these flattened into a forest. High above this sea of still-brown treetops, Shoq began to dance. As lithe as an otter in spite of his bulk, he favoured backward loops and dizzying, headlong spirals; but for variety's sake, he also chased his tail and ran a zig-zagging race with his shadow. Although he was dancing strictly for himself, his exuberant antics dispelled Lathwi's gloom. The feel of wind bracing her skin and gravity tugging at her guts stirred wild feelings within her. She might be caveless now, but she was still a dragon! Brimming with fierce pride, she shrieked for all the world to hear.

Shoq matched her cry with a roar of his own, then shot straight up into the sky. Higher and higher he climbed, his great wings straining for speed. His goal seemed to be the heart of a cloud. Lathwi's blood began to pound in her ears, her breath caught in her throat like a bone. Then, just as her vision began to fade, he abruptly folded his wings and plunged toward the ground. Her vision returned, but only as a blur, her stomach crowded her heart. The forest's skeletal canopy expanded, then expanded again, blotting all else from view. In spite of herself, she tensed, anticipating impact. Then Shoq pulled out of his headlong dive, so close to the trees that a few of the tallest branches tickled the soles of her feet.

Still panting from the excitement, she urged him to do it again. Tired now, he pretended not to hear.

"Were you frightened?" he asked, as they coasted along on the breeze which he had surreptitiously invoked.

"Not at all," she replied.

"What if I had dropped you?"

"Then I would have flown by myself."

"For a little while."

They flew on in silence, heading west simply because that was the way the wind wanted to go. As their journey progressed, the top of the forest sprouted a faint green nimbus which seemed to shimmer in the sun's waning light. Then a meadow spanned below them; it was dotted with the backs of grazing deer. The sight provoked a rumble from Lathwi's belly.

"Are you hungry?" she asked. The image with which he answered her was one of vast emptiness. She directed his attention toward the herd. *"Shall we hunt?"*

"*We shall,*" he crooned, and cut a high, wide circle back toward the meadow's edge. There, he swooped down on the herd with a roar, panicking its members into a helter-skelter dash for the trees on the far side of the field. Then he overtook a fat young buck and dropped Lathwi squarely on its back.

The deer's legs buckled as she slammed into it. Before it could recover its footing and shake her off, she seized its antlers with both hands and wrenched its head sharply to one side. Bones popped. The body she was straddling went suddenly limp. As it started to collapse, she vaulted to the ground. And by the time Shoq circled back around again and landed, she had already split its carcass from breastbone to groin with one of her dragon claws.

"Which do you want—the heart or the liver?" she asked.

"I want them both," he said, eying the carcass greedily.

Because it was bigger, she tossed him the liver. He snapped the hunk of dripping flesh out of the air, gobbled it down without chewing and then resumed his unblinking scrutiny of the stag's remains. Then, because it was not wise to keep a hungry dragon waiting for his meat, she hastily excised the heart and the better part of a hindquarter.

"The rest is yours," she told him, and then hauled her portion toward a patch of untrampled grass. When she was out of Shoq's immediate sight, she spat her purloined stone onto the ground, then sat down and began to feed.

The meat was tender and warm, an orgy of stomach-pleasing flavours. She tore into it with her teeth and nails, pausing now and again to slurp at the salty-sweet juices which were running down her arms and chin. The sounds of her feasting mingled with those of Shoq's. Like her, he ate noisily, and with gusto.

Twilight came and went while she fed, but she took no note of the darkening sky until there was nothing left of her feast except scraps of hide and raw white bone. She belched, welcoming the advent of night, then began to clean herself—first licking the stickiness from her hands, then rolling in the grass to scour her scales. By the time she was done, the heaviness in her belly had spread to her limbs and eyelids. Without further thought, she curled into a comfortable ball and promptly went to sleep.

A raven's distant caw roused her from her dreams. She opened her eyes to find a new day in full bloom. She wrung the last vestiges of sleep from her veins with a full-body stretch, then pawed through the grass for her stone. Finding it, she then rubbed it clean with her fingers and returned it to its hiding place beneath her tongue. Ready for the world now, she stood up and looked for Shoq. He was stretched out in a nearby patch of grass, his great belly angled toward the sun.

A mischievous grin curved across her mouth. Here was an opportunity too good to forego! Silent as a cat, she started to stalk her tanglemate. He stirred in his dreams. She sank down into a crouch and then pounced. As she slammed into the mound of his belly, her fingers burrowed into the soft spots beneath his arms.

His outraged bellow set a flock of birds to wing. His retaliatory swat sent her tumbling backward into the grass. Pealing with laughter, she bounced to her feet. An instant later, he bowled her over again. She rammed her fist into his nose, then got up and started to run away. With a flick of his tail, he tripped her. So they played, oblivious to all else, until she was too spent from laughter and abuse to get up from the dirt. Suspecting a trick, he thumped her one last time. When she did not avenge herself, he settled down next to her and rumbled contentedly.

"*That*," he said, his amber eyes glittering, "*was fun. What do you want to do next?*"

She rolled onto her back and stared at the sky as if divining for clues to her future. She knew what she wanted to do: she wanted to return to Taziem's caves and sleep off the post-sporting stiffness that was creeping into her limbs. Then, when she woke again, she wanted to resume her lessons. She knew these wants were impractical, but she could think of nothing else with which to replace them.

"I do not know what I want to do," she finally admitted. "I must give the matter some thought."

His contented rumble slurred to a stop. "*Thinking is no doubt what you do best,*" he said, shading the thought with traces of a reproach. "*I, however, have no stomach for it.*"

He lurched to his feet. She stood up as well, then reached for his head and touched noses with him. She did not want him to leave, but could not think of a reason for him to stay.

"*You know my Name,*" he said, projecting a blend of rue and resignation at her. "*Call me if you are in need. Or if you want to play.*"

"You know my Name as well," she replied. "If you Call, I will come."

He nodded, then withdrew a half-dozen steps and unfurled his wings. The motion sent a sudden swirl of dirt and grass her way. She closed her eyes. When she opened them again, her tanglemate was already a soaring bronze glint in the sky.

She lay back down in the grass and began to think. Presently, she fell asleep again.

The tapping of raindrops against her eyelids rousted her from her slumber. She sat up, then scowled as she glanced at the sky. A solid mass of dark grey clouds portended rain for days to come. She thought of Taziem, all snug and dry in her caves. She imagined herself there, too, then hissed at such pointless longings. Past fortunes were not going to stop the rain from dripping down her neck. She would do better to get up and seek out new ones.

So she abandoned the meadow for the span of trees beyond it. But while the forest offered her a modicum of protection against the gusting wind, its sparse spring canopy did little to deflect the rain. It was pouring now—a cold, relentless deluge. As she rambled through the woods in search of a nook or cranny big enough to shelter her, the muddy ground sucked the warmth out of her through the soles of her bare feet.

The day waned, but the storm did not. By now, Lathwi was thoroughly miserable. Her search for refuge had taken one frustrating turn after another by day's light; and she knew all too well that it would only get worse in the dark. She wanted to leave this awful place, to fly away and never come back. Now more than ever, she deplored the accident of birth that had left her wingless. Yet even as she bemoaned her ill fortune, the cloying smells of rain and sodden earth were suddenly joined by the faintest tang of wood-smoke. She hissed, recognizing Fire's breath. And where there was fire, there would be heat! An eager shiver scudded down her spine. Nostrils flared, she began to track the exhilarating fumes.

Dusk came and went, leaving her in darkness, but she did not quit the hunt. She followed the gradient through a stand of oaks, over a knoll and into a tiny glen. There, the smoke thickened into tendrils of pungent white fog which led her to a most peculiar wooden structure.

The sight confused Lathwi. For all of its strangeness, it seemed hauntingly familiar. She slowed to a stop in front of the structure, then stared at it, trying to dredge answers from her memory. The pelting rain stung her face and hands, but she barely noticed. Where had she seen this thing? What was its significance?

From out of nowhere, a word popped into her head: house. With it came a fragment of information—the longish square of yellow light outlined an entrance.

Although the recollection pleased her, she was far from satisfied. How did she know this? And why had she forgotten it until now? She stepped up to the outline and touched the planks which defined its shape; the wood was gloriously warm, heated from within. It dawned on her then: this was a place of power! That power had already drawn one secret from her. If she went inside, perhaps it would draw others. And even if it did not, at least she would be out of the rain.

She gave the planked outline a gentle shove. It did not budge. She tried again, more forcefully this time, but again it resisted her. Annoyed now, she stepped back, then dropped her shoulder and slammed into it with all her draconic might. The sound of splintering wood filled her ears. At the same instant, the barrier gave way and momentum slung her through the sudden opening. As she scrambled to regain her balance, a myriad of hot, concentrated smells blasted her in the face. She hissed, venting her surprise.

"Be gone, thief! There's nothing for you here!"

Lathwi pivoted toward the raucous sound, but her alarm melted into surprise as she spied its source. A human! He was standing in a far corner, his back pressed to the wall. His muddy brown eyes were wide with fright. He twitched a flat, shiny thing in her direction. The hand which held it was trembling.

"Go away, I tell you. Don't force me to use this!" Fascinated, she continued to study him. An abundance of reddish fur framed his pointed face; it shaded his eyes and upper lip as well as his lower jaw, giving him the aspect of a shaggy fox. His body was covered with a variety of animal skins. He was small, more than a head shorter than her, and scrawny. She stepped toward him, curious to see if he was as soft as he looked.

"I won't warn you again, thief! Be gone!"

His squawking rankled her ears. She projected a command at him: *be silent*! But the thought left no impression in his mind. Her curiosity soared. Did humans not mind-speak? She took another step, meaning to test him again at closer range.

With a strangled cry, he hurled the thing in his hand at her. It thudded against her scaled shoulder, then rebounded away and onto the wooden floor. Attracted by its shininess, she picked it up. Its shape reminded her of the dragon claws that she wore cinched at her waist, but in other ways, it was like no claw that she had ever seen. Its upper half was thin and flat, almost flexible; and its edges were as sharp as the point. The lower half was solid, agreeably thick; and felt comfortable in her hand.

"Who are you? What do you want?"

She wandered over to the tame little fire in the far wall to escape the moisture-laden wind that was blowing in through the hole that she had made. There, she sat down and resumed her examination of the not-claw. By the fire's soft light, it gleamed hunter's moon gold—the precise colour of Taziem's eyes. It was an auspicious omen.

"Answer me, dammit! What do you want?"

Lathwi scowled at the human, annoyed by his incessant chatter. His face was flushed and puckered, a comical sight; his hands were frustrated knots. He was hovering just beyond her reach like a gnat in need of swatting. She wondered what he could possibly want from her.

"Look, you. I don't know where you think you are, but this is my house, and I'm not going to—"

She cut him off with an excited hiss. House! That was the sound for this place! She remembered something else now, too—she had once been able to make these sounds! She raked her mind for other scraps of this awkward, unlovely language, but encountered only mystified silence. It was then that she realized why fortune had led her here: she was meant to study the human tongue! It made perfect sense now that she thought about it—while exiled among the land – bound, it would behoove her to speak as they did. Furthermore, this fox-like little man must be her new teacher. Why else would he be squawking at her so excitedly?

Eager to get on with the lesson which he had obviously already begun, she caught his eye with a flick of her wrist and then motioned him toward the patch of fire-warmed floor directly in front of her. His eyes narrowed, betraying his apprehension, but he made no move to join her. Instead, he folded his arms over his chest and glowered down at her.

"What happens if I decline your invitation?"

Although she did not understand the sounds, his stance was unmistakable. He was testing her. She responded to his challenge in true dragon style. She thumped her chest, then gnashed her teeth and then crooked a finger at his heart.

His reddened cheeks turned suddenly white. He glanced toward the opening that she had made, groaned at the rain that was pouring down beyond it, and then returned his gaze to her. A moment later, he grudgingly lowered himself onto the floor.

"Now what?" This time, the sounds left his mouth as a snarl instead of a squawk.

She pointed at him, then worked her jaws, pantomiming speech. The little man rolled his eyes.

"Dreamer! If this isn't the strangest night of my life, then I'll cheerfully die tomorrow. First you burst in on me like some storybook demon come to life and threaten to eat me if I don't join you on the floor, then you want me to talk! Who in hell do you think you are?"

She had trouble assimilating the torrent of sounds. The only time her jaws opened and shut that fast was when she was feeding. Still, she endeavoured to repeat the few sounds that she had managed to grasp. The stone in her mouth garbled her first attempt, so she spat it out and set it down next to the not-claw, then tried again.

"Who you?"

The man's brow furrowed with annoyance, and for a moment, she feared that her attempt at man-speech had offended him. But then, still scowling, he thumped his chest and said, "I am called Pieter. Pieter the Trapper."

"Pieter," she echoed. This time, she had no doubt as to what had been said. He had given her his say-name—the one that had no power. "Piterzatrapper."

He nodded, then pointed a firm finger at her. "Now it's your turn, stranger. Who the hell are you?"

She paused for a moment, trying to translate the nuances of her self-image into one coarse sound. "Lathwi," she said, at last. "I Lathwi."

"That doesn't tell me much," Pieter grumbled, although the crease in his forehead grew less severe. He nibbled on the fringes of his mustache, baffled by this uninvited guest. From this distance, he could see that she was a woman, but there was nothing even remotely feminine about her. She was well over six feet tall and at least two hundred pounds, with muscle accounting for every ounce as far as he could tell. Her face was angular and lean, criss-crossed with a multitude of scars; and any hair that she might have was hidden beneath the hood which was an extension of her peculiar black mail. She was, he thought, one of the most fearsome sights that he had ever beheld. Yet in spite her barbarous appearance and horrifying threats, there was something oddly ingenuous about her.

If only he knew what she wanted from him!

"Who?" she asked then, pointing at the fire in the hearth. Her voice was as shrill as a bird of prey's, yet unnervingly sibilant. The sound of it sent goose-pimples racing down his back.

"Fire," he said.

She repeated the word, then pointed to the blade which she had not yet returned.

"Knife," he said.

Again she pointed, then again and again. Each time, he fed her a word.

"Floor. Log. Kettle. Stew—food," he appended, when she crinkled her jut of a nose at the kettle's reddish brown contents. To prove it, he fished a chunk of venison from the pot and popped it into his mouth. Her look remained dubious, so he gestured for her to do the same.

She complied. The thick brown fluid burned her fingers, and the chunk-thing burned her mouth, so she spit everything back into the pot without a second thought. Sure that he was testing her, she then hissed, "Not food."

His astonished look pleased her. Clearly, he had not been expecting her to be so astute. Eager to continue, she then pointed to the next curiosity. "Who?"

"Bed," Pieter replied, and then scowled at his uninvited guest. "And speaking of which, it's time for me to turn in. You know, sleep." He folded his hands against his cheek and closed his eyes. "You're welcome to stay here for the night, but I've only got one bed, and it's mine."

To his relief, she showed no interest in contesting his claim, but simply curled up in front of the fire. "Sleep," she hissed at him. To his ears, it sounded like a command.

Muttering at her seemingly endless supply of nerve, he got up and shut the door. But it didn't fit quite right in the jamb anymore; and the wind came shrilling in through the resulting cracks. His scowl deepened. He was never going to be able to sleep with that racket in his ears! He glanced at Lathwi, fully expecting her to apologize for the damage she had wrought. To his profound annoyance, she was already fast asleep.

A clap of thunder rattled the cabin, shaking Pieter from his slumber. His mood, already rancid from a fitful night's sleep, spoiled even further as he glanced toward the hearth. Lathwi was still there, softly snoring into the floorboards. The wetness which gleamed on her mail told him that she had been out and back at least once already. He grumbled at her sneakiness, then slung himself out of bed and went outside to relieve himself. Afterward, he tramped over to a nearby shed to tend to his mule.

When he returned, all sopping from the rain, Lathwi was awake. She greeted him with an unnerving grin, then pointed at the door.

"Who?"

"Save your questions for later!" he snapped, as he wrung the water from his beard. "I've got more important things to do right now."

Although she did not understand the sounds, she knew by his tone that he was not ready to begin the lesson yet. That did not bother her—Taziem had taught her how to be patient. She curled herself back into a comfortable ball to watch and wait. Meanwhile, Pieter stirred the fire's dying embers with a blackened rod and fed it a handful of sticks. Then he took the kettle full of awful not-food outside and came back with sweet-smelling water. Later, when the water started to boil, he scooped a portion of it into a wooden bowl and sprinkled desiccated grass over its surface. The rising steam turned suddenly fragrant. He sniffed at these vapours for a moment, then lifted the bowl to his mouth and supped loudly. When he finally set the bowl down again, he smacked his lips and then favoured her with a smile.

"Ahhh, much better," he declared. "Nothing drives the rain from your blood like a bowl of hot tea."

She interpreted this sudden change in his tone as a cue to resume the lesson and so pointed at the door.

"Who?"

For one stunned moment, all he could do was gape at her. Then he shook his head, conceding defeat, and said, "What the hell. It's as good a way to spend a rainy day as any other."

"Who?"

Her puzzled frown, comical in its intensity, unravelled the last half-buried threads of his resentment. "Door," he told her. "You're pointing at a door."

The day passed, uneventful except for the rain and wind and the rate at which Lathwi learned to speak. For each new word that Pieter taught her, two others came tumbling out of her memory already ripe with meaning. The flood of knowledge excited her. She waited eagerly for a chance to show it off.

Her chance came that night, when Pieter pressed a hand to his breastbone and said, "I am a man. What are you?"

Without hesitation, she thumped her chest and replied, "I dragon."

His snort of amusement was not the reaction she had been expecting.

"Don't be ridiculous, Lathwi," he said. "You're not a dragon, you're a woman." As she tucked the correction away for future reference, he added, "But I must admit that I've never met a woman quite like you. Do you come from a warrior clan?"

"Who warrior?"

"A person who fights in wars for a living. A soldier," he said. Then, noting the frown that was prelude to another 'who?', he tried to simplify his explanation. "Someone big and strong, someone skilled with weapons like the sword and pike—"

She understood 'big' and 'strong' and knew that neither word applied to her. "I not warrior," she said, cutting his definition short. "I small. Weak."

His eyes turned suddenly round. "You? Small? Who told you that?"

"Mother say."

"Dreamer! If she considers you small, then I'd hate to see what she looks like."

"Say again?"

"Never mind," he said, and then pushed himself to his feet. "It's getting late. I'm going to take one last piss and then hit the sack."

"Who?"

"Sleep, Lathwi. When I get back, I'm going to bed."

This time, she understood: the lesson was over for now. She banished her disappointment with a shrug, then curled up in front of the hearth to review that which she had already learned. But the fire was down to a clutch of sullen embers now, and could not compete with the chill that was skating in through the cracks in the door. She got up and went over to the woodpile. There, she picked out the biggest hunk of wood she could find and hefted it into the fireplace.

At that very moment, Pieter came strolling back into the cabin. His jaw dropped. The hair above his eyes jumped up.

"Are you out of your mind?" he growled, closing the gap between them in three excited strides. "That's too much wood for that tiny fire! The embers will smother and then—"

With a whoosh, the log ignited. An instant later, it began to burn with cheerful enthusiasm. Pieter blinked back an overabundance of disbelief, then turned to gape at Lathwi. She did not seem the least bit surprised.

"That's not supposed to happen," he sputtered. "Did you do something to make it do that?"

She shrugged. "I Call Fire. Fire come."

"The fire came when you called it?"

His confusion puzzled her. How else was she supposed to bring fire into this world if not by summoning it? She could not breath it into existence like Taziem and her tanglemates could, but she knew its secret Name and could invoke it when there was need. So long as there was something nearby for it to eat, it did not mind answering her Call. Was he testing her again? Or was it possible that he did not know the power of Names?

"You no can call fire?" she asked.

"No," he replied, slightly wild-eyed now. "When I want a fire, I make it with flint and tinder."

The words meant nothing to her. She tried to think, to come up with a reason as to why he should be so unhappy, but the wind kept distracting her with its whistle. She invoked its Name to get its attention, then asked it to go away. The sudden silence was gratifying.

"You did that, too, didn't you?" he accused.

"You no can?" she asked. He answered her with a shake of his head.

She was amazed. Even the dimmest dragons knew the Names of Wind and Fire; and brighter dragons knew many more. Names were everywhere—all one had to do to learn them was listen. But, she reminded herself, Pieter was different. If he could not hear mind-speak, then he could not be rightly expected to hear fire or water, either. She wondered if the problem came from not-hearing or not-listening; and if Pieter was the only human so afflicted. Whether he was or not, though, it seemed like a most dismal way to go through life. She curled up by the now-crackling fire to further contemplate the matter.

Pieter, too, was lost in thought, but he was not nearly as philosophical. He was desperately trying to figure out a way to get rid of Lathwi. He didn't want a sorceress hanging around his house, conjuring up fire and The-Dreamer-only-knew what else. That was one of the reasons he had left the city of his birth so long ago. He wanted normal. He wanted safe.

And he wanted Lathwi gone.

But how to get her out of here? He could not just kick her out—fears of supernatural retaliation aside, he simply lacked the muscle for the job. And murder was out, too, for despite his solitary lifestyle, he was a civilized man. His thoughts drifted back to the city of his birth. Lathwi might like it there, he thought then. His aunt certainly did, and she was a sorceress. Liselle might even welcome the company of one of her own kind. Or, if nothing else, she would know where to send Lathwi next.

He decided then: he would take Lathwi to Compara. The journey would be time-consuming and inconvenient, but where sorcery was concerned, there were far worse prices to pay.

CHAPTER 2

The next morning, Pieter rose early. As he rolled out of bed, his eyes strayed toward the hearth. Last night's log had long since been consumed, but even so, there was still a tiny flicker of fire dancing among the ashes. That blatant confirmation of Lathwi's sorcerous abilities reinforced his decision to go to Compara. He frowned at the still-sleeping woman, then padded out of the cabin.

Outside, the ground was sodden: it squished and oozed beneath his boots as he strode across the clearing which he laughingly called his yard. No more rain was forthcoming, though—the dawning sky was as cloudless as a maiden's conscience. He thanked The Dreamer for small favours, then went to fetch his mule.

"Come on, hay-burner," he said, as he stepped into the shed, "it's time for you to earn your keep."

She was a homely creature: jug-headed and knobby-kneed, sway-backed, pot-bellied and slightly cross-eyed. But if The Dreamer had stinted her as far as looks were concerned, then it was most likely because She had been doubly generous with regard to brains. Buck was smarter than any horse, most dogs and even a few men he could name. Her ears flattened against the slope of her head as he approached with her gear, but she let him harness her with a minimum of resistance. When she was set to travel, he led her out of the shed and toward his workshop. There, he tethered her to a sapling and left her to graze.

Except for the faint yet lingering stench of old blood, mashed brains and tanning acids, his workshop seemed quite mundane: the racks on which he stretched and cured his hides were presently empty, his traps and knives were all carefully stowed away. He smiled, ever-pleased by its deceptive look, then strode over to a corner and scuffed at the layer of wood shavings and dirt which covered the floor. A grip appeared, then the outlines of a trap-door. As he tugged it open, a breath of cool air spiced with the scents of leather and fur caressed his face. His smile broadened. This secret cellar, designed to preserve his work from heat and thieves, hid two seasons' worth of pelts. He had not planned to market these pelts so early in the year, but since he was going to Compara anyway, he might as well profit from the trip.

One by one, he carried his precious bundles out of the cellar and secured them to Buck's back. When he was done, he restored the workshop to order and then headed for the door. On the way out, though, he remembered that Lathwi had not yet returned the dagger which he had thrown at her and so doubled back to raid his cache of work-blades. He strapped a hunting knife to his leg, then tucked a smaller blade into the top of his boot for good measure.

As he was leading Buck back toward the cabin, Lathwi appeared in the clearing. Without warning, her look of minor irritation turned to one of terrifying lust.

"Food!" she shrieked, and then came charging toward him with one of those obsidian-like knives of hers in hand. His heart slammed into his rib-cage. His hand darted toward his hunting knife. Then his mule went suddenly skittish, and he realized that Lathwi was referring to Buck and not him.

"No!" he shouted, throwing every ounce of authority that he owned into the word. "Not food! Definitely not food."

She slowed to a trot, confusion stamped into the folds of her frown. Almost white-eyed with panic, Buck continued to shy away. Pieter tried to soothe the mule with calming noises, but when she refused to settle down, he clouted her on the nose.

"What's the matter with you?" he demanded.

"It prey," Lathwi said, coming to a stop alongside of him. "It know it need run or I eat."

"This," he grated, shaking Buck's lead-rein in her face, "is a mule. A pack-beast, not a prey-beast. Not food. Do you understand?"

She eyed him dubiously, wondering if this was another of his tests. No, she decided then, convinced by the fierceness of his scowl. For some strange reason, he valued the beast's presence. The notion affronted her superior sensibilities. She had expected Pieter to be more discriminating about the company he kept.

"Not food," she said then, a sullen concession. But she was curious, too. "Why mule have furs on back?"

"We're going to Compara," he said, and then motioned her toward the cabin. As they walked, he watched her out of the corner of his eye, for he was still half-afraid that she was going to turn and pounce on Buck's unprotected flank.

He need not have worried, though. As soon as he uttered that last unfamiliar word, she lost all interest in the mule.

"Who Compara?"

"Say 'what', not 'who'," he told her, tired of hearing that screech-owl sound all of the time.

"What Compara?"

"Compara's a city." He elaborated then, simply because he knew that she would badger him half-crazy with questions if he did not. "A city is a place where many people live—"

"What many?"

"Many is a crowd, like the stars in the evening sky." An image of a cave overflowing with humans formed in her mind. She hissed her disapproval. "Not good," she told him. "Why mothers not send olders away?"

He laughed—a short, fox-like yip that startled her but not the mule. "Some mothers do, some don't. It doesn't make that much difference overall. For every man who leaves, ten others arrive. They come from all over the continent in the hope of finding fortune or fame—"

She hissed again, this time to express her delight. For while she still had no clear idea as to what a city might be, she knew what fortune was! And if it could be found in this Compara, then that was where she wanted to go. How smart of Pieter. In spite of his peculiar short-comings, he was quite a clever man.

"How get fortune in city?" They were back at the cabin now. Pieter tied Buck to a hitching post, then grabbed a set of saddlebags and went inside. She followed on his heels. "How, Pieterzatrapper?"

"Lathwi," he said, in a tone that reminded her of Taziem when she was in no mood for anything but meat, "if you don't shut up and let me pack, we're never going to see Compara."

She clamped her mouth shut, then hunkered down by the hearth. As she watched, he began stuffing things into those hard leather pouches that he had carried in with him. This, she guessed, was packing, but its purpose eluded her. What need had he of a small, flattened kettle or fat, dried seeds; strips of wizened, foul-smelling flesh or a small wooden box that rattled from within?

He didn't like her watching him, though. It made him nervous.

"Are you ready to go?" he demanded. She shrugged, then reached for her stone. He flinched as she went to pop it in her mouth. Dreamer only knew where it had been! "Wait," he blurted. "I think I've got something for you." He rummaged through his belongings, then tossed a soft leather purse at her. "Put it in there instead."

She picked the purse up, but did not seem to understand how it worked.

"Like this," he said, and bustled over to show her. He opened the drawstring with a flourish, then went to pluck the stone from her fingers. She hissed, an unmistakable warning. Quick as thought, he got out of her way.

"Suit yourself," he snapped then, throwing the purse to the floor. "I was only trying to be nice."

"Now get rid of that damn fire, would you? It's making my skin creep."

The hearth went dark. That gave him the creeps, too. He grabbed his saddlebags and bed-roll, then stomped out of the cabin.

In the meantime, Lathwi retrieved the purse and dropped her stone into it. Now that she knew its purpose, she had to admit that it was a practical device——especially for those who did so much talking with their mouths. She strode out of the cabin then. As she did so, the mule brayed a warning and tried to lurch free of the hitching post. Pieter yanked at her lead-rein, but Buck refused to calm down.

"Blessed Dreamer!" he grated. "We'll never going to get to Compara at this rate!"

Alarmed by that prospect, Lathwi decided to take action. She flung herself to the ground, then rolled back and forth until she was thoroughly covered with mud. Then, because she could still smell traces of her dragon-scent, she hunted down a mound of fresh mule dung and rolled in that as well. When she stood up again, she flashed Pieter a feral grin.

"Mule go now," she announced.

As if by magic, Buck stopped fidgeting and slowly raised her ears. And while her glances at Lathwi remained wary, her eyes no longer showed their whites. Pieter grabbed her lead and headed for the woods, too confounded for words. He knew that what he had just witnessed was only a trick and not true sorcery, but it was unsettling just the same. Lathwi had not only rolled in that dung, she had enjoyed herself while doing it! People—especially those of the so-called gentle sex—weren't supposed to behave like that.

"How get fortune in city?" Lathwi asked then.

He sighed. This woman was like a bad tooth—no amount of wishing was going to make her go away. And since she was all but impossible to ignore, he decided to try and make the best of the situation.

"It depends on the person," he told her. "Take me, for example. I have no need for the furs on Buck's back, but there are people in the city who will pay handsomely—"

"What pay?"

"Pay is what one person gives another person in exchange for something that the first person wants but cannot get for himself."

She understood most of the words that he was using, but even so, he was not making any sense. "Why not first person just take from second person?"

Pieter's mouth stretched into a thin, disapproving line. "That's called stealing, Lathwi. It's wrong. Illegal. You can be hanged for it. Do you understand?" he went on, almost certain that she did not. "People will kill you for stealing from them."

She shrugged. A thief who got caught should expect to be killed. That was what made the stealing so exciting. She fingered the little pouch that held Taziem's stone and smiled to herself. Not getting caught had its thrills, too.

"Tell more about fortune," she urged him. "How I get?"

"I know someone in Compara who is like you," he said, although it was becoming painfully clear that she and his aunt were nothing alike except for their sex and vocation. "She might be able to answer that question better than me."

Pleasure surged through Lathwi's veins like dragon fire. She had gotten the impression that Compara was exclusively a man-place. To learn that it was home to her own kind as well was a reason to celebrate. Unable to take wing and dance her delight, she filled her lungs with air and bugled instead.

Buck bolted into the brush, dragging Pieter behind her. Lathwi thought he was having some new kind of fun until she caught up with him.

"Don't ever do that again," he snarled, and then stomped away with the mule firmly in tow. The stiff span of his back warned her to keep her distance.

Humans, she decided, were a very moody lot.

They walked in silence throughout the morning and well into the afternoon. Then, as the sun started to dip toward the horizon, their path intersected a deer run. The musky scent tweaked Lathwi's salivary glands and tickled a grumble from her stomach. She caught up with Pieter, then tapped him on the back.

"I hunger," she said, as he turned to face her.

His gaze flicked from her to the sky, then to their surroundings. After a moment's thought, he pointed to the top of a nearby knoll. "That looks like a good place to make camp for the night."

She did not know what 'camp' meant, but she obligingly followed him up the little hill. There, she waited patiently as he tied Buck to a sapling and began rummaging through his saddlebags. When he looked up from his puttering to find her standing idly by, the corners of his mouth twitched downward.

"Since you don't seem to have anything better to do," he said, "why don't you go and find some firewood?"

"I hunger," she iterated, more firmly this time.

"I know, I'm hungry too, but we'll need a fire first, so go and get some wood."

As she combed the area for dead fall, she wondered why he wanted fire. It was not edible, and he did not look as if he were cold. She exhumed a branch half-buried by leafy debris, then speared the beetle that went scuttling up her arm with a nail. An instant after she popped it into her mouth, though, she spit it out again. Vile tasting thing. She wanted meat. Fresh, warm meat. That thought boomed through her head again and again, ruining her patience. She returned to Pieter with a meagre armful of branches and dumped it at his feet.

"I hunger now," she insisted.

He dismissed her complaint with a wave of his hand, then began to stack the wood into a complicated heap. When he was done, he opened the box that rattled from within and withdrew two small grey stones. These spat sparks when he tapped them together. One landed in a pile of dead, dry leaves and began to grow. Pieter blew on it until it sprouted a little yellow tongue.

"It won't be long now," he told Lathwi then. "Pan bread and beans sound good to you?"

"What that?" she demanded, suddenly suspicious.

"Food. You know, like stew, only with beans instead of venison."

Her eyes narrowed to slits, an accusation of duplicity. "Stew not food."

He answered her scowl with one of his own. "See here, Lathwi. If you don't like my cooking, feel free to go and forage for yourself."

She needed no further encouragement. Without a backward glance, she went off in search of something tasty.

He lobbed a good riddance in her direction, then started the beans. There was nothing wrong with his cooking, he told himself. Lathwi was just ungrateful, a pig-headed barbarian. He went to groom Buck then, and as he ran the curry-comb over the mule's hide, his list of grievances grew: she was selfish and lazy; a quick-tempered thief; and her persistence rivalled that of a starving tick's. And Dreamer, her habit of hissing at everything was nerve-wracking!

He was so wrapped up in his spleen-venting, he did not hear the footsteps closing in on his back until Buck shifted nervously and laid her ears flat. By then, it was too late. He turned to find three men standing in his camp. They were a hard-looking lot: dirty and travel-worn, poorly dressed but well-armed. The reek of outlawry clung to them like a second shadow. One of them—a brown-bear of a man whose eyes were like tobacco-stained callouses—tossed him a cat-and-mouse grin.

"Greetings, neighbour," he said, in a voice as deep as a river. "Mind if we share your fire?"

Pieter swallowed hard, trying to douse the clutch of hot rocks that had ignited in his stomach. Calm, he chattered to himself. He had to stay calm.

"Help yourself," he replied, trying to sound nonchalant. "I'm cooking up a batch of beans and pan-bread if you care to join me for supper."

A pock-marked blond with a ragged black patch over his left eye rubbed his belly. "Mmm, beans. My favourite."

"We appreciate your offer of hospitality," the third man said, while absently stroking the tangles of his greasy red beard, "but don't go to any trouble on our account. I think we pretty much found what we were looking for. True, Tebo?"

"True, Jasper." The voice came from behind Pieter. As he pivoted toward the sound, a wiry, black-haired man slung a double bundle of furs onto Buck's back.

"Nice work, trapper," this Tebo drawled. "These ought to fetch a pretty sum in Compara."

"My thought exactly," Pieter said, although the effort to remain glib was straining his nerves to their limit. "I don't suppose I could persuade you to leave them with me."

"You suppose right," the one named Jasper said, with an obscene sort of cheerfulness.

"Then how 'bout I fair-fight one of you for 'em?" Pieter asked, as Tebo led his fur-laden mule away.

"Mister, if we wanted to be fair about these sorts of things, we wouldn't be travelling in a pack," Jasper told him. "Besides, you might get hurt in a fight, and that would upset Drell." He grinned at the bearish man with the tobacco-stain eyes. "He likes you, trapper. He thinks you're pretty."

By now, Pieter could not care less about losing his mule or those damn furs or even his dignity. All that mattered to him was staying alive. So as the outlaws started toward him, four against one, he drew his hunting knife and then howled a name.

The forest abounded with tempting game: birds, rodents, wild boar and deer. Lathwi toyed with the idea of lying in wait for one of the larger prey-beasts, but decided that she was much too hungry for that kind of hunting and so followed a rabbit's tracks back to a clump of bramble-bushes instead. The plenitude of droppings in the area told her that there was a feast hiding within. She hid herself downwind from the warren, then withdrew a claw from her belt and waited.

A short time later, a fat buck poked his head into the clearing. His nose was twitching furiously, his ears were primed for the slightest sound of danger. She held herself completely still. The rabbit hopped past the brambles and toward her—closer, then closer yet. She was right on the verge of pouncing when a melting cry disrupted the forest's silence.

"Lathwi!"

In spite of herself, she started. The slight movement was enough to send her prey bolting back into the warren.

Annoyance rippled through her. Why was Pieter shouting? Did he not understand that she was trying to hunt?

"Lathwi!"

The cry's urgency roused her curiosity. There had to be a reason behind such vigorous squawking. Perhaps he was ready to resume her lessons. She eyed the warren, debating her appetites, then went bounding back toward the knoll and up its gentle slope.

As she neared the top of the hill, a string of strange noises snared her attention: scuffling feet, muffled grunts, a groan of pain or pleasure. Doubly curious now, she began to stalk the sounds. They led her straight to Pieter's camp and a most peculiar sight. Three unfamiliar men were holding Pieter belly-down on the ground. A fourth was pawing at his trousers. Pieter was bucking and squirming in an attempt to get free, but the others would not let him go.

Her mouth curved into a grin. These strangers must be Pieter's tanglemates, come to play with him. And Pieter must have called because he wanted her to join in on the fun. How clever of him! She liked games.

As she crept up on the cluster of bodies, she sized up her would-be opponents. The yellow-haired man was almost as scrawny as Pieter, and therefore no good match for her. Nor was she very impressed with the two men who were kneeling on Pieter's arms. That left the big, brown-haired man. He was the largest of the tangle, and promised the best sport. She bugled a challenge and then launched herself at him. He went tumbling. So did she. An instant later, they were both back on their feet and brawling.

He smashed his ham-sized fist into her jaw. She blinked back a swarm of floating stars, then countered his punch with one of her own. It collided with his nose with a satisfying crack. As he sniffed back a trickle of his own blood, one of his tanglemates grabbed her from behind. She elbowed him in the ribs, then danced around and kicked him in the groin. As he doubled over, she squealed.

This was fun!

The big man had a knife in his hand now. He flipped it from hand to hand as he circled her. She grinned, delighted with the trick, then hauled the not-claw from her belt. But before she had a chance to try the manoeuvre for herself, her adversary rushed in and slashed at her. Her scales deflected the blow. He lashed out again, aiming at her eyes this time. With a derisive hiss, she side-stepped the clumsy attack and poked her not-claw into his side. It slid in all the way up to the hilt. He stumbled backward, then fell to the ground. He did not get up again.

Now there was a surprise! She had assumed that he was scaled beneath all of that stinking leather. Why else would he be playing with something as sharp as a not-claw? As she marvelled at such foolishness, a hairy forearm wrapped itself around her neck and tensed.

"Bitch," a voice snarled in her ear. "You're going to pay long and hard for that."

The statement confused her. Why was he talking about pay? None of these men had anything that she wanted.

"Let go," she told him. "Not want play with you."

"Too bad," Jasper said, giving her neck another squeeze, "because play-time's just begun."

His obtuseness irked her, but she did not bother to tell him that. Instead, she sank her teeth into his arm. With a screech, he released her. Then, as she quick-stepped out of his reach, he unsheathed a knife.

"I'm going to carve you up," he informed her. "Then I'm going to feed the pieces to the birds."

Her annoyance dissolved into a lethal composure. Such unswervingly stupid persistence could only mean one thing: a challenge. She did not comprehend his reasons for wanting to turn this into a real fight—she had no territory to claim, and no fortune beyond Taziem's stone—but she did understand that he would not leave her alone now until she killed him.

So she bugled a formal acceptance of his challenge and then charged. Caught off-guard by her aggressiveness, Jasper hesitated. In that instant, she was on him, nails poised to rend. Her first swipe raked a set of bloody grooves in his beard; the second savaged his right eye. With a howl of pain and fury, he stabbed at her shoulder. The tip of his blade chipped as it struck her scales, leaving only a deep bruise behind. She kicked his legs out from under him then. An instant after he hit the ground, she leapt on top of him and began to bend his knife-hand toward the hairy wattle of flesh beneath his chin. He pitched and wriggled in a desperate attempt to unseat her, then abruptly shunted all of his strength into his arm.

The blade's downward progress skidded to a halt, then trembled in the space between them like an accusing finger. He tried to twist it upward and into her face, but could not make it budge.

"What in hell are you?" he demanded then, in a tone rich with newfound fear.

Her contempt for him soared to new heights, for that was a question he should have asked before he made his challenge. Still, she could not quite resist the chance to let him know exactly how stupid he had really been.

"I woman," she told him.

Then she pressed down on his knife-hand again; and this time, she used the strength she had developed while sporting with her own tanglemates. The blade trembled for a moment, then dipped downward. An instant later, it dipped again and plunged into his throat. The half-formed protest on his lips became a liquid sigh. Hearing that and nothing more, she got up and walked away.

Back at the camp, she spooked Pieter as he was pulling a knife from the blonde man's chest. He spun around, ready to strike, then forced himself to relax. His harried expression turned to one of complicated relief.

"Did you get them both?" When she nodded, he managed a wan smile and said, "Thanks. I wouldn't have stood a chance without you."

"You brothers play stupid games," she commented, as she glanced from one unmoving body to the next. "Not know when to stop."

"Those bastards weren't my brothers," he grated. "And they weren't playing games. If you hadn't shown up when you did, they would've—" He paled, then flushed anew. "—they would've murdered me."

He wiped his boot-knife off on the blonde man's jersey. As he did so, Lathwi remembered her own not-claw and went to fetch it. Pieter caught up with her just as she was passing Jasper's corpse.

"I thought you said you weren't a warrior," he said, as he admired her handiwork.

"I not," she replied, completely serious. "Not-brothers be soft. Stupid, too."

His grim chuckle slurred off into rigid silence as they drew to a stop alongside of Drell. Although the big man was bloody and his eyes were shut, his laboured breathing declared him to be very much alive. Pieter booted him in the head to get his attention.

"Get up," he said. "Get up so we can hang you."

With a bone-deep groan, the outlaw opened his eyes. He stared at Pieter, but did not seem to recognize his would-be victim. His face was slack and grey.

"Mercy," he mumbled. "My innards are all on fire." His whole body tensed then. His expression was one of pure pain. "It hurts. Ah, Dreamer, how it hurts!" He glanced at Pieter again. "Please, Mister, I'm begging you for mercy."

With a scowl as vast as a storm-front, Pieter unsheathed his hunting knife, then crouched down and showed it to Drell. "Is this what you want?"

Drell managed a feeble nod.

"Bastard," Pieter grated. "It's more than you deserve."

He cut the outlaw's throat then. Lathwi added mercy to her list of man-words.

"Come on," Pieter said afterward, "let's get our stuff and get out of here. All of this meat is bound to attract wolves, and I don't want to spoil their feast."

Lathwi pulled her not-claw from Drell's side and licked it clean. Because he had been a challenger rather than prey, she did not help herself to his flesh. And she had a feeling that it would not taste very good anyway.

Not far from their now-abandoned camp, they found Buck tied to a scrub pine. Her back was still mounded with furs. Pieter barely glanced at his own belongings, though; he was too busy gloating over the three horses which were picketed alongside of the mule.

"This one's carrying jerky," he announced, as he probed the splotchy brown and white beast's packs. "And waybread." A moment later, he moved on to the tan nag with the sagging back. "This one's got jerky and a hunk of pipe tobacco."

The last of the horses was a strapping bay stallion that snapped at Pieter as soon as he came within range. He batted its head away, then began to rifle through its saddlebags. A look of wonder crept across his face as he withdrew a leather purse and emptied its clinking contents into his hand.

"Lathwi!" he crooned then. "Come and see what I've found."

She headed toward him, but she was far more interested in the horses than anything they might be carrying. She had never been this close to so much prey before—none that she had not been planning to eat leastways. There was something exciting, almost indecent about it. Shoq would never believe her when she told him. He'd think she was playing a trick on him. She touched the bay's flank in passing. It flicked her fingers away with an annoyed twitch of its tail.

"Look," Pieter said, and then thrust his palm under her nose. It was mounded with flat, round discs which glimmered in the waning sunlight like Taziem's eyes. "We've inherited twenty, maybe thirty lucs."

She pinched one of the discs between her fingers, then raised it to her nose. Its smell was faint but unattractive: a combination of leather, human sweat and old dirt. It did not taste any better than it smelled. Unimpressed, she gave it back to him.

"What is?"

"It's gold," he replied, in a tone both reverent and smug. "Better still, it's our gold."

There must be something about this gold that she was not seeing, she decided. Otherwise, he would not be so excited.

"What gold do?"

"You don't know?" When she shook her head, he laughed. "Ah, Lathwi, you are a strange one. I've never met anybody who didn't know about gold."

"What do?" she demanded, even more curious now.

"It can buy things," he replied. "Furs. Horses. Land. The more gold a body has, the more he can buy. And the more he can buy, the more important he becomes."

Now his attitude toward the discs made perfect sense, for gold was obviously a form of power. And power was the essence of fortune. She glanced at the shimmering mound in his hands again, this time with a speculative eye.

"That many gold?"

"We're not rich," he admitted cheerfully, "but what we have here will buy a fair measure of comforts. And if gold is what you want, then we can always sell one of the horses when we get to Compara."

"Buy? Sell? What that?"

"It's a simple matter of gold changing hands," he said. "Those who have extra, sell. Those who want extra, buy. For example: we only need two of these horses. Someone who wants the third will pay us in gold to own it. We're selling, the other person is buying. Understand?"

"Why not other person just take extra?"

"That's stealing, Lathwi. And like I told you before, that's wrong."

"We take these horses from not-brothers."

"True," he quipped, "but they don't need them anymore. They're dead."

"So someone who want our horses need kill us to take."

"No, no, no!" he said, vehemently regretting his former glibness. "We didn't kill those bandits for their horses, we killed them because they were trying to kill us. The horses are a sort of by-blow, an act of providence. Understand?"

She rolled her shoulders. All she knew was that they had been stronger than those not-brothers, and as a result, the horses were now theirs. Everything else was a jumble of empty words.

He answered her shrug with one of his own, then started to pocket the pouch which held the discs. With a hiss, she stayed his hand. Although she did not know how to use gold yet, she was fully prepared to challenge him for its power.

"Mine," she said firmly.

A flush scalded the flats of his cheeks. Inwardly, he was steaming as well. She had no right to all of the gold! Half of it was rightfully his as a wereguild from the men who had tried to kill him.

Who would have killed him if she had not intervened.

The unbidden thought shamed him out of his greedy rage. He swallowed hard, then gave her the pouch. She took it from him without a word of thanks and then casually tucked it into her girdle alongside of her other purse. Such carelessness rekindled his resentment. She was going to lose it, he just knew it. And when she did, she was going to turn to him for more—unless he put his foot down now.

"That's all you're getting from me, you hear?" he told her. "Any gold that I get for my furs and the extra horse is mine to keep."

She shrugged, refusing to commit herself. Dragons did not make promises if they could avoid them.

"What horse do?" she asked instead.

A protest swelled within him. Was there no end to this woman's nerve? But even as he opened his mouth to give her a piece of his mind, he remembered again that she had saved his life, and that a little forbearance if not outright gratitude was due. So he wrung his hard words into a resigned sigh and then answered her question.

"Horses can do a lot of things. Some are used as pack animals; others pull plow, wagons and various other things. But mostly, they're used for riding."

"What 'riding'?"

"It involves getting up on a horse's back and making it carry you where you want to go."

That sounded like fun! "I do riding, too."

"Oh?" he asked, arching an amused look at her. "Have you ever ridden before?"

"No," she replied, seemingly unconcerned by such a minor detail. "You teach."

"I suppose I could do that." It would, he thought, make the journey go faster. His gaze twitched from her to each of the horses and back to her. "Here," he said then, trying to hand her the tan horse's reins. "This one should do right by you."

"Not want," she told him. "It pack-beast."

"Since when did you become such a discriminating judge of horseflesh?"

"Say again?"

"Never mind. You're right—this mare's as tame as they come. And that's exactly why you should take your first ride on her."

"Not want," she insisted. That beast was ill-made and obviously stupid, an affront to her dignity. The big brown one seemed more like a creature worthy of a dragon's company. "I ride this one."

"Lathwi, you don't know what you're saying," he argued, although he was not surprised that she had taken a fancy to a beast that liked to bite. "That bastard's mean—he'd throw you off and stomp you the first chance he got. Give this old mare a chance. She's got a better temperament."

She resisted his advice. After all, she had flown the skies and skimmed the treetops. How difficult could it be to sit on a beast's back? Furthermore, the bay possessed a lot of good meat. If this riding proved to be a disappointment, she could always console herself with a feast.

"I ride bastard," she said.

"Fine, have it your way," he said, tired of arguing with her. "But don't you dare try to blame me when all your bones are broken."

"How bones break?"

"You'll see," he said, and tossed her the bay's reins.

"Now?"

"No, not now. It's getting dark, and we've got to find another campsite. But don't worry," he said, smirking at the protest that cropped up on her brow, "tomorrow will come soon enough."

Lathwi opened her eyes to find herself curled up among the roots of a gnarled pine. The discovery confused her—she was certain that she had been drowsing in Taziem's caves a moment ago. Then she heard Pieter's bull-froggy snoring in the background, and realized that she had been dreaming. For some reason, that annoyed her.

Her stomach grumbled then, demanding food. She got up and went in search of prey.

When she returned, Pieter was pacing restless circles around the campsite. The scowl on his face was all for her.

"Where have you been?" he barked. "I've been packed and ready to go for an hour now."

"Went hunting," she said, undaunted by his snarly tone. She licked a last fleck of tasty yellow yolk from her lips, then burped. "We ride now?"

His scowl deepened. He had not slept well last night—the wolves that he'd wished on the outlaws' corpses had kept him up with their howling. And his first thought upon waking and finding Lathwi gone was that the dog pack had gotten her, too. Now here she was, well-fed and ready to go, thinking of no one but herself. She probably hadn't even heard the damn wolves last night.

Dreamer, but she could rub a man the wrong way!

"No," he replied, and was spitefully pleased to note her look of disappointment. "You have to learn how to saddle before you learn how to ride." Before she could digest that mouthful of words, he pointed to the stallion's tack. "Bring that stuff with you."

She gathered the pile of odd-looking gear into her arms then followed him over to the spot where the horses had been tethered. There, he ordered her to watch as he 'saddled' the splotchy beast. As he worked, he named the various pieces of equipment. She wondered why humans had to make everything so complicated. Why could they not simply get up on the horses' backs and go?

"Any questions?" he asked afterward.

She shook her head.

"So be it," he said, adding overconfidence to her list of sins. "Go and saddle the bay."

Then, fully expecting that vile-tempered bastard to deal a healthy dose of humility, he stepped back to watch the fun.

The stallion flattened its ears and then bared its teeth as she approached. Regardless of those subtle warnings, she drew to a stop alongside of him and slung the saddle onto his back. As she stooped to fasten the belly cinch, he swung his head around and snapped at her ear. She batted him away. He tried again. This time, he clipped her shoulder and caught a whiff of dragon. With a snort, he recoiled, then tossed his head back and forth as if trying to shake the smell from his nose. Meanwhile, she girded his saddle into place, adjusted the stirrups and began to bridle him. Still troubled by the disturbing scent, he accepted the bit without a fight. When the headstall was securely in place, she turned to Pieter and grinned.

"What now?"

"We walk until we find a meadow," he replied. For while he ached to see that smirk wiped from her face, he was not so malicious as to want to see it done by a low-hanging branch.

He started through the forest then, trailing a line of horseflesh behind him. Lathwi followed with the bay in tow, but she was far from satisfied with the situation. This was not riding as he had described it, this was walking; and she could do that without some beast at her back. She scowled at the row of swishing tails and swaying buttocks ahead of her. They did not need any of these animals, she thought, not even the mule. Pieter could have carried those furs on his own back. Indeed, it would've been better if he had, for then he wouldn't have brought so much other useless clutter with him. Men who kept beasts were like snails, she decided. When they went somewhere, they brought their houses with them.

Furthermore, she thought, glimpsing at Pieter's scrawny backside, a man who relied on a mule's muscles instead of his own grew weak. That was why those not-brothers had been able to best him so easily. She sniffed, scorning his feebleness.

At that moment, he happened to glance over his shoulder. Even from a distance, he perceived the contempt in her eyes, perceived too that it was all for him. His still smoldering resentments flared to new life. He could hardly wait for the chance to whittle her down to size.

That opportunity came in the guise of a sunlit meadow. It was small and flat and full of hidden potential. He tied Buck and the mare to a handy sapling, then slung himself into the pinto's saddle when Lathwi wasn't looking.

"This looks like a good spot for your first ride," he said then.

The sound of Pieter's voice startled Lathwi out of a daydream. She looked up to find him already perched on top of the mottled beast. The sight thrilled her. He looked far more powerful and self-assured on that animal's back than he ever did on foot. Perhaps this beast-keeping was not so bad after all.

"How you do that?" she asked.

He smiled at her—a tight, humourless bend of the mouth. "What? You don't know? I thought you knew everything."

"Not know how you do that," she replied. "You teach."

"Of course," he said, although the lesson he meant to teach her was quite different from the one she had in mind. "You can start by flipping the reins over the bay's head."

The stallion was feeding greedily now, and did not so much as twitch an ear as Lathwi did as she was told. Pieter was happy to see that, for it meant that the beast would not be so quick to cooperate with her this time.

"Now go around to his left side," he told her, when she looked to him for further instruction. "No, not that side, the other one. Don't you know your left from your right?"

She shrugged. Left, right—the words had no meaning to her. And besides, what did it matter, one side or the other? They both belonged to the same horse.

"Good," Pieter said, when she was where she ought to be. "Now stick your left foot in the stirrup." As she did this, the stallion strolled forward a few steps, forcing her to hop along with it like some great, black, one-legged wading bird. Pieter stifled an urge to snicker. "Now lift yourself up and swing the other leg over his rump."

She wound up on the ground on the other side of the bay. Pieter's smirk broadened, diagramming his spite.

"Try again. It's more of a climb than a jump."

This time, she landed in the saddle. It was as hard as a rock, and not very comfortable; but the view from here was excellent. She felt bigger suddenly. Stronger. She wanted to roar with pleasure, but decided to wait until this lesson had run its full course.

"What now?" she called instead.

"Use the reins to pull the bay's head up," he advised. "He won't want to give up his breakfast, so you'll have to pull hard."

His prediction proved to be correct. The first time she tugged on the reins, the bay tugged back and then resumed his grazing. The second time, he swung his head around and tried to bite her calf. She clouted him between the ears and tried again. This time, he grudgingly lifted his head.

"Now nudge him in the ribs with your heels. Gently—"

As intended, the qualifier came too late. The stallion started, then broke into a sudden gallop. As Lathwi lurched backward, remaining in the saddle only by sheer luck, Pieter roared with laughter.

A moment later, though, his mirth soured in his mouth. For the bay was racing across the meadow now, and Lathwi was nowhere close to being in control. She squealed once as her mount veered toward the trees, then again as it redoubled its pace. The poor woman, he thought, as he went charging to the rescue. She must be terrified.

Meanwhile, Lathwi continued to squeal. Although jarred and jolted and horribly off-balance, she was ecstatic. This riding was like nothing she'd ever experienced: breath-taking and violent, a blur of chaotic motion. It recalled the wind to her face and the thrill of speed to her blood. It was not as swift or grandiose as flight, but it would serve admirably for the moment—if she could figure out a way to communicate her wants to the beast.

"Turn him, Lathwi!" came Pieter's shout, from somewhere behind her. "Pull back on the reins!"

The reins? How curious. She had gotten the impression that those were meant to regulate the beast's appetite. She gave the straps an experimental tug. Without warning or loss of speed, the horse veered sharply to the left. She grinned, then yanked on the reins again. The horse veered again, this time directly into the path of Pieter's oncoming pinto.

The bay's first change of course sent relief gushing through Pieter's veins. The second took him completely by surprise. He hauled back hard on his reins, desperate to avoid a collision. The pinto skidded to a sudden stop and then reared, spilling him onto the grass. An instant later, the bay sped by. In passing, he heard Lathwi shout.

"That only way to get down?"

Although he could scarcely believe his ears, he was sure that there was light-hearted laughter in her voice.

Another hour or so passed before Lathwi could handle the bay with any degree of competence, and during that time, she took enough falls to mollify any remaining grudge that Pieter held against her. When they finally took their leave of that meadow, the meanness that had dogged them throughout the morning was gone.

They rode in companionable silence for a long time, each of them immersed in private thoughts. Pieter was thinking of his aunt, and the sort of welcome he was apt to get from her. On the one hand, she did not like surprises, good or bad; and this visit could definitely be viewed as a mixed bag. On the other hand, she was always glad for another chance to try and talk him into taking up life in the city again. She had been vehemently opposed to his moving away from Compara; at times, that was still a sore point between them.

And then there was Lathwi to consider.

She came riding up to him just then, as if she knew that he had been thinking of her. Although she still sat somewhat awkwardly in the saddle, she seemed very much at ease.

"I'll admit it," he said, flashing her an affable smile. "I'm amazed. I was sure that this demon-in-disguise would've killed you a thousand times by now. Instead, he almost seems to have taken a liking to you." He paused, debating whether to ask or not, then forced himself to be bold. "Did you use sorcery on him?"

"What 'sorcery'?" The tinge of fear which shadowed his tone implied that it was a thing of power. If so, then she wanted to know how it might apply to her.

He chewed on the fringes of his mustache, unsure of what to say. He knew all too well what sorcery was, yet now that he had been asked, he was hard-pressed to define it. Magic, witchcraft, wizardry: these were only variations of the same thought. Lathwi required words that explained themselves.

"Sorcery is a kind of secret knowledge," he told her at last. "A sorcerer— or sorceress, in your case—uses that knowledge to manipulate nature and other forces."

At that, her thoughts began to cycle at a furious pace. Taziem had taught her much that was secret. Did that qualify her as a sorceress?

"Tell more," she urged.

"I can't, I'm not an expert on the subject," he said. "All I can say is that sorcerers control things that ordinary men cannot—fire, wind, weather."

"I Call fire. Wind, too."

"I know," he replied, with a dry half-smile. "I, on the other hand, cannot. That's why you're a sorceress and I'm a trapper."

She hissed, venting her excitement. He had said it, so it must be true: she was not only a woman, but a sorceress as well. The distinction pleased her. Yet there was still much more that she wanted to know.

"Why you fear this sorcery?"

Once again, she rendered him speechless. It was only natural for a man to fear things that he could not control, he wanted to tell her, but that wasn't quite true. He could not control lightning, and yet he never went running when it crackled across the sky. Perhaps that was because lightning could only kill a man, he thought then. When sorcery struck, the results were often worse than death.

He glanced at her. She was still patiently waiting for an answer. A feeble curse died on his lips. He should have known better than to hope that she'd forget or let the matter slide.

"I'm afraid," he said, digging deep for an honest bone, "because I don't trust sorcerers to leave me alone."

"Why?"

"I don't know. Too much of any kind of power perverts a body's outlook on life." When she continued to stare at him, obviously expecting him to elaborate, he sputtered. "Could you trust someone who could summon wolves to eat his enemies or conjure fire to burn an unfaithful mistress in her bed or turn some unlucky trapper into a lizard simply because he was at the wrong place at the wrong time?"

As far as she could tell, trust was another human quirk. And because it did not apply to her, it did not interest her.

"Why this sorcerer not eat enemies hisself?" she asked. "He not have teeth?"

"It doesn't matter if he has teeth or not," he said, too agitated to quibble about details like cannibalism just now. "If he's like most folks, he'll only manage for himself until he's powerful enough to coerce someone else into doing the job for him."

There was nothing wrong with that, she thought. Every living thing strove to make life easier for itself. Did he not make his mule carry his things? Had he not claimed the horses so he would not have to walk anymore?

He was weak, she concluded again, this time with more clemency than scorn. He was afraid of power simply because he did not have enough of his own. But she did not say that aloud—it would serve no useful purpose. Instead, she began a lazy review of the conversation's other aspects. The part about playing tricks with fire interested her. She would not have thought to use her knowledge of Names in such a manner. She started to consider possible applications, mostly tricks on Shoq, but was distracted by a loud growl from her stomach.

"I hunger," she told Pieter.

"You're always hungry," he commented good-naturedly, and then squinted at the sky. The sun was still a fair distance from the horizon. "Can you wait a few hours? I want to make up for the time we lost in the meadow."

Her stomach growled again, loud enough for him to hear. The beginnings of a frown lined his brow, then abruptly gave way to inspiration. He swivelled around in his saddle, then began rummaging through one of his satchels. A moment later, he swivelled back around with two strips of what seemed like old leather in his hand. He stuffed one of these strips into his mouth, then offered her the other.

"Here, try this."

"What is?" she asked warily. He ate the most unlikely things. Stranger still, he seemed to enjoy them.

"It's jerky—preserved deer flesh," he appended, and then grinned at her instant look of revulsion. "I know it's not exactly your kind of food, but at least it'll keep your belly quiet until we're ready to make camp for the night.

"Do you want it?" When she hesitated, he added, "You did want to get to Compara sometime soon, didn't you?"

With a grudging rumble, she accepted the strip. It had a hard, greasy feel, and reeked of wood smoke and vague decay. If she had not watched him stick a similar piece into his own mouth, she would never have guessed that this was food. But because she had priorities, and Compara was one of them, she choked the jerky down—bite by galling bite. Her gorge rose and fell several times.

"Not bad, huh?" Pieter asked, as she swallowed a last mouthful of bile.

"No hunger no more," she replied, and then fell into a queasy silence.

The sun was close to setting by the time he deemed them ready to make camp. He steered his horse into a cozy little clearing among the trees and dismounted.

"Dreamer!" he groaned then. "I had forgotten what a day in the saddle can do to a body."

She didn't know what he was talking about until she went to get down from the stallion's back; and then it became all too clear. Her legs buckled as soon as they hit the ground. An instant later, her body turned into one long, excruciating cramp. She hissed, expressing consternation as well as pain. She had not hurt like this since the last time she had tried to fly on her own.

Pieter knew what her problem was. Indeed, he felt as if he were partially responsible for it. If he had stopped when she had first asked him, she might not be in such sorry shape now. Goaded by guilt, he rushed over to her with his bedroll and eased it under her head.

"Try to relax," he told her. "I'll be back to help you as soon as I can."

She groaned. He hurried off.

When he returned, he had an armful of wood. He dumped it onto the ground in front of her, then built a hasty pyre. "Get it burning," he said, and then hurried off again.

While she did not understand this obsession of his, she was in too much pain to argue. She pulled fire's secret Name from her sweat-soaked memory. The pile of wood ignited. The ensuing waves of smoky heat made her feel light-headed.

The next time the trapper came hustling back into view, he was toting a kettle of water. His thoughtless mobility filled her with respect. Never again would she accuse him of being weak!

"How are you feeling?" he asked, as he set the pot over the fire. "Has the cramping subsided yet?"

"No," she replied. Then, just so he understood that she did not intend to endure this same sort of unpleasantness on a daily basis, she added, "I not ride again."

He chuckled. "I'm sure you hurt like hell now, but after some broth and a good night's sleep, you'll be as good as new. And the more you ride, the easier it gets."

She grunted, a summation of doubts. He chuckled again, then settled down beside her and began to massage her scaled legs. She tensed and hissed a warning.

"Take it easy," he told her, refusing to retreat. "The broth is going to take a while to brew. Meanwhile, this will loosen up your muscles."

Although still dubious, she relaxed a notch and allowed him to continue.

He worked with dispassionate skill, more interested in her mail than the flesh which spanned beneath it. Like the rest of her, it was peculiar—as tight a mesh as he had ever seen, yet more supple than the lightest chain-mail. The few seams that he could feel did not come undone when he pressed on them.

"Where did you get this stuff, Lathwi?" he asked. "It's wonderful."

"Mother give," she told him, in a tone that matched her growing languor, "so I not bleed so much. She say smell make her hunger."

He snorted. This mother of hers sounded like one tough old bitch. "Do you know what it's made of?"

"She take hide from broke-back brother."

"Right." He knew she was spinning yarns at him now, but he didn't take her to task for that. The tales a person told could be as revealing as the outright truth, and he wanted to get to know her better for his aunt's sake, if no other. "Do you come from a large family?"

She smiled at the image which expanded in her mind—a tangle of well-fed dragons, each of them twice her size and still growing.

"Is big. Mother biggest. Smartest, too." In a wistful tone, she added, "She make me leave when chosen come back."

Ah, so that's what had happened to her, he thought then. She'd been outcast. Many peasant families did that to their daughters when there were too many mouths to feed. No wonder she was so fierce and uncivilized. No wonder her skills with the common language were so crude. She must have been on her own for years and years now.

Lathwi did not notice the pity that came crept into his eyes then. Her thoughts were still snuggled amidst a crowd of dragons. An ache swelled in her heart, displacing the one in her limbs. She pushed his hands away.

"No more rub," she said, as he started to protest. "No more talk."

He did not blame her for cutting the conversation short. Some things were just too painful to discuss.

CHAPTER 3

Shoq was sprawled across an outcropping of rocks that overlooked his favourite hunting ground. The mountain field was quiet, a lake of spring-green grasses. Soon, it would be filled with deer.

That prospect should have excited him, but it did not. For some strange reason, he did not feel like feeding. Or dancing. Or taking a long nap in the sun. At the same time, though, he was restless; on the edge of being bored. He knew he wanted to do something, he just could not figure out what that something might be. This did not surprise him. He had never been very good at thinking. He had always left that to Lathwi.

The Name-image which accompanied the thought triggered a wave of pleasure and longing within him. All at once, he knew exactly what he wanted. He wanted his armpits tickled and his nose boxed; his eyes deceived and his pride stroked. He wanted to see The Soft One again.

His snort sent twin dust-devils whirling across the rocks. Such a craving was ridiculous. Lathwi was on her own now, far gone from the caves which had kept their fortunes in common for so long. Barring accidents, it was quite unlikely that they would meet again soon.

That fact troubled him, more so because he knew that it should not. Adult dragons were solitary creatures; once they left the nest to pursue their own fortunes, they seldom had a thought for anyone but themselves. He had not longed to see Haqqaq, Lifyre or any of his other tanglemates after they had taken their leave of Taziem's caves. Nor had they gone out of their way to visit him. So why should it be any different with Lathwi?

Images of her cavorted through his mind, teasing him for being so foolish. Her mouth was a crescent moon filled with tiny white teeth. Her gloriously blue eyes were bright with amusement. The memories played with his senses. He could almost hear her laughing at him in the distance, almost smell the curious melange of her scent. Provoked by these too-real reminders, he came to a sudden decision: it did not matter if Lathwi was on her own now; he had to see her again.

But how was he supposed to find her? She had to be gone from that far-away meadow by now; and while he was hungry for the taste of her company, he was not particularly keen on the idea of passing an endless number of days in search of it. There had to be an easier way.

For a long moment, he considered using her Name. If he Called, she would have to come, the birth-bond between them would compel her. But that would be unwise, he decided then, guided by selfishness rather than scruples. She would not be pleased to come and find him in no obvious need. And if she was not pleased, she would not want to play.

His tail twitched with remembered delight as he recalled the games she had invented for their amusement: Hunter and Prey; Mock Challenge; Tricks on Tanglemates and Taziem. How much fun they could have if they were together again! They could play on the ground to their heart's content, then take to the sky and play some more. Come dusk, they could kill a stag and gorge on its sweet red meat. Afterward, they could curl up back to belly and sleep.

Yes! This was what he wanted to do—not just for a day or a score of days, but for always.

The thought inspired an idea. This was startling in and of itself, for he did not generally have ideas about anything other than food, sleep or play. But this idea was even more remarkable because it was brilliant, a solution to all of his problems. He would ask Lathwi to be his chosen!

Excited now, he began to fantasize in earnest. He would not be like his sire, Bij, who lived in the south and visited Taziem only to breed. He would find Lathwi a cave close to his own, or better still, persuade her to live with him. He would defend her territory against all challengers, and guard her fortune as if it were his very own. And when she finally came into Season, he would dance for her as he'd never danced before. She would choose him, as he knew she must, and then they would go soaring across the sky.

This chain of thoughts filled his nose with her essence again. A good omen, he thought, savouring the ghostly aroma. It made him think that she was somehow encouraging him from afar.

He needed no further urging. Resolved to go in search of her, he heaved himself to his feet.

A shriek erupted in the field below him. More out of habit than any interest, he craned his long neck toward the sudden noise and isolated the figure which was now running toward the woods. He could not make out many details from this distance, but he was sure of two things: it had a long black mane, and two rapidly pumping legs.

Lathwi! No wonder her scent had been so vivid. She was playing tricks on him again! But how had she found him? Had he, in a moment of unwitting excitement, Called her? Or had she hunted him down for reasons of her own? He dismissed the questions with a shake of his wings. Now that she was here, he did not care about anything else.

With a jubilant roar, he launched himself from the cliff and went flying after her. As the gap between them narrowed, he noticed discrepancies in her appearance. She was smaller than he remembered. Scrawnier, too. And instead of scales, she was wearing a loose white skin that snapped and fluttered behind her as she ran. These differences did not bother him, though. He was always getting confused over her true size. And that new skin of hers had to be another of her tricks.

How disappointed she would be to learn that he had not been fooled!

With that thought in mind, he swooped down and tripped her with his outstretched neck. She went flying face-first into the grass, but made no effort to get up and run away. Instead, she lay where she had fallen, forcing him to land. Once aground, he prodded her with a playful claw, but all she did was begin to tremble and wail.

He cocked his head, confused and more than a little annoyed: this was not the way that the game was played. He prodded her again, a little harder this time. Her wailing increased in pitch and volume.

"Be quiet!" he told her.

She chose to ignore him.

Goaded by the noise, his annoyance soared. He cuffed her—a warning blow that tore four parallel gashes in the back of her white not-skin. An instant later, those gashes began to turn red. He felt no remorse for the blood he had raised; when playing with The Soft One, some bleeding was to be expected. Now she was supposed to get up and retaliate.

Instead, she continued to wail—a humid, high-pitched sound that hurt his ears.

"If you don't stop that, I'll bite your lips off," he threatened.

Still she ignored him.

He rumbled. What was wrong with her today? Why did she seem so intent on spoiling their fun? Was she testing him? He was no good at thought-games; she ought to know that.

With an ungentle flick of a forearm, he flipped her onto her back. As their eyes met, she started to sob and gibber. He hissed, venting consternation and rage. This was not The Soft One! Lathwi's eyes were as blue as a summer sky, not brown like shimmering mud. Nor was her face so round and ugly.

And the noise! Lathwi had never made such awful sounds!

He swatted the impostor, meaning to shut her up. By chance, he slashed her throat. She gurgled a last, liquid protest and lapsed into welcome silence.

A moment later, the hot, salted smell of red blood curled in his nostrils, inviting him to feed. He did so with his usual gusto. It did not occur to him that there might be anything wrong with this. Indeed, to his way of thinking, it would have been the very height of indecency not to eat a thing that he had just killed.

As he fed, he thought of Lathwi. It would not be easy, but he would find her.

CHAPTER 4

The next day saw Lathwi back in the saddle. She was not wholly free of the aches and pains that she had acquired from yesterday's ride, but she had long since learned to live with such minor discomforts. She did hope, however, that Pieter had not been fooling when he told her that she would not hurt nearly as much after today's ride.

They rode past a fragrant stand of flowering trees, over a series of hillocks and then into a dirt track which spanned beyond sight in both directions. It was too straight and dry to be a creek-bed; and too broad and open to be a game trail. Lathwi was instantly curious.

"What this?" she demanded.

"It's called a road," Pieter said, looking quite pleased with himself. "The road to Compara."

As they travelled along this road, the surrounding forest turned patchy and sparse. At first, she blamed this thinning on disease or high wind, but then they rode past a stretch of land that was now barer than the bleakest alpine meadow. All that remained of the trees which had once stood there was a crowd of sullen-looking stumps.

"What happen here?" she wondered aloud.

"Looks like there are charcoalers in the area," Pieter replied.

"What that?" she asked.

"They're people who turn wood into charcoal." Before she could ask, he added, "Charcoal burns hotter and cleaner than wood, which is important to people who work with glass and steel. And those who live in the city like it because it's easier to store."

She did not understand a couple of the words, but even so, she grasped the basic concept: people were killing trees for their power. Not only that, they were doing it in a very foolish way.

"Cut too much," she told him. "What happen when no more trees?"

"Look around you," he told her, gesturing broadly. "The world is full of trees. There will always be more."

Her draconic memories told her otherwise, but she didn't want to talk about those terrible, long-gone days and so rode on in thoughtful silence.

They passed another tract of treeless land, then several more. These grounds were dark and freshly turned, as if wild pigs had been rooting here. The air stank mightily of animal dung.

Then the first shack came into view.

It was a wretched-looking thing—lop-sided and flimsy, with a filthy cloth flap for a door and rotting thatch for a roof. Ground-fowl scratched for bugs in the dirt around its threshold; a mangy goat drowsed in its shade. There were at least a score of other such hovels in the immediate vicinity, too, all clumped together like warts on a toad. For reasons which Lathwi could neither fathom nor explain, the sight of this squalid roadside cluster left her squirming inside.

"This Compara?" she asked, fervently hoping that it was not.

"No, Lathwi," Pieter replied, with a generous dollop of disgust in his tone, "this is only a crude peasant's village. Compara is much more civilized."

A series of shouts snared their attention then. They looked toward the sound to see a smooth-faced man with long, honey-coloured hair come running out from between two shacks with a swarm of angry-seeming men on his heels.

"Help!" the blonde man cried, as his pursuers caught up with him. "Won't someone please help me?"

Prodded by reasons which continued to elude her, Lathwi urged her mount closer. Although she barely noticed, Pieter did the same.

Two of the peasants were holding the blonde man by the arms now; a third was punching him in the belly. The blonde was dirty and grass-stained, and one corner of his mouth was leaking blood, but despite his dishevelled appearance, it was obvious that he was no peasant. His clothes were too fancy; his bearing, too refined.

"Here now," Pieter scolded, as they approached. "What's this man done to deserve such treatment?"

"He tried to ravage my wife," the man who had been doing all the punching snarled.

"That's not true!" the accused declared. "I would never touch a woman without her consent."

The swarm jeered, proclaiming him a liar and worse, but Pieter was not so sure. The accused was a handsome man, and well-spoken. It did not seem as if he would need to force a woman's charms from her. Then again, what men needed to do, and what they wound up doing weren't always one and the same thing. And not all outlaws were as obvious as Drell and his pack had been.

"What are you going to do with him?" he asked then.

"We're going to castrate the city-bred pig," the outraged husband replied, flashing a grin full of yellowed teeth. "If he survives, we'll set him free; if he doesn't, we'll take to our beds tonight knowing that we've done the world a favour.

"For a penny, you're welcome to stay and watch."

"Please, friend," the accused begged then. "Don't let them do this. I swear by The Dreamer that I'm innocent."

Pieter did not know what to do. While he had no desire to stand between these people and their justice, he did not want to see the wrong man lose his balls, either. He turned to Lathwi. Her expression was distant and strained.

"What do you think?" he whispered.

She did not hear him. Unease had been building within her like a thunderstorm; now it needed only a nudge to break. And until that nudge came, she could do nothing but watch and wait.

Meanwhile, the blonde man's captors wrestled him onto his belly and tried to bind his wrists. "Dreamer," one of them swore. "He's a slippery bastard."

"Most pigs are," the husband said, and then strode over to a neighbour's wood-pile. When he returned a moment later, there was a stout log in his hands. "This ought to hold him down while we tend to business." Then, as he handed the log to one of his accomplices, he glanced at Pieter. "How about it, Mister? Do you have a penny or not?"

Pieter turned to Lathwi again. She was sitting rigid in the saddle now. Her gaze was locked on the man with the log. As he went to thrust it through the bound loops of the blonde man's arms, she howled a protest and then urged the bay right into the crowd. Pieter's astonishment did not stop him from following her lead.

Startled, the crowd fell back. In the next instant, it surged forward again, swearing and shouting for blood. Hands reached for Pieter, trying to tear him out of his saddle. He drove them off with panic-induced dexterity, rein-whipping or kicking everything that came within range. As he fought, he glanced here and there for the accused, but he was nowhere in sight. Gone, he thought then. And: the bastard had probably been guilty after all.

"Let's get out of here!" he shouted at Lathwi.

But she was lost to a world where he did not exist. In that world, a black-haired youngling with desperate blue eyes was trying to escape the crowd of peasants that held her. As she struggled, bucking and squirming, somebody bound her arms behind her back. Somebody else set a chain of flowers around her neck. Then, through a blur of furious tears, she saw the log that was to serve as her hobble. It would all but wrench her arms from their sockets once it was in place. She could not let that happen. So she lashed out, again and again and again.

Then something hard slammed into her jaw, surprising her out of her trance. She blinked back a swirl of confusion and tears to find herself being pelted by stones. One caught the stallion in the flank; he squealed a protest and then reared. As she struggled to stay in the saddle, Pieter and his string of horses came racing toward her. His harried look acquired pained ridges as a fist-sized rock struck him in the ribs.

"Let's get out of here!" he shouted in passing.

Sane again, she gladly complied.

They rode all-out for nearly a league, then slowed to an easy walk so the horses could catch their breath. Pieter was glad for the respite, too, for his left side felt like it was on fire. He fingered those ribs gingerly, feeling for lumps, but they were only bruised, not broken. Then he glanced over his shoulder to see how Lathwi had fared. Aside from a pulpy lip, she seemed to have escaped unscathed. Even so, her look was grim. Was she thinking about the stranger she had saved? Was she, too, feeling like she had been handed the shitty end of the stick? He closed the gap between them to find out.

"How's your mouth?" he asked her.

She traced her tongue over the swelling, then shrugged to show her unconcern.

"Does it ache you to talk?" When she shrugged again, he felt free to question her further. "Then tell me something, Lathwi—why did you help that man?"

"What man?"

"The golden-haired fellow," he said testily, in no mood for games. "The one you rescued back there in the village."

Ah, yes. She remembered now—the one for whom the log had been intended. Coincidence had been his saviour, not her. If those peasants hadn't tried to hobble him, she would have cheerfully rode away and never looked back.

"Well?" he prompted, pleased for the chance to badger her for a change. "Why'd you do it?"

Now that was a different question. She could still see that black-haired youngling, still feel her helpless rage.

"Hate peasants," she said.

"Why?"

In spite of her efforts to keep it contained, the memory came surging back into prominence. She described the images as they unfolded before her mind's eye.

"When I be youngling, peasants do to me the same as they want do to man today. That log heavy, much hurt my arms, but peasants not hear my cries. They drag me to meadow and leave me."

This admission, so blandly made, shocked Pieter to the core of his heart. No child deserved so cruel a punishment, not even the worst hellion.

"How did you get away?" he asked.

"Mother come," she replied, smiling now as she relived this part. "Take me far away."

He regarded her with a mixture of awe and rue. Her life had more twists to it than a gopher-hole. Why would a mother save a daughter from a certain death sentence only to outcast her later on? And why would a daughter still yearn for that mother after such a devastating betrayal?

Those questions hummed in his head like bees, but he did not voice them aloud. He did not want to cause her any more grief, he told himself. And Aunt Liselle had taught him that some things were better left unsaid.

Lathwi did not notice his discreet lapse into silence. She was still soaring through the sky in Taziem's arms.

They made their camp in the forest that night, far from the road and unfriendly eyes. Pieter built himself a little fire, then sat down to a meal of pan-bread and jerky. Opting to go hungry until the morning, Lathwi settled down to sleep. But even as she started to doze off, the bay's uneasy nicker roused her again. A moment later, a snapping twig and then a steady crunching swept the last sleepy cobwebs from her mind. Anything that noisy had to be stupid, she thought; and stupid things were often good to eat. She uncinched a claw and then hid herself behind a tree.

Pieter appeared alongside of her. His arms were folded over his chest, his eyes were aimed at the sound. She tried to nudge him into hiding, but he did not budge.

"Something come," she hissed then. "Maybe it something tasty."

"It's a horse," he replied flatly. "And horses in these parts usually come with riders."

Her stomach grumbled, decrying the theory, but now that she thought about it, the crunching did sound like hoof beats. And moments later, an ochre-coloured horse with a white blaze came winding its way out of the leafy shadows. Its rider was the golden-haired man.

"Hullo!" he cried, as he verged on their camp. "Praise the Dreamer for guiding me here. I was afraid I'd lost you."

"What do you want?" Pieter demanded.

"I want to thank you and your friend for your help," he replied, unruffled by the trapper's hostile tone. "I'd also like to apologize for skipping out during the confusion."

"Apology noted," Pieter said. "Now off you go."

"I was also hoping to share your fire tonight," the man continued, with a self-conscious smile, "and to tell you my side of the story while we feast—" He patted the yearling doe which was slung over his horse's withers. "—on this."

"We aren't hungry."

"Really?" The stranger's eyes grew lively with sudden amusement. "Your friend looks famished to me."

One quick glimpse confirmed that assertion: Lathwi was staring at the carcass with wolfish intensity. Her nostrils were flared. Her jaws were clenched. There was a thin line of drool trickling down the side of her chin. Pieter knew then that further argument was useless.

"If you must, then join us," he grumbled.

"My thanks," the stranger replied, and then swung down from his saddle. As he hauled the deer down from its perch, he added, "By the way, my friends call me Jamus. I would be honoured if you would do the same."

"I am called Pieter," he said. "My companion's name is Lathwi."

"Well met," Jamus replied, flashing them a grin, "and good fortune to us all. Although you may not appreciate it yet, I am in your debt."

He dumped the carcass by the fire, then went to picket his horse. Pieter followed on his heels, just to make sure that this smooth-talking stranger didn't take anything that didn't belong to him.

Lathwi helped herself to a goodly portion of the carcass in their absence, and was already well into her supper by the time they returned. She ate with both hands at an incredible speed, and gulped down more than she chewed. Her swollen lip did not slow her down at all. She was supremely happy at the moment—and quite oblivious to the men and their incredulous stares.

"Lathwi," Pieter croaked, when he finally recovered his voice, "what are you doing? That's not cooked."

Obviously, she thought, exultant over that fact. But the abundance of meat had put her in a generous mood. Rather than comment on his acuity or lack thereof, she motioned him toward the carcass.

"Is good," she told him, between one bite and the next. "Eat."

Jamus shook his head. His mouth was a complex twist of amused disbelief and civilized revulsion. The look endeared him to Pieter, who was suddenly grateful for the company of a normal human being.

"Don't worry," he said, twitching him a long-suffering smile. "She's not crazy, just a little different."

At that, Jamus did an immediate double-take. And as he took a harder look at Lathwi, his jaw sagged with disbelief. "Dreamer keep me!" he blurted, too stunned for tact. "That's a woman?" "Hard to believe, isn't it?" Pieter dropped to one knee and began to carve thick steaks from the deer's loin. "When I first met her, I thought she was some kind of demon."

Fascinated, Jamus continued to stare. Even by the soft, kindly light of a campfire, she seemed more mannish than not. Her shoulders were too broad; her hips, too narrow; and she had no breasts of which to speak.

"I never would have guessed," he murmured to himself. "Never."

He reached into the pocket of his travelling cloak and retrieved a shiny silver flask, then took a long swig of its contents.

"Here," he said, tearing his eyes away from Lathwi long enough to pass the flask to Pieter. "Have a drink." Then, because his fascination demanded details, he asked, "Do you and your wife travel often?"

"She's not my wife," Pieter assured him, smiling at the thought as he sniffed the flask. "And this is our first and last trip together." Encouraged by the liquor's nutty aroma, he tipped a measure down his throat. His windpipe started to sizzle. "Good stuff," he wheezed, and then handed the flask back to Jamus. "Thanks."

"My pleasure."

In truth, he was delighted—not just with Pieter, who was proving to be likeable in spite of the unfortunate matter which still stood between them, but with Lathwi as well. He loved women—not just the beauties and the flirts, but the plain and the shy as well. Each posed a different challenge for him; each yielded a different sort of pleasure. When he speculated about the thrills that mannish, enigmatic Lathwi might have to offer, he got goose-flesh all over his body.

The steaks were sizzling over the fire now. Pieter fussed with them for a moment, then sat down to let them cook. Jamus sank into a crouch alongside of him and offered the flask again.

With a polite wave of his hand, Pieter declined. His blood was already tingling in his veins; another sip would have him giddy. And as much as he had warmed to Jamus over the last quarter-hour, he had no intention of getting drunk with a man whose character was still suspect.

"While we're waiting for our meat," he said, in a tone too firm to be casual, "why don't you give me your version of what happened back there at that village."

"An excellent idea," Jamus said, displaying no trace of rancour or resentment. He took another drink from his flask, then cleared his throat and began to speak.

"I am Jamus D'Arques, first lieutenant to Wynn Rame, the governor of Compara. I was returning from trade negotiations in L'Luus when I came upon that village. On any other day, I would've ridden on through with all possible haste, but as it happened, it was getting dark out, and I was road-weary, so I paid that big, brown-haired peasant with the rock-hard fists for the privilege of sleeping in his haystack. His wife gave me supper, too—cold bread and ham, as I recall.

"Ah, but she was a comely thing, with hair as brown as forest mushrooms, and breasts as full as melons. As I ate, she flirted with me; and I must confess, my friend; I flirted back. But because she was married, and I'm not an utter cad, I did not invite her to join me in the hay.

"This morning, she brought me bread and a mug of milky tea, and told me that she'd be pitching hay alone at noon if I wanted to get to know her better. And because she offered, and I'm only human—"

He sighed, a sound both wistful and bitter. "The only detail you need to know about that tryst is this: she was as happy as a lark right up until the moment her husband called for her. Then she turned frantic and started screaming like a she-panther caught in a steel trap. Shortly thereafter, I found myself being chased by the whole damned village.

"You know what happened after that."

"That I do," Pieter replied, determined not to let this rakish fellow wriggle off the hook so soon. "You cut out on us in the middle of a nasty mess."

"What else was I supposed to do?" Jamus retorted. "Wait for one of you to pluck me out of the crowd? Be reasonable, my friend. If you were caught in the middle of a riot with your hands tied behind your back, wouldn't you high-tail it, too?"

"Maybe," Pieter said, an admission as honest as it was grudging. "But if that's the case, then how did you manage to free yourself? And where did you get the horse?"

"That horse has been mine for the last five years now," Jamus asserted. "The lass who started the trouble brought it to me after I escaped from the crowd. She untied my hands as well. In return for her help, all she asked was that I take her with me." He shook his head at the nerve of some people. "Under the circumstances, I had to refuse.

"So," he said then, shedding the last of his apologetic look. "That's the long and short of it, my friend. If you wish, I'll leave now, with no hard feelings on my part."

"That won't be necessary," Pieter told him. "I believe you."

"And how does your lady—"

"Lathwi," he corrected.

"How does she feel?"

Pieter glanced at her. She was happily licking blood from her fingers. "Who knows?" he replied. "But since she hasn't asked you to leave, it's probably safe to assume that she won't mind if you stay a little longer."

"A most eloquent acquittal," Jamus said, curling his mouth into a sardonic half-smile. "I am touched to the core of my being.

"But in all seriousness," he continued, his smile now curving into a gentler bend, "I thank you both for all you did on my behalf. If there is anything I can do for either of you, you only need to ask."

The two men shared another drink from Jamus' flask, then fetched their steaks from the fire and began to eat.

Full now and immensely content with the world as it was, Lathwi sat back and watched as the men fed. They were dainty eaters, and amazingly slow; in the time it took them to carve a bite-sized piece and prong it into their mouths, she could have devoured an entire slab of meat. Eat it or lose it was a lesson she had learned early on from her tanglemates.

"Would you care for some of my steak?" Jamus asked then, mistaking Lathwi's unblinking scrutiny for hunger. "I'm sure I won't be able to eat the whole thing."

She disdained his offer with a hiss. "Not eat char."

"Personally," Pieter commented between bites, "I think a little char adds flavour to the meat."

"Roll deer in ash pit," she proposed. "Ruin meat faster that way."

"Forget I mentioned it," he grumbled, and then returned the whole of his attention to his dinner.

When he had finally eaten his fill, Jamus wiped his face and hands on a corner of his travel cloak, and then produced his flask again.

"How about a little drink of fire to wash it all down?" he asked Pieter.

Lathwi pounced on the ridiculous statement. "You no can drink fire."

"No?" A mischievous grin tugged at the corners of his mouth. He winked at Pieter, then leaned forward and pressed the flask into her hand. "How can you be sure if you haven't tried it?"

She raised the container to her nose and sniffed at the fumes which were radiating from its mouth. They were bitter and sharp, not at all like smoke from a fire. She arched a suspicious eyebrow at Jamus, who nodded encouragement, then at Pieter, who merely shrugged. Curious now, she tipped the flask back and drank.

An instant after the fluid hit her throat, it ignited. Heat billowed through her in sickening waves; her stomach broke out in a sweat. But even as she struggled to keep her gorge down, the nausea subsided and a glow took root in her head.

"So," Jamus said, grinning at her reaction. "What do you think of my fire-water?"

The glow spread from her head to all parts of her body. She remembered feeling like this once before—a time long ago when Taziem had let her suckle alongside of the rest of her newborn tanglemates.

"It like mother's milk," she replied dreamily.

He laughed. "If that stuff had flowed from my mother's paps, she'd never have been able to wean me!"

Homesick now, Lathwi drank again, a larger draught than the first.

"Easy now, don't drink it all," Jamus cried, enclosing the protest with more laughter. "Here, hand it back."

"Mine," she hissed, and then bared her teeth, ready to defend her claim.

Interpreting this as playfulness on her part, he grinned and stood up. "I'll wrestle you for it."

"I wouldn't do that if I were you," Pieter advised him. "She's serious. And if you so much as touch her while she's in this sort of mood, she's apt to tear you to pieces."

"You're joking!" Jamus accused him. He found it hard to believe that any woman would want to hurt him. And the idea of grappling with Lathwi excited him. "Aren't you?"

"I've seen her shred a man's face with her fingernails simply because he annoyed her," Pieter replied.

Jamus hmphed. Perhaps more circumspection was called for after all. He did an abrupt about-face, then headed for his saddlebags. When he returned, it was with another flask in hand.

"Fortunately, " he drawled, as he resumed his seat, "I like to travel well-prepared. But I'm warning you, friend: I won't take very kindly to having this one appropriated."

"Don't give it to her and she won't keep it," Pieter said. "As for me, I'm willing to share as long as you are."

The two men passed the new flask back and forth a couple of times, then settled back to enjoy the fire. "What we need now," Jamus said, "is a minstrel to sing us all to sleep."

"Don't look at me," Pieter replied, with a wobbly smile. "I can't carry a tune to save my life. When I was young, my aunt used to ply me with caramels to keep me quiet."

"How about you, Lathwi?" Jamus asked, caressing her with his tone. "You're a woman of many hidden talents. Dare we hope that singing is one of them?"

Pieter suppressed a tipsy giggle. Unless he was sorely mistaken, Jamus was actually trying to flirt with Lathwi! He shifted, hoping to make himself as inconspicuous as possible. This promised to be a very entertaining evening indeed!

As for Lathwi, she was far more interested in a piece of gristle that had lodged between her molars than anything that Jamus had said to her. When she finally worked it free, she spat it into the fire, then drifted into a gauzy nether world of her own making. Her unresponsiveness was a challenge that Jamus could not resist. He would find a way to interest her in him; now it was a matter of pride.

"It looks like it's up to me," he said, then cleared his throat and began to sing a love-ballad.

The stranger's warbling snared Lathwi's attention for a moment, but when she could make no sense of the words he was singing, she returned to her own dreamy musings. Shoq would like this not-water, she decided, taking another swallow. It turned one's thoughts into shiny beads of quicksilver: fun to watch, impossible to hold. Then again, Shoq's thoughts were probably like that all the time. She smiled at that, but her amusement abruptly gave way to a bout of longing. She closed her eyes to savour the boundless images of her tanglemate.

"That was beautiful," Pieter crooned, when Jamus brought his song to a close. "Might I persuade you to sing another?"

"Maybe later," Jamus replied, and then glanced at Lathwi in the hope that she would coax him for an encore, too. When he saw that her eyes were closed, a scowl of mock indignation ridged his handsome brow. "Damn, I didn't even manage to put a smile on her face. Does she always look that fierce?"

"No," Pieter said, inordinately pleased that he was not the only one whom Lathwi managed to confound. "Sometimes she looks downright terrifying." Then, because he didn't want to talk about her all night, he changed the subject. "This gish is excellent. Shall we have a smoke to go with it?"

"Splendid suggestion," Jamus said. Then, as the trapper fumbled for his pipe and weed, he asked, "Do you think she's ever been with a man?"

"I couldn't say," Pieter replied. "I've only known her for a few days. And in that short span of time, I've learned not to speculate about her past doings."

What they didn't know was that while Lathwi's eyes were closed, she was very much awake and listening to the ongoing conversation. This aspect of man-talk intrigued her. When dragons spoke to each other, only those addressed could hear.

"I'll bet she'd be a wild cat in bed," Jamus went on.

"I don't know about that," Pieter countered. "My guess is that she's more like a spider than a cat."

"Why's that?"

"After spiders mate, the female eats the male."

Lathwi allowed herself a private smile. It pleased her to know that Pieter held her in such high regard.

The two men lapsed into silence then. A moment later, their breathing patterns shifted, becoming deep and slow. At first, Lathwi thought that they were falling asleep, but then she caught a whiff of a strange-smelling smoke. It was acrid and sweet, cloying as wood smoke was not. She opened one eye to a slit. The other sprang wide open of its own accord.

Pieter was breathing smoke! It flowed from his nostrils like twin streamers of fog, then danced in circles away from his mouth.

"How you do that?" she blurted.

Startled by her sudden outburst, the two men bolted out of their boneless poses. An instant later, Pieter wagged a reproving finger at her and said, "You shouldn't sneak up on people like that."

She did not bother to point out that she had been in the same spot all night long. She was too intent on his newfound talent. "How you breath smoke?"

"This is a pipe," he said, holding up a long clay tube that bore a small, steaming bowl at one end. "It's got a bit of burning tobacco in it. When I put my mouth to the tip and inhale, smoke flows down the stem and into my chest. When I exhale, the smoke goes out my mouth." He demonstrated then. "See? There's nothing to it."

"I try now," she told him.

"Only if you promise to give the pipe back when you're done," Pieter countered.

Although dragons did not like to make promises, Lathwi's desire to make smoke was compelling. "I give pipe back."

"Say you'll return it tonight," he pressed, catching the deceptive flicker in her tone.

She grinned, congratulating him for his perceptiveness. If he had not made the effort to be more specific, she would have been able to keep the pipe indefinitely without breaking her word. Now she was obliged to accept whatever conditions he cared to impose.

"I return tonight," she said. "Give now. I try."

He handed her the pipe. She held it a moment, intrigued by the sensation of cool clay warmed from within, then raised the tip to her mouth. The hot, spicy odour of burning tobacco tweaked her nose. She paused, waiting for a sneeze that lost its momentum, then took a deep breath.

A forest of nettles clawed at her throat. A cold hand gripped her intestines. She coughed the smoke back up, then gagged as the dry, rancid taste of tobacco coated her mouth. For a moment, she feared she would vomit.

"What for you breath that smoke?" she demanded then.

"People smoke for pleasure," Jamus told her, his voice rippling with barely suppressed amusement. "Didn't you enjoy the feeling of sweet, cool smoke in your lungs?"

"No." Her head was whirling like it did after one of Shoq's dives. Her stomach was squirming, too. How could anyone mistake such misery for pleasure? "Make me sick."

Pieter chuckled. "I'll admit, it's an acquired taste."

"What that?"

"Something that grows more pleasurable over time," Jamus explained. "The more you do it, the more you like it."

"Why do more than once if no like first time? That not smart."

He dismissed that accusation with a shrug. "If people gave up on everything they didn't like the first time, we'd all still be hanging on to our mothers' teats."

That was not a true answer to her question, but she did not wish to pursue the matter further. She thrust the pipe back into Pieter's hand. "You keep. Not want."

"Whatever you say," he said, and then pulled a twig from the fire to relight the tobacco. She sniffed—not even Fire liked the awful stuff! Then the smell of it sent her stomach into another tailspin. She got up and headed downwind of the stench. Humans! she thought, as she curled up under a tree. She could study them forever and still not understand them.

Morning thundered down from the trees, an excruciating cacophony of bird song and rustling leaves. Lathwi peeled her eyelids open only to squeeze them shut again as rays of sharp-edged sunlight lanced into her impossibly tender brain. An instant later, her head began to throb to the beat of her heart. She groaned.

"Get up, Lathwi," Pieter boomed in a voice as great as a dragon-sire's. "It's time to hit the road."

"Shut up," she hissed.

"Good morning, Lathwi," Jamus said, as she struggled to her feet. "How are you feeling today?" The false sweetness in his voice suggested that he already knew the answer.

"Head hurt," she said. "Got stomach full of nettles."

His chuckle was not entirely sympathetic. "That's what happens when you drink too much gish."

"That not-water do this to me?" she demanded, glaring at him despite the ache in her eyeballs. When he nodded, she hissed. "Why you not say last night?"

"Would you have believed me?"

She continued to glare at him, but inwardly she had to concede his point. Up until this very moment, she had viewed him as superfluous, remarkable only as a convenient source of meat and exotic drink. She would not have believed him if he had told her that not-water would turn to poison in her veins overnight. She would not have believed him if he'd said that water was wet. So. She had learned one lesson here, perhaps more. Next time, she would be more circumspect.

She stared at him until he went away, and then stumbled into the woods to relieve herself. On her way back to camp, Pieter intercepted her.

"Jamus wants to ride with us," he told her. "I wouldn't mind having him along because there's safety in numbers. And besides, I like the man. You have the final say, though."

Safety did not usually interest her. Neither did Jamus. But since Pieter seemed to value the noisy man's company, she was willing to endure it—for now. "He want come, I not say no."

"I'll tell him that," he said, and then hurried off in Jamus' direction.

The two men conferred for a moment, then started to pack up their belongings. Meanwhile, she went over to the bay and began to saddle him. The stallion was in a feisty mood this morning and made her work harder

65

than she wanted to, but the exertion purged some of the gish from her brain. By the time Pieter and Jamus were ready to go, she was feeling more like a dragon than dragon dung.

They returned to the road, then continued on their way at a leisurely pace. As the morning wore on, it turned muggy and hot—a fact which the two men discussed at great length. Lathwi scorned such foolish talk. The weather was not going to change simply because they did not like it. Yet this was typical of them, she reminded herself. They did not seem to care about the conversation's contents, only the conversation itself. Jamus was worse than Pieter was in that regard—his vocal chords were better developed than his eyes, his ears or his nose. Indeed, he had probably talked yesterday's deer to death. She rumbled then, amused by the notion.

"What's so funny?" Pieter asked, in the mood to share a joke.

She did not feel like repeating the string of thoughts that had led to her tickling, so she rolled her shoulders and said nothing.

Her silence annoyed Jamus. For some reason, he was sure that she had been laughing at him. He glimpsed at her out of the corner of his eye, searching for minute facial clues that would confirm his suspicions, but she was as unreadable as a stone. Worse, she seemed genuinely unaware of his scrutiny. Her indifference whetted his curiosity even as it stung his pride. There had to be something he could do to capture her attention.

The idea came to him like a thunderclap: he would throw her and Pieter a party! Women adored parties. And ulterior motives aside, it was no less than she deserved. He'd issue Pieter an invitation first, he decided then. If the trapper accepted, she might be more inclined to follow suit. And if she felt a just little left out in the meantime, well—that was fine with him, too.

"So tell me, Pieter," he said, in a voice loud enough to be overheard. "What are you going to do while you're home in Compara?"

"Not much," the trapper replied. "I'll probably spend most of my free time with my aunt, which means quiet dinners by the fire and lots of rest."

"No offense, my friend," Jamus told him then, "but that doesn't sound very exciting."

"I've had more than my fair share of excitement on this trip," he drawled. "A week or so of peace and quiet will do me good."

"Peace and quiet are splendid antidotes for overwrought nerves, but in large doses, they can be just as taxing as any adventure. What you need, old boy, is a little variety."

"Such as?" Pieter prompted, recognizing a pitch when he heard one.

"I'd like to host a party in your honour," Jamus replied, "as a token of my appreciation for your friendship and aid. I'll have your favourite meats cooked to a fine turn, and all the gish that you can possibly consume. I'll hire the finest minstrel in Compara, and a troupe of dancers as well.

"Will you come, my friend? I'll do my best to make it a night you won't forget."

"I wouldn't miss it for the world," Pieter declared.

Jamus laughed and clapped the trapper on the back, then turned his smile on Lathwi. "And how about you, my dear? By rights, this party should have two guests of honour. Will you come?"

"No," she replied.

"Come on now, don't be such a spoilsport," he wheedled. "I'll bet that you'd have the time of your life."

"What 'bet', Pieter?" she asked. She had heard the word before, but had gotten no clear impression as to its meaning.

"A bet is a sort of game played by two or more people," he said. "Each player predicts the outcome of a particular event—such as a horse-race or a fight—and then promises something of value to the one whose prediction comes true."

She pondered the explanation for a moment, then said, "So Jamus predict I want eat ruined meat and drink not-water that make me stomach-sick and head-sore in morning?"

"That's what it sounded like to me," he agreed, unable to keep a smirk from his tone.

"Stupid prediction," she said.

"So it would seem."

She turned a toothy grin on Jamus. "What you promise?"

"Nothing," he grumbled, casting her a look as black as a storm cloud. "Nothing at all."

"Nothing got no value," she pointed out.

"I believe he has reconsidered the matter and no longer wishes to bet with you," Pieter told her. "Next time, shake his hand after he proposes a bet that you'd like to accept."

"Why?"

"That's how we sanctify our promises in this province."

"Saying promise not suffice?"

"Not always," he said, a hint of sadness creeping into his tone. "Some men will say anything to get what they want. Their promises don't mean a thing to them or anyone else."

"This hand-shaking stop them from making not-promises?"

"No," he said, both amazed and touched by her naivete. "Hand-shaking isn't sorcery, only a gesture of good faith."

She hissed, appalled by such moral depravity. Dragons avoided promises but never broke them; and while they might exaggerate a fact or withhold it from a telling, they never deliberately breathed an untruth into being. What sort of barbaric creatures were these humans? What sort of fortune could she expect to find among them?

Her turbulent thoughts revived the pounding in her head. She kneed the bay into a trot, purposely leaving the two men behind.

Eventually, Lathwi overcame her disgust and rejoined her companions. She had decided not to condemn Pieter for being human—his honest words and actions were ample proof that he had risen above his perverse birthright. And while Jamus was a less civilized sort, she was willing to put up with him for now, too, just so she could compare and contrast.

The afternoon slipped by without notice, then ended with a crimson flourish. As twilight began to draw the last hints of red from the sky, Pieter began looking for a likely place to camp. The day's ride, combined with last night's gish, had left him suddenly tired, and he wanted nothing more than to stretch out in front of a fire and relax. He could almost smell that fire's resinous smoke now.

He tensed, stung by a realization: his imagination was not that good! A moment later, Jamus sounded a quiet alarm. "Look alive, my friends. We've got company."

Two mounted men emerged from the left side of the woods. They were a swarthy duo, with coarse black hair cut close to their heads and eyes the colour of a moon-less night. The tiny loops of gold in their ears belied their homespun appearance.

"Gypsies," Jamus murmured, not unfriendly, but wary just the same. "Guard your purses if you have them."

The strangers reined their horses to a halt in front of them. The larger of the two raised his right hand, palm held outward, and then grinned. Lathwi was immediately intrigued, for his two front teeth were gold.

"Greetings, friends," he said. "I am Santana, leader of a scion of the Wandering Tribe. This," he said, gesturing to the dour-faced man to his right, "is my brother, Yorgi. How fares the road ahead?"

"Like most roads, it has its good and bad points," Jamus replied, assuming an easy, bantering tone. "The going itself is no problem; the road is firm and dry. But my friends here have encountered outlaws—"

"That lot won't be troubling you or anyone else," Pieter interjected, endowing the reassurance with a subtle warning. Santana rewarded him with an approving flash of gold.

"—and the village which lies a day's ride from here is filled with vile-tempered peasants," Jamus went on. "If you stop there, tell your men to beware a comely young woman with hair the colour of forest mushrooms. They could lose more than their hearts to her."

Santana's grin turned suddenly ambiguous. Afraid that he might have given offense where none was intended, Jamus hastened to change the subject.

"My guess is that you're coming from Compara," he said. "How fares the white-walled city?"

"Compara is her usual sluttish self," the gypsy replied, instantly cheerful again. "She's quick to give of her bounty to those who have gold, but equally quick to scorn those who do not."

The gypsy gave each of them a probing look then, saving Lathwi for last. A vague frown flitted across his brow as he eyed her scales and girdle of claws, but he dismissed it with another of his golden smiles.

"But we need not talk about such things in the middle of the road," he exclaimed. "Come, share our fires tonight. We are not rich, but what we have is yours. Eat with us. Drink with us. Let our women tell your fortune. And while you are among us, maybe you will purchase some of our humble wares to take back to your loved ones in Compara."

Pieter opened his mouth, ready with a polite refusal, but Lathwi cut him off before he could get a word out.

"Yes," she hissed, her eyes as lively as a pair of blue sparks. "I come. Want hear fortune."

Santana loosed a delighted yip and then reined his horse around. "Come, friends, our wagons are this way." As he and his taciturn brother went riding off, he added, "What a night this will be!"

Pieter groaned. In the short span of time since Lathwi had barged into his life, he had been attacked; nearly raped, robbed and murdered; and involved in a minor riot. He was in no hurry to add a night with gypsies to that list. Everybody knew what a volatile race they were—even an imagined insult could send them running for their knives. A smart man would high-tail it out of here while his hide was still intact, he told himself. But as much as the notion appealed to him, he knew he was not going anywhere so long as Lathwi had her mind set on staying. Because even though she was almost twice his size and a sorceress to boot, he—he rolled his eyes at the admission—felt responsible for her.

He exchanged a look with Jamus. The blonde man shrugged and said, "What the hell, we have sleep somewhere. And gypsy women are beautiful."

Pieter shook his head in mock dismay. Then he and his incorrigible new friend urged their horses toward the woods.

Lathwi was already far ahead of them. She was curious about these strangers. Furthermore, she wanted them to tell her fortune. As she threaded her way through the trees, she came upon a most peculiar sight: four small houses perched on wheels. She rode in closer to get a better look, then hissed with surprise and delight as she saw the dragons on the sides of the houses! They were only images, and not drawn to size, but even so, it was good to see one of her own again.

As she contemplated the painted figures, Pieter drew up alongside of her and started whispering.

"Choose your words carefully tonight," he warned, "for gypsies have notoriously quick tempers. They also have no qualms about stealing, so you might want to keep an eye on your gold."

She grinned. There might be hope for humans after all.

A wave of children came spilling around the corner then. "This way, this way!" they sing-songed, and began tugging at bridles and reins. Lathwi's bay snapped at one pudgy little boy who got too close, and for once, Pieter did not object to the beast's foul temperament. No one in his right mind would want to steal him, so they would have at least one horse left to them in the morning.

The children guided them to a makeshift corral. As they dismounted, Santana reappeared. On foot, he stood as tall as Jamus, who was only a half-hand shorter than Lathwi, but his dancer's lithe build made him seem smaller.

"Please," he urged. "Allow our young ones to care for your mounts. They are good with animals, and will treat them well."

Too well, Pieter thought, and then grudgingly handed his reins to a doe-eyed little girl with a missing front tooth.

Santana ushered them into a clearing studded with small campfires. There, a crowd of brown-skinned people formed a loose circle around them. "Friends," he said then, his chest swelling with pride, "welcome to our camp."

"Our thanks for your hospitality, Master Santana," Jamus replied. "A night on the road is never cold when spent among friends.

"I am called Jamus," he continued, clearly at ease with his ambassadorial role. "My companions are named Pieter and Lathwi. We are at your service."

"Well met," the gypsy leader said. "Allow me to introduce you to the family.

"This is Gem, my wife." A short, bosomy woman with ring-encrusted fingers stepped forward, then pinched a corner of her voluminous, multicolored skirt and dipped into a graceful curtsey. Lathwi stared, fascinated by her shiny, blood-red toenails.

"These are my children," he went on, and affectionately stroked their heads as he named them. "Tikki—" A willow wand of a woman-child with her father's exotic looks and her mother's unabashed breasts batted her eyelashes at them. Now it was Jamus' turn to be fascinated. "—Damiano—" This was the pudgy little boy who had almost lost a chunk of flesh to Lathwi's bay. "—and little Mim, our baby." She refused to come out from behind her mother's skirt.

"And over here we have my wife's brother, Tavi." A scar below this one's right eye gave his plain, clean-shaven face a hint of mystery. "Behind him is his wife, Silver," Hers was a delicate face framed by waves of black hair. "their oldest son, Luke," He was a pale-skinned boy on the verge of manhood. Like his uncle, he moved with a dancer's grace. Pieter distrusted his sly green eyes and self-confident air. "and their twin imps, Raul and Paulito."

The introduction moved to Yorgi and his family, then on to his wife's relatives. Lathwi did not try to keep track of names and faces. To her, they were all just one fascinating swirl. The younglings in particular amazed her. She found it hard to believe that humans started out that small.

Finally, Santana's gaze stretched beyond the circle and over to the only person who had not rushed over to meet the newcomers. She was seated in front of a small private fire, a wizened figure wrapped in a shawl and the world's dignity. Her hair was as white as moonlight.

"It is my privilege to introduce you to our mother," he said. "Katya, the Wandering Queen, wisest of us all."

She raised her hand as if in blessing. "You are our guests," she said, sounding as brittle as she seemed. "Be welcome at our fires."

Out of respect for her age and obvious authority, Pieter and Jamus bowed. She acknowledged their courtesy with a nod, then dismissed them with a slight flick of her wrist.

"Come," Santana said then, "let us retire to the fires. While we're waiting for our supper, we can have a drink and talk more about the village you mentioned earlier." He gave Pieter and Jamus a gentle push in that direction, then turned to Lathwi. "Please do not disturb Katya, friend. She is old and tires easily. Come, join the rest of my family instead."

Lathwi did not hear a word. Her attention was focussed on Katya. There was something compelling about this ancient human—her amazing decrepitude perhaps, or perhaps the way in which she spied on the world when she thought no one was watching. Driven by curiosity, she strode over and hunkered down beside her. An instant later, Santana and his brothers converged on her with hard lights in their eyes. Before any of them could lay a finger on her, though, Katya stayed their hands.

"This one means me no harm," she murmured.

"How can you be sure?" Yorgi asked, the first words that Lathwi had ever heard him speak. She wondered why he sounded so concerned.

"That is one of my gifts," Katya replied. "Now leave us be. I would speak with this strange friend of ours."

Grudgingly, the men withdrew. When they were gone, the old gypsy levelled her white-lashed gaze on Lathwi and asked, "So what is it that you want of me, child?"

The answer, adamantly elusive a moment ago, now seemed suddenly obvious. "Want you tell my fortune."

Katya heaved a nasal sigh, then pressed her right palm to Lathwi's forehead and shut her eyes. Her touch was cool, almost unnaturally so. Lathwi stifled an urge to pull away.

"Peculiar times," the gypsy muttered, when she finally withdrew her hand. "First magical warnings in the middle of the night, now an outsider with the impossible in her head."

"Say again?"

"I don't understand," Katya said, turning her troubled brown eyes on Lathwi. "Why do I see dragons in your mind?"

"Not dragons. Womans," she replied, and then flushed with excitement. This old one was clever.

"Not women," Katya insisted. "I am a woman. You are a woman. The creatures that I see in your head are dragons: a great black, a bronze, and many others."

"If those be dragons," she said, vexed by the confusion which this man-talk could cause, "I be dragon too."

Katya's eyes went round with disbelief, then narrowed back into deep-set slits. She peered at Lathwi for a long moment, a reading both blunt and intense. During that time, the lines in her aged face shifted from wonder to doubt and back again. Then she favoured Lathwi with a look of profound respect and regret.

"What you say is true," she said, sounding weary now as well as brittle. "I have seen the dragon in your heart. But you must know, Lathwi: few possess my special Sight. To most people, you seem to be no more or less than a woman."

Lathwi's immediate reaction to that last statement was hot, towering rage. Stupid people! Did they mistake snakes for worms? Eagles for flies? She was Lathwi, The Soft One; a daughter of dragons! She snapped to her feet, then started to pace back and forth in front of Katya's fire. Her obvious agitation attracted a swarm of frowns from Katya's protective kinsmen, but the old gypsy opposed their worries with a wave.

"Child, what have I said to cause you such distress?" she asked then, sounding more amused than concerned.

"I dragon," Lathwi insisted.

"So it would seem. And yet you have the semblance of a woman."

"No."

"Don't be contrary, child; it doesn't become you. And look at yourself through my eyes. You have neither wings nor tail. Your neck is shorter than mine. You walk upright as I do; talk as I do; and no doubt bleed red blood as I do, too. I see wisps of black hair peeking out from beneath your hood, and—"

"No more!" Lathwi snapped. She regretted the whim that had led her to this miserable place. She regretted meeting this sharp-eyed crone even more. For while it galled her to the bone, she could not deny the truth any longer. She was not a full-fledged dragon or even a wingless runt, but only and thoroughly human. She keened to herself, mourning the loss of the one distinction which she had cherished above all else.

"Here now," Katya chided then. "Why are you making such sad sounds?"

"Not want to be woman."

"Ah, I think I see." She waited until Lathwi paced by again, then reached out and grabbed her hand. "Sit with me for a moment, child." Too dispirited to refuse, Lathwi sank to the ground. "Now listen to me for a moment.

"My people believe that there is nothing more precious in the world than children. It does not matter if we beget them for ourselves or relieve them from outsiders—once the tribe accepts them, they are gypsies forevermore. Maybe this is so with you, too.

"Do you understand what I'm trying to say?"

"No," Lathwi replied, being deliberately obtuse.

"I'm saying that it doesn't matter what you started out as. For reasons that I can't perceive or hope to understand, you were claimed by the skyfolk. So regardless of where you go or what you do throughout your life, in your heart and in your mind, you will always a dragon."

The old woman's words soothed Lathwi's grief; and while she still felt a hollowness in the pit of her stomach, it no longer threatened to swallow her whole. Perhaps it was so, she thought to herself. Perhaps she did not need to abdicate her most prized distinction simply because she had acquired another, less savoury one. After all, nothing had changed—she was the same Lathwi whom Taziem had raised and sent away. Perhaps it was her fortune to be many things at once: first a dragon, then a sorceress, and now a woman, too.

"You almost as smart as Mother," she told Katya, meaning to honour her with such rare and high praise. Then, inspired by the association, she asked, "You teach me? I go where you go if you teach."

A flush banded the gypsy's withered cheeks, but Lathwi could not tell if it stemmed from pleasure or chagrin. "What about your friends?" she asked. "Could you leave them behind so easily?"

She shrugged. "You say you teach, I leave them."

"Let me see your hand," Katya said, and then sighed as she peered at the proffered palm. "I was afraid it might be so. Our paths seem destined to cross several times, but your future is not with us." She turned the hand over and patted it. "For what it's worth, child, I'm sorry. The tribe would have been pleased to take you."

Lathwi received the disappointing news with stoic grace. If Katya said that her fortune did not lie among the gypsies, then it must be so. But there was one more thing she wanted to ask before she and this wise old woman came to the parting in their ways.

"How you know about dragons in my head?"

An image formed in Lathwi's mind then. Although blurry and all too brief, it was a younger version of Katya casting her a conspiratorial wink.

Delighted as well as surprised, she flung a rapid succession of image-thoughts back at the gypsy, but Katya only shook her head.

"Your gifts are much stronger than mine ever were," she said, in a tone tinged with rue, "and that is both a blessing and a curse. For outsiders often fear that which they do not understand, and if they come to believe that you can perceive their thoughts, they may very well develop an urge to see you dead shortly thereafter. So take an old woman's free advice, and keep those gifts a secret.

"That is all I have to say, child. Please go now, and tell Santana that I wish to sleep. I will bid you farewell, but not goodbye, for I believe we will meet again."

Lathwi took no exception to this abrupt dismissal—such was the way of dragons. Before she left, though, she touched her nose to Katya's—a gesture of respect and fondness. The Queen of The Wandering Tribe flushed again, and then sent her on her way with a smile.

As soon as she stepped out of Katya's campsite, a crowd of curious younglings swarmed around her. The elders capered for her attention; the youngsters preferred to gawk at her from a safer distance.

"Where Santana?" she asked them.

They scattered like a school of startled hatchlings. A moment later, the gold-toothed gypsy came striding out of the shadows. A casual smile belied the swiftness of his gait.

"Did you wish to see me, friend Lathwi?" he asked.

"Katya want sleep now," she told him.

He hesitated for a moment—just long enough to glimpse into her eyes—then sped off toward Katya's fire. Sometime later, he came looking for Lathwi again. His approach sent a pod of younglings scrambling.

"Rascals," he said, sharing a paternal grin with her. "You would think that they'd never seen an outsider before." When she did not respond to this attempt at small talk, his expression turned suddenly somber. "You are a mystery to me, friend Lathwi. I do not recognize you, and yet I have this feeling that I should know you. Are you a long-lost cousin from another tribe?"

"No," she replied.

"Ah, well," he said, when it was clear that she was not going to comment further, "it doesn't really matter. I only ask because the feeling is so strong.

"Are you hungry? My mother has bade me to treat you as blood, and blood never wants for food or drink." Before she could refuse either, he shouted to his wife. "Gem, bring my mother's friend a plate of roast chook and a mug of beer!"

Even as the order spilled from his lips, a high-pitched squabbling erupted from the shadows on the other side of the camp. He flashed her an apologetic, almost embarrassed grin and said, "That is no doubt Tikki and her cousin quarrelling over hair ribbons again. Excuse me while I go and settle the dispute."

As he sped away, his buxom mate came bustling over with a mug in one hand and a heaping plate in the other. She was a graceful creature, but far too noisy; her skirts swished to the beat of her steps, her earrings and bracelets jingled.

"Here, friend Lathwi," she said, smiling as she handed Lathwi her supper. "Eat. Drink. There is plenty for all. I would stay and keep you company, but if I am not there to turn the spit, the meat will burn and I will never hear the end of it."

She hurried off then, swishing and jingling all the way. Lathwi tried to picture herself in the woman's place, but her brain rejected the image. Katya was right, she decided then. Regardless of where she was or what kind of company she kept, she would always be a dragon.

From his spot in front of Tavi's fire, Pieter saw Lathwi standing all alone in the dark. A pang of something close to pity urged him to get up and join her, but even as he started to act on the impulse, a trio of rowdy youths distracted him. They ran past Tavi's camp, then disappeared into the darkness only to come thundering out of the shadows at Lathwi's back a moment later. As she turned to see what was coming up behind her, one of the boys slammed into her. The other two skidded to a less calamitous stop and immediately began to brush the ruins of her supper from her mail. Their apologies were as loud as they were profuse.

Tavi flashed Pieter a toothy, boys-will-be-boys grin. Pieter was about to respond in kind when Lathwi seized one of those boys by the front of his shirt and hoisted him from his feet. The noisy camp went suddenly quiet. Even the resident tree frogs shut up.

"You got something that be mine," Lathwi said then, in a voice bristling with menace.

Pieter swore. Damned gypsies! Damned Lathwi, too. He took a step in that direction, hoping to calm her down before she got them into more trouble than they were in already, but then Tavi draped an arm around his shoulders—a casual hold that would've seemed friendly only a moment ago. Jamus, too, was being made to stay put. The two taut-jawed women who had him between them undoubtedly had knives in their skirts.

Meanwhile, Santana came bearing down on Lathwi from out of nowhere. His golden smile was strained now. The muscles in his arms were rigid cords.

"Put my nephew down, friend Lathwi," he told her. "He is a gypsy, he will not run away."

She shrugged, then set the boy back on his feet. True to his uncle's word, he stood his ground. His still-downy cheeks were ablaze with embarrassment now, but the look in his green eyes was of pure defiance.

Luke, my little wolf," the gypsy leader said then, "why is friend Lathwi so excited? Could it be that you have found something that belongs to her—something that might've been jarred from her person during that regrettable collision? If so, then give it back. I would not want her to think poorly of us."

The boy hesitated for a moment, then reluctantly handed her the claw that he had been hiding behind his back. He did not try to deny its theft or his guilt, but rather stood tall in her shadow and silently dared her to do her worst.

She rumbled her approval. In his stead, she would have done the same thing. Perhaps that was because he, like her, had started life as something other than what he was now, she thought, suddenly grasping the significance of his fair skin and green eyes. The notion appealed to her for no reason she could name. Moreover, it put her in a generous mood.

"You know what you steal?" she asked him.

"Steal?" Santana interjected, his face a caricature of horror. "Please, good Lathwi, do not use such harsh words. It was only a bit of boyish mischief—"

"Tell me," she persisted. "You know what is?"

"I thought it was some kind of knife," he told her then, flushing as his voice jumped an octave. "It's not, though, I can see that now. Here, take it back, I don't want it."

"Is better than knife," she declared, making no move to relieve him of it. "Knife soft, can break or chip. This be dragon claw."

A mutter rippled through the night air. Then, by ones and twos, the whole camp came drifting over as if spellbound for a better look.

"A dragon claw?" Luke echoed breathlessly, ogling the thing in his hands with a newfound mixture of awe and greed. "Where did you get it?"

"From dragon," she replied, feeling no need to be more explicit. "You want, I let you keep." As his eyes widened with comprehension, she added, "You try steal from me again, I eat you."

He lunged forward and hugged her, then raised the claw over his head and went running off and into the night. Less than a heartbeat later, a swarm of squealing younglings went chasing after him. Their raucous departure shook the rest of the camp out of its trance. Tavi clapped Pieter on the back and laughed as if they had just shared a joke, Tikki planted a kiss on Jamus' cheek, then flitted away before her elders could scold her for being so brazen.

"Your mother must have been one of us," Santana said to Lathwi, dazzling her with his broadest grin.

"My mother be dragon," she replied.

His grin went flat with wonder. "I cannot imagine how such a wonder could come to pass, but if you say it, then it must be so. It certainly explains a lot of the feelings I've had about you.

"Stay with us," he urged her then. "The Wandering Tribe has revered skyfolk since the world's first dawn. It would be a privilege beyond compare to have one living among us."

She shook her head. "Katya say my future not with you." His hopeful expression wilted. "It breaks my heart to hear that," he said. "but my mother is seldom wrong. If she says you are not for us, then I must believe her. But I will tell you this, friend Lathwi: you will be forever welcome in this camp."

Then, shifting moods again, he cried, "Enough of this serious talk! Let us celebrate while we still have a chance. Tikki!" he shouted. "Come and dance for us!"

"Which dance would you have of me, Father?" she asked.

"The Dance of the Flying Dragon. Yorgi, get your drum and give her the beat. Gem, help out with your flute. Make room, everybody. Make room!"

The gypsies formed a spacious circle. Tikki stood in its center, surrounded by shadows that the firelight cast at her feet. She waited for the excited buzz to die down, then nodded at her uncle.

The thump of a taut-skinned drum floated through the darkness like a disembodied heartbeat, then merged with the poignant voice of a sweet reed flute. Together, they evoked the image of a clear blue sky. Tikki's arms extended slowly open; the shawl which spanned taut across her shoulders gave her the aspect of wings. Stretching her neck into an elegant arc, she then began to dance. Her moves were basic at first: long, graceful strides accompanied by majestic strokes of her ersatz wings. The flutter of her ribbons and skirt suggested the presence of wind. Then the music quickened a little, and she began to embellish her steps with sinewy dips and whirls. Soon again, she incorporated acrobatic leaps and bounds which saw her in the air more often than on the ground. On and on she went, fuelled by passion and youth's raw power. And when she finally glided to a final, exhausted stop, she loosed her version of a dragon's roar.

Up until that moment, Lathwi had been rapt: the girl's dance had captured Shoq's surprising grace, her own memory had infused it with power. But that puny squeak was utterly wrong—it had sent her sky-dancing heart plummeting back to earth. This is what it should sound like, she thought, and gave voice to the proud cry of a dragon in flight.

For one stunned moment, the gypsies could only stare at her. Then, following Santana's lead, they bowed.

Pieter was dumbfounded. Everyone knew that gypsies did not bow to outsiders, not even to those who could have them killed for their pride. Then Jamus appeared beside him. His face was an amazed blank.

"Who in hell is she?" he whispered.

"She's Lathwi," he replied with a shrug. No other definition sufficed.

They rose early the next morning, a little bleary-eyed from the beer, but otherwise hale and still in possession of all of their belongings. Santana tried to persuade them into staying another day, but Lathwi's mind was already set.

"I go now," she told him, and then headed for her horse without another word.

"Many thanks for your excellent hospitality," Pieter said, embarrassed by her abruptness. "I hope we meet again some day."

"Call on me the next time you come to Compara," Jamus urged. With a wink, he added, "And don't forget to bring your pretty daughter."

The gold-tooth gypsy clapped each of them on the back—Jamus just a little harder than Pieter. "Farewell, friends," he said. "May the road ahead of you always be more pleasant than the road you leave behind."

A crowd gathered to see them off. Katya was not there, but the boy Luke was. He seemed taller today, and perhaps a shade less downy-cheeked as well. Unlike the other children, he didn't clamour for their attention, but merely saluted them with his dragon-claw as they rode by. Lathwi bared her teeth at him, then continued on her way without looking back.

"I almost hated to leave," Jamus said to Pieter, as they trotted along behind Lathwi. "Tikki and I were getting along splendidly."

The trapper snorted derisively. "Too splendidly, if you ask me. Another day in that camp, and that girl's mother and aunts would've carved you up like a holiday roast."

"You're just jealous because she picked me instead of you."

"Maybe; maybe not. At least I can be reasonably sure of spending the rest of my life with all my parts intact. You, on the other hand, are liable to lose one or more of the kind that count any day now."

"All the more reason to live each day to its fullest—if you know what I mean," Jamus added with a sly wink. Then, as if inspired by the thought, he caught up with Lathwi. She welcomed his arrival with her usual indifference, but he was in high spirits this morning and refused to be put off.

"You spent a lot of time with Madame Katya last night," he said. "If you don't mind my asking, what did you two talk about?"

"She tell my fortune," she replied.

"Did she tell you that you were going to meet a tall, golden-haired man and fall hopelessly in love with him?" he teased, batting his lashes at her.

"No," she replied, in a utterly humourless tone. "She smart, not talk nonsense. I want stay, learn from her, but she say it not my future."

He was glad to hear that someone had finally figured out a way to refuse her, but he did not say so aloud. His years of diplomatic service made him more circumspect.

"Oh well, these things have a way of working out for the best," he said instead. "Gypsies lead harsh lives more often than not." Then, because he was curious, he asked, "Why did they bow to you last night anyway?"

"They got respect for dragons," she told him.

"So that really was a dragon claw," he marvelled. "How remarkable. Is there any chance that you might give me one, too? It would make a wonderful addition to my collection of curiosities."

"No."

"Why not?" he asked, peeved now because he could not see how she could be so generous with a would-be thief and yet so stingy with him.

"Claw got no meaning for you. You want only because it curiosity." She made the word sound like an obscenity.

"Yes, but—"

"You want claw?" she challenged him then. "Be bold like youngling, try to steal. You survive, I let you keep."

That wasn't the way things were done in the civilized world, he wanted to tell her. Well-bred people minded their manners. But she wasn't well-bred, he reminded himself, and she wasn't civilized. And the truth was, he didn't want the claw badly enough to tangle with her.

"Oh, keep the damned thing," he growled, then wheeled his horse around and rejoined Pieter. There, he grumbled, "Blessed Dreamer, but she can be such a bitch!"

"True," Pieter agreed. "So when are you going to learn to let sleeping dogs lie?"

"Shut up," was his only reply.

The three of them rode on in silence for a long time to come.

They made camp in the woods that evening. Still tired from their sojourn with the gypsies, they fell asleep early and slept without rousing throughout the night.

In the morning, a chattering squirrel jarred Pieter from his dreams. He stretched to wring the vestiges of sleep from his veins, then sat up and glanced at his companions. Jamus was cleaning his teeth with a peeled twig; Lathwi was spying on him through slitted eyes.

She was due for a scrubbing, too, he thought, taking critical note of her dirty skin and mail. Liselle would have a fit if he brought her into the house encased in that much grime.

"Lathwi," he said, not quite sure of how to broach the subject with her. "If all goes well today, we'll be sleeping in Compara tonight."

"Good," she replied, and sprang to her feet. "We go."

"There's no need to rush," he told her. "The city is less than a day's ride from here. And besides, you need to do something before we leave."

"What that?"

"There's a stream not too far from here," he said. "I think you ought to find it and spend some time in the water."

"Why? I not thirsty. And I not want swim."

"This has nothing to do with drinking or swimming. You need a bath."

"What that?"

"I can show you what a bath is," Jamus told her. "I was just thinking that I could use one, too."

His offer roused her suspicions. The last time he had been so charitable, she had wound up poisoning herself with gish. If she had to learn about this 'bath', then she would rather have Pieter teach it to her. She much preferred his methods. The only problem was, he seemed perfectly happy to let Jamus conduct this lesson.

"Why I need this bath, Pieter?" she asked, hoping to trick him out of a useful clue or two.

"It's important for you make a good first impression on Liselle," he replied. "And she has rather definite ideas as to how a person should look and smell."

"I smell same as you," she asserted. "Why you not take bath?"

He scorned that suggestion with a snort. "I don't even come close to smelling like you do. And besides, I'm not the one who has to impress Liselle. She already knows me."

Lathwi hissed then, signalling her resignation. She did not know what this Liselle was, or why she had to impress it, but Pieter obviously thought that it was important to do so, so she would submit to Jamus' tutelage.

"I take bath," she told him. "You show how."

"I am your humble servant," he replied, and then turned his now-grinning face to Pieter. "Which way did you say that stream was?"

Pieter pointed and said, "I'll pack while you're gone."

"Take your time," Jamus advised him. "If all goes well, we'll be gone a long time."

Pieter was tempted to offer the blonde a wager on that, but refrained at the last moment. There was no such thing as a sure bet where Lathwi was concerned.

She heard the stream before she saw it; its chuckling voice filled the spaces between the trees with the sound of its secret Name. She smiled knowingly, then followed Jamus down the side of a ferny embankment. There, the air turned sweet and damp. Flashes of refracted sunlight dazzled their eyes.

"How now?" she asked.

"Strip," he told her. When she hesitated, he extended a hand. "Would you like some help?"

"No," she snapped, and batted his hand away. She wasn't happy with the idea of exposing herself in his presence. The extent of her softness was something she preferred to keep to herself. Regardless of her preferences, though, she was not going to back out. She had committed herself to this lesson; therefore she would strip.

She removed her scales with swift efficiency—first releasing each of the seams, then shucking the hide all at once. As her hood slid free of her head, strands of limp black hair slithered across her face. She frowned. Body hair was un-dragon like, an embarrassment like her softness. She would have hacked it off right then and there if Jamus had not distracted her. He was naked now, too, and what a revolting sight that was! His body was so soft, it almost jiggled in places; and so hairy, it seemed almost bearish. And she didn't know what to think of the thing that dangled between his legs. She knew what it was, all males had one, but for some reason, she had expected humans to be more like dragons in that regard. Sires kept their organs tucked away until such times as they were needed.

Jamus saw her staring at his groin and could not stop himself from smiling. It was rather impressive, he thought. And the sight of her standing there clad in nothing but long black hair and sunlight did nothing to diminish its stature. She was magnificent—a sculpture of solid muscle. Even her tiny breasts were rock-hard. And Dreamer, she had scars all over her! Some were faint and puckered, others were freshly healed. The thought of running his tongue over that violent network sent a shiver down his spine.

"Let's get in the water," he said, because he was afraid that his growing excitement might scare her away otherwise.

The stream was swollen from springtime rains and the last of the winter melt. An instant after he set foot in it, his blood turned to ice. He ground a yelp between his teeth, then forced himself to go deeper. Behind him, Lathwi hissed. She did not like being in this much water, especially when it was this cold.

"Get yourself wet," he told her, when they were in up to their waists. She splashed herself half-heartedly. He shook his head. "No, no. Like this," he said, and ducked beneath the water only to resurface an instant later. "Go ahead," he panted then. "It's not so bad once you get used to it."

Reluctantly, she did as she was told. When she came back up again, she found Jamus rubbing a foamy, lard-coloured knot between his hands.

"What that?" she demanded, instantly suspicious.

"It's soap," he replied, and then began to rub the foam in her hair. "No bath is complete without it."

"Stinks," she told him.

"Don't be silly," he chided. "It smells like violets."

"Violets stink."

"Whatever you say," he said, refusing to argue with her. "Now just try to relax. Bath-time can be a lot of fun."

He scrubbed her hair into a high lather, then commanded her to rinse. She bobbed down, then up again, now dripping with disapproval as well as water. If this was his idea of fun, he was less intelligent than she had supposed him to be. That smelly soap was making her nose itch, and the water was chilling her to the bone.

"Done now?" she asked.

"Not yet," he crooned, delighted to have such control over her. "Now we have to wash the rest of you."

He began with the muscled flats of her shoulder blades, then moved on to the rest of her scarred backside. She was tense at first, but he was skilled with his fingers and soon had her leaning into his surreptitious massage. His touches evolved into caresses then, lavish strokes which paid homage to her hips, buttocks, belly and breasts. Finally, he slid his soap-slick fingers into the bearded vee between her legs and gave her a brief taste of what could be. Then he ordered her to rinse.

"Now?" she asked, when she came splashing to the surface again. He thought he heard a different sort of hope in her voice.

"Not yet. It's my turn now," he said, and then handed her the soap.

She rumbled to herself. She felt surprisingly good now, all loose and tingly. Now she wanted to get out of this icy stream and bask in the sun. But since he wanted to test her, she was obliged to stay put and show him what she'd learned. So she took the soap and went to work. As she proceeded, the thing between his legs began to swell.

"Soap that, too?" she asked, simply because she wanted to be thorough.

"Definitely," he breathed. As she slid her soapy hands down the length of it, he gasped and then said, "Oh, Lathwi, that feels so good. Now put it in your mouth."

A doubtful scowl furrowed her brow. "Why for?"

"It's something every woman should try at least once," he told her. "Go on, give it a taste. If you don't like it, I won't force you to continue."

She shrugged. The path to being a woman seemed to be riddled with peculiar turns.

He closed his eyes as she leaned toward him, then arched his back as her breath skirted his loins. For one incredible moment, pleasure ruled his universe. Then a steel-jawed trap snapped shut on him, and pleasure turned to spangles of pain. He pushed her away with a garbled cry, then thrashed his way to shore. There, he hastily scooped up his clothes and went storming into the woods.

How curious, she thought, as she watched him disappear. A moment ago, he had been keen on being tasted. Now he was flapping around like some great wounded land fowl. Was this another example of acquired taste? If so, then how many times did he have to be bitten before he started to like it?

She shook her head at the quirks of men and waded back to shore. There, she hacked off her dripping hair with the not-claw and then started to get dressed. It was then that she noticed the smell: a sharp, distressing melange of sweat and other animal odours. It was coming from her scales. She was instantly appalled. This was what happened to those who kept company with men and beasts, she scolded herself. Their noses went dull, their habits turned bad. She would have to be more careful from now on, or someone would mistake her for prey.

She scrubbed at her scales with fine dry sand until they smelled dragon-clean again. Then, with the same fervour, she applied the sand to herself. In time, the stink of violets wore off.

"It's about time," Pieter chided, when finally she came ambling back into camp. "I was about to go looking for you." Then, noticing the crumbs of sand on her face and hands, his mock frown turned sincere. "I thought you were going to take a bath!"

"I take," she told him. "Now we go to Compara."

There was no point in arguing with her, Pieter decided. All he could do only was hope that Liselle would understand.

CHAPTER 5

A sound as sudden and bold as a thunderclap rolled into Taziem's caves, instantly rousing her from erotic day-dreams. She took a moment to stretch because it felt good to do so, and because she did not wish to seem too eager—then strode out to the landing and trumpeted a reply.

As her welcome faded from the air, a shadow glided over her head. It was as vast as a cloud, yet powerful and lithe. A moment later, this shadow became a mass of rust-red scales and muscle. It folded its wings with a dramatic snap, then struck a majestic pose.

"Taziem." The image-thought was one of canny black magnificence; its undertones were fraught with respect and pleasure. *"I have waited for your Call from the moment we last parted."*

"Bij." She offered him an exaggerated version of his Name-image: it was blatant flattery on one level; a subtle satire of his ego on another. *"Your wait is over."*

They rubbed noses, then entwined necks. This embrace sparked an ache in Taziem's loins; and Bij's sex-spiced musk filled her with an urge to roar.

"Shall I dance for you?" he asked then, flashing her an image of the sky.

"Is that wise?" she asked in return, meaning to goad him into a better performance. "Your journey was lengthy, and no doubt arduous as well. You must be tired—"

"Tired?" In a single fluid movement, he reared up onto his hindquarters and unfurled his wings. "Do I look tired to you?"

Before she could respond, he launched himself into the sky.

His dance was intricate and daring, a stylish spectacle of agility and strength. He went from a graceful strut to a raunchy swagger, then flung himself into a string of stunts which combined time-honed skills and youthful verve. As he flaunted himself, the spark in Taziem's loins turned into a slow, delicious fire. She began to whimper, then to writhe; her wings unfolded of their own accord. When she could not bear the humming in her blood any longer, she hurled herself into the sky.

Bij loosed a triumphant roar, then abandoned his dance and went tearing after her. She teased him at first, racing round and round the mountaintop at break-neck speed. But she was too excited to play for long, and so high above an alpine meadow, she let him catch her. Their necks entwined. Their wing-strokes became synchronized. Then, with a shriek, Taziem began her Season in earnest.

After that first exhaustive coupling, Bij hunted down a stag for each of them, and they gorged. Then, all appetites slaked for the moment, they returned to Taziem's caves. She had sealed off her inner chambers days ago to keep her Chosen from raiding her hoard of diamonds, so they curled up back to belly in one of the outer caverns. The only thing she wanted to do now was relax and exchange a little gossip, but Bij was too fidgety and restless for that.

"There is a faint reek about this place," he told her, rumbling with disapproval. "It smells suspiciously human. Have those two-legged intruders been giving you trouble?"

A private image of The Soft One flared in Taziem's mind. She quickly extinguished it again. Bij would not understand her reasons for bringing Lathwi here, or for allowing her to remain for so many years. Indeed, his comprehension would be limited to a single point: she had suckled a human instead of swallowing it whole. And he would be outraged. In his fury, he would make this Season a misery for her. Worse, he might force her to choose another mate. She did not relish either prospect. Therefore, she meant to keep Lathwi's existence a secret from him.

Fortunately, that was no great challenge. For while her chosen was one of the mightiest dragon-sires still alive, his strengths were all physical. When it came to mental ability, he was no match for her. No one was.

No one except perhaps Lathwi.

But that, too, would remain her secret.

"I have had no trouble with humans," she told him then, perfectly truthful in a sly sort of way. "Am I correct in assuming you cannot make the same claim?"

"Quite correct."

The thought was grim. Its underlying sentiment was one of rage. With a flick of her eyelids, she encouraged him to elaborate. He obliged with a resentful torrent of images.

"At first they invaded my territory by ones and twos—seemingly witless fools who spent their days sifting through streams or burrowing into mountain-sides. Then one of them discovered a substance called gold. Now the entire southern range is crawling with the noisy, stinking creatures. They are razing my favourite hunting grounds, and slaughtering my favourite prey. I have driven them away time and time again, but they always return, and always in greater numbers."

Taziem shrugged, unconcerned. Bij tended to exaggerate when men were involved. And besides, exaggerated or not, it was his territory that was being invaded, not hers.

"And that is not the worst of their affronts," he went on, veiling the thought with menacing shadows.

"No?" The archness of her reply mocked his penchant for theatrics.

"Then what is?"

"They have begun to hunt the younger dragons—not for fortune or territory, but for sport." He paused, giving her time to suck in a scandalized breath, then added, "They do not even eat the meat afterward."

She did not rue the passing of a few unknown younglings. Stupid dragons died every day; and any dragon who had fallen prey to men must have been stupid indeed. Nevertheless, the news troubled her, for she had seen no sign of such depravity in Lathwi. Was her fosterling an aberration? Or were Bij's humans the flukes?

Her chosen caught no glimpse of her uneasy thoughts. He was still fuming.

"It is intolerable. Completely intolerable. How dare they hunt our young? We are skyfolk, superior in every way. And there are few enough of us left in the world as it is."

"Blame that on Galza," Taziem replied, filling his mind with an image of red-eyed malice. "It was She and Her krim who nearly exterminated us in the waning days of Ever-Light."

"Yes, yes, I know the tale." The thought bristled with impatience. "Galza tried to destroy us only to be destroyed Herself by the Stone Oma. It would seem that the humans are now intent on fulfilling Her goal."

Her tail slashed back and forth across the cavern floor, a gesture of growing irritation.

"How can you possibly compare humans and their puny acts of spite with Galza's relentless venom?" she demanded. "She killed thousands, Bij. Can you imagine a number that large?"

"*No*," he admitted, "*but—*"

"And so what if humans have killed a few stupid dragons? If every youngling from every clutch lived to adulthood, the world would collapse beneath our weight. There would not be enough food to feed us all, or enough diamonds to keep us all amused.

"Would you willingly cede a portion of your territory to a caveless youngling?"

"No."

"Would you spare a challenger's life?"

"So it could return to challenge me again some day?" he demanded indignantly. "I think not."

"And yet you complain about our dwindling numbers. You might as well roar at the sun for setting every day."

"Perhaps," he growled, undaunted by her scorn, "but what does any of this have to do with the humans? Great or small, they remain a threat to our well-being."

"*To your well-being*," she asserted, although she was not wholly convinced of that, either.

"*They are a threat*," he insisted.

"All right then, let us suppose that they are. What do you think we should do about it?"

He sprayed an image of red blood and wholesale slaughter at her. She rejected the proposal with another hiss.

"Not all humans seek our destruction, Bij. Killing them indiscriminately, for no better reason than hate, would be an act worthy only of krim."

His nostrils flared, a gesture of resentment and wounded pride. *Do you have a better solution?*

"Not yet," she replied, the obvious implication being that she would in due time, "but I can tell you this much: there are stupid humans and not-so-stupid humans. A clever dragon would learn to tell the difference between one kind and the other before he began issuing challenges. Otherwise, he might receive a nasty surprise."

"How have you come to be such an expert on humans?" he demanded irritably.

"I am the Learned One," was her haughty reply. "I am on my way to becoming an expert on everything. But enough of this talk about humans already. Have we nothing better to do?"

She embellished the suggestion with a series of erotic images. He rumbled approvingly, then urged her toward open skies.

CHAPTER 6

Malcolm came to Compara clad in tatters and grime—a beggar's guise to which his deformities lent easy credence. The sentries at the gate did not ask him what business he had in the city; indeed, one of them cast him a coin of miniscule worth as he hobbled by. He flashed the imbecile a smile full of blackened teeth, then continued on his way at a cripple's guilt-inspiring pace.

At first glance, the white-walled city seemed an elegant place. Two – and three-story white-brick buildings with clear glass windows and ornate facades lined the main thoroughfare; and the people who shopped here were handsomely dressed. But beneath its hoity-toity petticoat, Compara was as rank as any dockside whore. Open sewers hemmed the back streets; garbage heaps and vermin multiplied in the alleyways. The houses and shops in this part of town were insulated from the squalor by walls of white-washed brick. As Malcolm made his way through this feculent maze, he looked for cutthroats and worse out of the corner of his eye. But no blackguard bothered him today, perhaps because he seemed so destitute.

He meandered in and out of the worst parts of Compara, then came to an abrupt stop as the city garrison spanned into view. It was a daunting structure, with high stone walls and manned battlements. Even the bruise-coloured shadows which it cast were imposing. He scowled, ever-jealous of the strong, hale-limbed soldiers who stood watch at its iron gates, then moved on to the sprawling outdoor bazaar which lay beyond the stronghold's shade. Although the day was rapidly coming to a close, the market was still jammed with last-minute shoppers. These were mostly common-born folk: plainly dressed women and domestic servants; children, soldiers, and the usual array of beggars and thieves. He mingled with this motley crowd for a while, then stole a hunk of bread from a weary vendor's stall and ducked into an alleyway to wait for nightfall.

The cemetery smelled of freshly turned earth and rotting flesh, but Malcolm did not care. He had come in search of a servant, not a flowery atmosphere.

As he prowled from grave to grave, just biding his time, a patch of absolute blackness began to flicker in and out of the peripheries of his vision. He grinned then, for this was a non-born, the very thing that he'd been hoping to find. It and its kin were mere graveyard haunts now, vultures that fed on the power of decay, but back in the age before the world's first dawn, they had been The Dark One's minions.

And soon, at least one of them would be so again.

He sat down with his back against a tombstone, then cast a morsel of pure power into the night. Like a shadowy tiger, the nonborn came slinking toward the bait—a shy, suspicious stalk which abruptly ended in a pounce. An instant after it consumed the lure, Malcolm began to reel it in with his Will. It shifted from one nightmarish shape to another in a frantic attempt to escape, but it could not overcome Malcolm's magic.

"Be at ease, nonborn," he told it, after he had bound it to his service with a spell. "I wish you no harm."

"Then release me," it replied in a hollow monotone. Its mouth was naught but a shadowy hole. "If you try to keep me as a slave, I will perish."

"Nonsense. You will thrive in my service." With the insouciance of a man feeding his favourite dog, he tossed it another morsel of power. It snarled, resenting his attitude, but could not stop itself from gobbling up the tidbit. "See? I can be a generous master. If you please me, you shall feed as you have not fed in centuries."

"What do you want of me, mortal?"

"For starters, you may show me to the catacombs."

"Why? There is no power among those long-dead bones."

"Ask me no questions, darkling," came his warning, both sharp and sweet, "for I can be mean as well as generous; and you will not like the taste of my displeasure."

Irritation distorted its featureless form. An instant later, it sullenly motioned for him to follow.

It led him out of the cemetery, down a lengthy series of deserted streets and into a section of the city which he had not explored. The buildings here were squat and rickety; the paving stones beneath his feet were cracked and broken. Even in the dark, he could tell that this was an old neighbourhood, long abandoned by its original inhabitants and now settled by immigrant squatters. The air reeked of rancid grease, exotic spices and refuse. Somewhere in the gloomy distance, a woman was ranting in a foreign tongue. But just as he was about to rebuke the nonborn for playing games with him, it glided to a stop in front of an ancient, rust-encrusted gate which barred the alleyway between two dilapidated shops.

"This will take you to the catacombs," it informed him.

His perceptions shifted then; and that which he had mistaken for a private alley became a separate, sheltered passageway. His budding scowl took a sudden, speculative slant.

"Good," he murmured to himself. "Very good."

"I have done your bidding," the nonborn said then. "Now release me."

"You may go for now," he replied, with a negligent wave of his hand, "but I have not released you. When I call, you must come."

It snarled at him, then melted back into the night.

Malcolm didn't hear that terrible sound. He was already on the other side of the still-locked gate, and racing toward the entrance to the catacombs. There, he wrested a resinated rag torch from its dusty, cobwebbed slot and continued on his way by its smoky orange light. As the passageway sloped into the earth's bowels, he wondered why no one used the catacombs anymore—they seemed as good a way as any to dispose of the dead. Then again, shit was buried. So were entrails. Maybe it was fitting that people preferred to be buried, too.

The passageway jagged into a staircase then. Its steps had been carved out of rock and river-clay—a slick, uneven descent that was a cripple's nightmare. He pressed his back against the rough-hewn wall, then began to creep his way down the decline. Each step felt like a tightrope; and each edge, a cliff. Sweat beaded on his split upper lip, the muscles in his bad leg threatened to cramp. When he finally reached the bottom stair, his relief flared bright as a bonfire.

His would-be domain was a narrow cavern whose walls were riddled with shallow enclaves. Its length was indeterminable by the scant light of his torch; ten feet looked the same as a mile. He ventured onward, probing ahead with senses keener than his eyes. As he proceeded, a variety of homeless bones grabbed at his ankles and feet. Perhaps this was why people had opted for coffins and solitary graves, he thought: worms did not toss bones around like rats and fortune-hunters did. He snorted his contempt. As if it mattered if a body rotted in one piece.

The catacombs diverged at irregular intervals, but he did not bother to explore the offshoots; with one sorcerous glance, he knew that they would not serve his purposes. He was searching for solid rock, for stone immured magic better than any other material. If he could not find so fortuitous a vein, he would have to build his stronghold elsewhere; and that would take time and power that he did not want to spare. So he continued down the main passageway. The air grew dry. The floor became less smooth. Then he came to a branch that the diggers had abandoned quite early. It was more of a node than a chamber, he thought, as he went prowling into it. But it was carved out of beautiful, insurmountable river-granite; and that's what really mattered. With a little work and some serious sorcery, he could turn this place into an underground fortress.

He rubbed his hands together, meaning to get started on his ambitions, only to be distracted by a massive yawn. How long had it been since he had slept—one day? Two? All of a sudden, it seemed like forever. He extinguished his torch, then crawled into the nearest enclave. It was empty, but he would not have cared if it had been otherwise. As soon as he laid down, he was asleep.

The Dark One's gyre whirled before him. Her laval eyes surveyed his newly warded domain.

"I approve," She said, all but overwhelming him with Her charnel breath. "Not even the feckless Queen of Dreams will be able to hear us now."

He bowed, trying to hide the smile that Her rare praise had fostered. "My only aim is to serve You, Great One."

She mocked him with a humourless laugh. "Your only aim, Blackheart? I think not. But never mind; I have no strength to waste on idle banter. Let us begin the Summoning."

"What must I do?" he asked.

"When I open the Door to the nether-region in which your so-called demons dwell, you must reach out with your Will and draw them into your world. Do not attempt to snare more than one at a time—you do not possess enough strength for such a feat. Work quickly, for I will not be able to hold the Door open for long.

"Are you ready?"

He took a deep, centering breath, then nodded. The eyes in the center of the gyre flashed, then abruptly folded shut. Minutes or hours later, the maw spat a single word.

"Begin."

He lashed out with his Will. It went streaking into the void between time and space, and rammed into a faceless mass. The collision drove psychic shockwaves into his brain, but he withstood the pain without flinching and began to retract his Will. A heartbeat later, his first conscript appeared with a deceptively mild pop. He casted for another and then another like a greedy fisherman's boy. Each time he made contact, he lost a measure of his strength, but he resolved to keep going until he was utterly spent.

As it happened, though, The Dark One's strength expired first.

"The Door is closed," She announced. Then, as Her eyes snapped open again, the six demons that Malcolm had Summoned dropped to their knees and began to wail. They were hideous things, both slimy and hirsute; with low, sloping foreheads and flat, piranha-like faces fringed with razor-sharp teeth. Stubby leather wings protruded from their shoulder blades, a double row of bony spurs guarded the length of their spines. Both their hands and their feet were tipped with evil-looking claws. She stared at them for a long moment, then broke into a murderous grin.

"Your memory pleases me," She said. "When I am restored to glory, you and yours will be well rewarded."

"How may we serve you, Galza—" one of the six began.

"Fool!" She hissed, flaying the offender with a whip of elemental might. "Never speak My name while you are on this world. The Dreamer must not be roused."

"I will not err again," the tormented demon croaked.

"See that you do not." She let it suffer for a moment longer, then abruptly recalled Her scourge. "The rest of you would be wise to learn from its mistake."

"I will keep a stern watch over them for You, Mistress," another of the demons said.

Her gaze strayed toward the speaker. It was a hand or so smaller than the other five, but its red, cat-like eyes possessed an intelligence which made it seem much larger.

"And who might you be?" She asked, a strong undertow of amusement in Her tone.

"I am Xallax'naj'kurjymym," it proudly announced.

"A naj?" Her gaze swerved back to Malcolm. The humour in Her tone had now infected Her eyes as well. "How bold of you, Blackheart. You have Summoned one of the ruling class into your service."

"His service?" The naj's snout crinkled, exposing a set of jagged teeth. It could have been an expression of dismay or disdain.

"Indeed," She replied. "Malcolm Blackheart is my chief servant on this plane. You will obey him as you would Me."

Its sudden disgruntlement was all but palpable in the chamber, but neither it nor any of the other demons dared to contest that mandate.

Satisfied and still slyly amused, the Dark One spared Malcolm one last glance. "I will give you one last bit of information before I go, Blackheart. Use it only as a last resort. And do not summon Me again until you have found the talisman."

"I will not fail you, Great One," he vowed.

The words were wasted breath, for the gyre was already starting to collapse on itself. He stood his ground until the last speck of charcoal dust spiralled to a stop and then started toward the diagram. As he did so, the naj raced past him.

"I will tend to the talismans," it told him.

"Stop right there, Xallax'naj'kurjymym," he commanded. He had not worked so hard and so long only to be usurped by an ambitious demon. It froze, then half-turned to glare at him. Its expression was a mixture of curiosity and disdain. "You will not touch the talismans now or at any other time," he said, "unless I give you permission to do so."

"The Dark One said I was to serve you, Blackheart," it dared to remind him. "Allow me to do Her bidding."

"Henceforth, you will address me as Master," he told it then, deliberately submerging his annoyance. "And since you are so keen to be of service, you may fetch a bucket of water and scrub the diagram from the floor."

"I am naj, not a drudge like those others," it asserted haughtily. "It would be more fitting for me to safeguard the Dark One's relics."

"Naj or no naj, you will not touch the talismans. If you do, I will use the Spell of Unmaking on you. Or, if you prefer, I will Summon the Dark One and have you explain your effrontery to Her."

Although the naj did not quite believe that this twisted little man-thing had the strength to act on either threat, it retreated nonetheless. A great opportunity was in the making here; and it did not intend to let it slip from its grasp.

"You need not worry about me," it lied. "Only say what needs to be done and I will see to it."

"I much prefer this new attitude of yours," he said, although he knew better than to trust such a sudden change. "And right now, the floor needs to be scrubbed. See to it." He turned his back on the naj then, and began to retrieve the talismans. The demon bared its teeth, then went to fetch some water.

When the talismans were back in safekeeping, Malcolm tapped the last reserves of his strength and then commanded the demons to attend him.

"Four people of power live somewhere within this city," he said. "I want you to locate them for me."

"Are we permitted to ask why you are interested in these people?" the naj asked.

"I have reason to believe that one of them possesses the last talisman," he replied, feeding it that bite of pertinent information simply to see how it would react.

"Ah." Its slotted nostrils flared then, but there was no telling what that meant. "And what do you wish us to do once we have found these people?"

"For now, you are to do nothing but observe them."

"Even if we find the one with the talisman?"

"Especially if you find that one," he stressed. "I must know my adversary's strengths and weaknesses before I attack. And remember this while you are roaming the city streets: no one must know or even suspect that there are demons about in the world again. Secrecy is vital to the Dark One's plans."

"Fear not," the naj said. "We can all walk the shadows without being seen. As naj, I can also change my shape."

"Good," Malcolm said. But what he was thinking was: how convenient. This naj might be a useful tool after all. "Now go. Report back to me two days from now."

The naj departed without a backward glance. The others followed on its heels. In their absence, he breathed a sigh of relief, then flopped into his enclave and slept just like one of the dead.

The demons returned at the appointed time. He approved their punctuality with a curt nod, then immediately began his inquisition.

"What have you learned?"

"We have found the people for whom you are looking," the naj reported. "Of the four, only one has a stronghold equal to yours."

"Oh?" he asked, immediately interested. "Tell me more of this one."

It grimaced as if offended by the request. "All we know so far is that she is a sorceress of considerable power. The matter of her sex is hearsay, gossip which I overheard from a neighbour. The matter of her powers is a fact which I deduced from the excellence of her wards."

"I need to know more than that," he growled. "Haven't you been following her?"

"It is impossible to follow a person who does not leave her stronghold," it stated.

Malcolm ground his teeth against an urge to shout. This was that damned warlock's doing, he just knew it. May he rot forever on the Plains of Pain for that meddling death spell!

"What about the others?" he asked then, bracing himself for more bad news.

"They are two males and a female," the naj informed him. "All have been seen and studied. The female is addicted to a substance called curra which distorts her talents as well as her senses. Her dwelling is warded, but not unbreachable.

"Of the two males, only one seems formidable. He sells his magic to all comers. He is skilled, but also careless. I have detected tiny flaws in his defences."

"And what of the other?"

"He is an old man, grey-bearded and feeble. His wards are as decrepit as he is."

"Good," Malcolm said, more to himself than to his minions. Fortune had favoured him once more. Four vigilant adversaries would have been a true trial; one was merely an annoyance. And annoyance or not, this reclusive sorceress interested him. If she was anywhere near as powerful as the naj claimed she was, then she might serve his purposes even if she did not possess the talisman. After all, the Dark One was not likely to want an addict's poisoned body, or one that was degenerate with age.

As for the other sorcerer: who knew? The talismans were attracted to power, not caution. And since he was the easier of the two likeliest candidates, Malcolm decided to deal with him first.

"Naj," he said then, "I want you to concentrate on the magician. Find out where he goes, and when he's home alone. If possible, search his house for the talisman.

"The rest of you are to maintain a constant watch on the other sorcerers. Make careful note of their habits. In the recluse's case, report anything out of the ordinary directly to me."

"Allow them to report to me instead," the naj suggested. "That way, you need not be bothered with every insignificant detail that crops up."

"In the right hands, even the most insignificant detail can become a useful weapon," he replied, deftly turning aside this latest grab for power. "So I will hear every report for myself." Then, because he knew that the demon lordling would do so anyway, he added, "But you may see to any other details pertaining to the watch."

The naj accepted that meatless bone without a word, but inwardly it was seething. How could the Dark One have chosen such an insolent fool to be Her highest servant? If it had its way, it would tear that misbegotten lump of humanity limb from twisted limb—slowly, with as much pain as possible.

"Is there something else that you want to tell me?" the cripple asked then, disrupting its bloody fantasy. "If not, then you had best be on your way."

"There is something else," it replied, and then suffered a fresh pang of humiliation as Malcolm responded with a look of mock-attentiveness. "We are hungry. Will you allow us to hunt?"

He narrowed his eyes as if inwardly debating the matter, then replied, "Permission granted. But be discreet."

"We will rouse no suspicions," it assured him.

"Then be off already! I have better things to do with my time than sit here and look at you."

With a surly lick of its chops, the naj departed. It would not forget this or any other insult that the cripple cared to tender. For although it did not know how or when as of yet, it meant to repay him for them all.

CHAPTER 7

The forest was gone now, replaced by a rolling series of grassy hills. The road was changing, too, becoming wider and more congested as one sourceless dirt tributary after another emptied into it. There were also more travellers on it. Most of these were farmers on their way to market with small herds of livestock or the first pick of the new season's vegetables and fruit, but there was also a string of brown-robed people whom Pieter called pilgrims; a strutting peacock of a man and his equally gaudy entourage; a band of scruffy, leather-clad men on horseback; and a smattering of less conspicuous folks. Some of these people hailed Jamus in passing, and others cast Pieter a neighbourly smile, but absolutely no one reached out to Lathwi in any way.

"She's not going to have an easy time in Compara," Jamus predicted, as he and Pieter trailed along behind her. "She's too fierce. She scares people."

"She'll do fine," the trapper countered. "Liselle will have her civilized in no time."

"You've mentioned this Liselle several times now," Jamus said then. "Who is she? More importantly, is she pretty?"

"You're hopeless!"

"I know. But tell me anyway."

"She's my mother's younger sister," Pieter informed him then. "She took me in when the plague killed my parents. I was thirteen at the time; she was twenty."

"So that would make her what—thirty, thirty-two now?"

"Thirty-five."

"Is she married?" Jamus persisted.

"Not a chance," Pieter replied, sounding both amused and scornful. "She's far too particular for most men."

Jamus gave his eyebrows a suggestive waggle. "Maybe she hasn't met the right man yet."

"If you're interested, I'll gladly introduce you to her when we get to Compara. But let me warn you right now: she's as apt to turn you to stone as to slap you for any liberties you might be tempted to take."

"She's a sorceress?" At Pieter's nod, he suppressed a shudder. "Perhaps some other time then. I've recently had my fill of terrifying women." He glanced at Lathwi then, as if to refresh his memory. As he did so, inspiration struck. "Does your aunt know you're bringing Lathwi home with you?"

"No."

"Really?" He grinned, a blend of anticipation and glee. "How delightful. Perhaps I'll take you up on that invitation after all."

They came to the crest of another hill then. Lathwi had reined her stallion to a standstill, and was now staring into the valley below. Her expression was one of horror.

"What's wrong?" Pieter asked, as he pulled up alongside of her.

She pointed. He looked down and smiled. For there lay Compara, the White-Walled Jewel of the NorthLands. Like most cities, it was both grand and grotesque—a sleek scab on the face of the world. Its lofty towers jutted into the sky only to be obscured by the thin grey smoke of a thousand chimneys. The setting sun's ruddy light gave that man-made fog a bloody tinge.

"Ah, home at last," Jamus exclaimed. and then urged his roan into a gallop. As he charged off, he cried, "Good food, warm beds and friendly women, here I come!"

Spurred by the sight of another horse's dust, Lathwi's stallion began to follow. She drew him back to a standstill with a savage jerk of the reins. She did not want to descend into that awful city-thing. She could smell its foul breath even from this distance; and its sprawling contours reminded her of an enormous termite mound.

"People live in that?" she asked Pieter.

"They sure do."

"Disgusting."

"It can be," he agreed. "But it can also be exciting once you know where to look."

"Not good, too many houses," she went on, as if she had not heard him. "There be no place to hunt. What people eat? Other people?"

He chuckled. "Cityfolk tend to be a little weird, but they certainly aren't cannibals. When they need food, they simply go to the market and buy it."

"They use gold to feed themselves?" At his nod, she hissed. "Waste of power."

"Not if the alternative is going hungry." When she did not concede that point to him, he added, "Don't be afraid to spend your gold, Lathwi. You'll find ways of getting more."

She did not want to spend her gold. She did not want to live in Compara, either. The mere thought of dwelling within that giant hive made her claustrophobic. She belonged in the open air—like the gypsies. With the gypsies. But that was not an option, she reminded herself. Katya had said so. For better or worse, her fortune was connected to this city. And the sooner she found it, the sooner she could move on.

With that in mind, she urged the bay down the hill.

Compara quickly surpassed Lathwi's worst expectations. There were people all over the place; and they all seemed to be making one kind of noise or another. Her ears ached from the clamour they generated, and her nose was runny from their collective stink. She turned to Pieter, seeking distraction, but he was talking to Jamus. Both men had a glad, homecoming gleam in their eyes. She thought of Shoq then. He would not like Compara, either, she decided, although he would think it great fun to send this giant human herd stampeding down these noisy cobblestone streets. The image cheered her immensely.

Meanwhile, Pieter turned off from the main road and led them into a quieter part of Compara. The houses here did not stand so close together; and beyond the tall white walls that hemmed them in, Lathwi could see treetops and hear songbirds.

"Nice neighbourhood," Jamus commented.

Shortly thereafter, the road they were following came to a shady dead-end. There was only one house down here: a large stone cottage. Fragrant smoke curled from its chimney.

"Ah, good, she's home," Pieter said. "Let's go in and say hello before we stable the horses."

"An excellent suggestion," Jamus replied.

He dismounted then, and unlocked the wrought-iron gate with a key that he'd been carrying in his boot. Lathwi and Jamus followed him into a spacious courtyard that was on the verge of going to seed. Pieter frowned as he looked around. His aunt usually kept her yard in better order. He wondered if she had hurt her back or something, but then figured that she was probably just caught up in other undertakings at the moment.

"Go ahead and tie your horses up at the post," he told Lathwi and Jamus. "And be sure to wipe your feet on the reed mat before you go inside."

Jamus did as he was told, but curious Lathwi barged past the cottage's heavy stone door without a thought for anything but what might lie beyond it. As she crossed the threshold, a tingle like static electricity raced through her. A moment later, a woman came running toward her. The look on her tiny face was one of outrage and alarm.

"Who are you?" she demanded. "Why have you come?"

Before Lathwi could answer these perfectly reasonable questions, Pieter stepped forward and opened his arms to the approaching woman. Recognition flared in her sea-green eyes, then paled to dismay.

"Pieter!" she croaked. "What are you doing here? And what are you doing with that—that person?"

He chuckled at his aunt's consternation. It seemed that Lathwi had the same effect on everyone!

"Liselle," he said, "I want you to meet Lathwi. She's the reason I've come to Compara."

"Do you know she's a sorceress?" Liselle snapped, still staring at Lathwi with open distrust.

"Yes," he replied, a little puzzled by her behaviour now. "That's why I brought her here. But how did you know?"

The truth was, Liselle's outer wards had warned her. It had been a faint alarm, triggered by some vague intimation of danger to herself, but she was not taking chances these days. So rather than answer her nephew's question, she continued to scowl at Lathwi.

Lathwi returned Liselle's stare, but did not say a word. There was something odd about this runty woman, something as compelling as it was elusive. She glanced past her eyes and into her head, trying for a peek at her thoughts. She caught a glimpse of some wild and nameless fear, an undercurrent of concern for Pieter, then sudden fury and nothing more.

"Who are you?" Liselle hissed then. "What do you want?"

"I Lathwi," she replied, wholly unruffled by the woman's hostile tone. "I want know what you got."

Jamus stepped forward to serve as a moderator then. He found Pieter's aunt quite attractive: petite and a just a bit plump, with creamy white skin; long, coffee-coloured hair; and a heart-shaped face. When she was upset, as she was now, her sea-green eyes snapped like northern lights. He was curious to see what they would do when she was calm.

"Pardon me," he began. "But what my good friend Lathwi is trying to say is—"

"Who the hell are you?" Liselle demanded then. "And why do you speak for this woman?"

"Liselle!" Pieter said, grinding her name into a rebuke. This was not like her! True, she could be brusque at times, but she seldom resorted to outright rudeness. "These people are friends of mine. I expect you to treat them as such."

Liselle's cheeks turned suddenly rosy. She pressed a hand to her forehead as if feeling for fever, then offered Jamus a wan smile.

"Please forgive me, good sir," she said. "I've never been good with surprises. I'm Liselle, Pieter's kinswoman. Who might you be?"

"My name is Jamus D'Arques," he replied, "and I, too, have been taken by surprise. For while your nephew spoke of you often during our journey, he never once mentioned your beauty."

"To his credit," she retorted, "my nephew is not prone to bouts of wind." Then she turned her gaze on Lathwi again. "Tell me what you want of me."

At that moment, Lathwi knew what it was about the woman that she had sensed but not recognized: power. It was oozing from her pores now—a display of strength and fear. And now she knew why fortune had brought her here.

"Want you teach me."

Hard ridges beetled Liselle's brow. "I don't have the time or the patience to train an apprentice. Especially one as old as you."

"She's not exactly a beginner," Pieter said, arguing on Lathwi's behalf simply because he did not want her following him back to his cabin. "Show her, Lathwi. Make the fire in the hearth disappear."

"No!" Liselle blurted.

But she was already too late. The fire vanished with an airy whoosh, leaving the fireplace dark and cold.

"How did you do that?" Liselle demanded, all wide-eyed with wonder now. "And why didn't it make any noise?"

Lathwi shrugged. "I ask Fire to go, it go."

"Yes, but what incantation did you use?"

She looked to Pieter for help with the unfamiliar word, but he was busy consoling Jamus. Compara's fair-haired son had a stunned, pasty look about him now, as if he had just been hit in the head with a brick.

"I can't believe you knew and didn't tell me," he was gabbling. "She could've turned me into a piece of jerky for teasing her the way I did."

"Pieter," Liselle said then, "why don't you and Jamus bring Lathwi's gear into the house and then take your horses to the stable."

"Does that mean that you're going to let her stay?" he asked, unashamed of the hope that he heard in his tone.

"For now."

The concession both relieved and encouraged Pieter. He hurried Jamus out of the house before his aunt had a chance to change her mind.

"It was prudent of you to hold your tongue in front of them," Liselle told Lathwi then. "But now that we are alone, you may speak freely. So tell me: what kind of incantation did you use to make the fire disappear?"

"I not know what 'incantation' be," Lathwi confessed.

Liselle ground her teeth against an exasperated groan. While she could pass hour after hour with her nose in a book in pursuit of arcane obscurities, she had little patience for extracting information from real live people. Still, she had to have answers from this strange woman. Both of their lives might well depend on it. So she took a deep breath and tried again.

"Let's forget the technical terms for the moment," she said. "Just tell me everything you said or did to make the fire go out."

Lathwi did not like to repeat herself, but she did so now simply because she thought she was being tested. "I say fire's Name, it go away. You want I call it back?"

A flush dawned on Liselle's winter-pale cheeks. "Are you telling me you know how to work magic with Names?"

"Yes! Names!" For someone who oozed power, this woman seemed incredibly dense. Was there something wrong with her hearing? "Secret Names."

Liselle's thoughts went soaring. Up until a moment ago, she had considered the Magic of Names to be an extinct art or even a myth. There were no known books or manuscripts on the subject, only a few offhand references to it in the oldest of old wives' tales. She would not have believed Lathwi's claim if she had not been present when the big woman made that fire disappear without a sound. But she had been present; and she did believe. And while she did not know how this new form of magic might serve her in the days to come, the mere fact that it had shown up at her doorstep in these troubling times gave her a fluttery sort of hope.

That giddy feeling gave way to anxiety as she turned her thoughts back to Lathwi. Was she really desperate enough to look for hope in a scar-faced barbarian? Desperate enough to trust that barbarian in spite of the warning from her wards? After all, her situation might not be that dire. A series of unnerving omens did not necessarily portend real danger.

Yet she could not dismiss those omens so casually.

The first had come to her over a month ago while she was out in the courtyard admiring the evening stars. "'Ware the rogue sorcerer!" a disembodied voice had howled. "As he has slain me, so shall he slay you! With my death, I curse him! Curse him! Curse him! May his living heart be torn from his chest and eaten before his eyes!"

If that had been the only such incident, it might have faded from her mind eventually. But three weeks later, she had come home from a morning at the bazaar to find a cat on her doorstep. It had been in pitiful shape, all protruding ribs and sores. When she went to pick it up, it had sunk its fangs into her left thumb and swallowed a drop of blood.

"The Blackhearted One is coming," it had hissed then, in a near-human voice. "He seeks a body for his Mistress. As I was drawn to you, so will he be, too. Ward yourself well, Sorceress, and beware."

Then the unknown witch's familiar had loosed a last meow and died. As a gesture of respect and appreciation, she had buried it in a sunny corner of her garden. That was the last time she had been outside.

And last week, her wards had been thoroughly probed.

Just then, her thoughts rippled—a distortion caused by another mind's touch. An instant before she recognized that touch as Lathwi's, a bolt of unreasoning fear stabbed at her, and she evicted the presence with emphatic force. An instant later, she rounded on the woman. The look of pained surprise on her scarred face arrested Liselle's need to scold.

"What did you see?" she asked instead.

"Me," Lathwi admitted. "You. There be lots of shadows and confusion, too. So many images surprise me. Not always see when I look."

"That's the way of mind-scrying," Liselle replied. "Or so I've been told—I have no talent for it myself. But I can sense when it's being done to me, Lathwi, and I'll tell you this much right now: if you want my help, you'll stay out of my head unless I invite you in. Is that clear?"

"I hear," Lathwi told her, being careful to make no promises.

"And since we're on the subject of rules," Liselle went on, almost in the same breath, "here are a few others that I expect you to abide by while you're staying here.

"One—" Her index finger snapped to rigid attention. "You must pay your own way. That includes buying your own food and clothing.

"Two—" Another finger popped up. "I am not a slave to you or anybody else. Therefore, you will cook and clean for yourself. And I like things clean," she added, glancing at the grit which adorned Lathwi's face and mail.

When Lathwi did not comment, the sorceress unfolded a third finger. "You wish me to teach you of sorcery. I will endeavour to do so, but my time is not free. Will you pay my price?"

"I have gold," Lathwi replied, willing to exchange one form of power for another. But her would-be teacher scorned the suggestion with a flick of her wrist.

"I have no need of gold," she said. "Past patrons have left me well-off in that regard. What I want from you is no more or less than what you want from me. I want knowledge, Lathwi. I want you to teach me the Magic of Names."

"Names be secret," Lathwi informed her. "I no can teach to you, you got find where they hiding for yourself." As the sorceress' brow puckered into a frown, she added, "I show you how to look if you want."

Liselle's frown deepened. The offer was straightforward and yet subtle, just enough to keep her hooked. Perhaps this peculiar woman was not such a barbarian after all.

"So be it," she said then. "Come. Let us seal the pact with our blood."

"Why for?"

"It's a common bonding ritual," Liselle replied. "Sort of like a handshake only more so."

Ah yes, handshaking—that meaningless display of honest intent. Lathwi found such customs absurd, but if that's what she had to do to secure herself a teacher, then she would not argue against it. So she followed Liselle through the common area, into an unlit passageway and up to the last in a series of closed doors. As she drew this door open, a friendly gust of sulfur came winging out of the room.

"This is my laboratory," Liselle said, and then motioned for Lathwi to step inside.

As Lathwi crossed the threshold, her senses tingled just as they had when she entered the house. She hissed, vexed by the sensation. It was like a floating itch, only worse.

"You felt something?" Liselle asked. The catch in her voice implied that she was more than casually interested.

Lathwi nodded. "What is?"

"My wards," Liselle replied uneasily. "For some reason, they're reacting to you."

"What be wards?"

"We can discuss that later," she told her. "Right now, I want to get on with our blood-oath."

She closed the door then. An instant later, an array of torches flared to life, dispersing the gloom which had folded over them. Lathwi blinked back a sea of floating stars, then looked around. The room was large, with thick walls and high ceilings. A variety of cupboards, shelves, and tables framed its perimeters; these were cluttered with containers of every size, shape and colour.

"Give me your knife," Liselle said then.

Lathwi did as she was told. Liselle clenched her teeth, then carved a shallow groove into the flat of her right palm. As bright red blood welled up from the wound, she handed the not-claw back to Lathwi.

"Now you," she said.

One swift stroke later, Lathwi's palm was bleeding, too. She watched, all eyes and curiosity, as Liselle clamped their wounded hands together. As small as she was, she had quite a firm grip.

"I promise to teach you the ways of sorcery rightly and true," Liselle said then, "and to honour the peace between us. This I swear by my power and pride. May the Dreamer strip me of both if I willingly foreswear myself."

An electric thrill tore through Lathwi's body, startling in its intensity. She tried to pull her hand from Liselle's grasp only to discover that she could not move those muscles. She hissed. What trickery was this?

"You must make your promises and sanctify them with your power," the sorceress told her then. "Otherwise, we're going to be stuck like this."

Lathwi hissed again. Promises? She had not agreed to make any promises! But even as her temper began to blaze, a splash of cold logic doused it. She was in this predicament because she had not considered this woman's offer carefully enough. Therefore, this must be her first lesson in sorcery: be wary, study a proposal before pouncing. It was an elegant exposition, subtle and yet obvious. Taziem would have had no qualms about using it herself. The realization made her feel better about the promise which she must now forfeit. And now that her shock had worn off, she knew exactly what to say.

"I promise I not eat you," she said. "Swear this by my Name."

Oath-magic sizzled through her veins again. An instant later, her hand slid free of Liselle's grasp. She gave the bloody palm a suspicious sniff, then began to lick it clean. She noticed no difference in the taste.

Meanwhile, Liselle went over to a nearby cupboard and fetched a more hygienic salve. As she doctored herself, her thoughts spun in troubled circles. What kind of promise was: 'I not eat you'? Had she, in her need for protection, bound herself to a cannibal? The voice of reason ridiculed such a notion. Lathwi was Pieter's friend; and he did not befriend monsters. The big woman was probably just a barbarian after all, accustomed to different patterns of thought and speech. Liselle would just have to get used to that.

"Since you're going to be staying here," she said then, "I guess we ought to find you a place to sleep. Come along. And don't touch anything."

The wards buzzed once again as Lathwi strode out of the laboratory, but Liselle tried not to let that bother her. If nothing else, she consoled herself, at least she was now safe from being devoured in her sleep.

As they headed back down the hallway, Liselle introduced her new apprentice to the other rooms in the house.

"This is my bedroom," she said, pointing to the first door beyond the laboratory. "You have no business in there, so stay out unless I invite you in.

"And over here, we have the storage closet." She opened that door and offered Lathwi a glimpse inside. "I could have Pieter clean it out and put a cot in for you if you wanted to bed down in there."

The room was small, dark and stuffy. Lathwi gave it the briefest of looks, then moved on to the next door.

"What here?"

Liselle chuckled. "I don't think you'll want to sleep in there. That's the water closet."

"What that?"

"Take a look. I'm sure you'll appreciate its advantages over a chamber pot."

Curious now, Lathwi opened the door. As she did so, the reek of human waste slapped her in the face. She slammed the door shut again and then hissed. No dragon voided its bowels or bladder so close to its own nest: the mere notion offended her. But since she could not fly off to the woods every time she needed to relieve herself, it looked as if she would have to endure the indignity. It was either that, or frequent the fly-infested trenches which lined the back streets—and that was no choice at all.

They moved on to the room at the open end of the hall. "This is where Pieter sleeps when he's here," Liselle said. "But I suppose you could use it when he's gone."

Lathwi squinted into the darkened chamber. Her first glance revealed nothing of interest: the shadowy outlines of an oversized bed that smelled of feathers and fur; an empty closet; a musty chair. Then, spurred by a whiff of cool air, she looked up and spied a door in the ceiling.

"Where that go?" she asked.

"To the attic," Liselle replied. "But there's nothing up there except some old furniture and drying herbs."

"How get there?"

"Like this."

Liselle grabbed the knotted cord which was dangling from the latch, then gave it a yank. As the door yawned open, a double-jointed ladder came sliding out of the dark and toward the floor. The instant after it touched down, Lathwi started to climb. As she ascended, the air turned cool and crisp—a welcome change from the stuffy, smoke-laced atmosphere below. She inhaled deeply, savouring the tang of drying grasses, then heaved herself up and into a pool of yellow light. Wondering at its source, she looked up to find the moon framed within the panes of a lofty window. She hissed, venting pleasure.

"I stay here," she said, as Liselle came climbing into the attic after her.

"Don't be ridiculous," the sorceress replied, scorning the dusty, oil-clothed room with a glance. "You'll freeze in the winter and roast in the summer. Not only that, the place is home to a host of wasps and more than a few mice."

"I stay here," she cheerfully iterated. Not even Taziem could see the stars from her nest!

Although Liselle hated to admit it, the idea of Lathwi living in the attic appealed to her. It was out of the way, so Liselle would not have to adjust her personal routines and habits so much. And it was already a wreck, so she would not have to nag the big woman about keeping it clean.

"I'll tell Pieter to bring a cot up here if this is what you want," she said.

"Not need cot."

"Don't be—"

The faint clicking sound of a lock being turned cut her off. She tensed for a moment, then relaxed again as Pieter's fox-like laughter went floating through the house.

"I'll see that you get a cot and anything else you might need," she went on then. "But you'll have to wait until the morning. Right now, I want to visit with my nephew."

Lathwi shrugged. She could wait forever for a thing she did not want. Then she followed Liselle down the ladder, out of the room and into the kitchen. Pieter and Jamus were having an animated conversation at the table.

"I still say I should get a commission for my help," the blonde man was saying. He looked as smug as a well-fed cat.

"What help?" Pieter demanded. "All you did was buy the fellow a beer!"

"What are you two squabbling about?" Liselle asked, as she took a seat alongside of her nephew.

"We stopped off at the inn after we stabled our horses," he replied, "and while we were there, we met a man—"

"I met him," Jamus asserted. "He was sitting all alone at the end of the bar, so I bought him a beer and invited him to join us. He did. And as luck would have it, he happened to mention that his mare had just gone lame."

"So?" Liselle asked.

"So I sold him my extra horse," Pieter said. "And now this scoundrel wants a cut of my profits.

"Which reminds me." He swivelled around to face Lathwi, who had curled up on the floor in front of the fire. "You owe me two dilucs. I paid for your horse's stabling out of my own pocket."

She shrugged, then retrieved her money-purse and tossed it at him. It landed on the table with a heavy clink. He fished two odd-shaped pieces of gold from its depths, then tossed it back to her. Instead of returning it to its place on her belt, she plunked it down on the hearthstones as if it were nothing more than a sack of candy. As an afterthought, she set the pouch which contained her stone alongside of it. Now that she had found a nest, she did not need to carry her fortune with her all the time.

"Well, my friend," Jamus said to him then, "I'd love to continue our debate, but the night grows old already and my own household awaits. Come and see me tomorrow when you're done dealing with merchants. I'll stand you a round simply for enduring such dreary company."

"I'll do that," Pieter replied. "I'll stand you another as commission."

Jamus chuckled, then stood up. Emboldened by Liselle's not-quite-covert scrutiny, he caught her hand and kissed it.

"Lady," he said, "please accept my many thanks for your splendid hospitality. With your permission, I would like to drop by every now and again to see how my dear friend Lathwi is faring."

"You must ask your dear friend for such permission," she replied, with a smile as peppery as her tone, "for it will be her time and not mine that you'll be wasting."

Ah, how he appreciated a quick-witted woman! Especially one who liked to spar with men. He had to see her again; his love of a challenge demanded it. Grinning now, he turned and winked at Lathwi.

"You won't mind if I visit now and again, will you?"

Lathwi shrugged, seemingly indifferent to the prospect of seeing him again. Her lack of enthusiasm did not bother him, though; so long as she had not refused him outright, he was free to call. Pleased with the way things were turning out, he flashed the women another of his devastating smiles, then bade them farewell. Pieter saw him to the door.

"Where in the world did you find him?" Liselle asked, as soon as he returned to the table. "He doesn't seems like the type who would enjoy tramping around in the wilds."

"He ran into him in a village on our way to Compara," he replied, his eyes lively with mischief. "The residents there were loathe to part with his company, but Lathwi here finally persuaded them to let him go."

"Oh?" She slanted an eyebrow at the big woman, inviting her to elaborate, but the discussion did not interest Lathwi, and so she said nothing. Annoyed by the apparent conspiracy to keep her curious about the honey-haired man, she abruptly switched subjects.

"So how long were you planning to stay here, nephew?"

"A week," he replied casually. "Perhaps a day more or less."

"So long? Don't you have work to do back there in that stretch of woods you call home now?"

"Nothing that won't keep until I get back."

"I see."

Although that was all she said on the matter, Pieter got the distinct impression that she was not pleased by the news. Which was strange, because her most common complaint was that his visits to Compara were too short, and too infrequent. He rifled through his memory for things he might've said or done to offend her, but all he could come up with was Lathwi. Was his aunt angry at him for bringing her here? If so, then why had she accepted the big woman as an apprentice? Liselle was not the type to rearrange her whole life just to indulge him. Something else must be going on, he decided. Something that had nothing to do with either him or Lathwi. Perhaps he had picked an inconvenient time to visit. Perhaps…

A yawn usurped the thought; and in its aftermath, all he wanted to think about was his old feather bed. He smiled an apology at his aunt, then said, "If you don't mind, I'd like to turn in for the night. A week's worth of sleeping on the ground has finally caught up with me."

"That sounds good," she replied. "I think I'll do the same." Then, turning to Lathwi, she said, "The attic isn't fit for—"

"The attic?" Pieter echoed. "You're sticking her in the attic?"

"I want be there," Lathwi told him.

Liselle lobbed him a haughty look, then proceeded. "As I was saying, the attic isn't fit for habitation yet, but if you want, you can sleep with—"

"I sleep here by fire," Lathwi replied, and then curled up into a sinuous knot. "Morning come, you teach."

Without further comment, she closed her eyes and started to snore. Pieter chuckled.

"What's so funny?" Liselle whispered.

"That's the way she spent her first night in my cabin, too," he said, not bothering to lower his voice.

"Oh?" She nabbed him by the arm, then ushered him down the hallway and into his room. There, she began to quiz him in earnest. "So who is she? And what is she to you? Even as a boy, you never picked up strays and brought them home."

"She's a stray all right," he said, unlacing his leather over shirt as he spoke, "but I didn't pick her up. She came crashing into my cabin one rainy night not too long ago; and when I say crashing, I mean crashing. The sight of her, all mud and black-mailed muscle, damned near scared the shit out of me."

"I can imagine," she replied. "But what can you tell me that I can't see with my own eyes?"

"She's quick-witted," he said, after a moment's thought. "And quick-fingered as well. If she likes something, she'll up and take it, so don't expose her to things that you'd be sorry to lose. And take care not to touch any of her stuff, either—sharing is by invitation only. If you forget that, she's apt to clout you in the head. And she packs a vicious punch."

"We swore a blood-oath while you were gone," she told him then. "I promised to teach her sorcery. She promised not to eat me. Why would she say something like that?"

"Lathwi was outcast as a child," he explained, "so she grew up wild. That was just her way of saying she won't hurt you. She said as much to me when we first met, too. And she has saved my life at least once since then."

That was the most heartening news Liselle had heard all night. Perhaps things were going to work out after all, she thought. Perhaps a strong-armed thief with a sense of honour was precisely the sort of ally she needed in these troubling times.

She reached out and embraced her nephew, blessing him for bringing her hope. Then, still high on that hope, she went to bed.

Malcolm was feeding the nonborn scraps of power when one of his demons came loping into his innermost sanctuary.

"Master!" it croaked, as it skittered to a stop in front of his chair. "The Recluse has had visitors!"

He shooed the nonborn off to the shadows as if it were a horrific horse cat, then focussed the whole of his attention on the drudge.

"Tell me more," he commanded.

"They arrived at her stronghold just before sunset—two males, one female." It paused. Its leer swelled to ghastly proportions. "One of them has the talisman."

"How do you know?"

"My kind can smell magic," it replied. "Especially that which belongs to the Dark One."

A delicious shiver coursed down his spine. So this was what it was like to be fortune's favourite son! Never in his life had so many things fallen so neatly into place. And now that he was sure of the talisman whereabouts, he could begin to bring the last phase of his quest to a close.

"Which one of the visitors has the talisman?" he asked, unabashed by the hunger he heard in his voice.

"I cannot say for sure," it admitted, "for I could not get close enough to make that distinction before they entered into the stronghold. But neither man had it on him when they came out again."

That did not surprise him. Indeed, the only surprising news was about the talisman itself: he'd assumed that it had been in Compara all along. He bit his lower lip, a sacrifice of blood and pain for being so careless. If he had chosen to attack The Recluse first instead of that pompous magician, he might never have recovered the relic. As luck would have it, though, no harm had been done. At least not to him, he added smugly, recalling his latest victim.

"Tell me more about these visitors," he told the demon, hoping to hear something that he could use to his advantage.

"I can say nothing about the female," it said, "for she has not come back out of the house as of yet. The males did not seem extraordinary in any way, but the naj may be able to tell you more as it was able to get closer to them."

"Ah, yes. The naj," he purred, hiding a burst of rancour behind a feline half-smile. "And where might that ambitious little sleep-stealer be at this moment?"

"It is following one of those men through the city. It said you might have an interest in his whereabouts."

He grunted his approval—the demon princeling might be the most dangerous of his slaves, but it was without a doubt the most astute as well. Anything and everything that passed beyond the sorceress' door was of the utmost interest to him now.

"Return to your vigil," he said then. "Tell the others that they are to follow anyone who emerges from The Recluse's house, but only from a distance. Under no circumstances are they to interfere with the people whom they are shadowing.

"Is that clear?"

"Abundantly so, Master," it rasped, and then went loping out of the chamber.

As soon as the drudge was gone, Malcolm loosed the smile that was singing in his heart. His quest was finally drawing to a close! He wanted to scamper down the streets of Compara and leer at its hale-limbed citizens. He wanted them to know that he, a miserable cripple, was to soon be their next king. He rubbed his chapped hands together, savouring the images of rape and murder that were now rioting through his head, then abruptly slapped himself sober again. Only a fool celebrated victory before the fact!

Even so, his heart continued to sing.

In the morning, Liselle came shuffling into the kitchen to find Lathwi by the hearth. The big woman was still curled up in a compact knot, but Liselle could tell that she was not asleep. Her eyelids were open to slits, and the eyes beneath them were too still.

"Good day, Lathwi," she said, as she began her morning routine. "I hope you weren't too uncomfortable last night."

"Sleep good," Lathwi replied, instantly wide-eyed and eager. "You teach now."

Such abruptness nettled Liselle, who was neither patient nor especially cheerful upon rising. "I'm not ready to teach you yet," she replied testily, "and I won't be until I've had my breakfast and a cup of tea. So if you want to get started anytime today, you'll stay out of my way."

But as the sorceress went about the business of making her porridge and tea, she began to feel guilty for rounding on Lathwi for what could rightly be viewed as a simple show of enthusiasm.

"Is Pieter still here?" she asked, hoping to start up a conversation and thereby assuage her conscience.

"No."

"Oh? When did he leave?"

"Before you get out of bed."

"I see. Did he say when he would be back?"

"No."

"Oh. Well. I suppose it doesn't matter. Do you want some of this porridge? I've made more than I can eat."

"No."

Liselle gave up and finished her breakfast in silence. Afterward, she dumped her dishes in a basin of soapy water. She was feeling better now, well enough to know that Lathwi had not meant to make her feel like a chatty old fool. The woman just wasn't much of a talker. And that wasn't such a bad thing—or at least it wouldn't be once a body got used to it.

"Come with me," she said to Lathwi then. "It's time for your first lesson."

To Liselle's vast surprise, the wards did not react when Lathwi set foot in the laboratory this time. She didn't know how such a wonder had come to pass. Maybe the blood-oath was responsible. Or maybe Lathwi herself had undergone some sort of subtle change overnight. Regardless of the cause, though, Liselle was deliriously relieved, for it meant that Lathwi no longer posed a threat to her!

"Close the door," she told Lathwi then. "It must always be shut when you work in here."

"Why?" Lathwi asked.

"Because power attracts power."

"Say again?"

Liselle sighed. She had hoped that someone who knew the Magic of Names would also have a passing familiarity with the basic rules of sorcery, but that was obviously not the case.

"Let's sit over there," she said, pointing to a nearby bench. "We need to talk about a few things."

Lathwi did as she was told without question or comment. The look on her scarred face was intense, almost voracious.

"As I was saying," Liselle began again, "power attracts power. This means that under normal circumstances, no magic can be performed without drawing the notice of other magical beings, be they human or otherwise. The Magic of Names might be an exception to this rule, but I doubt it. More likely, it's simply too specific to generate noise on any perceptible scale."

"Say again," Lathwi said. A frown baffled her forehead now. "Too many words, not enough meaning."

Liselle flashed her an embarrassed smile. "Sorry about that. Sometimes I get a little carried away. Just remember this: every time you use magic, you expose yourself to other sorcerers, not all of whom can be trusted. The greater the magic, the greater your peril; for as long as you are using sorcery, your mind is vulnerable to attack."

Lathwi hissed, a sound of complaint. "What purpose be sorcery if no can use?"

"People use sorcery all the time," Liselle assured her. "The smart ones take precautions beforehand. The most basic of these precautions are called wards."

Lathwi glanced toward the door then. Liselle approved her memory with a nod.

"That's right, those were wards you felt. I have two sets: the outer one prevents unfriendly magic from making its way into the house; the other encloses this room, and renders me and my sorceries silent. I tell you truly, Lathwi; this room is the safest place in the world for me. You'll be safe here, too."

Lathwi shrugged. Safety rarely concerned her unless her own was coming into immediate jeopardy. But she was curious about something else Liselle had said.

"You say you got wards one over other. So why you need close door before you make magic?"

Pieter was right, Liselle thought then. This woman was quick. And that was good to know.

"Only my inner wards are capable of silencing sorcery as it is taking place," she explained. "Any magic which escapes this room will be perceptible. It will also stress the outer wards, for they were designed to keep magic out, not in. And if those wards are stressed beyond a certain point, they will collapse. From that moment on, everyone in the house will be vulnerable to whatever might want to come inside.

"I don't want that to happen, Lathwi," she said, with an ferocity born of secret fear. "Therefore, you will close the door to this room before you practice your lessons. And you will never, ever practice magic anywhere else in this house.

"Do you understand everything I've told you so far?"

Lathwi nodded.

"Good. Now, have you heard enough for one day or would you like me to continue?"

"Continue."

"As you wish. But first you must tell me what you know about sorcery."

"Sorcery be power to command forces that other men no can control," she said then, quoting from the conversation that she and Pieter had had while on the road to Compara.

"Power and knowledge," Liselle appended. "One without the other is useless at best and terribly dangerous at worst. And while I can teach you the lore, you must already possess the power to use it."

That assertion intrigued Lathwi. To her, knowledge and power had always been one and the same thing.

"Tell more 'bout power," she urged.

"Well, for one thing, it stems from the Will—"

"What that be?"

Liselle raked her fingers through her hair as if hoping to find an answer among the strands. This was the first time she had ever been asked to define a notion that was so simple and yet so complex.

"The Will is an integral part of human consciousness," she began, "and the driving force behind desire. In certain individuals, this characteristic is more developed than—"

Lathwi hissed, venting frustration. So many words, so little meaning! Not for the first time, she longed for the compact eloquence of dragon-speech.

"All right," Liselle said, gathering up the scattered threads of her thoughts for another try. "Let's consider a different approach. Think of the Will as mental muscle: the more you have of it, the stronger you are. And the stronger you are, the more forces you can manipulate—"

"Show me," Lathwi demanded. "Easier to understand if I can see."

"What a remarkably good idea," Liselle exclaimed, a bit irked with herself for not having thought of it first. "And I've got the perfect exercise in mind. It'll work best if we are sitting on the floor."

Within the span of a blink, Lathwi was seated on the ground. The determined look in her blue eyes made her seem more fierce than usual. Liselle eased herself down next to her, then aimed a blunt-nailed finger at a shelf on the other side of the room.

"See that black jar over there?" she asked. "I want it. I want it more than anything else in the world, because it's filled with diamonds and gold. The problem is, I can't move my legs, so I can't go over and get it."

A sudden flash of greed encouraged Lathwi to get up and claim the jar's contents for herself. But when she tried to act on the impulse, her legs remained stubbornly folded in a sitting position. She rumbled. This tiny woman was sneakier than she seemed to be.

"Oops," Liselle said, letting hints of a smile skirt the corners of her mouth. "Did I fail to mention that you cannot move your legs, either? How forgetful of me.

"But never mind that, let's get back to the jar. I must have it. I must have it now." She stretched her arms toward the urn. Her eyes took on a distant glaze. "Fortunately, my Will needs no legs," she said, a trace of strain in her tone. "Even as I speak, it's speeding toward the jar. It cannot be seen or smelled or felt, but if you listen carefully, you may be able to hear it."

Lathwi did hear a faint, almost musical sort of buzzing in her ears. But before she had a chance to concentrate on the sound, the sorceress spoke again.

"My Will is wrapped around the jar. Now I need only to recall it."

The jar hopped into the air and began to glide across the room. Its flight was as smooth and steady as a summer breeze. Lathwi watched, slack-jawed with amazement, as it floated into Liselle's outstretched hands.

"Now that I have the jar," the sorceress said then, "I no longer want it. I want to put it back on its shelf. And because I still cannot move my legs, I must use the power of my Will to do so.

"Look into my mind now. Witness the jar's flight from a different perspective."

Lathwi did not need to be asked twice. With a deftness born of rabid curiosity, she slipped into the smaller woman's awareness. An image of the jar was waiting for her there—a peculiar band of scintillating white light was wrapped around its throat. This band contracted, then surged forward. The jar began to fly again. Lathwi grinned. This demonstration was so much clearer than a jumble of words.

When the jar was safely back on the shelf, the band slid free of it and came zipping back into Liselle's mind. There, it unravelled into a tangle of fragmented thoughts: pride and satisfaction; wonder and hope; an impression of some faceless menace. Before Lathwi could examine any of these threads in depth, a frosty blend of sound and thought pealed through her mind.

"Remove yourself," it said.

Lathwi withdrew immediately, but only because she wanted to learn more about this Will-thing. Otherwise, she would've gladly spent the rest of the day and more exploring Liselle's mind. It was, she decided, a thoroughly fascinating place.

"All right," the sorceress said then. "Now it's your turn. Give me your knife." When Lathwi balked, obviously suspicious of the demand, Liselle ridiculed her with a look. "Did you think I was going to let you practice with my jars?"

That had been Lathwi's precise thought, but she did not bother to say so. Instead, she tugged her not-claw free and handed it to Liselle. The sorceress got up then and started across the room. Lathwi tried to follow, but her legs still refused to budge.

"Now," Liselle said, setting the blade next to the jar, "all you have to do to get your knife back is reach out and grab it with your Will. Try it."

Lathwi pitched a confident thought at the not-claw. If Liselle could do it, she reasoned, then so could she.

Nothing happened.

"You're not concentrating," the sorceress informed her.

She tried again, then again and again, but met with no success. Liselle shrugged, then headed for the door.

"I'll be back later to check on you," she said. "At my knock, stop whatever you might be doing."

"This be stupid exercise!" Lathwi protested. "Fetching and carrying be work for legs, not thoughts."

"Perhaps," the sorceress granted. "But do keep trying just the same." As she started to close the door behind her, she added, "There will be no further lessons until you have mastered this one."

The door snicked shut. Lathwi's frustration turned to dread. What if she did not possess this Will-thing? What if fortune had abandoned her? A dragon with no fortune was no dragon, and a sorceress with no power was no sorceress. All she would be was a woman, soft and pink like prey.

She rejected these thoughts with a vehement hiss. She had power. She had concentration. And she had not come all the way to smelly Compara just to give up! She retreated to her memories then to review the day's lesson. Will, Liselle had said, was the driving force behind desire. Will was also that peculiar band of light she had seen with her mind's eye. As she shifted back and forth between these two perceptions, a key association lurched into place: that band was not one desire, but a whole host of them woven into a single adamant strand. Now she understood why she had failed. She had been concentrating on the wrong things!

Properly focussed now, she began to knit the bright white filaments of her desire into a whip-like cord. This cord was livelier than a dragon's tail, and it fell apart whenever her concentration slipped, but she returned to it again and again until all of its loose ends were tucked away. Then, tingling with suspense, she aimed her new-forged Will at the not-claw. It raced past the boundaries of her mind and across the room, then curled itself around the knife like a fast-growing vine. An instant later, she recalled it with an enthusiastic mental tug. Only her cat-like reflexes saved her from being speared in the throat.

For one euphoric moment thereafter, all she could do was gloat. She had done it, her fortune was true! Now she could walk the paths of power. Then a critical inner voice started to decry her achievement. It had been clumsy. And careless. Liselle would not be impressed. And if the sorceress was not impressed, she would not share any more of her secrets.

So she set aside her glee and began to gather the ravels of her Will together again.

The not-claw was halfway back to the shelf when a knock at the door distracted her. The knife clanged to the floor. An instant later, Liselle strode into the room.

"Congratulations," she said, when she spotted the fallen knife. "Some people take days to get that far. Others never catch on at all."

Lathwi deflected the praise with a frown. "I be clumsy. Need practice more."

"You've done enough for one day," Liselle told her then. "Sorcery is draining work, especially for beginners."

A protest swelled within Lathwi. There was nothing strenuous about playing thought-games! And she did not want to quit just yet. But even as she opened her mouth to voice these complaints, she realized that her brow was beaded with sweat. Moreover, the dull ache in her stomach was not due to hunger pangs.

"Is true," she said instead, a stunned admission. She stood up, then staggered a step to catch her balance. In the next instant, she went wide-eyed with surprise again.

"My legs work now."

"They would have worked before if you had really wanted them to," Liselle said, an undercurrent of amusement in her tone. "But never mind, that's another day's lesson. Let's get out of here."

Lathwi waved her on. "You go, I follow soon."

A concerned frown rumpled Liselle's forehead. "Do you want some help?"

"No. You go, no worry. I come quick."

"All right," Liselle said, drawling her reluctance, "but if you're not out in a minute or two, I'll be back. And if I catch you practising—"

"I no practice," she assured her.

Robbed of all excuses to stay, Liselle grudgingly left the room.

Lathwi waited until she was sure that she could not be heard, then stole over to the shelf where the black jar was resting and eased its lid aside. To her vast disappointment, it was empty.

Liselle was smart, she thought, and then went in search of a nap.

The next few days passed as a blur for Lathwi. When she was not practising in the laboratory, she was either gorging on the side of fresh meat which Pieter had purchased for her, or sleeping in the attic which he had swept out. She would not have noticed the trapper's considerations if Liselle had not pointed them out to her. The whole of her attention was centered on her budding magical skills.

She was on her way to the pantry after another day of obsessive practising when she spied Liselle sitting in the rocking chair next to the hearth. There was an unfamiliar object in her lap. Instantly curious, she hurried over for a closer look. It was a thin stack of yellowing, leaf-thin skins contained within a leather jacket. Each of the skins bore marks like chicken scratchings on its back.

"What that?" she asked.

"A book," Liselle replied, and turned from one page to the next.

"What do?"

"It tells me things."

"How?"

The sorceress loosed an impatient nasal sigh. She was in no mood for conversation tonight. All she wanted was to be left alone with her research. But it was clear that she would have no peace until she placated Lathwi's curiosity.

"Look here," she said, tracing a fingernail along a line of script. "See these markings? Each one of them represents a different sound. When these sounds are strung together in specific patterns, they form words. These words in turn form specific thoughts. The ability to draw these marks is called writing. The ability to decipher them is called reading."

Lathwi grinned. If she understood Liselle correctly, then books were collections of other peoples' thoughts. And that meant that reading was like eavesdropping—only better. She could not wait to give it a try.

"You teach me reading," she said.

"I suppose I could," Liselle granted, and then hastily added, "But not tonight. I've got work to do."

Before she could return to her book, though, Pieter came striding out of his room and toward them. There was a spring in his step, and a glint in his eyes.

"Good evening, ladies." He planted a bewhiskered kiss on his aunt's cheek, then turned to Lathwi and said, "Where have you been hiding these past few days?"

"I not hiding," she replied, perfectly deadpan. "I be practising magic."

"So I've heard."

"Have you found a buyer for your furs yet?" Liselle asked.

"As a matter of fact, I've found several," he told her, grinning with obvious relish. "All that needs to be done now is the haggling."

"How long will that take?"

"A day or two. At worst, a week."

"I see." A frown tugged at the corners of her mouth, but she twitched it aside. "There's a stew on the fire if you're hungry."

Lathwi rolled her eyes. What was it about these people and stew?

"Thanks," Pieter replied, "but I was planning to take my dinner at the inn tonight."

"Must you?" Liselle blurted, and then hastened to put a mundane face on her secret fears. "Compara can be dangerous after dark, especially for a man alone."

Resentment flashed within him then. Here he was, almost thirty years old now, and yet his aunt still treated him like a schoolboy in knickers. But as much as that griped him, he loved Liselle too much to hold it against her, and so made an effort to humour her.

"All right then, I won't go alone," he said, and turned to Lathwi. "Do you want to come to the inn with me? It will be my treat."

Although Lathwi had no idea as to what an inn might be, she decided that it had to be more fun than staying here and watching Liselle do something that she herself could not. So she flashed the trapper an adventurous grin.

"We go."

Liselle was not pleased to hear that. But she could not make them stay without revealing her fears, and she could not do that because then Pieter would want to stay in Compara and try to protect her, and that simply would not do. She wanted him to return to his home in the backwoods. He would be safe there, safe from fears which she could not yet name.

"Then go already," she told them, snappish now because she hated being so powerless. "And don't forget your keys. Otherwise, you'll find yourselves sleeping in the street."

They ducked out of the house and into a starry spring night. Lathwi breathed deeply, glad to be under open skies again. Pieter did likewise for different reasons.

"Has she been that moody all day?" he asked, as they started on their way.

Lathwi shrugged. She paid little attention to anyone's mood but her own. He nibbled on the fringes of his mustache, then tried again.

"How are you two getting along?"

"Good."

"Do you like her?"

"She smart like mother."

Her mother was the last thing he wanted to talk about tonight, so he abruptly changed the subject. "Since we're out, and it's on the way, let's stop in at the stable. You ought to know where you're keeping your horse."

The suggestion took her by surprise. In her eagerness to learn new things, she had completely forgotten about the stallion. But now that he had mentioned it, she supposed it would be useful to know the beast's whereabouts.

"You smart, too," she told him.

"I hope you're paying attention to the way we're going," he said, as they strode from street to street. "I don't plan on getting separated, but accidents happen from time to time; and it's no fun being lost in Compara at night."

"I no get lost," she confidently assured him. Years of hunting in vast tracts of mountain and forest had honed her sense of direction to a fine point. And while it might seem otherwise, she was taking careful notice of her surroundings.

They came to a broad building which smelled mightily of horse dung and dried grasses. Pieter ushered her through its wide, half-open doors, then planted his hands on his hips and called out in a falsely belligerent tone.

"Raffi, quit molesting your mares and get out here. I've brought a friend for you to meet."

A short, incredibly fat man with the scruffy beginnings of a beard came shuffling out from one of the stalls with a dung-clotted shovel in his hands.

"Who dat with da big mouth?" he demanded, squinting in their direction. "Could it be dat crazy trapper—" Then, catching sight of Lathwi, his broken-fence of a grin chasmed into a disbelieving 'O'. "Good Goddess, Pieter! Who da hell is dat with you?"

"This is Lathwi," the trapper replied. "She's here to check on her horse. And if she doesn't like the way you're taking care of it, she'll eat you."

"Which one her horse?"

"That bay stallion I brought in with my mare and Buck."

The stabler made a disparaging face. "Figures. Dat one nasty horse, you betcha. Chomp me good right here, he did." He patted the roll of fat that girded his hips, then laughed. "He not like it when I chomp him back. You remember dat when you think you hungry for Raffi," he said to Lathwi, wagging a chubby finger at her. "Now come, see you crazy horse."

He led them to the back of the barn, then gestured at a stall to his right.

As Lathwi strode forward to investigate, he said, "Lemme know if you got complaints. I not be sorry to see dat ingrate go elsewhere."

The bay snapped at her as she entered his stall. In one fluid move, she sidestepped his lunge and grabbed his halter; in the next, she punched his nose. He grunted irritably when she let him go, but made no further attempt to bite her. She did not blame him for being in a bad mood, for while he had a clean nest and plenty to eat, there was no sky over his head and no place for him to run.

"You satisfied?" Raffi asked, when she stepped back into the center aisle.

"He need run," she replied.

"You want, I exercise dat horse," he said. When she did not answer him right away, he added, "I do free for da friend of my friend."

She shrugged, giving the man leave to do as he pleased. Then, hungered by the concentrated smell of horseflesh, she turned to Pieter. "We go now."

Raffi's doughy face sagged with hurt and surprise as she started toward the door, then rebounded back into a wan smile as Pieter clapped him on the back.

"Many thanks, my friend," he said to the stabler. "Come to the inn when you're done with your work and I'll stand you a beer." Then, when he caught up with Lathwi, he took her to task for her rudeness. "It wouldn't have hurt you to be nice to Raffi. After all, he did offer to exercise your horse."

"I not ask him to do."

"That doesn't matter. When someone does something nice for you, the least you can do in return is say 'Thank you'."

"What 'thank you' do?"

"It's an expression of appreciation."

She hissed. "More words with no meaning. Why people talk so much? City noisy enough without them flapping their lips all the time."

"Perhaps," Pieter said. "But just remember this: you'll catch more flies with honey than sour wine."

Now what was that supposed to mean? Why would she want to catch any flies at all? She shook her head then. People had the strangest habits.

The inn was one street down from the stables. It was a large brick building full of windows and flickering lights. The most notable thing about it was its unfenced courtyard.

"It's busy tonight," Pieter commented, as they passed a hitching-post crowded with mud-spattered horses. "I hope we can get a table."

They strode up a set of scarred wooden steps and past a trio of men who were lounging on the porch. The air reeked of tobacco and gish, a stench which grew worse as Pieter led them into a dimly lit room. There were men everywhere here. Some leaned against the long, shelf-like table which spanned the length of the wall to her left. The rest were seated at a hodge-podge of smaller tables. Seated or standing, though, they were all staring at Lathwi. She did not blame them; she would've been surprised to see a dragon in a place like this, too.

Pieter nudged her in the ribs, then pointed toward the fireplace. "I think I see an open table over there. Let's grab it before someone else comes in."

He began feeling his way through the crowded room. She followed. But she was more of a bull than a conger in tight spaces, and so banged into several obstacles that the trapper had deftly avoided. One such collision sent a comber of beer splashing out of a brawny, bearded man's cup.

"Watch where you're going, bitch," the man snarled, and then gave her a retaliatory shove. She paid no attention to his challenge. She was too busy wondering why Pieter wanted to come to this wretched place. And her bafflement soared to even greater heights when she saw the table that he'd been so eager to grab. It was slick with smears of coagulated grease in some spots, and sticky from spilled gish in others.

"I know it's not the most elegant place in the world," he said, responding to her look of disgust, "but the food is good, and the price is right. And speaking of food—do you want something from the spit? Or are you dedicated to a diet of strictly raw meat?"

Under any other circumstances, she would've waited until they returned to Liselle's house to feed. But her day in the laboratory had left her famished, and time weighed heavily on a hungry dragon's mind, so she decided to try the inn's fare. After all, how much worse than jerky could it be?

"I take from spit," she replied.

A short time later, a reed-thin man dressed in greasy linens shuffled up to their table. He had snow-white hair, and skin to match. His eyes were a delicate shade of pink. Lathwi was immediately intrigued.

"Never see pink eyes before," she said. "They hurt?"

The albino blinked. His polite smile curled into a look of wonder. More to himself than to her, he said, "Now here's a rare bird. Plenty of people have taunted me about my pink eyes, and plenty more have tried to cheat me because of them, but this is the only one who ever wondered if they hurt.

"What's your name, stranger?"

"Lathwi."

He muttered the name several times as if trying to adapt the foreign sound to his own palate, then said, "Strange name for a strange person. But since you asked, Lathwi, I'll tell you. Yes, these eyes of mine hurt, especially when they're exposed to bright light. Which is why you won't often catch Zill in the sun."

"Hey, Pink-Eyes!" a big man with a braided beard yelled. "Quit cozying up to the bitch and her panderer. We need more beer over here." To emphasize his point, he slammed an empty tankard against the table. His table-mates sniggered as it shattered in his hand.

"Southerners," Zill hissed, giving the word a thousand jointed legs. "I'd piss in their beer if Kyle didn't need their gold so badly."

"Ignore them," Pieter advised, meaning to practice what he preached even though he did not appreciate being called a panderer. "Maybe they'll go away."

"Easy for you to say, Blue-eyes," the albino said, and then grinned to take the sting out of the retort. "But what can I get for you two tonight?"

"We'll both have a plate of whatever's on the spit," the trapper told him, "and a tankard of beer to wash it all down. Ask the carver to make Lathwi's portion as raw as possible."

"I'll do the slicing myself," Zill said with a wink, and then shuffled over to the Southerners' table. They subjected him to another round of loud insults, many of which were lewd innuendos involving Lathwi. Pieter scowled, offended by such behaviour, then tried to distract himself with small talk.

"Zill is a good man," he told Lathwi. "We've known each other for a long time now."

"You be brothers?" she asked.

"Not in the physical sense of the word. But people can be born of different mothers and still be friends, you know."

"What 'friends'?"

"Friends are people who share a special affinity for one another," he replied. "In times of peace, they stay together simply because it pleases them to do so; in times of trouble, they stick together to guard each others' back."

"This special affinity formed at birth?" she wondered, thinking of Shoq and her other tanglemates.

"Not necessarily. People can and do form friendships throughout their lives."

Just then, Zill reappeared at their table with two mugs in one hand and two platters of meat in the other. As he set Lathwi's dinner in front of her, he cast her another wink.

"It's cooked," he said, "but just barely. If you like it and want more, let me know. I took a whole joint off the spit just in case."

"Thanks, Zill," Pieter said, but the albino was already on his way to another table. He turned his smile to Lathwi and her heaping plate. "Speaking of friends, it looks as if you made one tonight."

Lathwi shrugged. Having a friend felt no different from not having a friend, leastwise not while she was hungry. She examined the mound of pinkish flesh in front of her then. It smelled a little smoky, but not as foul as jerky. It did not scorch her fingers when she touched it, either. She popped a small morsel into her mouth and chewed warily. Encouraged by the sweet warm juices that trickled down her throat, she then started to feed in earnest. An instant later, Pieter started to pester her.

"Lathwi," he whispered, "civilized people eat their meat with a knife when they're in a public place. Like this," he urged, as she glanced up from her plate. He carved himself a bite-sized strip, then lifted it to his mouth with the tip of his knife. "Go ahead, give it a try."

She hissed, immensely annoyed with him for interrupting her while she was trying to feed. Nevertheless, she slipped the not-claw from her belt and hacked her meat into inelegant slivers. When she was done, she began to prong those slivers into her mouth one right after the other.

"Stupid people," she rumbled between bites. "What be so civilized about slashing tongue to ribbons?" A moment later, she turned her scowl to her untouched mug. "What this?"

"Beer," he said.

"Civilized people eat that with knife, too?"

"Just shut up and eat," he growled, beginning to rue the whim that had prompted him to invite an ignorant barbarian to dinner. "Use your fingers if you want. Or perhaps you would prefer to gobble straight from the plate like a dog."

Just then, one of the Southerners plowed his way over to their table. He was a huge man, more than a hand taller than Lathwi and maybe half again as broad, with piggish brown eyes and a humpback nose. His greasy brown beard was twisted into a snake's nest of tiny random braids—a southern affectation which marked him as a man of status. Pieter was not happy to see that, for in the south, men moved up in the rank and file by murdering their superiors.

"What's the matter, little man?" the stranger jeered, in a loud baritone which was all slushy from gish. "Didn't your poppa teach you how to keep your merchandise in line?"

"You must be thinking of somebody else, Mister," Pieter replied, all politeness and frost. "I have no merchandise at this table."

"Oh?" the man countered derisively. "Where I come from, only one kind of woman shows herself in an inn. And only one kind of man accompanies her."

Pieter ground his teeth against an urge to toss his beer in this bastard's face. He did not want any trouble tonight, he reminded himself. Did not, did not, did not.

"That may be," he said then. "But as it happens, things are different in this part of the world. So why don't you go back to your beer and leave us to ours?"

"What if I don't want to leave? What if I tell you I've taken a fancy to your scar-faced bitch? What if I give you a little something for her use?"

Up until that moment, Lathwi's only concern had been the meat on her plate. But even as she went to stab another bite for herself, something hard hit the table and then bounced to a stop in front of her. To her amazement and delight, it was a dazzling blue-white diamond. Hunger forgotten, she put her not-claw away.

"That's twenty times her worth," the Southerner bragged to Pieter then. "But I'm hard up, and the other laddies will want to use her, too, so take your fee and run along. We'll send the woman home tomorrow."

"The woman comes and goes as she pleases," Pieter said, eyeing the diamond as he might a poisonous snake, "so if you have a proposition, make it to her, not me."

The Southerner despised Pieter with a look, then turned to dominate Lathwi's view. "Well, woman?" he asked. "Do you want the diamond or not?"

Fast as a striking dragon, Lathwi grabbed the Oma-stone. An instant later, the man with the broken nose grabbed her by the elbow.

"All right then, let's go," he said. "I've got a room upstairs." When she ignored him, he gave her arm a hard tug. "Move it!"

She twisted free of his grip and hissed a warning, then went back to admiring to the diamond. It was her first, and therefore auspicious. With it, she could start her own nest.

"It looks like she's not in the mood for your company after all," Pieter said.

"I'm not paying her to want my company," the Southern retorted, "I'm paying her to fuck it." He seized Lathwi by the elbow again. "Now come along, wench. This is the last time I'll be asking you nice-like."

Her annoyance swelled to Shoq-sized proportions. Could this fool not see that she did not want to play? She snaked free of his grasp, then gave him an emphatic shove. Rendered clumsy by a bellyful of gish, he stumbled backward and into a suddenly vacant table. He swore gustily, then stalked toward her again with a look like daggers in his eyes. Pieter tried to block his way, but the Southerner brushed him aside like a pesky gnat and then closed in on Lathwi.

"So," he rasped at her, "you like to play rough. Good. So do I."

Then he dealt her a resounding slap to the face.

A thin scum of silence settled over the room only to be broken by the sound of customers scrambling for safer ground or perhaps a better view. "Three dilucs says he gets her to his room before I finish my beer," a voice from the vicinity of the now-crowded bar cried.

"No bet," another sneered. "Everyone here knows you're the slowest drinker this side of the mountains."

Meanwhile, Lathwi gave her jaw a speculative rub. She was not angry at the man for striking her—it was a feeble blow compared to some that she had received from Shoq. But his contempt for her warnings was intolerable. She set her Oma-stone down on the table, then stood up to teach him the meaning of respect.

"Now you're being sensible," he said. "You took me by surprise last time; you wouldn't be that lucky twice. Come on, let's go up to my room and play in private."

She bared her teeth at him, his final warning. "I not want to play."

"Oy!" he laughed to the audience at large. "You should see the teeth on this bitch! What a wild ride this is going to be!"

Still chuckling, he grabbed her by the waist and took a step toward the door. She tripped him in mid-stride. As he lurched forward, she seized a fistful of his beard and slung him with all of her might. Boosted by an accidental pulse of Will, he went sailing halfway across the room and into a nest of chairs. Wood splintered. Mugs shattered. The Southerner shifted as if he were trying to get up and then went suddenly limp.

For one astonished moment thereafter, the whole room was quiet. Even the hearth-fire seemed to hold its breath. Then the Southerner's accomplices went scrambling over to check on him; and everyone else started chattering. As this commotion built up steam, Zill appeared beside Lathwi. He was grinning from ear to ear. "You've given Pink-Eyes a delightful treat tonight," he told her in a low, excited tone. "But now it's time for you to go. I don't imagine that that piece of southern shit will be a lot of fun when he wakes up."

Pieter was very much inclined to agree; and so without pausing to consult Lathwi, he plucked the diamond from the table and hurried off after his albino friend. Lathwi went loping after them—through the kitchen and out of the back door.

"Be sure to visit again when next you come to Compara," Zill urged them from the doorway. "But stay away until then. Those Southerners will no doubt be looking to carve the price of a diamond from your hides."

Pieter pressed three shiny gold coins into Zill's palm. "For the damage," he said. "And until next time, fare well."

They took the back way home—through alleys and over fences, past a party of derelicts feasting on garbage and a pair of skulking lovers. Pieter ran full-speed out of fear for his hide; Lathwi kept up with him simply because he had her stone. By the time they reached the safety of Liselle's courtyard, he was sweaty and huffing for breath. Lathwi was barely winded. He muttered about that as he opened the door to the house.

Liselle was still sitting in her rocking chair by the hearth when they came spilling into the kitchen. As she set her book down to look at them, a pleasantly surprised smile curled across her heart-shaped face.

"You're home early," she commented. Then she noticed Pieter's heaving chest and sweaty brow, and the corners of her mouth went flat with instant dread. "What happened?"

"Lathwi happened," he growled. With a cumulus frown, he dug the diamond out of his back pocket and slapped it down on the table. Then he began to pace back and forth in front of the hearth. Now that he was safely home, he could afford the luxury of annoyance. "She draws trouble like horseshit draws flies."

"Tell me what happened," Liselle demanded, as Lathwi came hurrying over to reclaim the diamond.

Lathwi did not understand why the sorceress was so keen to hear about such a tedious event. It had hardly been worth her own notice even as it was happening. And all she wanted to do at the moment was admire her first Oma-stone. Her gaze strayed toward the diamond then. Its firelit facets drew her toward communion.

"Well?" Liselle prompted. "I'm waiting."

"Man with broken nose give me Oma-stone," Lathwi replied then, just to shut Liselle up. "He want me to play, but I no want, so I make him go away. Zill say it time to go then, so Pieter and me run home."

Having said all that she meant to say, she then strode off to the attic to contemplate her newfound prize in peace. Liselle scowled at Lathwi's receding back, then turned to her nephew.

"Well?" she asked archly. "Would you care to elaborate?"

Pieter was astounded. That damned Lathwi had made their run-in with the Southerner sound like a holiday outing in the meadow! As he paced across the floor, he began to babble.

"The inn was crowded when we got there. And almost as soon as we set foot inside, some Southern bastard went after her. Don't ask me why—he was mean-drunk and looking for a fight. She snapped up the diamond he offered her as whore's wages, then told him to get lost. He tried to bully her into going upstairs with him then, but she—" Pieter didn't know if he wanted to laugh, curse, or cry now. "—she tossed him across the room."

"Was he a small man?" Liselle asked. "A dwarf perhaps?"

"He was twice my size!" Pieter bleated. "Not only that, he outweighed her by at least thirty pounds."

"And she pushed him away."

"She threw him halfway across the room, I tell you. Ask Zill, if you don't believe me. Ask anyone who was there."

"That's all right," she murmured then. "I believe you."

With that conviction came a wave of fresh fear. Because it was obvious that Lathwi had used sorcery to defend herself tonight; and while she'd had every right and reason to do so, Liselle was afraid that she'd escaped one danger only to set herself in the path of something even more perilous.

"I don't know," Pieter said then, misreading his aunt's troubled expression. "Maybe bringing Lathwi here wasn't such a good idea after all."

"What makes you say that?" she asked warily.

"She's too wild for city life, too unpredictable. What's going to happen to you when I leave?"

"I'm quite capable of taking care of myself," she told him, although inwardly she was squirming with doubts. "When you leave, I'll miss you terribly and think of you often, but believe me, life will go on."

"I must've taken a wrong turn on the way home tonight," he said, fixing her with an incredulous stare, "because this doesn't sound like the aunt I know and love. That wonderful woman prefers an orderly, uneventful life. She doesn't like surprises or disruptions."

"Things change. So do people—even me, I'm afraid."

"Have you gone mad?"

"I'm learning to take care of me and mine. If that's madness, then the whole world's crazy."

"I'm beginning to think so," he said, still eyeing her suspiciously. "Are you sure you want her here?"

"My life may be orderly, Pieter," she told him, "but it is rarely uneventful. And at this particular point in time, Lathwi belongs here with me. There are things that we need to teach each other, things which may prove to be important in the not too distant future. Because of that, I'm willing to put up with quite a number of surprises and disruptions.

"So stop fretting, nephew. Lathwi and I will manage."

"If you say so."

"I do. Now run along. I've still got some reading to finish."

Although he was not totally convinced, he did as he was told. He still had a couple of days left in Compara; and so would see for himself how the two women managed. And if he did not like what he saw, he would find a way to send Lathwi packing.

"The golden-haired man is some sort of an exalted lackey for the fool who rules this dung-heap. As far as I can tell, he has no significant ties to The Recluse."

A look like hunger streaked across Malcolm's face as he eyed the woman in front of him. She was undeniably stunning, a black-haired fantasy with bold hips and full breasts. Her long, come-hither lashes shaded a pair of sly, cinnamon eyes. She was everything a man could possibly want—so long as he could overlook the fact that she was not a woman at all.

"And what of her other visitors?" he asked, making it clear that his lust was for knowledge rather than the naj's illusory physical charms.

"The female is still a puzzlement," it said, affecting a winsome pout. "She does not often leave the house, and when she does, it is always in the company of others. My guess is that she is a stranger to this place."

"Perhaps," Malcolm murmured, and then paused to consider another report that he had received. One of his drudges had shadowed this mysterious female to an inn last night. While she was within, magic had been done—nothing dramatic, only a faint puff of Will. Afterward, she and the red-haired man had gone racing back to The Recluse's stronghold. Why? Had they been fleeing magic? Or had magic spelled their escape?

"Continue to watch her," he said, voicing his decision even as it formed in his head. "There is something about her which I mistrust."

"It will be as you say," the naj said, breathing the affirmation like an innuendo.

"Now tell me of the red-haired man."

The naj's simper abruptly chasmed into a blood-thirsty grin. "He is kin to the Recluse, Blackheart. Moreover, he has unlimited access to her house. I am of the belief that he can be used."

"Indeed he can," Malcolm rumbled, already in the process of devising a plan to fit the ingredients at hand. "Indeed he can."

CHAPTER 8

They were sitting around the kitchen table—Jamus and Pieter on one bench, Liselle on the other. As usual, Lathwi was sprawled on the floor. The remains of a sumptuous dinner were cooling under their noses.

"Lady," Jamus said, embracing Liselle with an admiring glance, "you are truly a woman of prodigious magical talents. That was a feast fit for The Dreamer." "I'm glad to hear you enjoyed it," she replied. She was in high spirits this evening—partly because of the company, and partly because of a glass of sweet straw wine. "But your thrice-emptied plate was all the praise I needed."

"High praise indeed," he chuckled good-naturedly, and then donned a smile which was both ironic and sly. "Perhaps you'll allow this humble glutton to return your hospitality." She arched an eyebrow at him then. He took that as a sign to go on. "I'm hosting a party for Pieter tomorrow night. I'd be most delighted if you would grace us with your presence."

The amusement in her sea-green eyes vanished, leaving a cool, distant sheen behind. "I thank you for the invitation, but I'm afraid I'll have to decline."

"But why?" Pieter blurted. "I'm leaving in the morning, you know."

"I know. And it's only fitting that you spend your last night in town with your rowdy friends. I wouldn't know what to do with myself in that kind of crowd."

"What if Lathwi came with you?" he wheedled. "She could keep you company."

Liselle turned to Lathwi, who was sharpening her nails on a bit of stone. The big woman's air of preoccupation did not fool her—she knew how much Lathwi liked to eavesdrop.

"What do you say, Lathwi?" she called out, in a falsely jovial tone. "Are you going to this party tomorrow?"

"No," Lathwi replied, without looking up from her nails.

"Come on, don't be such a spoilsport," Pieter scolded. "What else were you going to do tomorrow?"

Up until that moment, Lathwi had not given tomorrow any thought, for dragons were inclined to let each new day unfold according to fortune's whim. But since Pieter had asked, and she was a bit bored, she tried to anticipate the future. She saw herself practising magic in the laboratory, then feeding, then returning to her attic nest to sleep, but then dismissed the vision with a restless hiss. She had spent too much time on her backside lately; her already soft form was in peril of growing softer. She needed fresh air, open space. Suddenly, she knew exactly what she was going to do tomorrow.

"I go hunting," she announced. Then, meaning to rest up for that event, she got up and headed for the attic.

"That's going to take some getting used to," Liselle commented.

"What's that?" Jamus asked solicitously.

"Her rather unceremonious way of coming and going," she explained. "She always leaves me with the feeling that I'll never see her again."

"That'll pass," Pieter assured her. "As the weeks wear on, you'll probably find yourself wondering about ways to get rid of her."

Jamus pushed to his feet then. "I hate to take my leave of your excellent company so early," he said, "but I'm afraid I must go. The Governor-General is expecting me tonight.

"Lady," he went on, capturing her hand with a flourish, "it has been a privilege to dine with you. I cherish a hope that you'll change your mind about the party tomorrow."

"Don't hope too fervently," she replied, a warning iced with sweetness. "Disappointment is bad for the digestion."

"Then I'll suffer from colic for the rest of my days." He kissed her hand, then gently released it. As he headed for the door, he clapped Pieter on the back and said, "I'll see you tomorrow, my friend."

"Tomorrow," the trapper echoed with a grin.

The next morning, Lathwi was up and gone from the house before dawn. Although it was still dark outside, she had no problem finding the stables; all she had to do was follow her nose. Horses nickered nervously as she let herself into the barn. A moment later, Raffi emerged from a stall to bar her way. Although it was obvious by his bleary eyes and rumpled appearance that he'd been sleeping, there was nothing groggy about the way he was holding his pitchfork. He squinted at her for a moment, then grunted and dropped his guard.

"What you want so early in da day?" he asked.

"Need horse and tack," she replied.

"Tack's in da tackroom," he said, vaguely gesturing at the other side of the stable. "You wait, I get for you."

Not only did he fetch her gear, he carried it over to the stallion's stall and lent her a hand with the saddling. It did not occur to her to refuse his help—the bay was in far too feisty a mood. As soon as the horse was ready to go, she climbed onto his back and urged him toward the door. An instant later, she remembered Pieter's lecture on favours and reined him to a halt again.

"Thank you," she said to Raffi, who was staring up at her like a wounded fawn.

Those two little words had an remarkable effect on the stabler. His eyes gleamed with sudden pleasure; his sagging jowls perked into a smile.

"You watch you back," he told her. "And next time you need dat horse, you come a little later in da day."

She did not answer, but only started on her way.

As she made her way through the city, its shadowed walls took on lavender hues which then slowly turned rosy. For one breath-taking moment thereafter, Compara was beautiful: quiet and still, suspended by sunrise. Then the creak of an unseen oxcart shattered the spell, and Compara returned to its usual squalid self. Disgusted anew, she urged the bay into a trot. As soon as he cleared the city gates, she gave him free rein to run as fast as he pleased.

It did not take her long to forget Compara.

Pieter wandered into the kitchen, still dishevelled from sleep. His aunt was already seated at the table, as neat and crisp as a newly minted coin. He peered at her through puffy eyes for a moment, then asked, "Is there any tea left?"

"The pot's by the fire," she replied, in an obscenely cheerful tone. "If you want some, help yourself. I'm not your servant, you know."

"I know," he commented, as he went shuffling past her. "Servants know better than to flap their tongues so early in the morning."

"Early?" She snorted derisively. "What a sluggard you are! Lathwi was up and on her way two hours ago."

"That's no secret." Steaming mug in hand, he sat down across from her. "She woke me out of a sound sleep when she came down from the attic. I never did much more than drowse after that."

"Poor thing," she said, totally without sympathy.

He grunted, then slurped at his tea for a while. When he deemed himself awake enough to hold a decent conversation, he said, "Have you by any chance changed your mind about the party tonight?"

"No." If resoluteness had had a colour, it would've been the same shade as her eyes just then. "And I'd appreciate it if you didn't raise the subject again. I have my reasons for declining; and you must trust me when I say that they're good ones."

"As you wish," he said, lacing the words into a resigned sigh. "I only pressed it because I wanted to spend some more time with you."

"I know," she replied. "But maybe we can wring an extra moment or two from some other part of the day. What are your plans?"

"I'm making the exchange with my buyer this morning," he told her. "I'll probably pick up some supplies afterward and then come home for a bath. After that, I'm off to the event which I'm forbidden to mention."

"Busy day," Liselle commented, tongue-in-cheek.

"You know how it is." He stretched like a well-fed cat. "A man's work is never done."

"That's because they spend half the day loafing in bed."

He made a sour face at her, then went shuffling back to his room. When he returned a short time later, Liselle gave him a critical once-over, then said, "If you want, I'll trim your beard for you when you get back."

"That sounds good," he replied, and headed for the door. "I'll try to get home early."

Then, with a wave, he was gone.

She heaved a sigh laden with complex regrets, then got a book from the laboratory and returned to her rocking chair to read. But before she had turned more than a dozen pages, the front door burst suddenly open, and a wiry little man clad in a servant's drab brown livery came running toward her.

"What the—!" A jolt of fear-rich adrenaline slung her out of her chair. It also rendered her shrill. "You have no business here! Get out before I do something we'll both live to regret!"

The trespasser hurled himself at her feet and started to grovel. "Forgive my intrusion, Mistress," he cried, "but I'm desperate! My master has been most hideously cursed."

"Then take him to Weiss of Ormula," she snapped, still all but rabid from the fright she had been given. "Removing curses is one of his specialties."

"We have been to the Ormulan's home already," he told her. "He isn't there. And no one seems to know where he's gone or when he's coming back." A chill foreboding skated down Liselle's spine. It told her where the cocksure but careless Weiss de Ormula had gone. It also told her that he was never coming back. She groaned, damning herself as a self-centered fool. She'd assumed that The Rogue was only hunting for her. Now it was obvious that all of Compara's sorcerers were in danger.

If only she had been smarter. Braver. Better informed. The Ormulan might have stood with her against a common enemy. And two were always stronger than one...

"Please, Mistress," the servant begged her then. "Have pity on my Master. If you refuse him, he will surely die."

Liselle ground her teeth against an urge to shout. She needed to think, dammit! Who were Compara's other sorcerers? Where were they living now? And would they join her? But as much as she wanted to send the servant away empty-handed, her conscience forbade it. Only the worst sort of coward set her own fears above a dying man's need.

"Where is he?" she demanded, no more gracious for her morals.

"Outside in your courtyard."

"If he can make it through my door, I'll look at him. Beyond that, though, I'll make no promises."

The servant went racing out the door. When he returned, there were three others with him. Two were garbed in servant livery like himself, the third was swathed in canvas sacking. Her wards chirred faintly as that one crossed the threshold, but permitted him to pass. That meant that there was indeed some sort of malevolent magic afoot here; and that it was of no direct threat to her. Relieved, she guided the accursed and his anxious servants to the laboratory. There, she bade the accursed to remove his hood so she could have a look at him.

He reached up with a canvas-wrapped hand and slowly drew the sacking away from his head. Her breakfast lurched in her stomach as his face came into view. It was streaked with the foul colours of gangrene, and so bloated, she could barely see his eyes and nose. The stench which oozed from his distended pores was that of a violated grave.

Liselle flinched at the size and scope of the task ahead of her. She was going to have to use ritual magic to get rid of this curse—and that brand of sorcery involved prodigious amounts of power.

"I may be able help you," she told him, "but the attempt will be hard on both of us. Are you prepared to suffer?"

He replied with a barely perceptible nod.

"You won't be able to change your mind once I begin the rite," she cautioned. "And it is possible that my magic will not suffice, and your suffering will be for naught. Knowing this, do you still wish me to make the attempt?" Again the nod.

"So be it," she said, and gestured at his servants. "Remove his garments."

They scurried over, then stripped the canvas from their master's body. Naked, he was even more appalling to behold. His whole body was swollen: arms, belly, buttocks, toes. And all of it was marbled with subcutaneous rot. Spots which had clotted to the sacking were now raw slicks of greenish ichor. There was an horrible graveyard stench about him.

"Go now and fetch clean clothing for him," she bade the servants then. "Bring more sacking, too, for I can't promise a cure. When you return, stay in the courtyard until you are called. If you need something to occupy your thoughts in the meantime, feel free to apply yourselves to my woodpile."

They bowed to their stricken master, then vacated the laboratory. She locked the door behind them, then went in search of the tools she would need for the ritual. The first item on her list was a small, wrought-iron brazier. She eased it down from a shelf, then filled it with a mixture of dried herbs and ryzec. The herbs would freshen the air so she could concentrate, the ryzec would enhance her powers. She would pay for that extra strength afterward, but she tried not to think about that as she lit the brazier and inhaled its smoky fumes. The first whiff made her dizzy; by the third, she was feeling terribly energetic and alert. She took one last breath for luck, then retrieved three sticks of coloured chalk from a jar and returned to her supplicant.

"From here on, you must not move," she told him. Then she dropped to her knees and went to work.

First, she drew a equilateral triangle in yellow chalk: in its center were the accursed's swollen feet. She enclosed that figure within two concentric circles, both of which were drawn in red, then filled the area between the two rings with white, five-sided stars. When she was done, she pocketed her chalk, then stepped into the star which lay directly in front of her supplicant. She exchanged one last rueful glance with him, then focussed her thoughts. A moment later, she began to speak Words of power in a raw, inhuman voice.

In response, the triangle began to glow. She seized its ghostly outlines with her Will, then raised them into a sheer yellow pyramid that came to a peak above the accursed's head. This magical construct began to thrum with healing potential. The man within went rigid with pain. Liselle did not notice his agonized pose; she was too busy generating her protective spheres. The inner one enclosed the pyramid like a seamless red bubble; if all went well, it would contain whatever force she drove from the accursed. The outer one enveloped her as well as her other constructs, and would serve as a last-ditch defence against the unknown. As soon as those were complete, she activated the star in which she was standing. It flared white with the power to compel.

Ready to commence the ritual now, she focussed on the man within the pyramid. The veils of power which surrounded him lent a sickly orange cast to his gangrenous mien.

"Begone, vile rot!" she commanded, in an arcane tongue. "Relinquish your claim, forsake this curse."

A creamy black voice crept into her skull. "Curses may be broken," it whispered, "but never forsaken. Compel me if you can; leave me to my purpose if you cannot."

What was this? A talking curse?

The spheres flickered, a reflection of her astonishment. She regained control of them with fear-quickened dexterity. Sobered by the near-blunder, she then clenched the fists of her Will and began the exorcism in earnest.

Jagged tracks of golden lightning forked down from the pyramid's peak to form a sizzling cocoon around the hapless man. At the same time, the star projected a solitary beam of argent light at his head. Gobbets of pus began to ooze from his pores. These dripped down his body and toward the floor like clots of foul, semi-molten wax. Without a hitch in her concentration, she skipped over to the star on her right and clenched her Will again. Pus began to stream from the man in thick rivulets. His swollen body began to shrink. She leapt to the next star and then to the next. A black mole appeared on the back of the man's neck. Once visible, it ballooned to the size of a monstrous goiter and sprouted a set of leathery wings. Then a creamy black whisper echoed through her skull. "Enough!"

But she did not relent until she had gone full circle around the man. The last driblet of pus was gone from his body now, and he was now back to a normal size. The thing that had once been moored to his neck was now perched upon his shoulder. Its face and wings were those of a bat, and its lower body was that of a vulture's; but she sensed that this was not its true shape.

"You are more powerful than you appear, mortal," it told her. "Your enemy will be surprised."

Apprehension sizzled through her like an electric shock. This was a nonborn—the last living legacy from an age which most dismissed as mythical. Its unexpected presence worried her, as did its reference to her mysterious enemy. She said a silent prayer of thanks for protective spheres, then began to delve for answers.

"I know of your kind, nonborn," she asserted. "You have no love for living flesh. Who compelled you to this curse?"

"While it is true that I have been compelled to another mortal's service," it said, "my so-called master had no hand in this curse. That I undertook on my own."

"Why?"

"To meet you, sorceress."

Fearful alarms clanged in her head. Perversely, it was curiosity that quelled them. "What reason could you have for wanting to meet me? And who's this master of yours?"

"I would give you his thrice-accursed Name if I could," it replied, baring its frustration and hate in a snarl, "but he has bound me to silence. All I can say is: beware of him, for he is your enemy."

"Can you tell me where he is?"

"He is close. Very close."

"Where?" she pressed.

"Look among the city's bones—" When it tried to say more, its jaws snapped shut with an abruptness that smacked of compulsion.

As cryptic as this was, she gobbled up the clue and then immediately went fishing for more. "So," she said, "we share a common enemy. But that does not explain why you possessed this man."

"No?" it retorted, mocking her with a grin. "How else could I have contacted you without my master's knowing?"

"How would he know otherwise if you did not tell him?" she countered.

The nonborn answered immediately and with great relish, glad for a chance to thwart The Rogue's compulsions. "This stronghold is being watched."

Although she had suspected something of the sort, the news still came as a shock to her. Her thoughts reeled—a dance of fear and sudden fatigue. Her constructs flickered again. The nonborn shifted on its human perch, but made no attempt to take advantage of her momentary lapse.

"So," she said, doggedly regaining control over herself and her sorcery, "you outwitted your master. But what now? Surely your geas will not allow you to conspire against him."

"That is true," it admitted. "Yet in my own way, I do mean to oppose him." "How so?"

"I want you to destroy me."

The request horrified her. She had never used her magic to harm another creature, not even one so fell as this. "Why would you ask such a thing of me?" "Long ago, I refused to serve my Maker when She bade me and my kind to lay waste to this world. Now, ages later, I would rather end my existence than be compelled to serve the fool who seeks to revive that ancient grudge."

Liselle was amazed. She had always viewed the nonborn as a dangerous lot—powerful and amoral. Yet here was one who was ready to sacrifice itself in favour of its principles.

"Are all of your kind like you?" she asked.

"No," it said, without inflection. "Are all of your kind like you?"

"No," she admitted, then abruptly changed the subject. "What if I refuse your request, nonborn? I am a sorceress, not an executioner. What if I turned you loose in the hope that you would then go and slay yourself?"

"Fool!" it hissed, its eyes blazing red. "If I could slay myself, I would have done so already and spared myself the indignity of trafficking with humans. But I cannot, so therefore you must do it instead.

"Do not turn me loose, sorceress," it warned, steeping its tone in menace. "If you do, I will have no choice but to possess somebody else who will in turn have no choice but to come to you for help. Would you like my next victim to be a certain honey-haired man? Or would you prefer someone closer to your heart—a kinsman perhaps?"

"You wouldn't dare!"

"No? I might've dared it already if your enemy did not have similar designs. Even as we speak, that one is plotting to—"

"To what?" she demanded, suddenly on the verge of panic. "What does that bastard want with my nephew?"

The nonborn shrugged, a maddening gesture of impotence. "I cannot say. My tongue has been bound. But the longer you dally here with me, the more time your enemy will have to put his plot into motion. Make a quick end of me, sorceress—or the one dearest to you will surely suffer."

"So be it." She was ablaze with fear and fury now; and if saving Pieter meant killing a darkling creature from the distant past, that's what she would do. She would deal with her conscience later. "You shall have your wish."

With a furious pulse of Will-driven power, she shattered the pyramid. The man whom it had been supporting crumpled to the floor and lay there in a swoon, but the nonborn remained aloft as if it were balanced on an invisible wand. Her Will pulsed again. The inner and outer spheres shrank, forming a single red-hued capsule around the creature. She paused then to marshal her ryzec-augmented strength, and then stuffed the capsule into a hole in time and space. A scream rang out as she sealed that hole back up again, but she would never know if it had come from the nonborn or her own self.

The ritual was over and done with now. She staggered away from the powerless diagram, then gagged for breath that was slow to come. As she struggled to compose herself, her supplicant stirred. He glanced at her, then down at himself. Disbelief dawned across his now nondescript face. He patted his chest, belly and legs, then shouted for joy and surprise.

"Mistress! You did it!" He bounced to his feet, then craned his neck around for a look at his backside. A smile threatened to split his face in half. "Dreamer be praised!"

"Don't touch me," she snapped, as he came dancing toward her. Will-power alone was keeping her on her feet right now. The slightest nudge would knock her down. "Your servants are waiting outside. Celebrate with them."

She headed for the door then. The man followed, gushing and babbling all the way. "You may not know this, Mistress, but I am a wealthy man. Name your price for curing me, and I will gladly pay it."

"For starters, you can release that lock," she told him. Her hands were trembling uncontrollably; she could not get a grip on the bolt.

"Anything, Mistress. Anything at all."

She dragged herself into the kitchen in the admittedly farfetched hope of finding Pieter there, but he was nowhere to be seen. Had he come and gone again already? She looked around for telltale signs: muddy footprints, an empty mug, a stray package or two. But everything was as she had left it. Therefore, he had not returned yet. Therefore, he still had a chance.

Unless her enemy had him already.

"Mistress," the man said, jarring her from her thoughts, "you do not seem well. Is there something I can do?"

"Call your servants," she snapped, irritable from worry, fatigue and the ryzec. "Make sure nobody sees you."

As he hurried off to obey her, she ran a trembling hand across her sweaty brow and tried to reassure herself. There was still time. There had to be. Her enemy would not be so bold as to work his malice in broad daylight.

Would he?

The man's servants came piling into the house. Laughing and crying at the same time, their master danced a merry reel for them. Liselle watched his antics with a jaundiced eye, jealous of his energy. Most of it had been hers a scant hour ago.

"Goodman," she said then, a quiet croak that snared his attention nonetheless. "You have asked me to name my price. Hear it now and then go home."

"As you wish," he replied, still grinning from ear to ear. "But would you mind if I dress while you're talking? I suddenly feel a bit foolish standing before you like this."

"You may dress," she granted, "but not in your street clothes. For the next seven days, you must continue to wear sacking."

His grin wilted. "I don't understand. Am I not cured?"

"You are. But you will most certainly suffer a relapse if you do not wear the canvas throughout the week." She did not like to lie, but in this case, it was the best she could do for all concerned. "Furthermore, no one must know that I cured you today. If anybody asks what you were doing here, say as much or as little as you please so long as you do not give the truth away. After all, whoever cursed you is still out there. If he finds you before I find him, I can make no guarantee for your continued well-being."

"I shall follow your instructions to the word," the man vowed, already in the process of donning his canvas disguise, "Now please, speak of your price. I am eager to repay you."

"I will accept three half-weight bags of gold for my trouble," she said, figuring that she might need the money now that she was truly under siege. "If it pleases you, you may donate an equal sum to The Dreamer's temple anonymously."

"It pleases me," he replied, his voice now muffled by folds of sacking. "Both you and the temple shall have your gold in the morning. Is there anything else I might do for you to alleviate my debt?"

"No." There was nothing anyone could do now; she had to do it all for herself. By herself. "Leave now."

"As you wish," he said, bowing as if to a queen. "But if you are ever in need of a favour, remember Lionel Celeste."

He and his servants departed then. As soon as they were gone, she locked the door and then collapsed into her rocking chair to await Pieter's return.

The first thing Pieter saw when he came straggling into the kitchen with an armful of packages was Liselle. She was slumped in her rocking chair, fast asleep. Her tiny face was slack and ashen. A frown ridged her brow. He recognized the look immediately—it was the aftermath of serious magic. He didn't wonder about the sort of sorcery she'd been doing. He didn't want to know.

He slung his packages onto the table, then tramped over to her chair. He took no pains to be quiet, for he knew from past experience that absolutely nothing could wake Liselle up when she was in this condition. Poor dear, he thought, as he lifted her into his arms. He had never seen her this drained before—back when he had been living here, she'd always made it to bed before collapsing. Then again, he reminded himself sagely, he had left Compara years ago. And none of them were getting any younger.

He carried his aunt into her room and set her down on the bed. As he twitched the coverlet over her, her eyelids fluttered and her frown grew more pronounced. "Pieter?" she mumbled. "Where are you?"

"I'm right here," he replied.

Her eyes snapped wide open then, and she bolted upright on the bed. Her hands groped at thin air.

"Pieter!" she cried. "Please! You mustn't go!"

The panic in her voice quickened his pulse even as it raised the hackles on his neck. He seized her hand, then squeezed it.

"All is well, Liselle," he told her. "I'm right here."

She continued to stare past him and out into space. It was then that he realized that she was caught in the grips of some dream. A nightmare, he appended, recalling her cry. A nightmare in which he played some vital role. If he had not seen and heard it for himself, he would've never guessed how upset she was about his impending departure.

Poor dear, he thought again, beaming down at her with sudden tenderness. Despite her assertions to the contrary, she had not really changed so very much. Moreover, he was glad of it.

Still smiling, he eased her back into a prone position and then gently closed her eyes with a pass of his hand. She starting mumbling again, but the words were all gibberish and quickly tailed off into silence. He stayed by her side until he was sure no other outbursts were forthcoming and then went to take a bath.

It was an arduous process. First he had to drag the tub out of the storage closet and into the kitchen. Then he had to pump the water into a kettle and heat it up. By the time he had the tub filled to his liking, he was keener for a nap than a party. That languid craving grew even stronger as he eased himself into the steaming water.

Maybe he ought to stay home tonight, he mused, as liquid warmth seeped into the spaces between his bones. He did have some packing to do; and there was Liselle to fret about, too. Maybe he should stick around just in case those nightmares of hers returned. But even as he entertained the notion, a part of him rebelled against it. If he backed out of the party at this late moment, Jamus would be furious and rightly so—his newfound friend had gone through a lot of trouble and expense on his behalf. Besides, Liselle was not likely to stir again before tomorrow.

He soaped himself as he debated the matter, then ducked beneath the suds to rinse. When he surfaced again, his mind was made up: he was going to the party.

Lathwi stretched to pop the kinks from her spine, then began to pick her teeth with a sliver of bone. The carcass of a yearling buck lay nearby; the moon's pale light pooled in its wounds. It was a tasty beast. She had eaten fistful after raw fistful, a tactile frenzy that would have no doubt horrified Pieter. And afterward, when she could eat no more, she had curled up in the tall meadow grass and snoozed while her stomach worked and her horse-sore muscles healed.

Now she felt wonderful: full and rested and all sported out. All she needed to do was decide what she wanted to do next. She toyed with the idea of spending the night here in the meadow—it was extremely nice to be alone again, free to do and think as she pleased. She could spend the whole night contemplating the heretofore unappreciated sounds of silence. Tempting as the notion was, though, she rejected it. Staying here tonight meant returning to Compara in the morning, which meant that she'd be riding when she could be learning sorcery from Liselle. And at the moment, she desired knowledge more than the forest's peace and quiet.

So she slung the carcass across the stallion's shoulders and set off for the city. Mindful of low-lying branches and other nocturnal hazards, she held her mount to a walk through the woods. As soon as they reached the road, though, she let him have his head—not because she was in any great hurry to get back to Compara, but because she was hungry for speed and the feel of wind in her face. But while the stallion obliged with a headlong run, he could not quench her craving. If she had had the least excuse then, she would've Called Shoq. She wanted to soar through the sky with him and tickle the clouds and trumpet her pride as they outraced the wind. But she had no need at the moment, no need at all unless it be a pair of wings; and that was something that her tanglemate could never give her.

Her mouth chasmed into an inspired 'O'. Shoq could not give her wings, but perhaps Liselle could! The sorceress was smart, she might know of a magic which could make Lathwi fly. She would be a true dragon then, sky-dancer and cloud-teaser. There could be no greater fortune!

Excitement turned the road into a featureless blur, and when the gates of Compara finally loomed out of the darkness, she rode through them and on with no hesitation. The streets were nearly deserted now, but that inn where Pieter had taken her to eat was still quite lively. Laughter broke out as she went riding by its courtyard. Someone shouted. Uninterested in the commotion, she continued on to the stables. Raffi was shovelling dung out of a stall when she got there.

"Lucky for you I be extra busy today," he said, as she dismounted. "Otherwise, your devil-horse would have had ta spend da night wit you." Then, as she hauled her kill down from the stallion, a hint of benign envy crept into his eyes. "I wish I had time ta hunt. Meat from da butcher don't taste the same."

She shrugged, then began to remove the stallion's tack. He sighed, then pitched in. A moment later, he started to scold.

"You bring dis fella back in some kind of a mess," he said. "Look—he covered all over with burrs and sweat and blood. Take hours ta clean him up. You want, I do for you. I no can sleep anyway."

"Thank you," she said, acknowledging the favour.

"Go home," he replied gruffly, and then took off for the tackroom with her saddle.

She shouldered the yearling's carcass and headed for the door. Three steps later, she decided that she didn't want to haul so much dead weight all the way back to the house and so began to hack off a hindquarter for herself. Just as she was finishing the job, Raffi came ambling back from the tackroom.

"Why you still here?" he demanded.

"You want, you keep," she said, glancing at the rest of the buck's remains.

Raffi's jaw dropped open, then clicked shut again. His eyes were twin moons of disbelief.

"You too generous!" he exclaimed. "I can't eat dat much meat."

She shrugged, for that was his problem, then shouldered the haunch she had claimed for herself and started on her way again. He babbled thank-you's in her wake, but the words had no effect on her.

Three streets down from the stable, the sound of booted feet on the run erupted behind her. As she turned to see who was chasing her, someone slammed into her blind side. Caught off-balance, she staggered to the right and into the mouth of an alley. There, someone blind-sided her again, driving her deeper into the darkness. Then six broad-shouldered figures materialized in the alleyway with her. Although it was hard for her to discern details in the dark, she noticed that each of these figures bore a stout length of wood.

"Oy, lads," a vaguely familiar voice intoned. "Look at who we have here." One of the figures stepped closer—close enough for her to see its tangled beard and hunchbacked nose. "It's the thief." Then he twitched his piece of wood at the haunch which was resting on her shoulder. "Where'd you steal that, thief?" Recognition flared within her—this was the dull-witted man from the inn. She did not understand his interest in the meat. Did he mean to challenge her for it?

"What you want?" she asked.

He spat as if galled, then snarled, "I want my diamond, bitch. And I want it now."

She scorned him as a fool. Did he actually believe that she was stupid enough to keep such an auspicious stone on her person? Or that she would surrender it simply because he now regretted its giving?

"Mine," she reminded him, which was an insult in and of itself. "You give, I take."

"You were supposed to give me something in return. You were supposed to come to my room and do what women do best."

Step by deliberate step, he closed in on her. His five companions followed.

"Do you know what we do to thieves in the southland?" he asked, as he advanced. "We beat 'em bloody. And do you know what we do to thieving whores? We beat 'em bloody, then cut off their noses."

Now that was the most peculiar practice she had heard of yet, she thought. What possible use could somebody have for somebody else's nose?

"So if you know what's good for you," the man went on, "you'll hand over my diamond, then spread your legs for me and the lads. Who knows? We might even let you enjoy it."

"Go away," she told him. "Or you get hurt again."

His eyes narrowed. He wrung his length of wood as if it were her neck, then said, "I'm not drunk tonight, bitch. And that lucky punch you landed the other night is another reason you're going to suffer."

He lunged forward then and rammed his club into her gut. She stagger-stepped backward and into a wall. As she gasped for air, the other men came rushing toward her, all swinging wood. One slammed into her left thigh; another collided with her hip. Pain bloomed beneath her scales. Fury detonated in her head. With a roar, she threw herself into the fray.

She struck out with the hindquarter, swinging it like an oversized cudgel. One man went flying backward; another fell to his knees while still in range. That one she hit again—a vicious clout to the face. He pitched forward with a moan. Someone clubbed her knees then. The pain was explosive, like a streaks of lightning down her legs, but she remained on her feet and kept on swinging until somebody tore the haunch from her grip.

That gave her a chance to uncinch a dragon claw.

Moments later, a man cried out in surprise and pain. As he limped away from the fight, his viscera gleaming darkly in his hands, the rest of Lathwi's attackers turned savage. One of them dealt her a brain-rattling blow to the skull; another pummelled her ribs. She battled on like a creature possessed, but could not rout this cowardly pack of jackals. They were too quick for her now, too canny. More often than not, they anticipated her strokes or deftly turned them aside.

She slashed at a man who danced within range. By chance or design, a club came arcing out of nowhere and slammed into her claw-hand. Bones snapped like brittle kindling, the claw fell to the ground. A moment later, a crush of bodies pinned her to a wall. She tried to break free, but there was a fire in her lungs now, and her legs were on the verge of buckling. The only parts of her body that did not hurt were those that were already numb.

For a long moment after, the only sound in the world was that of ragged breathing. Then Lathwi heard the snick of a blade leaving its sheath. She blinked back a salty haze of tears to see the man with the tangled beard standing in front of her. There were purpling half-moons beneath his eyes and half-clotted rivulets of blood beneath his nose.

"You've got a lot to pay for, bitch," he rasped. "And I intend to take every luc of that debt out of your uncivilized hide."

He angled a big hunting knife back and forth in front of her eyes as if trying to dazzle her with reflected moonlight, then pressed its tip into the space between her left eye and the bridge of her nose. Its edge, she noted, was very sharp.

"This is for Tomas," he told her, and then slowly carved a diagonal trench across the top of her left cheekbone.

Her mind became a bog of pain and helpless outrage. If she had had one wish then, she would have used it to convert her fury into physical vigour so she could tear this cowardly fool into quivering shreds. As it was, she barely had enough strength to hold herself still as he set the tip of his blade to the corner of her right eye.

"And this is for Nev."

He scored the top of her other cheekbone, then stepped back to admire his handiwork. A moment later, he shook his head as if dissatisfied and set his knife on the lower left side of her nose—the spot where flesh flared into nostril. "This is for cheating us."

She gasped once as the blade dug into the lower half of her cheek, then again as the quickness of that breath filled her lungs with fresh fire. If only she could cough that fire up—

"This is for fighting us instead of fucking us."

—and spit it in this man's loathsome face.

Stunned to near-numbness by a sudden thought, she barely felt the hunting knife's eager bite this time. She could not spit fire, but she could summon it!

"And this one is all for me."

As he pressed the knife's edge to the base of her nose, Lathwi invoked the secret Name of fire. The answering mote hopped into Broken-Nose's beard like a flea. The Southerner loosed a puzzled grunt, trying to place the smell of burning hair, then dropped his knife and shouted as his head erupted in flames. His companions rushed his aid only to catch fire themselves. In a matter of heartbeats, the whole lot of them were brightly ablaze. Without a backward glance at her, they ran screaming out of the alley.

Lathwi wanted to give chase, but collapsed into a deep, dark gulf instead.

"You can't leave yet," Jamus complained, as Pieter made ready to do just that. "It's bad luck for the guest of honour to be the first to leave the party."

"That's nonsense," Pieter scoffed, and then drained the last sip of wine from his cup. "Besides, I'm coming back, so this doesn't really qualify as leaving."

"But why do you have to go at all?"

"Because I locked Lathwi out of the house."

"So?" Jamus argued. "Let her climb the fence and sleep in the courtyard. You know as well as I do that she can take care of herself."

"She can also break a door down when it suits her to do so," Pieter countered. "And if Liselle wakes up tomorrow to find her door in ruins, she's going to make those nearest and dearest to her miserable for weeks to come. So you see, old man—I'm actually doing this for your benefit."

Jamus arched an eyebrow at the insinuation, but decided not to pursue it. He would rather believe that Liselle held some sort of affection for him than know that her nephew was teasing.

"I could rouse a servant and send him over to the house in your stead," he proposed.

"Don't do that. Your servants have earned their rest."

The truth was, Pieter wanted to go home so he could look in on Liselle. He felt guilty for giving her nightmares, and for going out and having a good time while she was suffering. He didn't want to tell that to Jamus, though. It sounded too sissified. And he really had locked Lathwi out.

"Here," he said, handing the golden-haired man his empty cup. "Fill this up, then set it aside in a safe place. That way, I'll be guaranteed at least one drink when I get back."

"All right," Jamus grudgingly replied, "but don't you be gone too long. Otherwise, I'll move the party to your aunt's place and we'll sing bawdy songs in the courtyard till dawn."

Pieter grinned at the thought, then clapped his friend on the back. "Don't worry, I'll be back. I promise."

He started on his way then. The air was crisp and cool, an invigorating antidote for a night of near-constant eating and drinking. He walked at a brisk clip, whistling under his breath. It felt good to be out and moving.

He was less than three blocks from home when a figure came running out of the shadows and toward him. He tensed, an reflex born of instinct and wine, then relaxed again as that figure acquired a woman's unmistakable curves. To his amazement, she ran right up to him then and latched herself to his arm.

"Please," she begged. "You must help me."

Despite the darkness which surrounded them, Pieter could see that this woman was beautiful—a voluptuous, dark-haired sylph with delicate features and beguiling cinnamon eyes. He swallowed hard. Protectiveness welled up within him.

"What goes on here, lady?" he asked.

"Forgive me for being so bold," she replied, entreating him with those fascinating eyes, "but I am being followed by a trio of men who wish to do me harm. May I walk with you a while?"

"Of course." The idea of refusing such a request never crossed his mind. "If you wish, I'll gladly see you home."

"No!" She tightened her grip on his arm. "If you take me home, those rogues will know where I live. I'll never be safe again."

Her distress was both endearing and curiously exciting. He patted her pretty little hand and soothed her with a soft shushing sound.

"If you don't want to go home," he said then, "we'll go elsewhere instead. Where would you, lady?"

She leaned into him like a caress-hungry cat, then eyed at him through her lashes. "Is your house nearby? If it is, perhaps we could go there. Those footpads wouldn't follow me into another man's house.

"Please?" she asked, when he hesitated. "I'll only stay until I'm sure I'm safe. And believe me—your kindness will not go unrewarded."

That veiled promise triggered a whirlwind of delight and disbelief in his head. This sort of thing happened to Jamus, not him! He thought of Liselle then, and her profound sleep. She'd never know; and what she didn't know wouldn't irritate her.

"As it so happens," he told her, "I live just down the road from here."

Minutes or hours later, they came to a stop in front of Liselle's door. The woman had clung to Pieter every step of the way; and was clinging to him still. He was puff-chested and giddy, high on his good luck. As he eased the door open, he pressed a finger to his lips.

"Quietly now," he whispered. "My aunt is sleeping."

The woman took a step toward the doorway only to stumble backward. Her upper lip curled into an unbecoming pout then. In the scant light, it looked like a snarl.

"I cannot enter," she said, as she reclaimed her hold on his arm. "There is a forbidding here."

"Really?" He squinted at the door. "It looks the same to me."

"I would like to meet your aunt," she said then. "Call her."

"Not tonight," he replied, more than a little confused by the request. "Like I said, she's sleeping—Yeow!" Her grip had turned suddenly painful. "Ease up on my arm, lady. You're apt to tear it off otherwise."

"Call her."

The woman's smile was too large for her face now. Too large and too toothy. And the hand that was wrapped around his arm was no longer slim and finely boned, but gnarled like an old tree branch. A terrible realization formed in the pit of his stomach then: this was the secret fear that he'd seen in Liselle's eyes, the reason she had been behaving so oddly. Dreamer! Why had she not said anything?

"Call her. I will not tell you again."

"No," he whispered.

There was nothing womanly about its face anymore. Its cheekbones had shifted, becoming flat and hard; its nose had receded into mere slots above a wide strip of pointed yellow teeth. As he gaped at it, it began to twist his arm into an agonized starburst.

Absurdly, all he could think of was Liselle. Desperate to protect her against this walking nightmare, he lunged for the doorway. The creature pulled him back, but not before he jerked the door shut and flung his keys into the darkness.

"Fool," it said, scorning his heroics. "She will hear you nonetheless."

With that, it yanked him off his feet and into a fetid embrace. As pain shot down his spine and into every fibre of his being, he spent all of his strength on one last desperate cry for help.

The naj slunk into the torchlit chamber and up to the foot of The Cripple's dais. There, reeking of human blood and entrails, it waited for permission to speak.

Malcolm did not need to question the gore-flecked naj to know that his ploy had somehow gone awry—its downcast eyes and unusually submissive air were far more eloquent than any words. Even so, he proceeded with the interrogation just for the spiteful satisfaction of seeing the demon squirm.

"Well?" he demanded. "Where is she?"

No clarification was necessary. The naj knew all too well who the she in question was. It glanced at the cripple through hooded eyes and nervously licked its chops.

"I do not have her," it admitted. "She would not come out of the house."

"And why was that? Didn't you follow my instructions?"

"I did everything you told me to do," it replied, on the verge of grovelling now. "But while her kinsman screamed for his life, she did not make the slightest move on his behalf."

"Really? How interesting." And annoying. This Recluse was proving to be a woman of unusual strength. "I'll have to try a different bait. Or maybe just a different servant," he added, half-turning to eying the naj slyly. "Maybe you're no good for anything more than fetching and carrying."

The demon lordling bristled, then drew itself up to its full height. "I did not catch The Recluse tonight," it said, "but I did learn something that might be of use."

"Do tell," Malcolm urged it. "If it's as useful as you say, I might spare you the punishment you deserve for failing me."

"I learned a name," it told him then, eager to avoid The Cripple's magical lash. "Her kinsman shouted it out before I killed him, so it must belong to The Recluse."

"What is it?" Malcolm asked, truly interested now.

"Lathwi," it replied.

CHAPTER 9

Shoq swooped out of the sky toward the rocky flats of a mountain meadow. As he angled in for a landing, sheep scattered, bleating with terror, but he paid them no heed. His eyes were all for Lathwi. Even from this distance, he could tell that she was surprised to see him. She made no attempt to run away from him, but only stood where she was and gaped. Pleased by her reaction, he came aground with a flourish and then went strutting toward her. A dragon's length away, he stopped and slowly extended his neck. It was then that he realized that her odour was all wrong—it boasted the tinges of musk and red blood which he found so alluring, but these were fouled by an overwhelming miasma of animal fear. He rumbled, irritated by this trick. Sometimes Lathwi was too clever for her own good. Still, he was willing to forgive her so long as she played with him. It had been so very long since he had had any fun!

This too was The Soft One's doing. She had been acting strangely as of late: sometimes shy, sometimes contrary, and always annoyingly elusive. Just this once, he wanted her to be her old self again.

A futile wish. For even as his triangular head loomed toward her flat, stub-nosed oval of a face, she began to mewl and tremble. Then fat drops of brine began to drip from her eyes, further spoiling her scent.

Shoq's bronze lips curled back in disapproval, exposing two rows of bone-polished teeth, and her whimper arced into a high-pitched scream. He hissed, then projected a command at her: *quit this senseless noise and play with me!* Instead, she collapsed into a tiny gibbering heap and hid her eyes behind her hands.

At that, he knew her for an impostor. The real Lathwi would never have been so ridiculous as to try and make him disappear by covering her eyes. He lashed out at the fraud with his tail. Bone snapped. A howl pierced his ears. Then a geyser of bright red blood squirted forth from the ruins of her leg. Now, perversely, she tried to run away; tried to flee on her hands and knees. But he was beyond the point of forgiveness now. He pounced, breaking her back, then seized her neck in his jaws and shook her.

Afterward, he began to keen to himself. He had looked everywhere for the real Lathwi; searched every field and meadow, but to his dismay, he had encountered nothing but impostors. The world seemed full of them. He could not bear the disappointment any longer. He had to see Lathwi again; had to see and smell and touch The Soft One. This was not a desire, it was Need. So he Called her secret Name—once, twice and then a third time just for good measure.

As he waited for her to respond, he began to feed on the impostor's remains. If she got here fast enough, he thought, he would give her the liver.

CHAPTER 10

Lathwi was trapped in a bog of utter darkness, and so exhausted from her struggles to escape its hold on her that she could barely muster the strength to continue breathing. Let go, the voice of Oblivion urged. Let go and float away.

Too weak to resist that seductive tug, she began to slip the moorings which held her to the earth. As she did so, the darkness disappeared, and she found herself suspended above a room full of people. This didn't strike her as unusual until she realized that one of those people was her own self. How soft she looked in that strange bed! And how damaged! There was more bandage to her than flesh.

"I've done all I can do," she heard somebody say. "The rest is up to her."

Somebody else started to cry.

Understanding flooded through her then: the choice was hers. She could either climb back into that body or leave it behind for good. It did not seem like much of a choice—-she had no desire to be that small and weak again. And while she felt a curious sort of attachment to one of the people in the room, the bond wasn't strong enough to make her want to stay.

Lathwi!

The sound of her secret Name filled her with wonder and concern. And while she was powerless to respond to the Call, the desire to do so sealed her fate. She went streaking back to her battered body and into a deep, forgetful sleep.

Spangles of pain flared across the empty canvas of her awareness like fireflies on a moonless night. She tried to crush them beneath the heel of her Will, but they scattered unscathed, and dared her to try again. She hissed, venting her annoyance.

"Liselle, come quick!" a voice boomed then. "I think she's waking up!"

She rolled her eyelids open to find a shadow haloed by dusty sunlight standing over her. She blinked back a blur of photosensitive tears, then scowled as Jamus' golden features came into focus.

"Lathwi!" he shouted. "Dreamer be praised! Do you know who I am?"

She could have been blind and still recognized this fool by his penchant for asking stupid questions. And because her answer had to be obvious by now, she did not bother to voice it aloud.

"No more shout," she told him instead. "I hear fine."

Liselle came sweeping into the room then. She appeared thinner than

Lathwi remembered; older, too. The lines which rayed from the corners of her eyes were fresh and deep. The arches which defined the boundaries of her mouth were slack.

"Lathwi," this new Liselle said, in a voice that wavered between fear and relief and private pain. "How do you feel?"

Lathwi thought the question odd until she tried to sit up. Pain shot through her sides and into her extremities. A whirlpool started spinning round and round in her head. With a surprised hiss, she collapsed back onto her back.

"Don't try to move," Jamus told her then. "Whoever beat you up did a good job of it. You've got broken bones in your right wrist and lower left leg, at least a half-dozen cracked ribs, and an assortment of other fractures—the most notable one being in your skull. I must confess: I'm very impressed. A beating like that would've killed anyone else."

"Do you remember what happened?" Liselle demanded then. "Who did this to you?"

"I be on way back from hunt," she replied. "Broken-Nose and others push me into alley, then hit me with sticks." She bared her teeth at that part of the memory. The scabs on her cheeks cracked beneath their bandages. "I fight back, but I too soft, too weak to make them stop."

She closed her eyes then, galled by that fact, but found no solace in the dark.

"Too weak?" Jamus hooted. "Great Dreamer, woman, give yourself a little credit! Those men were mercenaries. And they had you outnumbered at least three to one. Yet despite those rather significant disadvantages, you survived—which is more than two of them can say. No warrior of any caste or race could hope to do better."

"He's right, Lathwi," Liselle murmured. "You did well. And you were lucky."

"I no like what you call luck," Lathwi replied, and then rolled onto her hip in search of a more comfortable position. The sensation of soft hides sliding against her flesh pleased her at first, but then triggered a wave of alarm. She should not be able to feel the hides! Se jerked the skins aside and confirmed her suspicions. She was totally naked save for the curiously hardened bandages which encased her arm and leg.

"Where my scales?" she demanded, ready to get up and go searching for them in spite of the pain that was now gnawing at her bones. Without them, she felt exposed to an extreme; and the multitude of yellowing bruises that mottled her body were an harsh reminder of just how soft she was.

"Your mail is in the loft along with the rest of your belongings," Liselle said, stepping in to cover her up again. "We had to remove it in order to tend to your wounds."

"Bring here," Lathwi told her.

"Why?"

149

"I need go find a man with broken nose."

"You're in no condition to be chasing after professional killers," the sorceress argued. "And you won't be for a long time to come, either. So why don't you do yourself a favour and forget about that man?"

Lathwi pointed to the bandages on her face. "These be Broken-Nose's notion of fun. He give to me after he break my bones. He want cut my nose off, too. I not forget that man, Liselle. Not possible."

"All right then, don't forget him. Just don't go after him right away. You need to stay here for a while."

The hint of urgency in Liselle's tone roused Lathwi's suspicions. She studied the sorceress for a moment, trying to make sense of her haggard, red-rimmed eyes; and the thin, bloodless line of her mouth. But thinking hard made Lathwi's head spin, and that in turn made her stomach uneasy. So she gave up on trying to solve the riddle of Liselle by herself.

"Why you care where I go or not go?"

"Pieter's dead," Liselle blurted then, and then choked on a sob.

The news startled Lathwi, but she was not devastated by it. All creatures died in time, even the long-lived dragons. Surely Liselle understood that.

"Pieter's dead," the sorceress repeated, as if prompted by the thought, "but he died no natural death. Somebody—" She groped for a less horrible description of his murder, but then gave up and spat out the brutal truth. "He was torn to pieces. His remains were strewn from one end of my courtyard to the other."

"You think Broken-Nose do?" Lathwi asked.

"No," Jamus replied, with none of his usual flippancy. "As far as we can tell, you and Pieter were attacked almost at the same time."

"Then who?"

"The Rogue," Liselle said, in a tone dripping with gall. Prompted by Lathwi's puzzled frown, she went on. "This rogue is a sorcerer who's declared war on the rest of the sorcerous world. I believe he murdered Pieter in an attempt to draw me out of my stronghold and so murder me, too." A guilty sheen of tears glazed her eyes then. "He would have succeeded if I had not taken ryzec earlier in the day."

Lathwi rumbled. This information was interesting in a mild sort of way, but she could not see how it pertained to her comings and goings.

"You think this Rogue try to kill me, too? That why you want me to stay?"

"I believe he'll try to kill you no matter what you do," Liselle replied. "The reason I want you to stay is—" She paused to choke back bile. This was so hard to admit aloud! "—I don't think I can withstand him by myself. I need you, Lathwi. I need your strength and your power."

"Strength?" Lathwi snorted, a disparaging sound. "Look at me—I be weak as old prey-beast. How I help you when no can help myself?"

"You're not weak, just inexperienced," Jamus told her. "A little bit of professional training would cure you of that in a hurry."

"He's right," Liselle hastened to say. "And if you stay here with me, I'll pay for all the training you can stomach."

Lathwi examined her priorities. Broken-Nose was one of them. But while she still ached to hunt him down and eat his liver, she could see where it might be smarter to first learn where his soft spots were. And a smart dragon took advantage of the opportunities which fortune cast in her path. She was smart; therefore, she would stay and take this training. But before she said so, she wanted to see how many other promises she could wrangle out of Liselle.

"If I stay, you still teach me sorcery?" she asked.

"Of course," Liselle said.

"You teach me reading, too?"

"It would be my pleasure."

Lathwi paused to contain her growing excitement, then gave voice to the hope which she had conceived on the ride back to Compara. "You teach me how to grow wings?"

"You've got more nerve than a one-eyed knife-dancer," Jamus exclaimed, bristling with sudden indignation. "If it weren't for this lady, you'd still be lying in that alleyway where we found you. And how do you repay her? By extorting pledges from her in her time of need! Fah, you're no better than the thugs who beat you up."

His accusations annoyed Lathwi. Why should he care if she tricked promises out of Liselle? The sorceress was no fool, she would not make any bargains that she did not wish to keep. And how dare he compare her to Broken-Nose and his pack of jackals? Those cowards would have cut Liselle's nose off to get what they wanted from her.

"Don't be so quick to condemn her," Liselle chided him. "I'm asking a great deal of her, perhaps more than she knows. It's only fair that she asks things of me in return."

Then she swivelled her gaze back to Lathwi. "There is a way by which you might grow wings, but you'll have to become more adept at sorcery before I'll consent to teach it to you. Is that acceptable?"

"Yessss," Lathwi replied. She would've agreed to almost anything so long as it contained the promise of dragon wings.

"Then you'll stay?"

"For now."

Relief washed over Liselle's face, but it brought her no joy. Her expression remained flat and grey.

"So be it," she said, and then pulled Lathwi's covers up again. "Now get some sleep. I'll bring you something to eat later."

Lathwi closed her eyes. A moment later, Liselle and Jamus shuffled into the hallway and began to talk in heated whispers.

"You can't trust her to keep her word," Jamus hissed. "She's a barbarian, her sense of honour is skewed. She could leave you in the lurch on a whim. But there are others who would help if you'd let them, those who held Pieter dear and who would, if given half a chance, hold you dear as well."

"Jamus," Liselle fired back, "who made the arrangements for Pieter's burial?"

"I did," he replied, "but what—"

"And who ordered a squad of the governor's men to patrol the boneyards in hopes of uncovering my enemy's hide-out?"

"I did. But—"

"And who has soldiers combing the slums of Compara for a curra-chewing sorceress who might very well be dead already?"

"Me—"

"And still you claim that I'm not letting you help. How much more can you expect to do?"

"For starters, you could let me move you into a place of safety," he replied.

"I've told you a hundred times already: there is no safe place for me outside of this house."

"Then let me station a guard in the house."

"No, thanks. You've already got one man posted outside. I don't need anyone else watching me."

Jamus licked his lip, a gesture of surprise and newfound respect. He hadn't mentioned that guard to her. "Maybe he's not there to watch you. Maybe he's there to watch Lathwi."

"Quit your harping on her," Liselle snapped then. "Like it or not, I need her here and she's staying—"

"Only because you bribed her," he jeered, his own temper rising alongside of hers.

"At least she's forthright about her motivations. I'm not so sure I can say the same about you. How am I to repay you for your assistance? By inviting you into my bed?"

For a long moment, an icy silence ruled them both. Then Jamus strained a breath of air through his clenched teeth and said, "From what you've told me, milady, the man who murdered your nephew is plotting some sort of war against the citizens of this city. It's my sworn duty to prevent such an ill from happening. And since you're my only link to this sorcerer at the moment, I mean to protect you as best as I can. But know this, Liselle, and believe it: I expect nothing in return but your cooperation.

"Now, if you'll excuse me, I must go."

Angry footfalls stormed down the hallway then. A moment later, a pair of slippered feet went sulking off in the other direction. Sure that there was nothing more for her to hear, Lathwi allowed herself to fall asleep.

Jamus' anger curdled into an ugly miasma of grief and guilt as he strode out of the house. For although rain and traffic and the carrion crows had wiped all trace of murder from the courtyard, he could still see the mangled pieces of Pieter's corpse, and still smell the blood and shit that had clotted in the grass that night. If only he had not let the trapper leave the party, he told himself. If only he and the others had come looking for him sooner.

And poor Liselle! By the time she finally came out of her drugged slumber, Pieter's remains were already in a box. Jamus had had to show her the head. She had clung to Jamus then, and drenched his shirt with her tears.

And how did she repay him? With hurtful accusations and mistrust! He deserved better from her. Much better.

Preoccupied with his thoughts, he did not see the woman in his path until they collided. She landed on her backside with a startled squeak; he staggered back a step to catch his breath. His immediate thought was one of amazement: whomever he had run into was very solid indeed.

"Pardon me, good sir," his victim said then, "but could you please help me up? I think I've twisted my ankle."

Stammering apologies, he hastened to her aid. She was a plump woman, not old yet but no longer young. The touches of time which feathered her cinnamon eyes lent a dignified depth to her pretty face. She favoured him with a shy half-smile as he eased her onto her feet, then winced as she tried to stand on her own.

"Lean on me, Mistress," he told her then, "and I'll help you home."

She studied his face as if searching for signs of secret malice, then eyed the rest of him as well. What she saw must have relieved her, for she sanctioned him with another of her shy half-smiles.

"Thank you," she said. "You're too kind."

"Think nothing of it," he replied. "After all, it was I who knocked you down. Now tell me: where do you live?"

"My house is that way," she told him, and pointed toward a poorer section of town.

He flashed her a smile and then spouted a lie. "What a coincidence. I was heading in that direction anyway."

They started down the road then. She had an arm around his neck; he had her by the waist. As they walked, he became increasingly aware of her scent. It was warm and yeasty like fresh-baked bread, yet deliciously spiced with hints of sex. His eyes strayed toward her ample breasts. His thoughts were quick to follow.

"I find city-life terribly stimulating," she said then. "Is it so for you, too?"

Caught in the middle of a fantasy, he started and then flushed. "Huh? Oh, yes," he stammered. "Very stimulating indeed."

Her scent was driving him to distraction. It urged him to knead the soft flesh of her waist, to caress the rounded slope of her buttocks. His hands were all but trembling now. Other parts of him were protesting his restraint, too.

"Here we are," she announced then.

They were standing in front of an old wooden gate. The courtyard beyond was overgrown with weeds and smelled vaguely of decay. The house looked like a gap-toothed derelict.

"You live here?" he asked, too surprised for tact. In his mind, she dwelt in a mansion filled with feather beds and silken sheets.

"Life has been hard since my husband died," she said, eyes downcast as if with embarrassment. Then, as he shifted, meaning to let her go, she looked up again and hastily added, "But not so hard that I cannot offer hospitality to a gallant stranger. Will you come in and refresh yourself? Whatever I have is yours."

The invitation spurred his pulse to a lusty gallop, for there was no mistaking the glint in her eye. This voluptuous pigeon wanted him! And oh, how he wanted her back! But even as the thought stiffened within him, Liselle's frowning image slapped it down again. Behold a philandering fool, it cried. Behold a man who traded help for sex. He tried to refute the charge, but that was hard to do when his trousers were around his knees.

Ah, Liselle! He had treated her badly, and she had only been telling the ugly truth.

The woman was smiling at him now. Her pretty face was all aglow. He patted the soft flesh around her waist, then gently withdrew his support.

"Mistress," he said, as he opened the gate, "I'm honoured by your invitation." She sallied into the courtyard, clearly expecting him to follow. Instead, he closed the gate behind her. "Unfortunately, I have a previous commitment to keep.

"Good day to you. I hope your ankle feels better soon."

He hurried away then without a backward glance. So he did not see the rage which consumed the woman's face, or the shadows which then swallowed her up.

Liselle sat by the hearth with a book of sorcery open in her lap, but the words blurred whenever she tried to look at them, so she gazed into the fire's flickering depths instead. Its tongues conjured images of Jamus.

He had been kindness itself over these past few weeks, a stalwart pillar of strength. She did not know what she would have done without his help and support. Even so, she did not dare to trust the honey-tongued rake too much. He could make a stone love him if he were so inclined. And in spite of her wishes to the contrary, she was not a stone.

Even now, as she mourned her past and agonized over her future, she had to admit that a part of her was attracted to him. This was a terrifying admission, and one which she must keep strictly private. For now she knew what The Rogue would do if he found any more soft spots on her.

Ah, Pieter! Forgive her!

Her thoughts blew through the house in search of solace, but memories of her nephew lurked everywhere: in the kitchen, down the hallway, even in the furs beneath her feet. He had been dead for over two weeks already, but she still could not shake her grief. It ran on and on, as deep and bitter as the guilt which ran alongside of it. She had pulled out fistfuls of her hair, torn her garments, cried until her eyes and nose were raw, but nothing made her feel better because it was her fault that he was dead. She should have driven him away that very first day. Or, failing that, she should've stayed awake that last terrible night. Ah Dreamer, if she had only known! She would've helped him, freed him maybe; or if nothing else, taken her place alongside of him. But she had been weak from start to finish, and poor dear Pieter had died because of it. She'd never forgive herself for that.

And she wasn't going to let it happen again, either.

That's why she needed Lathwi.

Lathwi would teach her strength and the ways to endure a world of pain and grief without flinching. Lathwi would show her how to survive, regardless of the scars incurred. And as soon those secrets were hers, she would attack The Rogue with the whole of her hate intact and rend his body even as he had rent Pieter's. There would be no mercy, no quarter begged or given. Lathwi would teach her that, too, and she would learn the lesson well.

In the meantime, though, she had other work to do.

She drew the book closer and began to read even though her mind cried out for rest. There could be no rest for her yet. Pieter's murderer was still at large.

Alone within the confines of his stronghold, Malcolm limped back and forth across the cold stone floor and cursed. Things were not proceeding according to plan, and that didn't please him at all.

The Recluse was his foremost source of aggravation. She was proving to be a most difficult target: cannier than a ten year old trout and surprisingly hard-hearted. Who would have guessed that she'd allow a kinsman to be murdered rather than put herself at risk? Up until now, he had regarded that kind of ruthlessness as his own special trademark.

Her calloused instinct for self-preservation wasn't the only burr in Malcolm's drawers, either. There was the matter of the new boneyard patrols, too, and her sudden interest in the curra-chewing sorceress' whereabouts. Neither detail was worrisome in and of itself: D'Arque's minions could prowl the catacombs for years without ever finding this stronghold; and The Curra-Chewer was a loose thread that he could snip at any moment. But the two so suddenly combined set off alarums in his head, for they suggested that The Recluse knew more about his doings than she ought to. And the only ones who could've possibly told her about those doings were demon-born.

It made sense. The compulsions with which he had bound his slaves would make treachery difficult but not impossible; and a geas-guarded tongue would explain her rather haphazard countermoves. In addition, there was one demon in his thrall who had the means, the motive and the intelligence to connive against him.

The naj.

He knew that the demon lordling resented its subservient status, and that it would cheerfully take his place if given half a chance. But he was not so sure that it would risk The Dark One's displeasure by actively conspiring with the enemy. That tiny uncertainty was all that stood between the naj and The Spell of Unmaking right now; that and a grudging respect for its abilities. He did not want to destroy so precious a resource until he had the last talisman in his hand—unless, of course, he had to.

So he would bait a series of little traps for the naj. Then he would wait and see.

And as for The Recluse—well, perhaps he could trap her in the same web.

He summoned one of the lesser demons with a psychic snap of his fingers. Several minutes later, it came skulking into the chamber with a worried look on its hideous face.

"You're the one who is watching The Curra-Chewer, are you not?" he asked.

"I am," it replied.

"Can she be caught outside of her wards?"

"She can," it told him, "but not easily, for the drug she ingests makes her uncommonly quick. It will take two to accomplish the task: one to give chase, the other to grab her as she bolts for her stronghold."

"I see." He tapped his chin, a thoughtful gesture, then said, "Instead of two, I will assign three of you to the job. The third will act as a look-out, and, if necessary, distract any humans who may be hunting for our rabbit."

"What sort of distraction?" the demon asked, in a tone that rippled with cruel possibilities.

"So long as you don't kill anyone or reveal your true nature, I don't care how it's done. And once you have The Curra-Chewer in your custody, you are to bring her straight to me.

"Alive," he appended sternly, noting the evil smirk that slithered across his minion's lipless mouth, "and relatively unharmed. Is that clear? Or are you too dull-witted to be trusted with such a task?"

"I will not disappoint you," it replied.

"See that you don't," Malcolm warned, and then dismissed the demon with a wave of his hand. As it half-turned to take its leave, he added, "Oh, and by the way."

It tensed like a dog expecting the whip. "Yes, Master?"

"The naj is not to know about this. If it asks, tell it nothing, then report its interest to me."

"I will do so," the demon replied, and then went loping on its way as if it were happy to have escaped unscathed.

Malcolm sat back in his chair and congratulated himself: two snares for the price of one. He wondered what he would catch.

CHAPTER 11

Bij leapt from the landing with a majestic roar and then propelled himself through the sky with bold, swift strokes of his wings. Distance soon dwarfed his massive form: it shrank into a blood-red speck, then disappeared within the plumes of a far-off cloud. Taziem watched until she was sure he wasn't coming back, then loosed a rumble and retreated to the scanty comforts of her outer caves. There, surrounded by scintillas of their mingled scents, the she-dragon reminisced about this latest encounter with her chosen.

All things considered, she decided, she was glad to see him go.

It had been a short Season for them, and less pleasant than some she could recall. For while their couplings had been as exhilarating as ever, the interludes in between had quickly acquired a sour tang because of his obsession with humans. She curled her lip at the memory, an expression of weariness and scorn. Despite his great age and experience, he had a very little imagination. He refused to admit that people could be intelligent in any significant way, or that they might be something more or less than a passing pain in the tail. And his callow remedy for that pain was wholesale slaughter and good riddance to them all.

Fool! Did he truly believe that it would be that easy?

Indeed he did. For while he could rail against men hour after hour, he knew close to nothing about them. He had not studied them for any length of time, had not seen for himself how clever and persistent they could be. And Bij compounded his ignorance by refusing to listen to her.

But that was his problem, she reminded herself. If he did not want to listen to a dragon wiser than himself, then let him learn from hard experience instead. As for herself, she was perfectly content to leave men alone so long as they continued to do likewise.

Her stomach growled then, and a wave of dizziness lapped at her thoughts. She hissed, resenting the immediacy of this next phase of pregnancy. She had hoped to have a few days to lounge in her nest and think interesting thoughts. Her belly rumbled again, more emphatically this time. The fast-growing embryos within wanted to be fed. Moreover, they wanted to be fed now.

Unable to deny that internal demand, she lurched to her feet and headed for the landing. There, she catapulted into the sky and toward a distant hunting ground where she would begin the gluttonous binge that would leave her as bloated as Bij's obsession.

CHAPTER 12

A fortnight passed—two of the longest, most stressful weeks that Liselle had ever endured. This wasn't due to The Rogue, who had ducked back into deepest hiding after Pieter's murder, but Lathwi. Awake now and on the mend, the woman was without a doubt the world's worst patient: quick-tempered and demanding; opinionated and argumentative; and as stubborn as the day was long.

First, there had been the water closet incident.

The morning after Lathwi's return to full consciousness, Liselle had been reading by the fire when a heavy thud echoed down the hallway. Fearing only Dreamer-knew-what, she'd gone bounding into Lathwi's room to find her in an agonized huddle on the floor. The shapeless cotton nightgown she was wearing was limp with sweat.

"What do you think you're doing?" Liselle demanded.

"Need to use water closet," Lathwi panted in reply. Her broken limbs were throbbing from the fall she had just taken, and it felt like she was breathing red-hot needles because of her cracked ribs, but she was determined to get to the midden so she would not foul her nesting place. She ground the pain into a paste between her teeth, then dragged herself onto her elbows and knees, and started to crawl toward the hallway.

"What are you doing?" Liselle cried, appalled by the big woman's willingness to suffer, and then raced over to the bed to fetch the thunder-mug which she had set there. "Here, use this! I'll empty it for you when you're done."

The idea of somebody else cleaning up after her wastes offended Lathwi even more than the thought of soiling herself or her bed. She warned the sorceress away with a scowl, then continued on her way. Inch by agonizing inch, she worked her way out of the room, down the hall and into the water closet. She would've crawled all the way back to bed afterward, too, if Liselle hadn't gotten her a crutch in the meantime.

Liselle shook her head, still bristling with remembered awe and outrage. Anyone else would have accepted the mug and still considered themselves a hero for bearing the indignity. What was it that drove Lathwi to such extremes?

Those extremes provoked another confrontation a few days later, during the physician's weekly visit.

Liselle supposed that she herself had instigated the incident by tattling on Lathwi. But at the time, she had been mad because the pig-headed bitch refused stay in bed where she so obviously belonged.

"Got to challenge bones," Lathwi tried to explain before the doctor's arrival. "I stay on back till pain goes away, I never get up again."

"That's nonsense," Liselle argued. "You've got to give your body some time to rest and heal."

Lathwi shrugged, then proceeded to take another painful lap around the room. And so when the physician finally came to call, Liselle told him all about his patient's misdoings; and he, a sour-faced ex-military man with set opinions about how women should behave, went huffing into Lathwi's room just as she was climbing back into bed. Blustering with righteous indignation, he rushed over and grabbed her crutch.

"That's enough foolishness out of you, young woman," he said, shaking the forked stick in her face. "If I catch you out of bed again before I give you my consent, I'll give you a thrashing you'll never forget."

Her eyes narrowed into slits. Her upper lip curled back to bare her teeth. Without further warning, she then seized him by the throat with her good hand and pulled him to within an inch of her nose.

"You hit me," she said in her most threatening tone, "I eat you."

Surprise rippled across the physician's puckered face, then hardened into a look of tight-lipped acquiescence. He lowered the crutch, then started his examination. As he did so, his rigid air began to decompose. He muttered something several times, then finally turned to Liselle with a hint of suspicion or perhaps wonder in his flinty eyes.

"Did you use some sort of healing spell on this woman?" he asked.

"No," Liselle replied. The yellow pyramid was her only source of healing power; and that only worked on arcane woes. There was nothing magical about broken bones. "Why do you ask?"

"Her recovery is most remarkable," he explained, turning to look at Lathwi again. "Her ribs are more than half-mended already; and judging from the range of motion that I've seen, so are the bones in her wrist and leg. Even her facial scars are starting to scab off and turn pink."

Lathwi did not seem the least bit surprised or pleased by this pronouncement. It was as if she had expected no less of herself. Her flawless composure in the face of such good news roused the physician's curiosity.

"Well, woman," he said gruffly. "What say you? Do you know what brought this medical wonder to pass?"

"Hard work," she told him, just as she had tried to tell Liselle earlier. Then, because he had asked, and she did not care if he knew, she disclosed the other factor that had made her quickened recovery possible. "Mother's milk, too."

He snorted derisively, then packed up his instruments. On his way out the door, he turned to Liselle and said, "I'll be back next week. In the interim, keep her diet simple—no distilled spirits or red meat."

At the time, Liselle had accepted his instructions with the meekest sort of gratitude. Now, after a week of Lathwi's near-constant complaining, she was ready to stuff them down his lizard-like throat. Their latest go-around on the matter had taken place this very morning.

Lathwi had been sitting up in bed when Liselle entered the room with her breakfast. As soon as she saw the bowl of boiled cereal, she hissed and then turned her head away like a spoiled child.

"Not want porridge," she said, accenting the last word like the vilest of curses. "Want meat."

"You can have some broth for lunch," Liselle countered.

"Not want stupid broth. Want red, raw meat."

"You heard the physician. He said no distilled spirits or red meat."

"Physician no like me. He say just for spite."

"Maybe," Liselle said, although by now she was convinced that any spite involved was aimed at her. "But until he says otherwise, that's the way it's going to be. So why don't you just shut up and eat?"

Lathwi pushed the tray away. "Not want. You teach me reading now."

"You need to eat," Liselle insisted. Then, determined to have her own way for a change, she added, "I'm not going to teach you a blessed thing until that porridge is gone."

With that, she had turned on her heel and marched out of the room.

A full hour later, Lathwi called her back into the room and then pointed at the empty bowl. "Porridge be gone," she said, with no trace of anger or rancour in her tone. "Now you teach me reading."

Despite her attempts to suppress it, a ghost of a smile curled across Liselle's lips. She had finally bested Lathwi in a contest of wills! And as trivial as that victory might be, still it gave her a feeling of formidability and control. Girlishly giddy now, she carried the breakfast dishes out to the kitchen and then returned with a tray layered with fine white sand.

"Sand for cleaning scales, not reading," Lathwi stated. "Where book?"

"In order to read, you must first recognize the runes," Liselle said, and then traced two figures in the sand. The first one seemed like a poor rendition of a foot; the second was more beetle-like.

"This rune is called 'dhe'," she said, pointing to the first figure, "and that's the sound it represents. The one next to it is called 'ai'. By themselves, they are symbols. Together, they form a word." She exaggerated the shape of her mouth as she strung the two symbols into a single sound. "Dhai— which is the word for the span of time between dawn and dusk.

"Do you understand?"

Lathwi was speechless with admiration and delight. At first, these rune-things had seemed like frogs on a pond—lots of noise, but little to eat. But when Liselle put the two frogs together, they became an entirely different beast. Day—she knew that word, Pieter had taught it to her. Now his not-mother had given her its shape. The symmetry within the lesson pleased her.

At Liselle's prompting, she sketched her own version of the runes into the sand and spoke their Names. "'Dhe.' 'Ai'. Dhai," she recited. Then, spurred by a playful impulse, she reversed the order of the sounds. "Aiidhe. What that mean?"

"Aid is another word for help," the sorceress explained dryly. "And now that you've grasped the fundamental concepts of reading and writing, let's move on." She erased the slate with the palm of her hand, then fingered a new shape into the sand. "This rune is called argh…"

The lesson continued, rune after rune after rune. Then, as Liselle drew what looked like an inverted dhe in the sand, her eyes suddenly misted over. "This one is called pye," she said mournfully. "Pye for Pieter."

Lathwi dutifully reproduced the shape and its sound, but Liselle didn't respond with her usual nod or grunt. Instead, she lowered her head and just sat there in silence. This did not strike Lathwi as odd: Taziem had often gone chasing after an exciting thought in the middle of a lesson. Then Liselle began to shake and sniffle. Taziem had never done that!

"You sick?" she wondered.

Liselle looked up. To Lathwi's horror and fascination, her green eyes were brimming with tears. "Oh, Lathwi," she moaned. "Don't you miss him?"

"Who 'him'?"

"You know," she replied, and then blurted, "Pieter!"

Lathwi did not want to talk about Pieter. It served no useful purpose. So she shrugged and then stated the obvious in the hope of reminding Liselle that they had more important things to do. "Pieter gone."

"How can you say that so calmly?" the sorceress grated. There was both an accusation and a plea for enlightenment in her tone. Lathwi chose to address the plea, although she was rather surprised that she should have to explain something so basic to one as learned as Liselle.

"Long or short, all paths come to same end someday."

Liselle's teary eyes began to drip. "True. But Pieter didn't deserve to come to the end of his so early in life or in so vile a manner. It's my fault he's dead."

"You kill?"

"Not with my own two hands," Liselle replied. "But I might as well have for all the good I did when he needed me. I should've stayed awake that night. I could've done it if I had only tried a little harder."

"You no can challenge sleep," Lathwi told her. "Sleep always win."

"Then I never should have let him stay here in the first place!" Liselle argued.

Lathwi snorted then. "I see. You want be not-happy."

"I do not!" She drew herself erect, then scrubbed her eyes dry with the back of her hand. "What an awful thing to say about a person."

By now, it was clear to Lathwi that the sorceress didn't want to hear what she had to say, so she hauled the tray back onto her lap and began to review the runes that she'd learned so far. As she did so, Liselle stared at her, all resentment and grief. How could the woman be so cold? And how dare she imply that Liselle enjoyed being miserable? It was just that she felt so responsible. And so terribly guilty. She should have—

Sudden impatience grabbed her by the shoulders and shook her then. Lathwi was right. She wasn't mourning Pieter, she was torturing herself. The dead had no use for should-haves, could-haves or did-nots.

And, she thought then, the living had no time for them.

"That's all for today," she told Lathwi, and stood up to leave. As an afterthought, she added, "Thank you."

Lathwi shrugged, then sketched another rune in the sand: pye. For Pieter.

And porridge, she thought, as the smell of boiled cereal edged its way out of the thunder-mug where she had dumped it. For no reason she could name, she smiled.

"This book stupid," Lathwi complained, as Liselle came strolling into the room with lunch.

"Really?" Liselle asked, in an utterly unconcerned tone. "Let me hear something you find offensive."

She tracked down a particularly absurd passage and began to read in a slow, steady voice:

"Roses are red,
Violets are blue.
Sugar is sweet,
And so are you."

"That was very good," Liselle told her. "And have you noticed? Your speech is improving. Pretty soon, you'll be as well-spoken as the governor himself."

"Is stupid," Lathwi stubbornly insisted. She recognized the words. Roses and violets were flowers; red and blue were colours; and sugar was the substance that made candy so sweet. But what did any of those things have to do with her? "Make no make sense."

"I told you to read it, not critique it," Liselle said. "Think of it as a vocabulary exercise."

"My vo-cab-u-lary," she countered, taking elaborate care to emphasize each syllable, "is full of flowers and songbirds and butterflies. Those things got nothing to do with magic."

The sorceress laughed. "Are you sure? There are plenty of people who would argue that point with you."

"I want to read your books."

"Forget it," Liselle said, as she set the lunch tray on Lathwi's lap. "Those books are too dangerous for a beginner like you. You could accidentally put a curse on somebody just by sounding out a difficult patch of words."

"But—"

"No buts. Until you learn to read without moving your lips, you're going to have to content yourself with whatever harmless material I can dig up for you. Is that clear?"

"Clear," Lathwi grumbled. Although she was unhappy with the order, she could not argue against it. For every now and again, she did move her lips when she read.

"Good," Liselle said. "Now hush up and eat your lunch. Feed yourself with your broken hand, it'll be good practice. "Go on," she urged, when Lathwi made no move to pick up the spoon. "A little nourishment will do wonders for your mood."

"You want make mood better," Lathwi rumbled, "you take broth away and bring me meat."

"Oh, no!" Liselle exclaimed. "I'm not going around this mulberry bush again. You can either eat the damn broth or go hungry until supper—I'll give you to the count of three to decide."

She scowled at the bowl's watery contents, then loosed a churlish grunt. "Leave it. Maybe I eat later."

"Not a chance. I found one of your lunches rotting on the bottom of your thunder-mug already. I have no desire to repeat the experience.

"So what's it going to be—feast or famine?"

In reply, Lathwi grabbed the spoon and took an overly loud slurp of broth just for the spiteful pleasure of seeing Liselle stiffen. The sorceress was even more obsessive than Pieter had been about matters pertaining to food, eating and incidental body noises.

"Do try harder to rise above your barbaric upbringing," she said, a distinct edge to her banter now. "It's not that much to ask in exchange for a roof over your head, is it?"

"Not slurp meat," Lathwi said, employing the same sort of persistence that had stretched Taziem's patience to its limits at times. "Meat is civilized food. Broth…is not."

"If you so much as mention meat again, I'll stitch your mouth shut while you're sleeping," Liselle threatened, fully prepared to back her words with action. "And if that doesn't work, then I'll—"

A loud rap cut her off in mid-threat. It was followed by a familiar "Hello?", and then the sound of leather-soled feet tramping down the hall. "Is anybody home?"

Lathwi rolled her eyes. Jamus knew full well that they were both here. So why did he bother to ask?

A moment later, he strode into the room. His normally immaculate face was streaked with sweat and dirt. His hands, Lathwi noted, were hidden behind his back.

"Greetings, ladies," he said. "May I join you?"

"It would appear that you have already done so," Liselle retorted, trying hard to keep the corners of her mouth on an even keel. "What brings you here so early in the day?"

"I was at the stables exercising Lathwi's stallion," he replied, "and since I was in the neighbourhood, I thought I'd drop by and see how our favourite patient's doing." He turned to Lathwi and grinned. "You're looking well today. It won't be long before you're exercising that foul-tempered beast for yourself. And personally, I'm starting to live for that day. He bucked me off twice this morning just to prove he could do it."

"He behave better if you bite his ear," Lathwi advised, and then switched to a more interesting topic. "What you got behind your back?"

He laughed. Now that he was aware of his own mercenary tendencies, he was far more tolerant of them in others.

"You know very well what I've got," he chided, and then tossed the kerchief full of candies at her. As she snatched it out of the air, he added, "Enjoy."

Lathwi was happy to comply, for while she despised most other kinds of human-food, she'd taken a strong and immediate liking to chocolate. It smelled wonderful, sweetly pungent. And its taste was as luxurious as a nap on a sun-warmed rock. She gobbled one morsel after another in quick succession.

"If she gets sick from all that candy," Liselle said to Jamus, "you're the one who's going to have to nurse her back to health."

He snorted. "She's not going to get sick. Look at her, she's as healthy as that damn horse of hers. But if you want me to oversee her care for a while, just say so. She's more than welcome to stay at my house."

"Wouldn't that be convenient," she scoffed in return. "You'd finally have a woman who couldn't run away from you."

"For your information," he huffed then, "most women come running TO me, not away." That took them both by surprise. He flushed, immediately sorry that he'd said it; she berated herself for having poked him in the privates. As she fumbled for words with which to fill the gulf that had suddenly yawned open between them, she happened to look at Lathwi. Chocolate ringed her mouth. The tip of her nose was smudged, too. The sight was so comical, she just had to laugh. "Lathwi!" she exclaimed afterward. "You're going to need a bath to get clean."

"Two baths in one year?" Jamus teased, happy for the diversion. "How terribly civilized of you, my dear."

Lathwi peered at him through half-hooded eyes. If she had had a tail, the tip of it would have been twitching now. "I take many baths since bones broken," she told him. "Most times, Liselle be there to help."

"Good for you," he began, but she was not done with him yet and so cut him off. "Liselle say it not ne-ces-sary for both people to take clothes off. Or for me to taste—"

"Your vocabulary is coming along splendidly," Liselle interjected then. But she was grinning like a cat who had a fresh mouthful of feathers.

Jamus coughed up a clot of embarrassment, then grumbled. "My father was right—education gives women wicked thoughts. She would've never said something like that a few weeks ago."

"I be knocked senseless then," Lathwi reminded him.

"I think I liked you better that way," he retorted, and then turned to Liselle again. "By the way, my men found one of the sorcerers you were asking about last night."

"Which one?" she asked, and then bit her lip.

"The old man."

"And?"

"He's dead. Has been for a while. His house looks like it's been ransacked, but nobody seems to know if anything was taken."

So, Liselle thought, her enemy was still out there. She knew she had no right to be surprised or even disappointed by the news, but she was just the same. These last few weeks of inactivity had fostered an insane half-hope that he had given up and gone away.

"What about the addict?" she asked. "Has she been found yet?"

"Not yet," he admitted, with just a hint of exasperation in his tone. "Curra-chewers are as quick as gutter rats, and this one's jumpier than most. Every time my men get close to her, she runs; and none of them can seem to get a firm fix on her bolt-hole."

"She's probably got it hidden behind an illusion," she mused aloud. "Good. That means the curra hasn't completely scrambled her wits." She gnawed on her lip for a thoughtful moment, then added, "Let me do some experimenting. Maybe I can find a magical way of pinpointing her location. In the meantime, though, tell your men to keep on trying. I have a feeling she has good reason to be jumpy."

He arched a half-playful, half-reproving eyebrow at her. Only then did she realize that she was telling him how to do his own job.

"That's a very pretty colour on you," he remarked, as her cheeks went suddenly rosy. To his surprise and delight, that flustered her even more. At times like this, he could almost believe that she really did like him! He decided to make his retreat before he did something to change her mind.

"Well, dear ladies," he exclaimed, "it's been fun, but duty calls. I hope you'll allow me to visit again some day."

"Come tomorrow," Lathwi said. "Bring more chocolate."

"Good idea," Liselle chimed in. "I'd like some, too."

He gaped at them for a moment, then shook his head and grinned. They were, he admitted, too much for him.

And that was kind of nice, too.

The next morning, Liselle came breezing into Lathwi's room with a breakfast tray in her hands and a fat book tucked beneath one armpit. Lathwi was up and eager to begin another day's lessons, but the sorceress briskly disappointed her.

"I have a lot of work to do today," she said, as she set the tray on Lathwi's lap, "so you'll have to amuse yourself." Then she handed her the book. "Here. This ought to help."

Lathwi ogled the book with an almost comical mixture of surprise, glee and greed. It was a big book, with a cracked leather cover and thick, yellowed pages that smelled of dust and mould. The title page read: The Origins of Magic.

"You letting me read magic?" she gurgled.

"Of course not," Liselle replied. "I already told you you're not ready for such a text. What you have there is a collection of legends and myths. It's quite entertaining," she added, as the big woman's grin started to collapse. "I read every single one of those tales at least ten times as a child. If you don't like it, though, you can always go back to that book of doggerels."

The sorceress breezed back out of the room then, leaving Lathwi alone with the book, a bowl of cooling oatmeal and her disappointment. She wanted to read magic, not doggerels or a collection of legends and myths—whatever that was. She ran a speculative finger down the book's spine—it called to her in spite of her pique. Who knew what thoughts lurked inside? Who ever knew unless they looked?

And as for the oatmeal—well, although it wasn't common knowledge, a dragon could eat just about anything when it was hungry enough.

And she was finally hungry enough.

So she shovelled the foul-looking paste into her mouth, bite by tasteless bite. When she was done, she set the bowl on the floor, then thumbed the book open and started to read from the beginning.

Back in the days of EverLight, two suns shared the sky, and the world was a marvellous place. Beasts talked, flowers sang, rivers flowed back and forth in their beds according to whim. Men were ignorant, but knew it not, and lived in peace with all creatures as The Dreamer slept on in Her bed beneath the earth's rocky crust. When She stirred, and the mountains trembled, those whom She had created sang lullabies until She fell into a more tranquil sleep. And when Her snores rumbled throughout the sky, they stamped their feet and shouted until She rolled over again. For years beyond counting, Her dreams were serene, and life was good.

Then, for reasons unknown to mortal men, Her dreamings turned suddenly tumultuous. Rivers raged up and over their banks, drowning all that lie in their paths; the once gentle wind became a fury which uprooted stands of trees like twigs. Men tried to serenade Her back into a sweet sleep, but things got increasingly worse. Vast chasms opened in the earth like anguished jaws, salted rain fell from the skies. Then, with a cataclysmic roar, a mountain to the east burst its top and began to bleed liquid fire. In the midst of this lurid flow, a full-blown nightmare appeared.

She was as dark as the bowels of an unopened grave, all but Her eyes which glowed like the fires from which She had sprung. Her body was vast yet grotesquely formed, and while she could take different shapes, none of these were pleasing to behold. This was Shadow, The Dreamer's darkling Daughter; and as soon as She saw Her mother's other creations, She was overcome by the blackest jealousies, for they were hale when She was not. Shadow tried to destroy the world then, but She was new to the ways of power and Her spell went awry. Beasts lost the ability to speak. Men acquired a taste for violence and meat.

Years passed. Shadow grew in might and malice until one day, She lay Herself down on the fertile plains of Veroan and went into a dreaming trance. Soon thereafter, a blight began to gnaw at the grasses which surrounded her great bulk. This blight spread outward in all directions, leaving naught but a ring of desolation behind. The plainsmen rode against Shadow wielding new-forged spears and swords, but The Dreamer's fell Daughter was impervious to their might, and She dreamed a new terror into being. These were darkling creatures who changed their shapes and devoured human flesh. Yet while many of the nonborn embraced their Maker's campaign of fear and death, an equal number went into hiding instead. So Shadow gave up Her one attempt at creation and went questing for a more reliable stock of soldiers. And when She returned, She had an army of demons with Her.

The world became a waking nightmare for all of mankind. Fields and forests were razed; towns and villages were laid to waste. And those few who escaped the demons fell prey to nonborn and dragons. Soon, humanity teetered on the brink of extinction.

It was then that Jerome The Steadfast appeared. He gathered as many survivors as he could find and led them east to a cave in the mountains which was known as The Dreamer's Ear. There, they began a great noise-making—not to lull the Sleeping Goddess, but to rouse Her from this most ruinous dream. For sixteen days, they tramped their feet and clapped their hands; blew on whistles, banged on drums; sang, shouted and wailed. They did not stop for food or sleep, and so their din was peppered with the howls of starving children and dogs. Then, halfway through the seventeenth day of their clamorous vigil, a giant horde of demons and dragons appeared in the sky. A similar army began to swarm up the mountain's side. In the face of such overwhelming might, Jerome and his followers fell silent. The earth trembled then, as if to mock them. Jerome's people feared this as some new evil of Shadow's, but Jerome gave a great shout of hope and joy. Then, with the last of his failing strength, he broke into song again. In response, the lesser sun flared to white-hot brightness. No one saw what happened next, for Ar's sudden brilliance blinded Jerome and his followers, but what they all heard was terrible. There came a scream, then a pause, then a snarl of fast-moving power and a thunderous crash. The air grew thick with the smells of ozone and ash. The snarl struck out again and again and again only to be countered by a concussive boom and more ash.

Mother and Daughter fought for hours without end; and in that time, sight returned to Jerome and his folk. The snarls became bolts of blackest excrescence which sizzled across the sky; the booms became scintillating explosions as The Dreamer reduced the blackness to ashes with Ar's adamant light. This ash had no ill-effect on the men it touched, but when it fell on Shadow's fiends, it brought them pain and a melting death. Eventually, Her whole army was destroyed. She tried to flee then, but it was too late. The Dreamer caught Her by the heel and then cast a sphere of light around Her. That sphere flared to a star's brightness for a moment, then abruptly vanished. With its disappearance, Ar faded and did not shine again.

Thus, The Dreamer's Daughter was destroyed. And with Her passing, night came to the world and the age of wonders passed…

With a hiss, Lathwi slapped the book shut. At the same moment, Liselle shuffled into the room. The sorceress looked tired and ill-used, like a old bone that had been gnawed once too often, but she had enough energy to display her surprise.

"What's the matter?" she asked.

"Myths and legends be other words for not-truth," Lathwi declared, injecting a full measure of rancour into her tone.

"I suppose you could say that," Liselle conceded. "But that's a rather extreme definition. Most people regard myths as stories that the old wives made up to explain things they couldn't understand."

"People believe these stories?"

"People aren't so naive nowadays," Liselle assured her. They know that mythical tales need to be taken with a grain of salt."

"Salt is for food, not not-truths."

Weary and disappointed because of her fruitless attempts to locate The Curra-Chewer with magic, Liselle was in no mood to butt heads with Lathwi over colloquialisms right now. But it was obvious that something was bothering the woman, and as the saying went—there was no time like the present. So she gathered up the shards of her patience, then sat herself down on the corner of the bed and tried to clarify herself.

"In this instance," she said, "salt is another word for skepticism, which is another word for doubt. One regards a myth with doubt because it comes from prehistoric times and has undergone countless changes since its first telling."

"Changes?" Lathwi did not like the sound of that.

"Yes, changes. As a myth is handed from one generation to the next, those who retell it add, subtract or exaggerate seemingly extraneous details to suit their own fancy. These embellishments are incorporated and compounded throughout the years until someone like our good scribe here finally decides to put the final version down on paper.

"So. While you may find nuggets of truth sprinkled here and there among the pages of this book, most of it is merely a patchwork of mankind's imagination. If you approach it as such, you will be taking it with a grain of salt."

The explanation horrified Lathwi. How could humans have been so supercilious with regard to their past? Dragons were experts in the art of exaggerating the impertinent details of everyday life, but when it came time to review the past, only the complete and unadulterated truth sufficed. Because false memories served no useful purpose; and the lessons which they displaced were then lost forever.

"My mother recall the end of EverLight differently," she said then, determined to set this perverted telling straight. "She say it was dragons who bore the brunt of Galza's spite."

"Who's this Galza?" Liselle asked.

"The one called Shadow. In my memories, she is called Galza—The Dragonbane," she translated, as an afterthought. "And in my memories, it was dragons who were hunted down and killed by demon-krim; dragons who fled to the mountains; and dragons who finally brought about Galza's end."

Instead of looking surprised or troubled or impressed, Liselle flashed Lathwi a triumphant grin. "There! Without realizing it, you've just illustrated my point about the way myths work. Your mother taught you one version of the story, my mother taught me another, and our scribe's mother probably taught him the version that you read today. Yet despite the discrepancies between these versions, it's obvious that they all share common threads."

"No," Lathwi insisted. "Scribe's version be wicked as well as wrong because it tell people that dragons sided with your Dreamer's daughter. I tell you truly, Liselle: dragons have two words for enemy. One be krim. The other be Galza."

Liselle was stunned. This was the first time that she'd ever heard Lathwi speak so passionately, and at such length. And the subject that the big woman had chosen to champion was intriguing to an extreme.

"But how do you know your mother's account is accurate?" she asked. "You weren't there to see what did or didn't take place. Neither was she."

"Mother not there," Lathwi conceded, "but her mother's mother's mother's mother was. Bryllia fought krim and fled from them. She roared with fury when Galza's malice claimed her mate. She watched the Stone Oma rise from the mountain's side and seize lesser sun in her jaws. She witnessed Galza's final defeat and the world's first dawn. These memories and more Bryllia gave to her young, who gave them to their young and they to their young in turn. So the present recalls the past exactly as it occurred."

"Exactly?" Liselle scoffed. "Word for word? That's a pretty remarkable feat."

Lathwi deflected the other woman's scorn with a haughty look. "The language of dragons be composed of thoughts and images, not meaningless words. It be beautiful as well as exact."

Sure that she was being teased, Liselle adopted a more playful tone. "Oh? And how did you and your family happen to acquire the dragon tongue? Was that something that you inherited from your mother's mother's mother's mother, too?"

For one incredulous moment, Lathwi could only gape at the sorceress and wonder if she was being mocked. Then her astonishment sloughed away and a shiny new skin of awareness took its place: as impossible as it seemed, Liselle honestly had no idea as to who or what Lathwi really was.

"My family speaks the language of dragons because they are dragons," she said. Then, just in case Liselle failed to grasp the significance of that statement, she added, "I am a dragon, too."

Now it was Liselle's turn to stare and wonder if she was being mocked. But while she was extremely tempted to dismiss Lathwi's claim as nonsense, she could not quite bring herself to do so. Indeed, the more she thought about it, the more it explained: her fearless nature and copious scars; her strange garment and fondness for raw meat; even the blood-oath promise she had made. Pieter had said she'd been outcast as a child. And children almost never survived that cruel sentence unless someone found and fostered them somewhere along the way. Who was to say that that someone could not be a dragon?

The implications were staggering. Like the rest of the human race, Liselle had always regarded dragons as beasts—great, majestic beasts, but beasts all the same. But if what Lathwi was saying was true (and she had never heard her utter an outright lie), then dragons were not only more intelligent than anyone had ever suspected, they were also self-aware and cultured to boot. Oh, the questions she wanted to ask! How, when, why? But to her consternation, the most absurd thought in her head wriggled out of her mouth first.

"Do dragons really eat people?"

Lathwi shrugged. "Sometimes."

"Have you ever eaten anybody?" she went on, compelled by morbid curiosity.

"I never been that hungry," Lathwi replied.

A host of other questions crowded into Liselle's mouth then, but before she could voice any of them, Lathwi pushed herself into a sitting position and asked, "You finish your work in the laboratory?"

"Yes, I'm done for the day."

"Good," she began to haul herself out of bed. "I go practice magic now."

A protest swelled within Liselle. She wanted Lathwi to stay right where she was and tell her more about dragons and their ways! But even as she opened her mouth to say so, she realized that it was pointless. Lathwi was still Lathwi; and she would come and go according to her own whims and desires. The only thing that had changed was Liselle's perceptions.

Suddenly, the exhaustion that her excitement had been staving off reasserted itself. So as Lathwi hobbled her way toward the laboratory, Liselle went in search of her own bed.

Another day passed. Lathwi's disdain for human myths and legends did not. She spent the better half of a rainy afternoon trying to read another of the tales, but finally lost her patience and tossed the book aside. She turned to Liselle then. The sorceress was sitting in a chair by the bed. As usual, her nose was buried in a book. A real book, Lathwi thought covetously. A book about sorcery and power.

"I not move my lips when I read today," she announced.

"Good for you," Liselle replied, as she turned a page. "You give me new book to read."

"Not today, Lathwi. I've got too much research to do. If you need something to occupy your thoughts, feel free to go to the laboratory and practice your lessons."

Lathwi wanted to argue, but decided not to. That would only irritate Liselle, and that would diminish if not defeat her chances of seeing a real book anytime in the near future. So she slithered out of bed and onto her crutch, then hobbled her way to the laboratory. There, she set her receding aches and pains aside, and then gathered her Will. That most basic act of sorcery was now as natural to her as clenching a fist. And the exercises which she performed next seemed easier than ever before.

She made a vase fly around the room—up and over, down and back. When that got tedious, she Willed another urn into the air, then another and more. Separately, they bobbed like ducks in a pond. Together, they rippled like the ridges on a dragon's back. When that became boring, she Willed them back to their places all at once.

Now for the new lesson, she thought, regaining a speck of enthusiasm. Liselle called it translocation: the ability to move an object from one place to another without dragging it through real space. It was supposed to be a complicated procedure, one that required memory and imagination as well as power and desire. Lathwi thought it was fun.

She summoned an image of the not-claw. When its details were as clear as crystal, she envisioned it at the far end of a pitch-black cave and then sent her Will streaking after it. A heartbeat later, a faint psychic tremor told her that she'd made contact. She folded her ethereal grip around the image, then quickly withdrew. The tunnel collapsed behind her.

Now the not-claw was in her hand, solid and sharp-edged. Its appearance did not excite her, though, for she had spent the last three days Willing it hither and fro. She needed a different target, something interesting and new...

An image of a small, leather bound book popped into her head then, almost of its own accord. She hissed, instantly pleased with the idea. Translocating a book out from under Liselle's nose would not only make good practice, it might also prompt the sorceress into giving her a real book of her own. After all, she had satisfied the requisite for reading magic today. Why should she have to wait to reap her reward?

Grinning now, she called that pitch-black cave back into being and then reached into it as if it were a honey pot. An instant after she brushed against the book-image at the other end, though, the tunnel flared white and began to sizzle in a most alarming sort of way. Quick as a thought, she retracted her probing Will. As she did so, something landed in her lap. She blinked back a moment's surprise, then thumbed the thin, dog-eared book open to a random page and began to read.

"Roses are red,
Violets are blue..."

Just then, the laboratory door flew open; and one very red-faced sorceress came storming in.

"I suppose you thought you were being clever," Liselle grated, as she strode toward Lathwi. "I suppose you thought it would be fun to surprise me."

"What I do wrong?" Lathwi wondered, trying to figure out how she'd wound up with the book of doggerels.

"You still don't understand, do you?" Liselle accused. "When you form a magical link with something, even something as inert as a book, your mind is open to attack. If I hadn't been so quick to recognize your touch, I might have hexed you while you were trying to fast-finger that book. You could've been seriously hurt or even killed."

Lathwi snorted. Liselle couldn't kill a spider or a fly with her own hand, so how could she possibly pose a threat to someone twice or even thrice again her size?

Liselle's glare became as potent as an electrical storm, and her thoughts were all howling wind and thunder. The time had come to teach this hulking she-barbarian a different sort of lesson! So she balled her Will into a fist, then abruptly lashed out. The first blow paralysed Lathwi's arms and legs; the second imprisoned her mind. Lathwi tried to break free, but for all of her superior strength and natural ability, she was no match for a trained adept.

"So," Liselle hissed then, "you scorn me because I'm too small to hurt you with my fists. Stupid fool." She snatched the knife from Lathwi's belt and brandished it. "I could cut your throat from ear to ear, and you wouldn't be able to lift so much as a finger to stop me. Or," she added, as she threw the knife away, "I could kill you with a wish."

Without warning or reason, Lathwi broke out in a cold, stomach-churning sweat. An instant later, her heart started pumping pain into her chest and arms. It was so terrible, it blotted out all thought. Her vision blurred, then started to turn black. Her awareness started to dim. All that was left was the pain...

Liselle snapped her fingers. The pain disappeared. All was normal with Lathwi again except for the sour taste in her mouth. She sucked in a relieved breath only to vomit it back up a moment later. There was a fist knotted around her lungs now; she couldn't breath. As she gasped like a land-stranded fish, her vision began to fade again.

Although Lathwi's frantic wheezing appalled Liselle, she waited until the woman was on the verge of passing out before easing her grip. She had to learn, the sorceress thought, as her victim gulped at the air. She had to understand that she was neither the biggest nor the best when it came to sorcery. And so as soon as Lathwi got her wind back, Liselle doggedly resumed the gruelling lesson.

A clutch of white-hot rocks flared to life in Lathwi's stomach. She doubled over from the pain, then tensed as her sphincter muscles threatened to collapse. Desperate now as well as convinced, she swallowed a sea of hot, churning bile and croaked, "Stop!"

"Why should I?" Liselle demanded, loosening her grip but not relinquishing it. "What have you learned?"

"You could kill me," Lathwi admitted bleakly.

"Any competent sorcerer could," Liselle maintained, "no matter how harmless that person might seem outwardly. And if that person attacked you through a mind-link, death would not be the worst you could expect.

"Do you understand me? Or do I need to proceed with the demonstration?"

"I understand," Lathwi replied. Only a complete fool could've failed to grasp a lesson so thoroughly taught. And only a fool would dare to admit it. "Now let me go. Or kill me."

Amazing, Liselle thought to herself. Only Lathwi would dare to issue ultimatums while still on the torturer's rack. Was that courage? Or more arrogance? Did she dare to hope that these were not one and the same to her?

Yes, she decided, and retracted the talons of her Will.

Lathwi felt the life flood back into her limbs, but she made no effort to move. Her ribs ached from all the gasping that she'd done, and the rest of her insides were still numb. Instead, she looked up at Liselle and nodded—a rare gesture of thanks and respect.

"Don't force me to repeat this lesson," Liselle warned. "And don't ever try to steal one of my magic books again. As you may have noticed, they're protected."

"You sneakier than you look," Lathwi told her, and then gestured at the door. "You go now. Leave me alone to think and practice."

Liselle had spent a great deal of power as well as anger on her apprentice this afternoon, and so welcomed the idea of returning to the solid comfort of her rocking chair. But she wasn't about to let Lathwi order her around in her own house, so she stood her ground and flexed her newfound authoritative muscle one last time.

"Don't do too much more in the way of practising," she cautioned. "Although you may not realize it yet, you burned up a lot of energy during today's lesson."

"I mostly think," Lathwi assured her.

As soon as the sorceress was gone, Lathwi eased herself onto her back and began to massage her throbbing ribs. Each sore spot she fingered reminded her of Liselle. Never again would she scorn that one as weak! And never again would she trust size as a measure of might! She had never suffered so horribly, or so helplessly. She did not begrudge Liselle her methods, though. Indeed, if the sorceress had been any less brutal, the lesson probably wouldn't have been so thoroughly impressive. Even now, convinced as she was, Lathwi could not help but marvel at the unlikeliness of it all. Who would've guessed that so small and meek a creature could possess such fearsome powers?

Not her!

But she knew better now. And now, for the first time, she understood how someone might come to fear sorcery.

An image of Pieter's furry face accompanied the thought. She did not often think of the trapper unless Liselle brought his name up first, and sometimes not even then; because those who were gone, were gone, and nothing could be done about it. Yet it seemed right to think of him at this moment; to recall all that he'd taught her; and to acknowledge the irony of his end. That which he had feared most had finally come to fetch him.

This, then, was his last lesson to her: she must have no fear. Of anything.

She reached for the not-claw which Liselle had let fall so long ago. But even as she tried to resume her practising, another image of Pieter distracted her. She hissed, venting her irritation, then went suddenly wide-eyed as two thoughts collided to form a new idea. If she could pull a knife or a book out of another space, perhaps she could do the same for Pieter.

This morning, she might have done a bit of experimenting in the vainglorious hope of impressing Liselle. But not now. Wise dragons did not make the same mistake twice. So she got up and hitched her way into the kitchen. There, she sat down on the floor and stared at Liselle until the sorceress looked up from her book with a half-weary, half-wary now-what on her heart-shaped face.

"I am wondering about a thing," she said then.

"What is it?" Liselle replied.

"Why we not use translocation magic to bring Pieter back?"

Liselle blanched as she often did when she was reminded of Pieter; and for one annoyed moment, Lathwi thought she was going to have endure another of her weeping fits. But crying was the last thing on the sorceress' mind at the moment.

"Pieter's dead," she croaked.

"But the image of him in my head is still alive," Lathwi argued. "I use that to bring him back, he be alive again."

"It doesn't work like that," Liselle said, in a strident tone. "When Pieter died, his spirit separated from his flesh and went to sleep in the Dreamer's embrace. If you attempted to translocate him, you would either wind up with a body with no soul on your hands or a homeless ghost."

"What if I fetch both and reunite?" Lathwi persisted.

"Don't even consider it," Liselle warned.

"Why?"

"Because if you succeeded," she replied, in a tone thick with loathing, "Pieter would be a monstrosity. Men would run screaming at the sight of him."

Lathwi shrugged. That didn't sound so terrible to her. "At least he be alive."

"But that's just it!" Liselle blurted passionately. "He won't be alive! He'll be one of the walking dead, a zombie." When Lathwi cocked her head at the unfamiliar word, she took a deep breath to calm herself and tried again. "No brand of magic can restore the bond between spirit and body once that bond's been broken. Without that bond, the body is just meat that will continue to decay unless it's constantly maintained with spells. And without that bond, the spirit is naught but a helpless slave trapped in a rotting shell."

She leaned closer then and looked Lathwi squarely in the eye. "Would you wish a fate like that on your own spirit?"

The thought offended Lathwi to an extreme. Her reply to it was immediate and heart-felt. "No!"

"Then do not seek to inflict it on someone else's."

"I understand." She discarded the horribly flawed idea without a second thought. As she did so, her curiosity took another turn. "How you know these things?" she asked Liselle then. "You try to bring someone back?"

The sorceress lapsed back into the recesses of her chair like a bag of dirty laundry. Her expression was haggard, and fringed with sorrow. This made her seem smaller than usual.

"No, Lathwi, I've never tried to bring anyone back," she replied. "I learned what little I know about necromancy from a manuscript fragment that had written back in the dark age."

"Ne-cro-man-cee?"

"That branch of sorcery which deals with the raising of the dead," she told her. "At its best, it's a dangerous art. At its worst, it's unspeakably evil."

"I wanted to bring Pieter back. That evil, too?" Lathwi asked, wondering if she needed to add that unsavoury-sounding word to her list of distinctions.

"Not at all," Liselle assured her. "You considered the idea for Pieter's sake, but then chose to abandon it when you learned that it would do him more harm than good. That's not evil, that's simply a bright and discriminating mind at work. An evil person would have chosen to pursue the matter further in spite of his new-found knowledge. An evil person would've gladly torn Pieter from the grave if doing so would serve his twisted purposes."

With a start, she realized that she was talking about someone specific now, someone who had come to embody all the evil in her life. And as she marvelled at that subconscious mix-up, a notion struck her.

Could The Rogue be a necromancer?

That could explain the warning that the witch's familiar had given her: The Rogue seeks a body. That nonborn had also connected him somehow with the city's bones. But if that was the case, what body did he want? Compara had buried her fair share of heroes in her day, but none of them were renowned as people of extraordinary power. And what else but power would tempt a man to risk necromancy and the Dreamer's wrath?

Lastly, what did any of this have to do with her?

Oh, how she hated trying to press odd bits of different puzzles together in hopes of finding a match!

She began to rock back and forth in her chair—a slow, soothing motion that belied the furious pace of her thoughts. Sensing that the time for questions had passed, Lathwi got up and hobbled out of the room. After all that talking, she was ready for a nap.

In the morning, Lathwi emerged from her room at an eager clip, hoping to catch Liselle in another expansive mood. She had learned a lot yesterday, but not nearly enough to satisfy her appetites. The faster she learned, the sooner she'd have wings!

She found the sorceress standing near the kitchen door with her arms crossed over her chest. A long moment passed before she became aware of Lathwi's presence, and even then, it seemed as if she were looking elsewhere.

"Good morning, Lathwi," she said, as she meandered back toward the table. "You just missed Jamus. He dropped by to tell me that none of Compara's legends have been molested in their crypts. That's one more red herring for the bucket."

Lathwi tipped her head to one side—a look both comical and quizzical. Liselle couldn't help but smile at it; and as she did so, her self-absorbed funk receded.

"Never mind," she said then, "I was babbling to myself. Did you want something to eat, or are you ready to start the day?"

"There be meat in the house?" Lathwi asked.

"Not yet."

"Then I ready to begin. What you teach today?"

"Actually," the sorceress replied, with a sly lilt in her voice, "I was hoping that you might teach me something for a change, the magic of Names."

"Why you want to know?"

Liselle's first and immediate reaction to the question was annoyance. She was not accustomed to having her motives challenged, especially by someone who never felt it necessary to explain her own. Then reason intervened, and she blurted out the sorry truth.

"I'm desperate, Lathwi," she said. "My enemy is closing in on me—I can almost feel him breathing down my neck. But every time I think I've found a clue as to his whereabouts or purpose, it turns out to be a dead end. I need new ideas and insights. I need to know what's going on."

"I not see how Names can serve these needs," Lathwi told her. "People do not seem to know their own Names, so they no can Call each other or be Called. And it will take you many seasons to learn the Names of those things that be willing or able to help you."

Then, although it hadn't been solicited, she offered the sorceress a rare bit of advice. "You should track this enemy down, then split him in two and eat his liver. Then you need not worry anymore."

"I'd love to do exactly that," Liselle replied in a tone that quivered with frustration as well as longing. "But I'm a scholar, not a warrior. I need to know who my adversary is before I can face him; I need to know what he can do. And if we ever do come face-to-face, I'll need to know more than he does to prevail.

That's why I want you to teach me the magic of Names, Lathwi. I need all the options I can get."

Lathwi was decided now: these needs were real and true. So she waved the sorceress toward the hearth and said, "Make the fire bigger."

Liselle looked from Lathwi to the hearth and back again, then blinked back a splash of confusion. "I thought you said you weren't hungry."

"I did not say I was not hungry," she replied. "I said I did not want to eat unless there was meat. You must learn to listen better, for some things only tell you their Names once."

Although she was still confused, Liselle did as she was told and then turned to Lathwi again. "Now what?"

"Sit down on the hearth and open your mind to the fire," she instructed. "Watch it, touch it, taste it. Listen with all your heart. Sooner or later, it will give you its Name."

"Couldn't you just give me the Name?"

"No Name but my own is mine to give. If you want Fire's Name, you must ask a fire."

Having said all that she intended to say on the matter, she then pivoted on her crutch and headed for the laboratory. Liselle scowled at the big woman's decidedly cryptic teaching style, then gave her skirts a resigned twitch and sat down on the stone floor in front of the hearth. As she stared at the now-roaring fire, wondering how she was supposed to touch or taste it without getting burned, gentle combers of heat broke over her. They lapped at her nose, her cheeks, the hollow of her throat; the knots in her spine began to melt. She leaned closer to better savour these thermals. Her pale skin started to glow.

It was a pretty fire, she admitted dreamily. Its colours were as rich as velvet, its many surfaces seemed as supple as silk. Impelled by a sudden surety that she wouldn't be hurt, she offered her hand to a lively orange flame. It flickered as if signalling its pleasure, then licked her fingers one by one. She felt nothing but its warm, benevolent breath and so did not withdraw.

The fire's roar tapered into a whisper. As she focussed on this sound, an image of rustling leaves took shape in her head, and a wealth of aromas filled her nose: heat, dry and ascetic; the more appealing tang of dirt, spring-green leaves and cherries. She began to grow then—a steady climb toward the sky. The warmth that embraced her was that of the sun's. An impression took root within her then. It burrowed its way through the multi-coloured orchard of her thoughts, then tapped the wellspring of her awareness. An instant later, it burst into flames, and a Word rose up from its ashes.

A feeling of immense privilege overcame her. What she had heard just then was not a name like her own, but a gift from the Dreamer Herself! It was pregnant with meaning, with power and import. To know it was to know its owner as well. Now she understood why Lathwi had been so secretive: this was a special brand of magic indeed!

Prompted by a sudden need to share her good fortune, she withdrew her hand from the fire and went scurrying off to the laboratory. Spangles of pain shot up her arm when she rapped at the door, but she was so excited, she barely noticed.

As soon as Liselle came scurrying into the room, Lathwi knew that she had tasted some sort of success. Her greenish eyes were aglow with pride. Her mouth was a toothy crescent.

"Fire talk to you?" she asked, and then grinned at the other's excited nod. "Tell me what it told you. Not aloud," she added sharply, cutting Liselle off even as she opened her mouth to speak. "You want to start a fire in here?"

Liselle flushed, chastened by her near-gaffe, then bent over and whispered the Name in Lathwi's ear. The big woman's face went curiously blank. Her torso started to tremble. A long instant later, she loosed a series of unnerving shrieks. Liselle could not believe her ears. Lathwi was laughing.

"What's so funny?" she wondered.

"That not Fire's Name," Lathwi replied between guffaws. "That is the Name of the tree that Fire was eating. You did not listen carefully enough." As the sorceress' face wilted, she stifled her mirth and added, "You do better tomorrow."

"I'm not tired yet," Liselle said, determined to be as resilient as Lathwi. "I'll give it another try now."

"Wait until tomorrow."

"Why?" she demanded, taking a perverse sort of pleasure in reversing their usual roles. "What's wrong with now?"

"You touch fire?" Lathwi asked. At Liselle's proud nod, she said, "Let me see that hand."

Liselle extended the palm in question. Lathwi casually smacked it. The sorceress yelped and jerked her hand away.

"Now is the time to soak that hand," Lathwi informed her then. "Tomorrow is the time to try again."

"I'll use my other hand," Liselle countered, unwilling to admit defeat. "When I'm done, I'll soak them both."

Lathwi shrugged. "Fire is kind to those it likes, but skin is still skin regardless. If you do not soak that hand now, you will have blisters tomorrow."

Liselle's frustration came to a boil in her eyes, then abruptly simmered into a cunning gleam. Noting that, Lathwi generously tendered her another scrap of unsolicited advice. "Do not try to learn Fire's Name with one hand stuck in a pot of water. If you do, Fire will get angry and burn you good. Fire does not like Water."

"I told you to stay out of my mind," Liselle snapped.

"I did not need to look inside of your head to see that thought," Lathwi replied, baring her teeth in a grin. "When I be youngling, I tried a similar trick. My mother knew what would happen, but did not find it necessary to warn me.

"My hand hurt for weeks."

That divulgence quelled the last of Liselle's rebellious inclinations. Moreover, it made her realize that Lathwi had been trying to do her a favour.

"In that case, I'm glad you aren't your mother," she said, an awkward apology for her former belligerence. "She sounds like a formidable creature."

"My mother," Lathwi firmly maintained, "is a dragon."

"I know," Liselle said, and then left the room to go and soak her hand.

CHAPTER 13

A most peculiar procession worked its way up the side of the craggy highland knoll: one glassy-eyed peasant boy; four frazzled, grey-bearded men clad in homespun; and eight motley but well-armed foreigners. The different groups kept as far away from each other as was possible under the circumstances.

The boy feared the elders. If he hadn't agreed to guide them today, they would have beaten him again and outcast what was left of his family. He feared the foreigners, too. They were loud and insulting and mean. They were also the ugliest men the boy had ever seen. Their leader was the worst of the lot. He wore a chain-mail helm which veiled his face, but it could not completely hide his oft-broken nose, or the freshly healed burns which gave his jaws a marbled, half-molten look. Three of the other men bore lesser burns; the rest boasted a variety of more mundane scars. All eight appeared capable of murder.

Which was why the elders wanted to hire them.

The hillside flattened into a small, sheltered plateau. The boy led his followers through a thick stand of trees and toward the meadow where he had last seen his sister. When he finally reached its grassy shores, he stumbled to a stop and began to tremble.

"Where now, boy?" the chief elder demanded then. He was a spindly old man with straggly grey hair and one milk-white eye.

The boy pointed to a patch of buttercups.

"Well then," the elder snapped, "let's get moving. The sooner we find her, the sooner we can leave this ill-favoured place."

Just then, a shadow skimmed across the meadow. With a shriek, the boy bolted back into the thicket and disappeared. The elders scanned the sky with suddenly nervous eyes only to be mocked by mercenary laughter.

"What a bunch of women you are!" their captain sneered. "It was only a passing cloud!" Then he gave the nearest elder a shove toward the meadow. "Get on with it, dung-eater. Our time is valuable."

The old men waded into the pool of yellow flowers, then began to poke at the dirt with their staffs. It did not take them long to find what they were looking over.

"Over here!" a stoop-shouldered elder with all of four hairs left on his head cried out. "She's right here."

The be-helmed captain strode over, then hunkered down in the weeds. When he stood up again, he had the better half of a shiny white femur in hand.

As he rubbed his thumb over the bone's severed edge, he nodded to himself.

"Leastwise the little snot wasn't lying," he said to his men. "Nothing but a dragon could've done this so cleanly."

He fingered the shard a moment longer, then flipped it back into the grass and turned to look at the elders who had formed a half-circle at his back.

"What I don't understand," he said then, "is why you're making such a fuss about this. What's one girl-child more or less?"

"She isn't the only one we've lost," Milk-Eye replied. "That damned dragon has devoured five of our daughters this past season—all healthy young maids of almost marriageable age."

"What a waste!" That came from a tall, blonde-haired man whose once-handsome face was now puckered with healing burns. He cupped his genitals and laughed. His companions sniggered, too.

"So," their captain said then, "you want us to slay this maiden-eater for you, is that it?"

All four greybeards nodded.

"How big is it?"

"The boy says it's at least seven times the length of my staff from snout to tail," Milk-Eye replied.

"Big," the captain mused then, "but not a sire. That's good. Those frights are impossible to kill." The conviction in his voice was not feigned. "And what would you give us to do this thing?"

The chief elder's one good eye acquired a doleful gleam. His tone became more ingratiating. "Our villages are poor," he said, "and this last winter was an exceptionally hard one. Still, our people are willing to impoverish themselves to rid themselves of that accursed dragon. Our offer is this: three pouches of gold—"

"Insulting," one of the mercenaries muttered.

"—five cattle, twelve sheep—"

"Do we look like shepherds to you?" another mercenary jeered.

Old Milk-Eye's expression soured, but he continued his recitation in the same wheedling tone. "—a pot of healing ointment, four jugs of mountain mash, plus shelter and food for you and your horses for the duration of your stay."

"Let's get out of here, Jarrad," the blonde man with the burns snapped. "These lackwits want us to risk ourselves for a pittance."

"Dummy up, Marl," Jarrad snapped back. "The rest of you put a sock in it, too. We're trying to strike a deal here." He turned his helmed face back to the chief elder then. His tone was one of warmth and reason, but his mouth remained as cold as flint. "Brash as they may be," he said, "my comrades have raised a valid point. We have no need of stock. We'll take three more pouches of gold instead."

"But we have no more gold!" the stoop-shouldered elder bleated.

"Sell the sheep and cattle!" Jarrad replied, skilfully mimicking the other's high-pitched whine. "Or else slay the dragon for yourselves."

The elders exchanged a round of panicked whispers, then stepped back to let Old Milk-Eye do the talking.

"The animals will be brought to market," he announced, "but we cannot guarantee you three full pouches of gold from their sale. We will have to drive them hard and fast, which will cause them to lose weight and thus lessen their value."

"Then either bid your drover to bargain well or have him sell more beasts," Jarrad replied. "Our asking price is six pouches of gold, not a single luc more or less. Furthermore, we will require mash with every meal and a woman to cook and keep us warm at night."

"Out of the question!" one greybeard blurted.

"Southern bastard," another growled. "Who does he think he is?"

Old Milk-Eye rounded on the dissidents with his staff, cracking shins and knuckles with a dexterity that belied his feeble appearance. As he laid into them, he snapped, "Mind your tongues, you stupid old goats! Our people knew they'd have to make sacrifices when they bade us to enlist the aid of mercenaries.

"You shall have your gold, Southerner," he told Jarrad then. "And so long as you do not harm her, you shall have a woman as well."

Jarrad clapped his calloused hands together as if in delight. "Excellent!"

"Do we have a deal then?"

"Maybe," he drawled, eying the old man slyly. "You'll have to agree to one more thing first."

"And what might that be?" the elder wanted to know.

"When it comes time for us to set our trap," he replied, "you must provide the bait."

CHAPTER 14

As Lathwi climbed past the ladder's last rung and into the sunlit loft, an electric thrill quickened her pulse. At long last, she was back to her old self! She bugled once to celebrate her return, then again simply because once was not enough.

Her jubilee brought Liselle to the foot of the ladder at a record speed. "What's the matter?" she shouted. "Should I call the physician back? He only left a moment ago, he can't have gone far."

"I do not wish to see that sour gas-bladder ever again," Lathwi replied. Then, because she wanted Liselle to go away, she added, "Do not worry, I am well. I will be down soon."

Liselle hmphed, then grudgingly abandoned her post. Her receding footsteps gratified Lathwi. There were times when a dragon needed to be alone. And this, her first hour without bandages or crutches, was one of those times. She stretched, savouring the feel of her newfound freedom, then went over to stand beneath the skylight. The incoming sunshine warmed her face. She thought about basking in that light until the rest of her was toasty, too, but then she saw her scales lying on the nearby cot and forgot about all else.

With a eager grin, she shucked the soft, shapeless gown she was wearing and slipped into her scales. As she did so, her eagerness turned to dismay. Nothing fit right! The hood was tight; the bodice and leggings were too loose. And while she could easily fix the hood's fit by chopping off her hair, there was no quick remedy for the rest. The gallons of broth that Liselle had forced her to consume had left her woefully thin.

She needed real food! And she needed it now.

With that goal in mind, she pivoted toward the ladder. The unthinking swiftness of the manoeuver provoked a painful twinge in her newly healed leg. She hissed, frustrated now as well as dismayed. How was she supposed to hunt when one misstep could put her in splints again? Feeling disgruntled and much abused, she climbed down from the loft.

"Now there's a sight for sore eyes," Jamus exclaimed, as she came striding toward the kitchen. "You're looking as fit as you were on the day we met, old girl." When she hissed at the blatant untruth, he cheerfully added, "Your disposition hasn't changed a whit since then either."

She hissed again, then gracelessly flopped to the floor in front of the fire.

"How's your leg?" Liselle asked.

"Sore," she admitted irritably. "It itches, too."

"Ah," Jamus intoned, as if she had just said something profound. "That would explain your somewhat churlish mood. Fear not, though—both are temporary conditions. You'll be brawling with the locals again in no time."

"I do not think so," she replied mournfully. "I got no muscle left. I need to eat. I need to eat meat."

"I know, I know," Liselle said in a harried tone. "And I've just now asked Jamus to stop at a butcher's stall on his way back to the garrison. Is there something special you'd like him to order?"

"I want meat, lots of meat," she said, fully prepared to repeat herself a hundred times if necessary. "I want it red, raw, and fresh. If it is not fresh, I will eat the delivery boy instead."

"I'll be sure to pass the message along," Jamus drawled. "Especially that last part. Oh and by the way," he added, as the thought occurred to him, "the swordmaster at the garrison is a friend of mine. If you're still interested in learning the ways of a sword, he's willing to teach you. "Shall I tell him to expect you?"

"Yess," she replied, without a moment's hesitation. "You tell him to expect me tomorrow."

"Now wait just a minute!" Liselle rasped. Two angry red shoals banded her cheekbones. Her green eyes were afire. At the moment, this display was all for Jamus. "Why didn't you discuss this with me before mentioning it to her?"

"I did," he replied, flabbergasted by her sudden change of mood. "All three of us discussed it that day she woke up. Remember? You said—"

"I know what I said."

Indeed, she remembered her promise all too clearly. But she'd been desperate then, half-mad with fear and grief. She would've said anything to stop Lathwi from charging off after her attackers. Now she felt the same way about swordplay.

If only Jamus had kept his big mouth shut!

"And I was wrong to say it," she continued, striving for a less heated tone. "I don't want Lathwi getting hurt again, not after all I've gone through to nurse her back to health."

"I will not get hurt," Lathwi assured her.

"You can't be sure of that," Liselle argued. "Accidents happen all the time. I think you should forego this foolish idea."

Lathwi studied the frets that ridged Liselle's brow with a dragon's suspicious eye. For while it was obvious that the sorceress was upset, something about her concern rang false.

"I do not think your fear is for me," she said then.

Liselle's cheeks flared red again, but her gaze turned suddenly elusive. "I am too afraid for you," she maintained. "Swordplay is dangerous business.

But if that doesn't daunt you, then think about The Rogue. If you give him the chance, he'll treat you as he did Pieter; and I don't want more blood on my conscience.

"So forget about going outside and playing with swords. Concentrate on your sorcery instead. Both of our lives may depend on it."

Ah, so there was the problem, Lathwi thought: Liselle was confused about their fortunes. Where the sorceress saw one path, she saw two which happened to be unfolding side by side at the moment. It was time to make that distinction clear.

"I will continue to study sorcery," she stated. "I will also learn to play with swords. Maybe this Rogue will try to spill my blood. Maybe he will succeed, maybe he will not—I cannot see tomorrow. But if I let maybes tell me how to live my life, I would never do any living at all."

"You're one of the most selfish women on the face of the earth," Liselle accused, and then abruptly turned her back to Lathwi.

Selfish: Lathwi knew that word. It described an abiding concern for one's own well-being, and so certainly applied to her. But what was so terrible about that? All creatures saw to their own needs first; they had to in order to survive and prosper.

"How are you different?" she wondered aloud.

The sorceress stiffened as if stung, then spun around on the bones of her butt and impaled Lathwi with a furious look. "I gave you a place to stay and taught you secrets of sorcery and nursed you back to health when you were nearly dead—all with very little thanks from you. That's how I'm different."

"Pieter invited me to stay here before you did," Lathwi reminded her. "And you only agreed to teach me your secrets after you discovered that I knew one that you did not. And as for tending to me while I was hurt, did you not do so in the hope that I would help you against your enemy afterward?

"Be wary of half-truths, Liselle," she cautioned then. "They are often more convincing to those who speak them than to those who hear them."

"Me? Half-truths? Of all the nerve!"

She snapped to her feet with a huff, then stomped out of the kitchen and out of sight. Moments later, a door slammed. Lathwi turned to Jamus then. He had the dazed look of a man who been caught in a windstorm.

"How did I insult her?" she asked.

"You didn't," he replied, absently combing his fingers through his unruffled hair. "Not exactly. You simply lack tact."

"What is tact?"

"That, my friend, is the ability to tell somebody the shitty truth without rubbing his or her nose in it."

"I do not understand."

A rueful smile twitched across his mouth. "No, I had a feeling you wouldn't. Let me put it another way…"

From the confines of her bedroom, Liselle could hear the faint buzz of voices; and although she couldn't make out any of the words, she knew that Lathwi and Jamus were discussing her shameful behaviour. And she was ashamed, horribly so, for now that she'd recovered from her tantrum, she could see that Lathwi was right: she was selfish. And even worse than that, she was a coward. Out of fear for herself, she had tried to shackle Lathwi with ugly chains of obligation and guilt. And out of fear, she'd convinced herself that such was her right. But that was wrong, contemptible; pathetic. If Lathwi didn't want to skulk in a house for the rest of her life—well, who could blame her?

Still, Liselle could not help but wring her hands at the thought of Lathwi wandering Compara's streets with absolutely no protection. The Rogue would gobble her up like a meat pie and spit out the tough bits afterward. Sweet Dreamer! There had to be something she could do to keep that from happening. But what? Advice was out—the only thing of value that she had to say was don't do it. And while Lathwi was well on her way to becoming an accomplished sorceress, she was still more inclined to react with muscle than with magic in a crunch, so teaching her a self-defence spell or two probably wouldn't be all that useful either. No, what Lathwi needed was something automatic, something that could protect her against a magical attack without her conscious participation.

What Lathwi needed, Liselle concluded, was wards.

The idea immediately intrigued her. As far as she knew, no one had written anything about the generation of personal wards, but it certainly seemed possible in theory. It would have to involve stone and ritual magic, perhaps even a little blood…

Oh, she could not wait to discuss this with Lathwi! Still fiddling with the bones of her inspiration, she went shuttling back into the kitchen. Her sudden entrance prompted Jamus and Lathwi to silence.

"Lathwi," she said without apology or preamble, "I have a favour to ask of you."

"What is it?" Lathwi asked warily.

"I want you to wait a week before starting your lessons with the swordmaster."

"Why? What difference will seven days make? When those have passed, will you ask me to wait seven more?"

"Lathwi," Jamus cautioned under his breath. "Remember what we were talking about just now? Go gently."

Neither woman paid the slightest bit of attention to him.

"I have an idea for a warding ritual that might save us both a lot of grief," Liselle replied, "but I'm going to need some time to work out the details and you're going to need to be here to help me." Lathwi's eyes narrowed into speculative slits then. Liselle interpreted that as a favourable sign and pressed on. "One week isn't so very much to ask, is it? If nothing else, it will give you a chance to work some strength back into that leg of yours."

"I will grant you one week," Lathwi said. She liked the prospect of actively using magic instead of merely practising it. And although she would never say so aloud, her leg would be better after a week of proper feeding and exercise. "Seven days from now, I will begin lessons with the swordmaster."

"So be it," Liselle told her, looking relieved if not exactly pleased. "Thank you."

"On that happy note," Jamus said, "I think I'll take my leave."

He stood up, then reached for the hat that was sitting on the bench next to him. Its black brim was platter-sized, its crown was a slanted peak. A long blue feather protruded from the band. As he set it on his head, he turned to Lathwi and grinned.

"What do you think of my new hat?" he asked.

"It is the most ridiculous thing I have ever seen," she replied.

"I said the same thing," Liselle said. "The hatter who made it couldn't get any self-respecting woman to buy it and so sold it to him instead."

Lathwi sucked in a scandalized breath. "You traded gold for that?"

"I should've known better than to solicit an opinion on fashion from a woman who lives to wear mail," he replied with a disgusted shake of his now be-feathered head.

"Indeed," Liselle commented slyly. "Your mode of dress is infinitely more practical."

He clamped his hands to his breast as if to stopper the wound that he had just been dealt. "Sometimes I wonder why I take the trouble to visit with either of you."

"You like a captive audience," Liselle scoffed.

"Ah, but it is I who am your prisoner," he said then. "And your cruel remarks have cut me to the quick. Will you not ease my pain with a kiss?"

To his resounding surprise, she got up from her seat and did just that. It was a sweet little kiss that barely grazed the corner of his mouth, but even so, it changed his blood to honey and music. He thought to pull her close and return the sweetness then, but she had already distanced herself again.

"Get yourself going, milord D'Arques," she said, biting back a smile as she gestured toward the door. "Lathwi and I have work to do."

Too dazed to do anything else, he did as he was told and then drifted in the general direction of the garrison. Every time he remembered that lopsided little kiss, he broke into a silly grin and a small cold sweat, for he had not touched his lips to any woman since the day he had resolved to change his philandering ways.

Abstaining was much more difficult that he'd imagined it would be. There was temptation everywhere: on the streets and at the bazaar, on the job and even in the tavern where he sometimes took his meals. Some were obvious whores with eyes only for his wallet's bulge, but most were just women in need of a man's touch. His touch, it seemed. A busty schoolgirl, a raw-boned seamstress, even that black-haired veil-dancer—they had all made themselves blatantly available to him. And oh, that devil of a veil-dancer! He had had to pinch himself in a very soft spot to turn her down.

Still, he had no lasting regrets. Liselle's unexpected kiss had made all of his sacrifices seem worthwhile. He was in love with the heart-faced sorceress—he could admit that now. And today, she had given him cause to believe that she might love him just a little bit, too. The possibility made him giddy.

He strolled into the arms of Compara's sprawling bazaar then. A host of smells assaulted his nose: soured sweat and roasted meat; raw fish, exotic spices and sour wine. Voices hailed him from every direction.

"Over here, good sir! I've got fresh apples today!"

"You! With the hat! Come hither and try my cheese."

"Milord! Come and buy one of my looking-glasses for your lady."

As he wound his way through the ever-shifting maze of carts, stalls and milling bodies, the back of his neck began to prickle. Warned by this soldierly sixth sense, he paused as if to admire a vendor's collection of shoddy crockery and then casually glanced behind him. After taking careful note of the faces he saw there, he headed for the butcher's stall. There, as he waited for service, his nape tingled again. He half-turned, but saw no familiar faces. And before he could conduct a more thorough survey, the butcher's blood-stained wife accosted him. They exchanged a few ribald pleasantries, haggled over the price of a haunch of beef. and then finally made arrangements for its delivery. But while he maintained a bantering tone throughout their conversation, any pleasure he might've derived from it was marred by the knowledge that someone was following him. He had a fair guess as to who it was, too.

The Rogue.

Jamus rolled the name around in his mouth like a chip of rancid candy. Who else could it be? He had no enemies other than an occasional outraged father or brother or husband; and these days, that lot had no reason to be tiptoing after him. But as Liselle's friend, and as an officer sworn to bring her nephew's murderer to justice, this Rogue would've had to take an interest in his whereabouts sooner or later.

And obviously, that time had come.

He had mixed feelings about that. On the one hand, his investigation was nearly at a standstill with nothing to show for its efforts. If he could lure that bastard or one of his henchmen out into the open, then it was no less than his duty to play the hapless decoy. On the other hand, there was more to life than duty. He hadn't forgotten what had been done to Pieter; and it was not a fate he relished for himself.

His nape bristled again. A chill skated down his spine, then gave way to annoyance. He was tempted to duck into the nearest alley and then pounce as his shadow came skulking by. That would put an end to this nerve-fraying game! That would make his back much safer, too. He ground the impulse between his teeth. Bait did not pounce; it dangled.

He continued toward the garrison then. And although his sixth sense didn't itch again, the space between his shoulder blades ached every step of the way.

"I know we've had this discussion before," Liselle said, as she watched Lathwi eat, "but I'll broach it again just in case you're too proud to say you've changed your mind."

"Won't you let me cook that for you?"

"No," Lathwi replied. Out of respect for the sorceress' ridiculous sensibilities, she'd consented to eat from a plate with her not-claw, but that was as far as she was willing to go. "You eat your food your way, I will eat my food my way."

Liselle gave the tiny beef roast that she'd spitted for herself a fretful turn, then blurted, "But that much raw meat can't possibly be good for you!"

The hearth-fire popped then—a cheery exclamation. The sorceress smiled and added, "See? Even Fire thinks you ought to cook your meat."

Lathwi rolled her eyes. The woman had known Fire's Name for three days now, and already she claimed to understand all its thoughts and moods. Not even The Learned One herself was daring enough to make such a boast, and she had been studying Fire for almost two centuries!

Ah, Taziem! How good it would be to see the she-dragon again. An image of black magnificence welled up in her mind, but it was not the same as the real thing.

Her plate was empty now; and for the moment, her hunger was slaked. She might have gone upstairs then to nap in the skylight's warmth and dream of her mother, but before she had a chance to act on the urge, Liselle snagged her attention.

"I've done some more thinking about the warding ritual," she said, "and it still looks as though it could work. So as soon as you're done with lunch, I want you to find yourself a stone."

"How big?" Lathwi asked.

"Thumb-sized, maybe a little larger," Liselle replied, improvising as she went along. "You'll be wearing it around your neck eventually, so it can't be too large."

"There are plenty of pebbles out in the courtyard," she said, and then jumped to her feet. "I will go and get one."

"No. Sit down. None of those will do."

"Why?" she demanded, as she resumed her seat.

"Those stones have stood in the shadows of my magic much too long. They bear my essence, not yours. You must find a piece of rock that has been close to no power but your own. That diamond perhaps."

Lathwi rejected the suggestion immediately. Her only diamond was already auspicious in its own right. So was the stone that she'd stolen from Taziem. She would have to find another elsewhere.

But where?

Her thoughts circled back to Taziem. The she-dragon's outer caves were littered with rocks of every shape and size. Some of them—perhaps the scrabble that lined the corners of her old sleeping niche—might've absorbed some of her power. She delved through her memory for the appropriate image, then held it up to her mind's eye. As she did so, another gust of longing blew through her.

"I know of a place where I might find such a stone," she said, there now in all but the flesh. "But it is far away from here."

"Distance isn't a problem so long as you have a clear image with which to work," Liselle reminded her.

"The image is clear," came Lathwi's dreamy reassurance. "As clear as a mountain lake. I feel as though I could step through it and be there."

She blinked as if stung by the thought, then focussed her suddenly lively gaze on Liselle. "Is that possible? Might I not use that image to translocate myself?"

"I'm afraid not," the sorceress replied. "No one can maintain a link and traverse it at the same time. The link would collapse, and its maker would be trapped in that void forevermore."

Lathwi contemplated the explanation for a long moment, intent on finding a loophole through which she could squeeze. Failing that, she dismissed her disappointment with a shrug. Taziem would not have been pleased to see her anyway.

"What must I do once I have this stone?" she asked then.

"You'll have to use magic to empower it," Liselle told her, "and that will require a ritual. I know that may sound ominous, but it's simply a work of sorcery that has more than one step to it. A more direct approach would cause the stone to shatter."

"Does that make sense to you?"

"It does," Lathwi replied. "When can I start?"

Liselle shrugged. "As soon as you find a stone."

Lathwi got up and headed for the laboratory.

A black-hided nightmare prowled the darkened catacombs with a predator's deadly grace. Its cat-like eyes were red, the colour of resentment. It was naj, it fumed to itself, an exalted member of the ruling class. Yet Malcolm Blackheart treated it no better than a common drudge.

Do this. Do that. Do it and be quick.

A rat scuttled across its path. With a silent snarl, it impaled the rodent with one of its talons and flicked it into its maw. As it crushed the tiny bones between its teeth into a paste, it imagined The Blackheart in their stead. He was a fool and an upstart; and some day, it meant to tear his heart from his chest and eat it while he watched!

But not yet, it thought, slowly retracting its overeager claws. And not as long as the last talisman remained in The Recluse's possession. For although the naj would rather bite off its tongue than admit this aloud, it knew it couldn't get past her defences without the cripple's help. Therefore, it would bide its time, enduring all insults to its self and its caste, until an opportunity arose. Then it would seize the moment with both hands and wring a new hierarchy into being.

The stench of human sorcery guided it toward a stretch of seemingly solid rock. As it passed through this warded facade and into the torchlit passageway beyond, an unpleasant itch flared in its mind. That was The Blackheart's touch, a fleeting probe to ascertain his would-be caller's identity—no one who entered his stronghold was exempt from it. Yet in spite of that forewarning, the odious little man let several minutes slip by before he deigned to join the demon lordling in the central chamber. The naj sharpened its teeth on the bones of this latest insult, but said nothing.

"So," Malcolm said, when he had settled himself on his self-styled throne. "You have a report for me."

"Yes."

His cloven lip curled upward, a parody of mirth. "Mind your manners, naj," he said, "or you'll find yourself wading in your own shit until the end of time."

"Yes, Master," it said then, sneering the title into an obscure obscenity.

"Very well then," he said, "I'll hear what you have to say. Begin with any news which might pertain to our dear, reclusive Lathwi."

"That one continues to cower within her sanctuary," the naj replied, "unseen and unheard. But I saw the other woman this morning."

"What woman was that?" He already knew the answer, but wanted to see how much or how little the naj would divulge.

"The big one, the one who came to Compara with Lathwi's kinsman," it replied. "Fyjjyx thought she'd been beaten to death, but obviously Fyjjyx was wrong. When I saw her this evening, she appeared quite healthy."

"And what does our recluse want with this woman?"

"I do not know. She was dealing with a delivery boy when I saw her, so perhaps she is a servant of sorts."

"A plausible guess," he granted. "Has your fair-haired fop said anything that might substantiate this theory?"

"I have not yet been able to seduce any information out of him," it admitted, and then scoured the floor at its feet with a scowl.

Malcolm loosed a derisive hoot. "What's this—another mortal capable of resisting your charms? Maybe you're losing your touch, naj. Maybe I should put Fyjjyx on his tail for a while. It might succeed where you've failed."

The insult outraged the naj. Fyjjyx was barely capable of shaping a thought, never mind a form that any human would find enticing. How dare that ugly lump of a man even suggest that a drudge might be better than a naj? Yet even as it raged to itself, it could not help but remember the numerous times that it had approached the golden one in alluring guise only to be rebuffed.

"I do not understand," it growled, venting its pent-up frustration. "The men in his service refer to him as a great lover of women. Yet he has declined every opportunity I have created for him thus far."

"Why don't you just rape him?"

"My magic is weak on this plane. I will not be able to charm his secrets from him if he is less than fully receptive to me."

"Then use some other method to find out what he knows," Malcolm said.

The suggestion both irritated and alarmed the naj. To give up now was to concede defeat to a mere mortal; and that was one humiliation it did not mean to tolerate. The golden one was the demon lordling's chosen quarry. It would not be satisfied until he had yielded heart and soul.

"What would you have me do instead?" it asked, in its most reasonable tone. "He does not take his colleagues into his confidence—I know, I have seduced several of them with that possibility in mind."

"How industrious of you," Malcolm purred. "But maybe he commits his thoughts to the written word instead."

"I would not know. I cannot read."

"I can," he said slyly. "So maybe you should be trying to steal his papers instead of his heart."

"I will do so if that is your desire," the naj replied, taking care not to betray its own thoughts. "But it seems a rather desperate course to pursue at this point in time. As soon as he discovers that his scribblings are gone, he will realize that someone is spying on him and tighten his guard. If he is sufficiently unnerved, he might even feel compelled to abandon his association with The Recluse and then he will be of no use to you at all.

"Is that prospect worth a few papers of indeterminate value?"

Malcolm pressed his forefingers into a steeple on which he then rested his chin. The demon's argument made perfect sense, which was exactly why he suspected it. Was it trying to worm its way into his good graces? Or to keep some secret out of his hands? He debated the matter for a moment, then shrugged it aside.

"Very well, naj," he decreed. "I'll leave the papers for another time. But," he added, just so the demon wouldn't think it had prevailed over him, "I trust you understand that my patience is not unlimited. If you continue to disappoint, I will feed you to the Dark One."

"I understand," it said. "You will not be disappointed."

"Make sure of it," he warned, and then abruptly moved on to other matters. "Has anyone found The Curra-Chewer yet?"

"No, Master," it replied, hoping to placate the cripple into forgetting his threat to feed it to The Queen of Death. Even a naj could fear that with no shame. "They come close at times only to be thwarted by the illusion which guards her sanctuary."

"How tiresome," Malcolm grumbled. "If they do not solve that pathetic little riddle sometime soon, I shall be forced to solve it for them.

"Nevertheless, tell Fyjjyx to maintain its watch on her. If she tries to bolt again, it is only to scare her back into her hole. And if The Recluse's dullards look as though they might finally stumble on to her sanctuary, it is to inform me straight away.

"Is that clear, naj?"

"It is."

"Then get out of here. I need to get some sleep."

The demon lordling took its leave without another word or a backward glance. But as it headed back toward the main tunnel, it fumed to itself: do this. Do that. Someday, the cripple was going to pay.

The week passed. Within that scant span of time, Lathwi had translocated a suitable stone from Taziem's cave, affixed it to a chain of her own braided hair and then polished it to a dull sheen with drops of her bright red blood. Now, on the eve of her first man-fighting lesson, she was ready to invest it with power.

She and Liselle were in the laboratory now, chalking the last of their preparations onto the floor. Earlier on in the week, Liselle had realized that she could use personal wards, too, so they were going to perform duplicate rituals, side by side. The sorceress fingered the stone that she had prepared for herself. An unimposing chunk of blood-buffed granite, it represented hope nonetheless. For if this experiment worked, she would finally be able to leave her sanctuary without fear of being bushwhacked. Armed with this newfound freedom, she could then act on Lathwi's advice and hunt her enemy down.

Oh, what a coup that would be!

Lathwi shared Liselle's excitement about the impending ritual, but her reasons were more immediate than its eventual outcome. She was going to work real magic today! She closed the last of her red-chalked circles, then switched to a shard of white chalk and sketched an eight-sided star two steps due south of her three concentric rings. When she was done, she looked to Liselle. The sorceress set her stone in the center of the smallest circle and then took a stand within the star. Lathwi did likewise.

"We will start by constructing Spheres of Power around our stones, as we discussed," Liselle said then. "Remember: raise the smallest sphere first; and maintain control of your Constructs at all times.

"Good luck, and may The Dreamer bless us with success."

Lathwi cleared her mind of extraneous thoughts and then turned her attention to the diagram. Imagining the innermost circle as an empty gas bladder, she puffed one breath of Will into it, then another and another. The circle shimmered like the horizon at dawn and began to swell. As it expanded, the stone floated up from the floor to mark its new center. She let it grow until it was full-blown, then immediately started to infuse it with her power. The sudden outpouring of energy made her giddy.

The second sphere was twice again the size of the first one. So was its capacity for power. As she filled it up, it drained the giddiness right out of her and left her craving a nap. She dismissed that urge with a scowl and doggedly moved on to the third circle. Constructing it was easy enough, for despite its larger size, it required no additional Will-power to inflate. But its empowering was sheer torture. Less than a third of the way through, she was tired to the bone; at the halfway mark, her vision started to turn blurry. She gritted her teeth and clenched her fists, wringing energy from caches that she didn't know she had. The sphere swallowed it all up and demanded more. Out of desperation, she then called upon the only source of power she had left: her Name. A heartbeat later, the third sphere was full.

She turned to Liselle then. The sorceress looked as bad as Lathwi felt. Her skin was grey and textureless except for the bags of skin that hung like thickened bruises beneath her eyes; and her shoulders drooped like blades of grass that had just been stepped on. Nevertheless, her spheres were intact, one within the other, and she was ready to move on.

"Now we must activate the star," she said, in a voice as fragile as gossamer. "This will sustain our bodies while our thoughts are elsewhere."

Lathwi wasn't exactly sure what that last bit meant, but she raised a slumberous scion of her Will and cast it at the octagon beneath her feet just the same. An eight-sided tower of radiant white light flared up from the ground then; and as it rushed past her, it lifted her from her feet and suspended her in mid-air as if she were a fly caught in a spider's web. She fought against its grip at first—an instinctive bid for freedom. But as soon as she realized that she was struggling for the dubious privilege of bearing her own weight, she gave up and allowed herself to be supported.

A moment later, Liselle's disembodied voice came sifting through the column to nestle in her ears.

"Now we have come to the final stage of the ritual," she murmured. "In order to accomplish it, you must first imagine yourself in the center of your stone and then slowly draw the surrounding spheres inward. The waves of incoming power must infuse the stone through and through; none of it must be lost or absorbed by you. This will become harder to manage as the stone approaches its saturation point, but you must persevere until every last bit of power has been sealed within your talisman.

"Proceed slowly, and with care."

Liselle's caveat faded into silence, a signal for Lathwi to begin. She resolutely plunged her imaginary self into the stone's core. Within the span of a dragon's blink, her world became a porous grey blur.

Encouraged by this little success, she reached out with her Will and tapped the first sphere. Its contents spilled forth like a high tide. The stone absorbed the first series of waves instantly. Then, as its initial thirst grew slaked, it began to drink slower; then slower still. Meanwhile, she was hard-pressed to keep the rest of the sphere's power from flooding away. Now she understood why Liselle had warned her to take care. Like water, power was hard to control when it was not contained.

Fortunately, the first sphere ran dry then, and no power was lost.

Wiser for her mistake, she broached the second sphere in a different way, creating a tiny aperture whose flow could be regulated with a thought. But while this approach did indeed restrict the influx of power, it also sired a new, unforeseen problem: pressure. For if the first sphere's contents were a glad tide, then the second's were storm-driven combers. They pounded against the walls of her Will, demanding release, and when she refused all but a trickle, they punished her for it. The spaces behind her eyeballs began to throb; her eardrums began to quiver. In the meantime, the stone drank at an ever more leisurely pace; and its once porous surface was turning slick as well as potent.

By the time she had siphoned the last drop of power from the second sphere, she felt like a rag that had been squeezed through a wringer once too often. Her thoughts were frayed; her Will, limp. She eyed the stone's energized alluvium with mixture of envy and longing, but sternly rejected the urge to filch a taste for herself. Liselle had said she must not, so she would not.

An instant later she tapped the third sphere, she wished that she had not, for the resulting pressure was titanic. It threatened to squash her Will and come rampaging forth in one vast and ruinous spurt. She staved off a rare moment's panic and then moulded her world into a solitary thought: maintain! Her eyeballs bulged in their sockets. Blood fountained from her nose. Her stomach contracted, threatening upheaval, and the oxygen in her lungs turned to semi-molten lead. But she maintained until the stone had swallowed its fill, and until the third sphere was no more. Then, finally daring to shift her Will, she sealed the now empowered amulet with her Name.

The next thing Lathwi knew, she was falling—out of the stone and back into her body. The last thing she saw before succumbing to sleep was the floor rushing up to meet her.

CHAPTER 15

Lathwi stirred, roused to sluggish semi-consciousness by the subliminal urgings of her bladder. At first, she thought she was back in Taziem's caves because the pillow beneath her cheek was cool stone, but then she saw Liselle sprawled in an insensate heap nearby and the veils which shrouded her memory parted. Ah, yes—she was in the laboratory. She had passed out last night after eking through the ritual. That had been an interesting experience, but not one that she would care to repeat. She fetched the stone from the now powerless diagram and fastened it around her neck. In spite of all that it had been through, it still looked and felt like an ordinary chunk of granite. She shrugged, then headed for the water closet.

She was heading into the kitchen for a quick bite to eat when a knock sounded at the door. Her appetites shifted like a windblown fire. She hastened to let Jamus in.

"Morning, Lathwi," he said, as he came ambling over the threshold. "Are you ready—" He stopped dead in his tracks and did a double-take. "Good Goddess! What happened to you? Have you been out brawling already?" Another thought hit him then. The roses in his cheeks went suddenly pale. "Where's Liselle? Is she—"

"Liselle is asleep," Lathwi replied flatly. "And yes, I am ready."

"Then why do you have dried blood all over your face?"

There was blood on her face? She brushed her cheeks and upper lip with the back of her hand. A crystalline flurry of ochre flakes went fluttering toward the floor. She recalled an unbearable pressure then and a geysering nose.

"It is nothing." She scrubbed the rest of the flakes away. "Let us go."

As soon as Lathwi cleared the courtyard, she broke into an easy run. It was a pleasant morning, just cool enough to be invigorating, and she was in a mood to exert herself. She raced up the cul-de-sac, then down the next street and toward the stable. To her rear, she heard leather shod Jamus falling farther and farther behind. She slowed down, for she needed him to show her the way to the garrison, then scrabbled to an abrupt halt as the stone at the base of her throat emitted a spine-tingling pulse. A moment later, Jamus came huffing to a stop alongside of her. He was holding his hat on his head with one hand, and his sword to his hip with the other. She was absently scratching her breastbone and staring at nothing at all.

"Feeling our oats today, are we?" he asked dryly, trying not to seem as winded as he felt. She continued to frown and rub at her sternum. "Are you unwell?" he asked then. "We can go back to the house if you want."

"No," she replied then. "I am well. A strange feeling overtook me for a moment, but it is gone now."

"Good," he said, and then started down the street again at a brisk but comfortable pace. "Icky doesn't have a lot of patience for people who disrupt his schedule."

"What is an Icky?" she wondered.

"Icky is the swordmaster you'll be studying with," he explained, his tone waxing affectionate. "But don't let him hear you call him that, or he'll string the both of us up by our thumbs. His proper name is Pawl."

Then, although Lathwi did not prompt him to, he went on. "We grew up together," he said. "I call him Icky because that was what his little sister always said when he came home from a hard day of training and kissed her tender cheek. Needless to say, she didn't have the same reaction to my kisses."

They were treading on the bazaar's outer fringes now. Even at this early hour, it was teeming with people, animals and goods. Jamus was so used to this sprawling marketplace, he rarely gave it a second thought anymore. Lathwi, however, was seeing it for the first time; and she was revolted. Its multitude of clashing sights and sounds and smells struck her as obscene; and the concentration of red-blooded bodies ached her head like not-water. She tried hard not to breath as she waded through this human infestation. Then Jamus pointed out the garrison and she loosed a glad shriek.

"You're late!" a voice boomed, as they strode into the garrison's great, dusty courtyard.

A tall, sun-bronzed man clad in a plain brown jerkin and drawstring trousers broke away from a cluster of soldiers and came walking toward them. He carried himself with confidence and grace. His frown was disapproving.

"Did you get lost or something?" he asked, upon joining them. "I expected you here at exactly seven bells."

"Pawlo, you mangy dog, you know very well that we were late simply to spite you and your tyrannical schedule," Jamus replied. While he was no runt by human standards, he seemed small in the other man's shadow—small, dollish and garishly overdressed. "And do stop glowering like that. You'll have Lathwi here thinking that you're some kind of ogre."

"Oh?" Pawl folded his well-muscled and oft-scarred arms across his chest, then pivoted to face Lathwi. His eyes were sienna-brown like his plaited, waist-length hair. They shone with warning and challenge. "Does he speak truly, woman? Is that what you think?"

"No," she replied, simply because she did not know what an ogre was.

"Good." His gaze turned a degree less threatening, but no less direct. "You've obviously got more sense than Jamie. Not that that surprises me; headless chickens have more sense than he does.

"Now." The word was a command for complete attention. She granted it to him instantly. "Jamie tells me that you're interested in learning how to use a sword." She nodded. "He also tells me that you're something of a sorceress." Again, she replied with a nod. "If I take you as a student, it will be with the understanding that you do not call on your arcane powers to aid you during our sessions. Does that strike you as unreasonable?"

"No."

The succinctness of her answer seemed to satisfy some crucial doubt within him, for he praised her with a grunt and then turned back to Jamus. "I'll put her through a few paces and see how she goes. Meanwhile, it wouldn't hurt you to go a few rounds with yon recruits. You're looking as soft as a pile of fresh dog droppings these days."

"As a matter of fact," Jamus sniffed, "I came here with every intention of working out."

"Then get going! And leave that overpriced toad-sticker of yours with me. You know the rules: no edged steel on the exercise grounds. Don't worry," he added, as Jamus slung his sword-belt at him. "You'll get it back when you're ready to leave—if I don't take a fancy to it."

"You and Lathwi should get along famously," Jamus told him dryly, and then strode off to join the recruits.

"What's that supposed to mean?" Pawl asked.

Her only reply was a shrug.

His eyes narrowed into speculative slits. He knotted his hands behind his back, then began to pace a slow, tight circle around her. The long brown braid that parallelled his spine swayed to the meter of his measured steps.

"Jamie told me you took a bad beating recently. He said you were outnumbered at least six to one." He stepped behind her, then paused. His voice floated over her shoulder. "He also said you gutted one and brained a second before you were overcome." Now the swordmaster was on the move again, coming around to her right. "Do you have any comment so far?"

"Jamus talks a lot."

"That he does," Pawl chuckled, and then strolled around to stand before her again. The lines which characterized his weathered face were softer now, more accepting. "But in this instance," he said then, "he was right to do so."

His eyes skimmed across her face as if to take inventory of her scars. His mouth puckered at the corners as he viewed her latest acquisitions. "Southern handiwork," he commented, treating the words like gobbets of phlegm. "I'd recognize it anywhere. How is it that you didn't lose your nose as well?"

"I summoned Fire," Lathwi told him. "My attacker found it hard to hold onto a knife while his face was on fire."

Something like mirth tried to flare in his eyes, but he smothered it with a stern blink. "So you set a man on fire, eh? How resourceful. Does the memory trouble you at night? Do you suffer from fits of remorse or guilt?"

"I like my nose. Keeping it has caused me no regrets."

"Well spoken," he said. "Maybe there's a sword in your future after all." He began to pace back and forth in front of her. "I don't accept many women as students," he went on, "for they tend to be squeamish and sentimental. Such tender inclinations make them more dangerous to themselves than to anyone else."

His pacing carried him over to the sword-belt that Jamus had set aside. He snatched it up, then unsheathed the blade; it glinted in the morning light like a strip of glacial ice. He turned then, and lunged. The sword's point came to rest against the base of her nose. She looked down the length of shiny metal and squarely into the swordmaster's stern brown eyes. This was a test she did not intend to fail.

"I could drive this thing all the way through your head before you could stop me," he said, "and you'd be dead before you hit the ground. You do not flinch from that possibility, eh? Good. For if you are to carry a sword, then you must be prepared to kill or be killed every time you draw it.

"Do not mistake my words—I do not advocate murder. A wise swordsman does not unsheathe his blade unless he has no other choice. Unfortunately, such will ofttimes be the case. Then the swordsman must be like the steel in his hand: cold, uncaring, lethal. He'll neither ask for quarter nor give it.

"So. Knowing this, do you still wish to be my pupil?" When she made no attempt to answer him, he grinned and lowered the sword. "Smart move. Now you may speak without fear for your nose. What say you?"

She flashed him a sly half-smile. "I say I have had my first lesson from you already. Now it is you who must decide if I am worthy of learning more."

Approval sparked in his eyes. He returned Jamus' sword to its handsome leather sheath, then glanced at the group of recruits. It had broken down into two smaller sets, and the two were now fighting each other. Pawl watched the goings-on for a moment, then shouted.

"Nudge!"

A downy-cheeked youth separated himself from the melee and then stretched his gangly body into an eagerly attentive pose. "Yes, Captain?"

"Bring us a couple of those staves."

Lathwi's eyebrow arched at the unfamiliar word, then flattened again as the manling came trotting over with two crude wooden swords in tow. As he set them at Pawl's feet, he snuck a quick and curious glimpse at Lathwi.

"My thanks, Nudge," he said, and then gently gripped the boy by the shoulder. "I was watching you spar over there. A determined opponent would've pushed right your flimsy defense and gutted you. Ask milord Jamie to show you a proper parry. From what I saw of his form, he could use the review."

"Yessir," the manling replied, and went dashing off.

Pawl grabbed one of the staves, then motioned for Lathwi to take the other one. As she went to pick it up, he cracked her across the knuckles with the flat of his mock-sword.

"By the hilt, always by the hilt," he said sharply. "If that had been a real sword, you'd have sliced your fingers to the bone. And pay careful attention to the way you take hold of the hilt. Fold your hand around it like so, aligning your thumb with the sword's edge."

She did as she was told. He praised her with a curt nod and said, "Now, without realigning your fingers, tighten your grip. Not that tight, though! Your hand will cramp. That's right, gently. Now stand up straight and hold your stave out in front of you like this." He demonstrated. She copied his pose. "It doesn't feel like much, does it?"

That made her wonder if he too could peer into minds and pluck out thoughts.

"It will," he went on, with a knowing chuckle. "After a couple of hours or so, you'll start wondering when your arm's going to fall off. And real swords are even heavier. I've spent many a pain-ridden day wishing that I'd taken up a soft life like Jamie's."

Her gaze absently strayed toward Jamus then. Pawl gave her knuckles another sharp crack. "Never look elsewhere when there's someone standing in your face with a sword," he said. "Nine times out of ten, that someone will skewer you for your carelessness."

To emphasize his point, he stabbed the tip of his stave against her breastbone. The force behind the thrust sent her staggering back a step.

"And that brings us to your next lesson: stance. Your feet are too close together. The space between them should match the width of your shoulders. Good," he said, when she adjusted. "Now slide your left foot slightly forward."

She shifted. He cracked her on the shin. Pain shot up the length of her leg.

"You had best learn left from right in a hurry, woman," he told her. "Elsewise, your shins are going to be black and blue forever.

"That's better," he said, when she had conformed to his specifications. "Now bend your knees. Make sure both legs are bearing an equal amount of weight. No, that's not right, Your back leg is doing too much work." She shifted, but he was not satisfied. "You're still favouring the left leg. Is that the one that was broken?" She nodded. Pawl said, "Too bad," and knocked her feet out from under her with a casual swipe of his leg.

She landed on her back with a dusty thud. He stood over her like a conqueror and pressed the tip of his mock sword to her throat.

"Without a proper stance," he said, "you cannot achieve proper balance. And without proper balance, you cannot wield a sword and hope to survive. Now get up."

Streaming dust, she climbed back to her feet.

They spent the rest of the morning testing the limits of each other's patience. Lathwi's grew a little thin and sour as frustration mounted within her, but Pawl's never wavered. When she did well, he told her so. When she made a mistake, no matter how minor, he either knocked her to the ground or cracked her with his stave. Her body began to ache all over. Her mind grew limp with fatigue. She forgot her reasons for wanting to use a sword. She forgot where she was and who she was with and how she'd come to be here. The only things that she dared not forget were her Name and the instructions which Pawl was drubbing into her.

Finally, Lathwi struck a perfect stance and held it for what seemed like hours. Pawl paced a series of slow circles around her, then pried the stave from her throbbing hand.

"You did well," he said. "Come back tomorrow."

He strode off then, leaving her alone. Suspecting some sort of trick, she maintained her rigid pose.

"Don't worry," a familiar voice advised her. "He won't be back today."

She spun on her heel to find Jamus lounging against the wall. His presence there irritated her, for she had not seen him leave his group or retrieve the sword-belt which now hung around his hips again. And the fact that he was nowhere near as bedraggled as she felt did nothing to endear him to her, either.

"So," he said then. "What do you think of Pawl?"

She grunted, then started for the garrison's gates. Her leaden feet left welts in the courtyard's dust.

An instant after Lathwi dragged herself into the house, Liselle descended on her like an annoying little gnat. The sorceress' green eyes were now a frantic shade of grey; and agitation exaggerated her every move.

"Lathwi! Praise the Dreamer, you're back!" she babbled. "I can't tell you how worried I've been. You should've never left the house this morning."

"You knew that I meant to leave the house today," Lathwi reminded her, in a disapproving tone. She was tired and sore and impatient with the world. All she wanted to do was crawl upstairs and sleep away the aftereffects of swordplay. "You knew seven days ago. You also gave me reason to believe that you would not trouble me about it so long as I left with this amulet around my neck."

"But that's just it!" Liselle declared. "Something went wrong. The amulets don't work."

Lathwi frowned, remembering the pulse that had coursed through her earlier. "What makes you say that?"

"I spent the morning testing my stone. And the sad fact is, it only retained a fraction of the power that I put into it. I guess we should've used a better sealing spell. Don't be too disappointed, though. As soon as I modify the ritual, we'll try again."

The prospect of repeating that debilitating ritual left Lathwi cold. And she wasn't convinced that such a repetition was necessary, at least not in her case.

"You cannot conclude that my amulet is powerless simply because yours is," she asserted. "That is sloppy thinking."

"It is not," Liselle fired back. "We started out with the same kind of stones and performed the same ritual at the same time. It's only logical to assume that we achieved the same results."

"I dispute such logic."

A half-irritated, half-condescending smile tugged at the corners of Liselle's mouth. The idea of a novice like Lathwi outstripping an adept like herself was preposterous. Had the woman acquired such unswerving arrogance from the dragons who had fostered her? Or had she been born like that? In either case, a little demonstration seemed to be in order.

"All right then," she said, "let's go and put logic to the test."

Lathwi rolled her eyes, but followed after the sorceress just the same. The sooner they settled this controversy, the sooner she could go to sleep.

"This won't take long," Liselle promised, as they strode into the laboratory. "And all you have to do is stand in the center of the room and let your thoughts wander. Don't watch me, don't try to guess what I'm doing, and don't summon your Will."

At last, Lathwi thought: a set of instructions after her own heart. She trudged over to her appointed spot and closed her eyes. A moment later, she began to doze off. Meanwhile, Liselle tried to decide on an appropriate curse. It couldn't be lethal or overly vicious, for her aim was to teach, not to hurt. But it could not be too subtle or slow-acting, either, for then her cheeky apprentice would probably miss the point. What she needed was something nasty but essentially harmless. Something like...

Hives.

A devilish grin accompanied the idea. It was perfect, absolutely perfect. A moment or two of unbearable itching was all it would take to explode Lathwi's mistaken sense of invulnerability. So she invoked the spell and then cast it at her apprentice. The big woman started as if she had been prodded in her dreams, but continued to cat-nap on her feet. Liselle scowled, then boosted the curse's intensity. Again, Lathwi's only reaction was a dreamy nod.

"Lathwi?" Liselle whispered then. "Are you still awake?" When Lathwi nodded, she asked, "How do you feel?"

"Sssleepy," came Lathwi's sluggish reply.

"Doesn't your skin itch?"

"No."

Liselle scowled, then flung a different curse at Lathwi. But Lathwi didn't succumb to a fit of uncontrollable laughter like she should have. All she did was scratch at her sternum and frown like a baby in need of burping. Disbelief whipped through Liselle then, leaving welts of fury in its wake. She stormed over to Lathwi and seized her by the shoulders. The glaring difference in their sizes stoked her rage.

"What did you do that I did not?" she demanded, shaking Lathwi again and again as if hoping to jar the secret loose.

Such a rude awakening left Lathwi in a daze. Why was Liselle shaking her? And why did she look as if she had just swallowed a mouthful of broken glass? She distanced the fey, red-faced woman away with a weary shove, then held her at bay with an outstretched arm.

"What is troubling you?" she asked.

"It's your accursed amulet," Liselle grated.

"What about it?"

"It works, damn you! It works when mine does not. What did you do differently?"

The rancour in the tiny woman's tone compounded Lathwi's confusion. Why should Liselle be unhappy about the amulet's competence? Was that not what they had sought to ascertain?

"I did nothing different," she stated calmly. "I recall your lesson on unsupervised experimentation very well."

"But you must've done something," Liselle insisted, more composed now but no less emphatic. "Otherwise, we would have gotten the same results. Think back. Did you do anything I didn't tell you to—anything at all? I won't punish you for it," she promised, when Lathwi continued to balk. "I simply need to know so I can do it, too. Please. Try to remember. It's important."

Although she was sure it would serve no useful purpose, Lathwi reviewed her memories once again. She watched herself construct the spheres, then condense them via the star. She remembered the pressure and the strain; the fatigue and the pain. And just when she thought she'd recalled every detail, she stumbled upon one thing more.

"My Name," she murmured. "I used it once to empower the stone and then again to seal it."

"I don't understand," Liselle said then. "Your name has no power."

"My use-name has no power," Lathwi corrected her. "But my secret

Name, the Name that embodies all that I am and all that I will ever be, is powerful beyond measure. That is the magic of Names. And that is why it is a secret."

"Oh," Liselle said, and then raised hopeful, humble eyes to her apprentice. "Could you perhaps tell me what my secret Name is?"

"If you do not know it," Lathwi replied, "how would I?"

Liselle's hopes sank like a lead weight in black water. It was cruel, too cruel. She had the key to her freedom now, and still could not use it! What was her Name? Where was it hiding? If trees and fires and dragons had Names, surely she had one, too. She ransacked the folds of her mind in search of it, but found nothing except silence. Her failure dropped her to her knees; and there, she began to cry.

Moments later, an awkward hand gripped the round of her shoulder. There was an abiding weariness in that clasp, and a dollop of impatience, too; but the underlying sentiment was one of bewilderment and concern.

"What troubles you now?" Lathwi asked.

"My Name," Liselle replied, choking the bitter words past her tears. "I do not know my Name."

Lathwi did not try to console her—there was no solace for some things. So she left the sorceress to her grief and went upstairs to sleep.

Lathwi was sprawled on her butt in the garrison's dusty courtyard. Her sword-arm was numb. Her leg itched. And her ears were still ringing from the clout to the head that she'd received a moment ago.

"Get up," Pawl told her then. "And this time, remember to keep your guard up."

He was teaching her the five basic sword strokes today: sweep, parry, lunge, reverse, chop. She had kept up with him at the start of the lesson, but now, several hours later, she was tired and he was still relentless.

"Watch me, not the sword," he said, and then dealt her a blow to the hip. "Never give your opponent an opening he can use."

He drilled her until she could not see for the sweat in her eyes, until she barely had the strength to lift her feet. She refused to give in to her weaknesses, though. As long as Pawl persevered, so would she. She clung to the thought with a dragon's stubborn pride. And finally, the lesson came to a close.

"That's all for today," Pawl told her. "Come back again tomorrow."

She handed over her stave without a word, then turned on her heel and went shuffling homeward. She did not see Pawl's look of wonder, or hear his admiring sigh.

Liselle was in the laboratory when Lathwi returned to the house, and when she finally emerged several hours later, she looked as haggard as a woman with twice her years. She shambled into the kitchen where Lathwi was feeding, then all but collapsed into her rocking chair. The flesh beneath her eyes was dark and swollen; the folds of skin which bracketed her mouth looked like ridges of dried paste. Her unwholesome appearance surprised Lathwi—so much so that she impulsively offered the sorceress her still-heaping plate of meat.

"Eat," she said. "It will give you strength."

"I'm not hungry," the sorceress replied, in a monotone fraught with bitter grief. "And I have no wish to nourish a failure."

Lathwi shrugged, then retracted her plate and began to feed again. As she ate, she contemplated Liselle's cryptic statement. How did one nourish a failure? Unable to solve the riddle on her own, she finally posed the question aloud.

"What is this failure you mentioned?"

Resentment blazed in Liselle's blood-shot eyes only to be smothered by shame and self-disgust. She buried her face in the cradle of her arms, then croaked a single word.

"What was that?"

Lathwi pressed. "I did not hear you."

"Me!" the sorceress blurted then. "I'm the failure! Do you want to hear it again? Me, me, me."

"I do not understand."

"Of course you don't!" Liselle grated. "How could you? Everything comes so damn easy for you: magic, sword-fighting, even health! You're big and strong and maddeningly fearless; and you've got a Name that permits you to come and go as you please. What would you know about failure?

"Meanwhile, I'm trapped in this house with no way out—all my attempts to escape have failed. I have an enemy whom I cannot comprehend; a possible ally whom I cannot find; and an apprentice whom I cannot hope to equal.

"Tell me, Lathwi: are you beginning to understand yet?"

Lathwi polished off the last scrap of meat on her plate, then scrubbed her mouth with the back of her hand and belched loudly. "I understand," she replied. "You are feeling sorry for yourself again."

At that, Liselle sat straight up and glared at her. The ravels of angry veins in her eyes looked like stabs of bloody lightning. "One of these days," she warned, "you're going to push me too far."

"And then what will you do?" Lathwi jeered. "Curse me? Kill me? Cast me out? More likely, you will plague me with more of your useless tears."

The sorceress sucked in an outraged breath, but before she could convert it into a vituperative blast, Lathwi went on.

"You say I have never experienced failure and so cannot understand it. You are wrong on both counts; and I have the scars to prove it. But I do not choose to cherish my defeats as you do. Instead, I either try again or move on.

"Choice is the essence of failure, Liselle. And life is full of choices. I understand and accept that. Can you say the same?"

Having said all that she wanted to say, she then pushed to her feet and headed for the loft. Liselle was glad to see her go. She needed some time alone—time to think and then to choose.

When Jamus arrived at Liselle's house the next morning, he was disappointed to find only Lathwi waiting for him. It had been two days since he had last seen the sorceress. He missed her face and incisive wit, her quiet brand of courage and the sparks that danced between them when they conversed. He was afraid that she might be avoiding him.

"Is she well?" he asked Lathwi, as they headed for the garrison.

"She was when I last saw her," Lathwi replied, with her usual shrug.

"Is she mad at me?"

"I do not know if she is mad at you, Jamus. The last time I saw her, she was mad at me."

That bit of news made him feel much better. As long as he was still in Liselle's good graces, he could bear the ache of not seeing her.

He and Lathwi walked on in companionable silence for a time. Then, as they neared the outskirts of the bazaar, the back of his neck bristled. He swore softly, but with gusto.

"What ails you?" Lathwi asked him.

"Someone's following me," he replied, in an undertone. "Who?"

"I don't know."

How fun! As younglings, she and Shoq had stalked each other for hours without end. It had been an exciting game, one which had demanded cunning as well as stealth. Playing it with a complete stranger was a challenge which she could not resist. She glanced to the left, and then to the right. There were people everywhere, any one of whom could be Jamus' shadow. The trick would be to isolate him from the rest of the herd.

"Head for that alley," she said, directing him toward the far side of the bazaar with a seemingly innocent thrust of her chin.

Confusion eddied through his mind, then turned into a gyre of surprise as he realized that she meant to help him. Then, as he thought about it, he supposed that he shouldn't be that astonished; after all, she'd come to his rescue once already. And while he knew her too well to believe that she was acting strictly on his behalf, he was suddenly grateful to her just the same.

She led him deep into the alley's trashy shadows, then pulled him into an alcove and started to strip off his outer garments. He loosed a garbled protest, contesting a spate of spontaneous fantasies as well as her unexpected forwardness, then broke into a grin as she placed his hat on her own head. Of course! They were of a similar height and build; with the right kind of camouflage, she could easily pass as his double from the rear. He was keen to collaborate now, so he removed his sword-belt and buckled it about her boyish hips. Then he draped his cloak around her shoulders. To perfect the guise, he gave the hat on her head a rakish tilt.

"My," he clucked, as he admired his handiwork. "What a dashing figure I cut."

"I will go back to the bazaar now," she told him. "Wait here until I am well into the crowd, then return to the mouth of the alley and keep watch. As I move from stall to stall, take note of those who might follow."

"Be careful," he urged her. "This could be dangerous."

She grinned at the prospect, then started on her way. Her imitation of his walk dismayed him—surely he did not swagger that much!—but since she was already out of easy earshot, he held his tongue and settled back to wait.

Lathwi moved from stall to stall with predatory grace, disdaining all who got in her way. She was hunting, and her quarry was afoot. It was simply a matter of flushing it out.

A fruit vendor bawled at her like a bull-calf in search of its dam. A potter tried to sell her a cracked vase. She had no use for such wares and so moved on. The bazaar's reek was making her nose itch now, and the noise was giving her an ache between her ears, but she continued to wade through its bowels until a flash of reflected light snared her attention.

A sly smile curved across her mouth. Now there was a thing she could use!

She swaggered over to the stall where the looking-glass was being sold and demanded to see a piece. The proprietor gave the hairs on his fat black chin-mole a thoughtful twirl, then set an assortment of mirrors on the counter in front of her. She chose one at random, then held it up and pretended to admire herself. And as she angled the glass this way and that, she spied on the world behind her.

It was a trick she had learned from Liselle.

A profusion of people shifted into view and out again: a bearded old man with shifty eyes; a pregnant woman with a tall wicker basket balanced on her head; a trio of youngling thieves, one of whom had his hand around a pilgrim's purse. The pregnant woman reappeared—closer this time and without her basket. She glanced at Lathwi's cloaked back then. As she did so, her eyes happened to meet Lathwi's in the mirror.

At that instant, the stone around Lathwi's neck began to throb—a series of sharp, breath-stopping pulses which were fraught with urgency. Surprised by the outburst, Lathwi lost her focus on the mirror; and although she regained it a scant moment later, the woman was already gone. She whirled, ready to give chase, then hissed as a hand closed around her wrist.

"Did you wish to purchase that mirror, mister?" the man with the hairy mole inquired, and then directed her attention to the club which he was holding not quite out of sight. "If not, then kindly give it back."

She tossed the piece of forgotten glass in his general vicinity. As he hastened to snatch it out of the air, she went in search of her quarry.

But the pregnant woman was nowhere to be found.

How could someone that gravid have disappeared so fast? And why had the amulet reacted so strongly to her?

Distracted by these thoughts, she would have wandered right past the alleyway where Jamus was hiding if he hadn't reached out and hauled her into it. It took her a moment to recognize him—without his gaudy trappings, he seemed naked, almost plucked. Perhaps he thought so, too, for he wasted no time in reclaiming his clothes.

"So," he said, as he slipped back into his costume, "how did it go? I didn't catch sight of any suspicious characters on your tail. Did you?"

"I saw a woman," she replied, and then began to describe the image she had seen in the mirror. "She had dark skin and long black hair. Her eyes were red like fresh clay. She was slightly taller than Liselle, and extremely quick in spite of her pregnancy."

Dismay flooded across his face. "She was pregnant?"

"Very."

"Dreamer," he muttered to himself. "As if I didn't have enough problems." Then, as he searched his memory for a name to go with Lathwi's description, discrepancies began cropping up. This woman sounded somewhat familiar, true, but he could not give her a time or a place or even a face; and these were particulars he rarely forgot. And if she was indeed carrying his child, why did she not simply confront him? What was the point in just following him?

He heaved a troubled sigh, then turned his gaze back to Lathwi. "Many thanks for your help," he said, "but I fear it was a waste of time. The woman you saw can't possibly be the same person who's been following me—I would've noticed her by now. Besides, I've got this feeling that my shadow isn't the least bit feminine."

Her only reply was a shrug. If he chose to dismiss the woman, that was his business. As for herself—well, except for a few unanswered questions, her interests lay elsewhere. She would keep her eyes and ears open, but did not intend to actively pursue the matter further unless it began to pursue her first.

"This is the second time you've been late," Pawl grated, as he paced disapproving circles around her, "and this is the last time I'm going to tolerate it. If you can't be on time, don't come at all. Is that clear?"

She nodded. So long as she wanted what he had to offer, she would abide by his rules. It would not be easy, though; like most dragons, she did not usually notice the passing of time unless she was hungry.

"Good," he said, and then proceeded to lead her through a gruelling series of exercises and drills. He demanded more of her this morning— more skill, more speed, more stamina—and when she disappointed him, he struck her with his stave. She did not object to this treatment; indeed, she resolved to best him at his own game. He lunged. She parried. The fact that he was more skilled than her added to the challenge. He lunged again, then pulled a reverse. She hissed as his sword streaked past her guard and into her belly. An urge to tense jangled through her then, but she relaxed instead and let the rhythm of the exchange guide her. Sweep, lunge, chop; parry, parry, chop. And while she never came close to touching him, she did whittle down the number of times that she herself was touched.

This was fun!

By the time the day's lesson came to an end, she was wet with sweat and all but panting. As she strove to recover her wind, she studied Pawl out of the corner of her eye. Dots of sweat glimmered on his upper lip and his leather jerkin was a half-shade darker around his neck and armpits, but otherwise, he looked as if he had just walked in from the street. Every hair in his long brown braid was in place, his chest rose and fell at an easy pace. She admired him for his composure, and wouldn't consider herself accomplished until she could either duplicate his condition or reduce him to hers.

"You learn fast," he commented.

"I have no fondness for bruises," she replied.

He laughed—a rich, melodic sound that contrasted his rugged appearance. "Few people do, but that doesn't always make them able students."

"I will do better with more practice," she said, hoping to draw him into another round of sparring.

"I do not doubt it," he replied. "Come back tomorrow. Be on time."

With that, he reclaimed her stave and headed toward the group which harbored Jamus in its midst. Moments later, she heard him snap, "No, no, you're pulling yourself off-balance when you do it like that."

To her immense satisfaction, the criticism was followed by the sound of a body hitting the ground.

CHAPTER 16

Liselle was in the laboratory. She had been there since the crack of dawn and did not intend to leave again until she had procured the information which she so desperately needed. The pentagram was ready, as was the vision-melange. Now all she had to do was swallow the separation dust and get on with it.

As she raised the packet of fine powder to her lips, she thought about the sorcery she was getting ready to attempt. Dream-questing was not without its dangers. And she was not without her reservations. But she had to do it, she reminded herself. She had tried everything else. And if this didn't work…

No. She would not let such thoughts take root. Failure was not inevitable, merely a possibility; and one that needed to be considered only if it came to pass. She must be strong today. Strong and confident. She squared her shoulders like Lathwi would, then strode over to the pentagram and sat down in its center. The vision-melange was waiting for her there. It was a grayish paste with the consistency of freshly mashed brains. Her gorge rose at the sight of it, but she smeared her heels, the insides of her wrists and the back of her head with it nonetheless. When she was done, she wiped her hands clean with the hem of her skirt, then pitched the now-empty container clear of the diagram. It landed on the floor with a porcelain pop.

Her face was tingling now, and a feeling like music was loose in her veins. That was the separation dust, urging her to begin. She activated the star that would sustain her body throughout the ordeal, then constructed the sphere that would protect her from all powers but her own. Then she lay down, taking care to align her melanged extremities with the star's corresponding points.

The floor turned rubbery and began to undulate—a slow, sensual series of waves that clashed with the spinning in her head. Instinct urged her to close her eyes and thereby shut out the disturbing sensations, but that was exactly the wrong thing to do. Closed eyes would turn the dream-quest inward: and that would lead to nightmares, madness and death. So she forced her eyes wide-open and stared at a faraway cobweb. As she did so, her heartbeat slowed to a near standstill and her breath turned suddenly cold. Then rainbows began to slide in and out of the ceiling—grand ribbons of colour which whirled through the room like kites at the mercy of wind or a child's whimsy. Their exuberance enchanted her. She wanted to reach out and wrap them around her like blankets, mingle her spirit with theirs. A perilous desire. If she allowed the rainbows to seduce her into such a merger, she would lose control over their magic. They could take her anywhere, then abandon her. She kept her hands pressed to the floor. The rainbows paused for a moment as if acknowledging her mastery, then started to thrum and twang like gaudy sitar strings. One impossibly low note vibrated the marrow in her bones, then painted the world black. She tried to open her eyes, but could not.

Madness, she thought, and then giggled. The possibility did not seem so terrifying now.

Another note sounded. It lifted her up and out of the omnivorous bog that had engulfed her. Her vision returned as a psychedelic blur. She forced herself to concentrate on the colours then. As she did so, they settled like river sediment and the blurs acquired shape. She found herself staring down at her self. How small and doughy and unimposing she looked! And she had forgotten to comb her hair...

Liselle's dream-self began to drift toward the ceiling, which now appeared to her as shifting grey slab frosted with the golden glow of her own warding spells. An instant later, she was above and beyond the house, afloat on a scintillating cloud of her own power. Below her, Compara fanned out in all directions. The people who lived within its white walls were discernible only by their auras. She admired this view for a moment, then squared her insubstantial shoulders and bade the rainbows to take her to The Curra-Chewer.

The sky winked out, taking her with it, and when it next appeared, she was hovering over a strip of derelict buildings and decaying streets. The auras in this part of Compara were mostly bleak: diseased yellow and green-grey despair, mottled misery and the ice-blues of chronic lassitude. Pity churned through her, then curdled into a horrified sort of amazement. How could people live like this?

A flicker of gold caught her eye then, and her amazement gave way to elation. Only people of power bore gold in their auras. That had to have been the addict!

After her, she thought, and just like that, the rainbows whisked her past a row of squalid shanties and into the ruins of an old fire-gutted inn. There, she flitted, appropriately ghost-like, from one blackened corner to another in search of the fugitive sorceress. A familiar flicker of gold scurried down a set of fractured stairs. Liselle's dream-self made it to the bottom of the staircase just in time to see the warded silhouette of a door swing shut. That magical outline proved Liselle's earlier suspicion: the addict used illusion to fool her hunters.

Her bolthole was warded as well—Liselle could feel the power radiating from the brick in the walls. But while these wards were strong enough to keep a dream-quester at bay, they could never withstand a direct assault by someone as powerful as The Rogue. How then had the addict managed to survive all this time? Had she outran, outhid or outwitted him? None of those possibilities seemed probable, for he had dispatched at least three other sorcerers of greater skill already. Had he simply decided that an addict was beneath his notice?

She drifted back up the broken stairwell and out of the building, then paused to memorize the site so she could later describe it to Jamus. As she did so, she spied a shadow that was not a shadow. It was lurking in the rubble of the inn's collapsed porch. It wasn't easy to see, for it was as black as midnight and bore no perceptible aura; but it did possess some sort of power, just enough to give it a presence. And while she had no idea as to what it might be, she was sure it was here because of the curra-chewer.

Her immediate thought was to go rushing homeward so she could send a rescue party after the poor woman. But even as that impulse jangled through her, she ruthlessly suppressed it. If she went home now, she would lie trapped in her own body, helplessly insensate until the separation dust had run its full course; and that wouldn't do anybody any good. The Curra-Chewer was simply going to have to fend for herself for a few more hours, until Liselle had finished what she had set out to do.

Ah, but now that the moment was here, she didn't want to go forward. To seek out her enemy in his own stronghold was folly beyond measure or repair…

As soon as she gave thought to that dreadful plan, the rainbows slung her into a void. When she emerged an instant later, she found herself entombed in darkness. If she could have turned back then, she might have done so, for this place struck terror in the sensible part of her heart. But neither fear nor regrets could deliver her from a nightmare which she herself had instigated. The rainbows carried her mercilessly forward— down a series of passageways and up to a wall which shimmered like a sheet of gangrenous power. She gaped at the entrance to her enemy's stronghold for a long moment. It was awesome; appalling; and daunting to an extreme. There was no way she was going to be able to get past it. But as helpless as she was against such overwhelming might, she was not ready to give up and go home just yet. Maybe she could find a flaw in the wards that she could exploit later.

She extended her dream-senses only to learn that she was not alone in the dark. Something else was in the passageway, and it was heading right toward her! She froze like a rabbit caught in the open. A moment later, a not-shadow surged into view. The Rogue's wards flared at its approach, then spawned an opening. The not-shadow barged through it. Liselle snuck in on its tailwind. To her all-consuming wonder, her passing went unchallenged.

The not-shadow stormed down a darkened tunnel and into a chamber. Liselle followed at a cautious distance. At first, she only intended to hover outside the chamber and eavesdrop, but then, drawn by the pallid glow of torchlight and her own audacity, she stole all the way into the room.

"What are you doing here?" a voice demanded then.

Once again, Liselle's dream-self froze. In her ethereal heart, a place where only she and maybe the Dreamer had ears, she hoped and prayed for mercy.

"I did not summon you," the voice went on. "Nor are you due to report."

"Nevertheless, I have news," the not-shadow replied.

Silence descended upon the room only to be broken by an annoyed rustling and then a series of odd, almost syncopated footfalls. A moment later, The Rogue came limping into view. She could perceive very little of his superficial self—that limp, a stiff back, his lack of height and width. Everything else was hidden by the terrible magnificence of his aura. It was both black and golden—a small sun occluded by a bank of malignant storm-clouds. The sight of it made Liselle want to gag and weep.

Her nemesis limped his way over to a chair that had been carved into the far wall, then sat down and gestured for the not-shadow to approach. It did so boldly.

"Tell me this news of yours," The Rogue said then. "For your sake, it had better be worth my while."

"It will be," the not-shadow replied. "But you will not be pleased at first."

Annoyance infected The Rogue's aura. It looked like a smoldering bank of ochre coals. "I warn you, naj," he said. "I am in no mood for your clever tongue today. If you push me too far, you might not live to regret it."

"I meant no offense, Master," the naj hastened to say. "I merely wished to prepare you for the news."

"And that is—?" Malcolm prompted.

"There is no Recluse. You have been stalking a phantom. In the meantime, the real Lathwi has been coming and going as she pleases."

Alarm raced through Liselle's dream-self alongside of a slipstream of joyless vindication. She had told Lathwi that something like this was going to happen! Amulet or no amulet, she should have never allowed her to leave the house. Now fell creatures were mouthing her name and no doubt sizing her up for slaughter!

The Rogue's aura was hot and bloody now, on the verge of eruption. "If my Lathwi is a phantom," he said, grinding the words between his teeth, "then who do you suppose is the real one?"

"The big woman—the one we dismissed as a servant."

"What makes you say this?"

"I chanced upon her in the bazaar this morning," the naj said, deliberately vague about the details of that encounter. "And although our eyes met for only an instant, she perceived that I was not as I seemed to be and nearly stripped me of my chosen form. Only a sorceress of surpassing power could have done that, Blackheart."

The Rogue lapsed into a furious silence. If the naj was right—! He couldn't bring himself to complete the thought. But he had to admit, the possibility had some circumstantial evidence in its corner. Like the last talisman. It had come to Compara at the same time as the naj's Lathwi. What if she had just been returning home from abroad then? What if she'd hired somebody to take care of her stronghold in her absence? That would explain why Fyjjyx had never seen anybody of power coming and going from the house.

And what about that little incident at the inn? Fyjjyx had caught a whiff of unwarded magic then. Had it come from the naj's Lathwi? Fyjjyx had not thought so, but it had lost the scent before it could finger her or anyone else.

Lastly, there was the trapper's murder. His Lathwi had turned a deaf ear to his screams—a feat he still found hard to believe. Indeed, it seemed more plausible to presume that she had not heard them at all. And the naj's Lathwi had been almost a mile away at the time.

"Fyjjyx would have let her die," the naj said then.

Liselle watched, half-mesmerized by horror and suspense, as The Rogue's temper surpassed its boiling point. His aura flared pure red, then sprouted a blackened tentacle of power. That tentacle snaked into a hole in time and space; and when it returned an instant later, it flung another not-shadow at the sorcerer's feet. The creature grovelled before him like a dog who knew it was about to be beaten.

"Master?" it whined. "How may I serve you?"

"You could have cost me a world," Malcolm replied, in an executioner's fell monotone. "I have no further use of you."

"But—"

The sorcerer began to spit out an incantation. Liselle didn't recognize any of the words, but their inborn foulness burned her spectral ears just the same. Then, as she looked on, jagged bolts of jet-black lightning appeared from out of nowhere and plunged into the not-shadow's back. It shrieked, a hair-raising cry of agony and dismay. An instant later, it began to melt like a rancid candle. Gobs of dissolving flesh hit the floor with sickening plops, then slowly liquefied.

"Clean that up, naj," The Rogue said afterward. He felt better now that he had purged himself of that murderous rage. And while Fyjjyx' punishment seemed somewhat excessive after the fact, still he had no regrets, for the naj had been here to witness it. Now it knew what he could do to a demon that displeased him.

"Excellent," he said, when the naj had finished its gory task. "And since you tended to that so capably, I'm going to let you clean up another of Fyjjyx' messes. From now on, the real Lathwi is your responsibility."

"What?" the naj grated, surprised out of its subordinate stance. "But what about D'Arques? Skillful as I am, I cannot stalk him and the sorceress at the same time."

Startled by the creature's reference to Jamus, Liselle loosed the magical equivalent of a gasp. An instant later, The Rogue sprang to his feet and began sweeping the chamber with his Will. Liselle didn't need to consult his aura now: she knew what he was looking for, and what he would do if he found her. Inspired by sheer desperation, she darted toward a nearby torch and invoked Fire's Name. It freely consented to hide her.

Malcolm probed every nook and cranny with his Will. He was sure that he had sensed another presence in the chamber a moment ago. But the only things he detected now were the naj and the fluttering torches. It must've been his imagination, he thought, as he returned to his seat. For nothing could've escaped his stronghold so quickly and completely.

"Where were we?" he asked the naj then.

"You have imposed the impossible upon me," it replied. "I cannot spy on two people at the same time."

"Ah, yes," he said, in a mocking tone. "An impossible task indeed. But I do not need second-hand information about Lathwi now that I know I can get it first-hand from the woman herself. Therefore, you may quit your watch over D'Arques."

"But—"

"No 'buts', najling," he warned. "And no more mistakes. Otherwise, one of the other drudges will be scrubbing you up from the floor. Is that clear?"

"Quite," the demon replied, choking back a snarl as well as a host of invectives. It feared this upstart cripple now; and that intensified its hatred of him. It could barely wait for the day when it claimed The Dark One's favour for its own. Its first act as Her new chief servant would be to sacrifice the old one with its own claws. Until then, though, it would have to proceed with the greatest of care.

"What do you want me to do with the sorceress?" it asked then. "Watch her? Or seize her?"

"What would you recommend?" Malcolm asked in return.

"If it were up to me, I would seize her."

"Why?"

"Because it's easier to execute an ambush when you know the target's comings and goings. She's visiting the garrison every day now, but that could change at any moment. And even if it doesn't, I do not think it would be wise to let her get too proficient with a sword."

"Worried about your gnarled hide, naj?" Malcolm taunted.

"Your hide is not immune to steel, either," it reminded him. "So why risk it when there is no need?"

"I'm touched by your concern, naj," he said then, "but you've failed to take one important detail into consideration here. Alone, the sorceress is of no use to me. I must have the talisman as well. Do you suppose she will simply hand it over once I have captured her?"

"No…"

"I do not suppose so, either. Therefore, you will only watch her until I tell you otherwise. Is that clear?"

"Yes."

"Good. Now unless you have something more to tell me, you may go."

The not-shadow turned on its heel then and stalked away. Liselle slipped away from the torch's concealing embrace and raced after it—down the tunnel and through the temporarily unwarded entrance. Once she reached the passageway, though, she abandoned her unwitting passkey and then took a moment to recompose herself. What a terrible experience that had been! She had never been more terrified in her life. And yet—

Her dream-self smiled. And yet, she'd gotten through it unscathed. Ah, and the things she had learned made the peril worthwhile. She could hardly wait to get back to her body so she could start putting her knowledge to good use.

She summoned the rainbows once again. Within the span of a blink, she was out of the darkness and soaring across a cloud-studded afternoon sky. She was surprised to find it so late in the day—it seemed as if only a few hours had passed since she had left her home. But that was one of the dangers of dream-questing, she reminded herself. A sorcerer who lost track of time might also lose his body if he was too far away from his body when the separation dust wore off. She was not worried, though. It was late, but not that late.

A dark glint appeared in the sky ahead of her then. To her dismay, she realized that it was a not-shadow—probably the same one she had followed out of The Rogue's stronghold. She had not known that it could fly. She had not known that it could endure direct sunlight, either. She glanced from it to the horizon and then back again. The sun was not ready to set yet. And this was very likely the only opportunity she'd ever get, so…

The thought sent her zooming toward the glint before she could change her mind or question her courage. But while the rainbows brought her to within an inch of the not-shadow, she continued to perceive it as an auraless blob. She fluttered all around it, searching for any clue that she might be able to use, then impulsively extended a tendril of her dream-self and touched it.

A flood of pure hatred swamped her unready awareness: it burned like acid and spread like gangrene; its malice knew no limit. She recoiled, a reflex born of self-preservation. An instant later, she forced herself to make contact again. The images which flooded her mind then were terrifying: blood and entrails; a taloned fist clenched around a human-sized heart; a curiously cloven mouth twisted into a rictus of agony. She endured these and other equally grisly scraps of thought with a detached sort of horror, but then she caught glimpses of an achingly familiar victim and abruptly lost her objectivity.

Pieter!

If her dreaming-self had possessed the ability to speak, she would have invoked The Rogue's black lightning there and then. As it was, all she could do was beat at the not-shadow with her spectral fists and hurl impotent curses in its face. As she railed at it, her strength began to wane. Fury ebbed, giving way to fatigue; suddenly, she had to struggle to stay aloft. One look at the horizon explained her abrupt decline. The sun was setting now; the separation dust was wearing off. She had to get back to her body. Now.

She hurled one last curse at the not-shadow—a promise of revenge. Then, as it winged its way toward parts unknown, she called her rainbows. They appeared to her as washed-out ripples; and when she wished herself home, they did not whisk her into the slipstream which ran between time and space, but rather began to haul her across the sky. The going was slow, a fitful series of starts and stops. Meanwhile, the sun sank ever closer to the horizon.

Her dreaming-self was tingling with exhaustion and fear now. She begged the rainbows to hurry. They obliged with a last burst of speed, then abruptly plunged her into a vicious headlong spin. The spiralling made her dizzy, then nauseated. She lost sight of the sky and the setting sun. All she could see was rooftops. A collision with one of them was imminent, inevitable; and it was said that those who slept through such a crash never woke up again. She tried to meet her end with her spectral eyes open, but at the last moment, she squeezed them shut. An instant later, her dream-self shattered into a million fractured realities. The rainbows fled like naughty kittens. The spinning came to a sudden stop. The next thing she knew, she was back in her body and staring at a wisp of cobweb.

Her amazement was short-lived, as was her relief, for with reunification came a swarm of physical woes. Her eyes were as dry as parchment. Her throat was clogged with dust. She sat up to try and clear her reeling thoughts only to be doubled over by stabbing stomach pains. She threw up, wave after wave of foul-tasting bile, then collapsed into a heap and lay there on the floor like a piece of spent bait.

But as much as she wanted to, she did not faint. A need to find and warn Lathwi kept her awake.

With her pulse beating in her ears like a slave galley's drum, she heaved herself over and onto her knees. There, she paused for a moment, wincing as every joint in her body began to ache, then climbed to her feet. But her inner balance was skewed, thrown off-kilter by all the spinning. She staggered backward, then slipped in a slick of vomit and landed on her butt with a hard, heavy splat.

The pounding in her head struck a frenzied pace. Tears of exhaustion and self-pity stung her eyes. But even as she thought about giving in to her body's need for healing sleep, an image of Lathwi dragging her broken, battered body to the water closet popped into her head. The big woman had refused to let conflicting needs compromise each other. If she could do that, then Liselle could, too. So she climbed back to her feet and staggered across the laboratory, dedicating herself to each step as she took it. At the door, she paused to let the thundering in her temples subside and then shuffled into the hallway. It was dark out here, and ominously still. She called out.

"Lathwi?"

There was no reply to her forlorn croak.

She groaned. There was only one place in the house that Lathwi could be where she wouldn't hear herself being called, and that was the attic. It seemed like such a long, long way to go. She started down the hall, sliding along the wall for support. When she finally came to the ladder that led to the loft, she groaned again.

It was the longest climb of her life.

As she hauled herself from rung to rung, the pounding in her head turned to a gyre which spun out chaotic thoughts and fears: she was too late, Lathwi wasn't here, she was outside fighting for her life against the same foul creature that had murdered Pieter. Why oh why had she not tried harder to keep her at home? She mourned the big woman for a drunken moment, then abruptly forgot what she had been thinking.

She had to find Lathwi.

Warn her.

Help.

Then she stumbled past the last rung and fell face-first into the loft. She lie there for a dazed moment, then lifted her head up like a baby who has not yet learned to crawl. As she peered into a streak of dusty moonlight, her first absurd thought was of what a slob her apprentice was.

An instant later, she spied Lathwi's cot: except for her knife, a small cache of coins and two glittering gems, it was empty. The sight turned her heart to dust in her mouth. Oh, Dreamer! What was she going to do now?

A soft purring sound insinuated itself in her ears then. She squinted into the shadows beyond the cot. Her jaw lapsed into an incredulous 'O'. For there was Lathwi, curled up on a fur, nearly invisible in her black mail. As Liselle stared at her, a delicate snore shivered past her lips.

The loft began to buck and spin as in celebration. For a brief moment,

Liselle was tempted to appropriate the empty cot, but then decided that it would take too much effort and passed out on the floor instead.

A sense of floating warmth permeated Liselle's dreamless sleep. It was a delicious sensation, as luxurious as a satin quilt, but when she tried to burrow deeper into its folds, it turned suddenly aqueous and flooded her nose. Sputtering and coughing, she started awake. The sudden movement sent water cascading out of the tub in which she was sitting, but in her confusion, she barely noticed or cared. How had she come to be in the kitchen? And why did she seem to be taking a bath?

Just then, Lathwi came strolling into the kitchen. She looked the same as she always did: strong, healthy, imposing. For some reason, that annoyed Liselle.

"Would you mind telling me what I'm doing in a bathtub at the crack of dawn?" she asked tartly.

"You stank," Lathwi replied.

No elaboration was necessary. Like marbles in a glass, Liselle's memories of last night abruptly clicked into place. With that shift, her sense of urgency returned as well. She motioned Lathwi toward the tub with an imperative wave of her hand, then grabbed her by the wrist.

"Listen," she urged then. "This is important." She paused to make sure she had Lathwi's full attention, then said, "You and Jamus were being watched yesterday."

"I know," Lathwi replied, in a tone as blase as a shrug.

"The watcher isn't human."

"I know."

"How?" Liselle demanded, thoroughly irritated now. "How do you know? What makes you so damn smart all of a sudden?"

Lathwi decided to answer the first question first. That one was merely a matter of reciting a past event. The second one would require a measure of thought.

"On our way to the garrison yesterday," she said, "Jamus felt that he was being followed. I put on his outer garments and wandered about the marketplace to see if I could draw the lurker out of hiding. As I was looking in a piece of mirror, a woman came stealing toward my back—"

"A woman?" Liselle scoffed, feeling absurdly vindicated. "That's not right. The thing I saw was like a shadow, only solid; and while I couldn't perceive any details with regard to its shape, it definitely wasn't feminine. What you saw in that looking glass was probably some silly schoolgirl mooning over a handsome man."

"Jamus came to a similar conclusion," Lathwi said dryly, "but I do not agree with it. My amulet reacted when our eyes met in the mirror. And although I only lost sight of her for a moment, she was nowhere to be found when I went hunting for her. And I am a very good hunter, Liselle."

Although one stubborn fragment of Liselle's pride still wanted to argue with her apprentice, she knew better than to heed its urgings. Lathwi's story gibed too well with the one she had heard from that not-shadow. And now that she'd had a moment to consider it, even the bit about the spy's form made sense. Sorcerers could shift their shapes, as could nonborn. So why not a not-shadow as well? And a womanly disguise was the perfect choice for someone who wanted to go unnoticed in a crowded marketplace.

"I stand corrected," she said then, injecting an apology into her tone. "Now, tell me this: do you know why The Rogue is having you watched?"

Lathwi shook her head.

"He thinks you are me."

Once again, the big woman's reaction defied expectation. Instead of acknowledging her predicament with the gravity it deserved, she bared her teeth in a feral grin and said, "That is good."

"Are you crazy?" Liselle blurted. "That's not good, that's dreadful! You're in terrible danger."

"A man who stalks a dragon thinking that it is a mouse is apt to get his head bitten off when he least expects it," she replied.

"Your head is as likely to roll as his is," Liselle told her.

She shrugged. "As long as your enemy is pursuing me, he will not be looking for you. This will allow you to sneak in and bring him down from the rear. Then you will not have to worry about the disposition of my head."

"But what if I don't succeed?"

She shrugged again. "Then perhaps I will lose my head."

Liselle's bath water took a sudden chill. She did not want Lathwi to act as a decoy for her. Nor was she keen to assume the responsibilities of a saviour. But she was caught up in a flash-flood of circumstances here; and her druthers were as flotsam. She could either do what had to be done, or be swept away with the rest of the wreckage.

And that was no choice at all.

She splashed her way out of the tub over to the hearth. As the fire's breath steamed her skin dry, she thought about the things she needed to do today. Rescuing the addict, she decided, took top priority.

"When's Jamus supposed to get here?" she asked then.

"He is not coming today," Lathwi replied, masticating the words along with the last shreds of her breakfast. "He said he had work to do."

"It figures," Liselle muttered. "The one morning I want to see him and he's not coming. Isn't that just like a man?" Then she speared Lathwi with a look. "I suppose you're going to the garrison anyway."

"I am," Lathwi replied, and then heaved to her feet to forestall the argument which she expected next. "And I must go now. I cannot be late—"

Without warning, Liselle abandoned her spot in front of the fire and went racing toward her room. Over her shoulder, she called, "Don't leave until I get back!"

When she returned a moment later, she had a square of folded paper in her hand. "Have this delivered to Jamus," she told Lathwi. "Make sure it gets to him this morning.

"Oh, and by the way," she added, as Lathwi headed for the door, "be sure to carry your knife with you at all times: The Rogue's minions are vulnerable to steel. The next time I see Jamus, I'll tell him to find you a sword."

A protest rumbled up Lathwi's windpipe: she wasn't ready to carry a real sword yet! Pawl had said so. But she didn't bother to share the swordmaster's opinion with Liselle. That would only provide the sorceress with another opportunity to delay her.

But her discretion was for naught. Halfway through the door, Liselle bedevilled her again. "Wait!" she blurted. "I almost forgot. There's one more thing I wanted to ask you."

"Ask," Lathwi hissed, deliberately keeping her back to the woman. "Ask quickly."

"Do you know anything about a talisman?"

"I'm wearing it."

"No, not that one," she clucked. "The Rogue could have no possible interest in that. I'm talking about a different talisman, one you had no hand in making. You would've picked it up before you came to Compara."

"It is possible that I picked such a thing up," Lathwi admitted, although nothing specific sprang to mind. "It is also possible that I put it back down again. I will have to look back at my memories.

"But not now," she added emphatically. "Now I am going to the garrison."

An instant later, she was gone.

As Lathwi made her way to the garrison, she slipped the note from her belt and unfolded it. She had no qualms about doing this. If Liselle did not want her to know what was in it, she reasoned, then she would not have given it to her in the first place.

Jamus, she read, taking care not to more her lips. Meet me at the garrison as soon as you can get away. I must speak to you regarding a matter which has been troubling us both as of late.

To her surprise, her own name graced the bottom of the slip. That puzzled her for a moment, for she had nothing to say to the man, but then logic came to her aid. Liselle was not supposed to exist; thus, she had to remain invisible even on paper. The only mistake the sorceress had made concerned the handwriting itself: even rushed, her script was neat and compact, a decorous pageant of ink. In contrast, her own was barely legible. But since she did not intend to let Jamus or anybody else see one of her own drafts, such an oversight was inconsequential.

There was, however, one other problem. She had no idea as to where Jamus was supposed to be this morning. And even if she had had a clue, she did not know the city well enough to track it down.

So how was she going to get this message to him?

Returning to the house to ask for directions was out of the question. The trip would take too much time, for she was on the outskirts of the bazaar already. And besides, Liselle didn't know where Jamus was, either.

As she pondered her dilemma, a hand clamped down on her shoulder. Caught by surprise, her reactions were all reflex. She whipped the not-claw free of her belt. At the same time, she pivoted on her heel and drew her left arm up to guard her temple. By then, her would-be assailant had backed off just enough to allow her a clear glimpse of himself.

"Pawl!" she blurted. "What are you doing here?"

"Good morning to you, too, Lathwi." The calmness of his tone belied the sparks of amusement and intrigue that livened his sienna eyes. "That's a nice blade you've got there. But it wouldn't have stood a chance against mine."

Up until that moment, she had not noticed the knife in his hand. And now that she saw it, she could not understand how she had managed to overlook it. By itself, the blade was over an inch longer than the whole of her not-claw; and with the hilt, it rivalled the length of her forearm. Yet in spite of its size, it appeared light and well-balanced—a pleasure to carry or wield.

"And in reply to your question," he went on, in the same conversational tone, "I'm here because I prefer fresh food to the stodge they serve at the garrison." Then he pulled a fat red apple from a shoulder satchel and casually carved it into wedges. "Want a piece?"

"No."

He shrugged, then resheathed his knife and began to eat. Lathwi returned her not-claw to her belt as well.

"You seemed a little jumpy back there," he commented, as they meandered toward the garrison. "I wouldn't have come up behind you like that if I'd known you were the nervous type."

"I was thinking when I should have been watching," she admitted.

"Oh? What's on your mind? Maybe I can help."

Once again, humanity's penchant for meddling amazed her. No dragon in its right mind would volunteer to help a virtual stranger, especially when there seemed to be no personal gain in doing so. Then again, no dragon declined a free meal when it was offered, either; and he did seem to be offering.

"I have to get a message to Jamus," she told him, "but I do not know where he is."

"Is it an important message?"

She fetched the folded note from her belt and offered it to him. Instead of taking and reading it as she had expected him to, he stared at her as if he were trying to look all the way through to the other side of her. This scrutiny made her uneasy. She wondered if she had done something wrong, and if she was going to get cracked in the knuckles or shins for it. He banished those worries with an amused snort and pushed the proffered note away.

"I like your style, Lathwi," he said. "And I'm fairly sure we can find a solution to your problem at the garrison."

That was good enough for her.

They continued on to the garrison; and as soon as they were inside, Pawl beckoned Nudge away from his duties with a wave of his hand. The manling rushed over, then stood gladly in his captain's shadow.

"Do you know where milord Jamie lives?" Pawl asked.

"Yes, sir!" Nudge declared. "I was there once. It's a beautiful place, all full of fancy rugs and shiny mirrors—"

"I know," the swordmaster interjected wryly. "I've been there once or twice myself. But the reason I asked is this: Lathwi here has a message for Jamie. She needs a trustworthy courier to deliver it for her."

The boy eyed her with unabashed curiosity. Her scars in particular seemed to fascinate him.

"I could do it," he said, with a shy sort of eagerness. "With your permission, of course."

"What if milord Jamie isn't home?" Pawl quizzed him.

"His servants will know where he is," Nudge replied. "I'll ask one of them to direct me to him."

"Well said!" He clapped the youngling on the back, then turned to Lathwi. "Well," he asked then, "what do you say?"

Lathwi handed the note to Nudge.

"It's important," Pawl cautioned, "so don't dawdle."

"I won't," he promised, and went dashing off toward the gate. A plume of tawny dust rose up behind him; and when it finally settled again, he was nowhere to be seen.

"He's a good lad," Pawl commented, seemingly unaware of the fond half-smile that graced his mouth. "He'll be a good soldier someday."

A thin, grim line superseded that smile then. His eyes acquired distance and flint. Suddenly, the genial man whom Lathwi had encountered in the marketplace vanished; and the master of swords took his place.

"Go over to the bin and get a couple of staves," he told her. "From what I saw this morning, we have a lot of work to do."

Jamus strolled into the garrison's yard just as Lathwi was dusting herself off after another brutal lesson. "I got your message," he said, as he approached. "I must confess—I'm intrigued. What's this matter of importance that has you so eager for my company?"

She waited until they were face-to-face before replying; and even then, she kept her voice pitched ultra-low and tried not to move her lips.

"Liselle wishes to see you immediately. Do not ask me for details," she went on, even as he opened his mouth to do exactly that, "for I will not discuss this with you out here in the open. As you suspected, we are being watched."

"I knew it!" he declared, and then laughed as if she had told him a joke. "Didn't I tell you so?" Then he seized her by the elbow and ushered her toward the gate. "But enough of that for now," he said, in the same boisterous tone. "Let's talk about your lesson. Did Icky abuse you again? He's good at that, he's always been a bully. Unfortunately, he's also one of the best swordsmen you'll ever meet. Did I ever tell you about the time he out-duelled a Kryvarian assassin?..."

He babbled all the way back to the house.

"...and so that's why I had to talk to you right away," Liselle said, ending her non-stop narrative on a breathless note. "I hope you'll forgive me for being so secretive."

Jamus reached across the table and captured one of her winter-pale hands. His smile was reassuring.

"There's nothing to forgive," he said. "Even a layman like myself knows that an illusion will only work so long as no one suspects it. I'm just glad that I can be of some use to your non-existent self."

"Then you'll help me?"

"Of course!" he exclaimed. "I'll relay the information regarding the addict's whereabouts to my men as soon as I get back to the garrison. We should be set to nab her by the end of the day. I'll pick up some curra for her, too."

Her expression soured. "Will that really be necessary?"

"Have you ever met a curra addict?" he asked in return. "No? Well then, my dear, allow me to tell you what you can expect." There was a slight edge to his tone now. It both reproached and mocked her for questioning his motives. "If they catch her while she's high, she'll talk for hours about nothing at all. As the drug wears off, though, she'll become irritable and distracted. A little while later, she'll start to sweat and shiver; and after that, she'll gibber and drool. At that point, she'll beg for curra—just one pellet to keep her sane! If you don't give it to her, she'll turn violent. How violent, I cannot say, for each person acts differently, but I once saw an addict charge four soldiers who had come to arrest her. She broke one fellow's arm and nearly scratched another's eyes out; and when they finally got the manacles on her, she immediately tried to chew her way free of them. She was not, I might add, chewing on the metal."

Liselle shuddered at the image which flared in her mind, then heaved a sigh chock-full of regrets. "You're right," she said to Jamus. "We should have curra on hand. It's just—"

She lapsed into a wistful silence. He scooted down the length of the bench, then draped a brotherly arm around her shoulders and prompted her. "Just what?"

"I hate using other people," she replied. "You, Lathwi, your men, the curra-chewer. I wish it were just me and The Rogue. I'd feel so much less responsible."

He coiled her braid around his hand and gave it a gentle tug. "Ah, my dear Liselle. You take too much upon yourself. It may well be your fate to face this Rogue, but the Dreamer would never be so cruel as to force you to make that stand by yourself. You have friends who would gladly risk that danger with you, friends who—"

His free hand began to caress the rounded curves of her face of its own volition. When she did not shy away from his touch, he dared to finish what he had started.

"You have friends," he repeated in a coarsened whisper, "who would risk anything because they love you."

He drew her close and kissed her then. She accepted the tender pillow of his mouth with an almost reverent solemnity, then abruptly flung her arms around his neck and deepened the kiss of her own accord. At that moment, long weeks of denial dissolved, washed away by a dizzying wave of emotion-charged desire. She was his, and he, hers: nothing else mattered or sufficed. Yet even as he shifted, seeking to celebrate that passionate truth, the moment shifted, too, and she drew away from him.

His eyes widened with surprise and a sudden fear. Could he have misread her? No! He knew women far too well to have mistaken the hard pliancy of her body and the honey sweetness of her mouth for anything less than a lover's invitation. He looked to her for answers then; and the pool of hopeless love and sorrow that he saw in her eyes confused him all the more.

"Come here," he said, reaching for her again. "Come and tell me what's wrong."

"I cannot," she replied, in a tone riddled with regrets.

"But why?"

"Because I have seen what happens to those whom I allow myself to love."

Ah, he understood now. She was trying to protect him. That was so sweet of her, so noble and brave.

But he did not want to be protected! He wanted to kiss her mouth again and run his fingers through her hair and make her say the words he so ached to hear. He knew he could make this happen. Her resolve was flimsy. The right touch in the just right place would do it. He reached out, then stroked a stray wisp of hair away from her temple.

"What a pity," he said then, and expelled a tragic sigh. At her questioning glance, he smirked and added, "I've never bedded a sorceress."

She blinked back a moment's shock, then returned fire. "That's not for lack of trying, though, is it?"

Their laughter was strained at first, but it snowballed into a fit of genuine humour. As they laughed, the gulf that had sprang up between them shrank to bridgeable proportions. He smiled at her; she smiled back. The pain on both sides was contained.

"Well," he said then, "now that that's behind us, let's get back to business. Is there anything else you want me to know or do?"

She gnawed on her lower lip. She was tired, emotionally spent. It was hard for her to think in such a state. "Did I tell you about the catacombs already?"

He nodded grimly. "I still think we should send a squad of soldiers down there and flush the rat out of his hole."

"He wouldn't budge," she told him, "not even if you sent the entire garrison down there after him. And any change in our routine would tell him more than we want him to know. So for now, let's keep things exactly the way they are, even the boneyard patrols.

"Oh, and before I forget again—Lathwi needs a sword."

"She's not ready to carry a real sword yet," he argued.

"The Rogue's minions can be slain with a sword," Liselle countered, "so ready or not, she needs one. You'd be wise to carry one as well."

He patted the hilt that jutted up from his hip. "I take it with me everywhere these days. And in view of the special circumstances, I'll see if I can requisition one just like it for Lathwi."

Gratitude swelled within her. It was a tender sort of pain. She reached out and clasped his hand, then pressed it to her heart. "Thank you so very much for everything, Jamus. I hope there will come a time when I can repay you."

"You already have, my dear," he replied. Then, because his resolve was even flimsier than hers, he slipped his hand free of her grasp and stood up. "I must go now. If all goes well, I should have good news for you very soon."

"Take care," she told him.

"Likewise," he replied, and then took his leave with a flourish that he didn't feel in his heart.

She expelled a sigh laden with might-have-beens and then lapsed into her rocking chair. Her insides felt as if they'd been scraped clean with a blunt knife. The fact that she had done the scraping herself did little to mitigate her sense of loss. She began to rock back and forth, forth and back. She wanted to sleep, to steep herself in healing dreams, but even as her body began to yield to that desire, Lathwi appeared at her elbow.

"I am ready to learn something new," she announced.

An urge to send the annoyingly carefree woman on her way rippled through Liselle, but she ignored it. Lathwi had done nothing to deserve such spiteful treatment. And sleep wasn't the only distraction in the world.

"Cast an illusion over that bench," Liselle commanded.

Lathwi went as still as a frozen pond. A moment later, a tall shelf of books appeared where the laboratory bench had stood. The transition surprised Liselle—not because it had been skilfully done, but because it had been done without the usual ration of psychic noise. Once again, she had forgotten about Lathwi's amulet. And once again, she found herself staving off pangs of jealousy because of it.

"Illusions are like lies," she said tersely, "best when kept simple. So in the future, use a less complicated image. In the meantime, let's talk about transmogrification."

"I do not recognize the word," Lathwi admitted.

Her honesty leached the sting from Liselle's resentment. "I'm not surprised," she said, in a less cutting tone. "It's not a word that crops up in an everyday conversation. But as intimidating as it sounds, transmogrification is nothing more or less than an elaborate form of illusion.

"Behold." Liselle strode over to the illusory bookcase then. "Here's an example of a simple illusion. It will fool the unsuspecting eye, but none of the other senses. As soon as I touch any part of it—" She reached out to grab one of the books. Her fingers folded around air. "—the illusion becomes transparent. This happens because you have pasted an insubstantial image over a solid object. The two exist as separate realities and cannot compensate for each other.

"Transmogrification, on the other hand, molds the image and the object into a single hybrid reality."

Lathwi's brow beetled itself into a perplexed vee. "I am not sure what a hybrid reality might be and what purpose it might serve."

Liselle sighed—a prayer for continued patience as well as the right words. "Whenever a sorcerer uses his powers to alter an object's configuration, he creates a reality that is half magic and half natural. Thus, that object can exist as itself and something else at the same time."

"That does not make sense," Lathwi argued. "How can a thing change and yet stay the same?"

"You're thinking about this too much and too hard," the sorceress scolded. "Just relax for a moment and listen to me. Transmogrification alters a thing's outward appearance, but leaves its essential nature intact. Therefore, no true Change takes place. For example: let's say I transmogrified a mouse into a cow. That mouse would then look and smell and feel like a real cow, but it would still think and act like a mouse. Thus, the cow is no more than an illusion; the mouse is still itself."

Lathwi thought about that for a moment. As she did so, her uncomprehending scowl broke up like a pack of wind-blown clouds. "So as long as the mouse remembers its Name," she summarized, "it will remain a mouse."

"I suppose you could say it like that," Liselle said. "But I prefer to think of it in terms of awareness instead. After all, a thing doesn't necessarily have to know its Name to be aware of who and what it is. Look at me—I'm proof of that."

Lathwi did not bother to dispute that statement. Her thoughts were already racing down a different and far more intriguing trail. "What would happen if you transmogrified this mouse into a bird? Would it then be able to fly?"

"No," she replied, with a shake of her head. "Because a mouse does not have the instincts of a bird. It would die on the ground beneath a hungry cat's claws, never realizing that it could easily flap its way to safety.

"Fortunately," she added, as Lathwi's face sagged with disappointment, "transmogrification is not the last resort. There is a form of magic called transformation which brings about true Change. In its grips, our mouse might fly around the world and back as if it had been born a bird.

"But never mind about that for now. You must learn how to walk before you can run."

"I am ready," Lathwi declared. "Teach me."

And so the lesson proceeded.

CHAPTER 17

The naj came streaking into The Blackheart's stronghold on the back of a summons. To its surprise, it saw that three of the drudges were here as well, crouched at the man's feet. The naj scorned them with a look, and then turned its gaze to Malcolm. He looked ridiculously small in his outsized chair, but the gleam in his eyes had a lethal edge.

"What goes on here?" it asked.

"D'Arque's men are closing in on the curra-chewer," the cripple gloated. "They should have her in custody before the day's end."

The naj bared its teeth in a grin. "So tonight is to be Lathwi's downfall."

"Exactly."

"Tell me what I must do."

"You, Hwavok and Gryztel are to return to her stronghold and hide yourselves until the addict arrives. Once she is in the house, you must get ready to attack. Hwavok and Gryztel, you will be responsible for distracting any people who might be lingering outside—"

"How is this to be done?" one of the drudges asked.

"Create a disturbance," he replied, "or scare them away. Kill them if nothing else works. I don't care what you do so long as you keep would-be reinforcements out of the house."

"And what would you have me do while these buffoons are churning up the dust?" the naj asked.

"You will be inside, dealing with Lathwi," Malcolm said. "She must be brought to me alive," he added, as an evil smirk spread across the naj's mouth. "And relatively undamaged."

"Why?" it snapped. "Alive, she is dangerous. Dead, she is naught but a bad case of gas."

Malcolm did not want to part with such a detail, but it was too important to leave to chance—especially when chance involved a naj with a grudge. "The Dark One will need a body to occupy upon Her return to this world," he said, "and since She cannot inhabit dead or impotent flesh, I must have Lathwi alive. If you cannot manage that, I will assign someone else to the task."

The naj's thoughts became an whirlwind of possibilities. There was an opportunity brewing here. But the naj needed to be at the right places at the right times for it to come to a head. So it bit back its pride for the last time and adopted an ingratiating tone.

"Do not send a drudge to do a naj's work," it said, "for it will surely prove ruinous to your plans. Now that I know of the Dark One's need for a body, I will be more than happy to oblige Her."

"I'm sure She'll appreciate that," Malcolm purred. He still didn't trust the demon lordling, but true to its claim, it was the best one for the job. So, despite his misgivings, he was going to send it after Lathwi and the talisman. And because of those misgivings, he was going to destroy it upon its return. "Just make sure you don't get carried away with your work."

"I will be careful," it assured him. "But may I ask one thing more?"

"If you must."

"How am I to gain access to her stronghold?"

Malcolm grinned, savouring this last delectable irony. "Fear not," he replied. "The addict will let you in."

CHAPTER 18

Although it was growing late, and she was tired as well as hungry, Lathwi persisted in the laboratory. She wanted to master the elements of transmogrification as soon as possible so she could move on to the mysteries of transformation. The thought of being so close to attaining her own wings was more provocative than her need for food or sleep.

Her first attempt at this strange new magic had been to give one of Liselle's jars the semblance of a mouse. It had seemed like an easy task at the time—she had seen plenty of mice in her day; as a youngling, she'd even eaten a few. But the image that had been so sure in her head hadn't translated well; and the jar had become a meaty grey blur with oversized ears, twig-thin legs and a long string tail. Since then, she had learned to select her images more carefully, and had made that same jar resemble her not-claw; a steamy bowl of broth; a log; and finally, her personal favourite thus far, Liselle's disembodied head.

That last illusion was still intact, and as she admired its admittedly exaggerated scowl, she hissed to herself. Oh, the mischief she could accomplish with this magic! How Shoq would roar when his meat turned into a patch of dragon dung!

Just then, the door rattled as if to remind her: sorcery wasn't supposed to be fun! A moment later, Liselle poked her head into the room.

"Lathwi!" she barked. "Quit what you're doing and come join us in the kitchen. The Curra-chewer is on her way."

The news meant nothing to Lathwi. She did not know this curra-chewer. Nor did she understand why Liselle was so keen to meet her. Still, it did not seem worthwhile to argue with the sorceress over the matter: her concentration was starting to fray anyway. So she dismissed the jar's quasi countenance with a flick of her Will and headed for the kitchen. Liselle was there already, pacing back and forth in front of the door like a soft-slippered ghost.

"Where are they?" she demanded, in a tone crackling with agitation. "They should've been here by now."

"Relax," Jamus told her. "They're my best men, they're not going to let her get away."

"That's not what I'm worried about."

He turned to Lathwi; the look on his face was aggrieved. "You tell her to calm down, Lathwi. She won't listen to me."

"That seems like a most sensible decision on her part," she replied.

"Hey now!—"

Liselle ignored their bickering. Her thoughts were all for the curra-chewer. At first, her intention had been only to rescue the poor woman from her peril. Then she had hoped to form an alliance with her. But the more she thought about the addict, the more things failed to ring true. How had she survived so long in her drugged condition, especially with a not-shadow at her door? She had to know something. She just had to. And now Liselle was determined to find out what that something was.

A knock at the door startled her out of her pacing. She tensed as if struck. Her cheeks went numb. She hurried over to Lathwi, then hid behind her like a shy child.

"Would you please let them in, Jamus?" she asked.

He cracked the door open and peeked outside. Satisfied with what he saw, he then stepped aside. A variety of sounds drifted in through the gap: the scuffling of booted feet, the clinking of chains, a muttered curse. Then a woman came into view. She was dirty and rail-thin, a fleshy skeleton clad in rags and shackles. Hanks of greasy red hair shaded her eyes. Her lips were green from curra-juice. As she shambled across the threshold, Liselle let out a tiny gasp.

Mongoose-quick, Jamus unsheathed his sword and used it to bar the addict's way. Then he glanced toward Liselle and demanded, "What's wrong?"

"Ward-magic," came her troubled reply. "She herself is not evil, but something about her is a threat to me."

"What kind of threat?"

"I don't know." She tapped Lathwi on the back. "Can you read her thoughts?"

Lathwi shrugged, noncommittal, then extended a tendril of her dragon-sense. A moment later, she retracted it again and then spat as if to clear her mouth of a bad taste.

"Well?" Jamus prompted. "What did you see?"

"Her head is full of hunger and confusion," she replied. "Her only clear thought is of curra."

His scowl intensified. "So what are we going to do with her?"

"Send her away," Lathwi suggested, in a tone thick with contempt. "Her mind is porridge; it cannot possibly contain anything of value."

"I agree," Jamus said. "In this case, the risks seem to outweigh the rewards."

"Maybe so," Liselle said, in a voice that was suddenly all stubbornness and steel. "But I've come too far to turn back now. Let her in. Then take her to my laboratory."

Jamus appealed to Lathwi with a look, but she had voiced her opinions on the matter already and did not feel the need to repeat herself. He curled his lip at her lack of support, then grudgingly admitted the addict into the house.

"Wait there," he told his men. "We may need you again later."

He eased the door shut and then marched the curra-chewer through the house. She plodded along like a dazed milch cow, looking neither left nor right. Her shackles clinked to the beat of her steps. Her brow was damp with sweat.

"Thank you, Jamus," Liselle said, when they came to the door of her laboratory. "Now I must ask you to leave us for a while."

"But—"

"No arguments, please. I want to work some sorcery, and I'd rather not do that with you in the room. If it will make you feel better, though, you can lend Lathwi your sword."

He knew quite well that handing his weapon over wasn't going to make him feel anywhere close to better, but he did it anyway because he had to contribute something to Liselle's protection or go crazy with concern.

"Remember," he grated, as Lathwi cinched the belt to her hips, "this is just a loan. Pawl will have a sword ready for you tomorrow." She shrugged, then strode into the laboratory after the other two sorceresses. As the door started to shut him out, he called, "I'll be right out here if you need me!"

Then he settled against the wall to wait.

The addict began to fuss and mutter like a baby on the verge of waking. Liselle looked up from the diagram she was drawing and frowned.

"If she gives you any trouble," she told Lathwi, "knock her out."

Lathwi snorted, amused by the thought. Trouble? From this little green-lipped zombie? It seemed highly unlikely. She did not even seem like much of a match for puny Liselle! But looks could be deceiving, she reminded herself, and the outer wards had reacted to this woman, so she kept a sharper watch than she might've otherwise. All the curra-chewer did, though, was scowl and scratch at her sweaty face.

"Bring her over here, would you please, Lathwi?" Liselle asked then, pointing toward the center of her pentagram. "Be sure she doesn't smudge the outlines."

Lathwi slung the muttering, green-lipped woman over her shoulder and toted her over to the star like a sack of grain. The addict offered no resistance, not even when Lathwi slung her back to her feet and told her to stay where she was or be eaten. Once again, Lathwi found it hard to think of her as a threat.

"All I need you to do now is stand guard," Liselle told her then. "If anything goes wrong, save yourself and Jamus."

Lathwi snorted, much amused by the differences in their priorities. A moment later, the sound of sorcery swelled in her ears. It was music both forceful and sweet.

The addict started awake. Her curra-stained lips parted as if in wonder. Then a tendril of Liselle's inexorable Will bored into her skull, and that awed look turned to pain. She tried to writhe away from whatever it was that was tormenting her, but she was caught in the Star of Compulsion now and its power held her still. A silent stream of tears began to drip down her cheeks. A moment later, she went suddenly limp.

"Curra-chewer!" Liselle said then. "What is your name?"

"Margita," she whispered in reply. "My name is Margita. What have you done to me?"

"I have burned the curra from your mind," Liselle told her. "Your thoughts are free again."

"But why?"

The woman's piteous tone wrenched Liselle's heart, but she choked back the guilt which rose like bile in her gorge. "I need to talk to you," she said.

"Curra," Margita pleaded. "Give me some curra and I'll talk to you until the end of time."

"I have curra, but you'll not see so much as a pellet of it until you tell me what I need to know." She was not proud of herself for exploiting an addict's cravings like this, but at the moment, she feared The Rogue far more than she valued her scruples. "Tell me why you're still alive."

Within the span of a blink, Margita's tearful expression shifted into an lupine snarl. "How should I know? I'm not a philosopher."

"Don't bandy words with me," Liselle warned. "I haven't the time or the patience for it."

"Then stop speaking in riddles!" Margita snapped.

"Very well. There's a shadow lurking on your doorstop, isn't there?"

The blood drained from the addict's face. This made her lips and the whites of her eyes look greener than ever. "How did you know?" she whispered.

"I've seen it. Is it yours?" When she denied it with a shake of her head, Liselle asked, "What does it want?"

"I...I don't know. I've tried to run away from it, but it always seems to find me. One time, the first time, it—" She squeezed her eyes shut as if to blot out the memory. The muscles in her jaw clenched. "it caught me and carried me away to a place of darkness and stone."

"What happened there?"

"I don't know. I was high; and half-mad with fear."

"Think," Liselle urged, and then reinforced the command with a pulse of her Will. Margita mewled as if in pain, but could not resist the compulsion.

"I remember a man with a twisted leg. He gloated over me as if I were a fair-day prize and then raped my mind with his powers. He was evil, unspeakably cruel. The things he said and did made me want to die…"

"So I ask you again, Margita: why are you still alive?"

"I don't know!"

"Ah, but I think you do," Liselle said, and clenched her Will again.

Margita reddened as if she were being squeezed in the middle. Sweat slicked her face. She loosed a strangled cry, then blurted, "He said I was to be the death of someone! He said this someone would find me and take me home and force me answer questions about him. And by the end of that same day, he said, that someone would be dead.

"Please!" she sobbed then, on the verge of hysteria. "I don't want to kill you! Let me go. Now! So that both of us can live!"

Liselle was numb, stricken cold to the very core of her being by the sound of her own death warrant. She should have foreseen this, she thought, as she shivered within that icy cocoon. She should have suspected such a trap from the very beginning. Instead, she had deluded herself into believing that she was being the clever one this time. Dreamer! How could she have been such a fool?

But recriminations were useless, she told herself. She needed to find a way to wriggle free of this ugly snare. One solution suggested itself immediately: kill Margita here and now. It would be easy while she was encased within the star; one well-placed thrust of Will would do it. She had disposed of that nonborn in a similar way not too long ago, and it had been far less of a threat to her than the addict.

Do it, an inner voice urged her. The curra-chewer meant nothing to her or anybody else. Her life, her work, was more important.

She ground the idea into a sour paste between her teeth. There were limits as to how low she would sink in the name of her own survival. Yes, she had destroyed the nonborn, but it had wanted to die. The addict wanted to live—just like she did. And when all was said and done, who was to say which of them was more worthy of the privilege? Therefore, she had to set her free.

But not unconditionally. There was something she could do that might buy them both another day. She raised a fresh scion of her Will and sent it snaking into the other woman's mind. With one gentle stroke, she whisked her hysteria away; with the next, she tamped a geas into place. Then she heaved a resigned sigh and then collapsed the walls of her Star.

Margita stumbled forward, out of the diagram and toward Liselle. Lathwi came charging across the room to intercept her, but Liselle checked her headlong rush with an upraised hand.

"It's all right," she said. "I've laid a compulsion on her. So long as she does not try to harm me, it will remain inert. But if she attempts my life in any way, it will kill her."

Her gaze shifted toward the addict. "Do you understand, Margita? It was the best I could for you."

"I understand," Margita replied, sounding as dazed and bedraggled as she looked. She licked her juice-stained lips, then added, "It is more than I expected."

"And less than you deserve," Liselle told her. "I only hope it will suffice."

"Under other circumstances, I would invite you to be my guest for the evening. But given the way things are between us, I think it would be best if you left right away. Jamus' men will take you back to your home or wherever else you may wish to go."

"What about the curra?" Margita bleated. "Will you give it to me as you promised?"

"If you wish it, it is yours. Come, I'll give it to you on your way out."

As the three women stepped out of the laboratory, Jamus all but pounced on Liselle. His eyes delved the lines of her heart-shaped face, a reading both anxious and relieved.

"Well?" he demanded. "How did it go?"

"As well as can be expected, I suppose," she said. Her heart was heavy now, and her stomach hurt. "Do you have that curra on you?"

"It's in my cloak."

"Would you please go and get it?"

He shot her a dirty look for withholding the details of the addict's interrogation from him, then swept past her and toward the kitchen. She took one step in the same direction, then doubled over as the pain in her stomach came to a sudden boil.

"Lathwi," she groaned, "get Margita out of here."

Then she bolted for the water closet.

Lathwi rumbled, a sound of concern, then turned to find the curra-chewer staring up at her. There was a wild, almost panicked look in her eyes.

"What did that one call you?" she asked.

"Lathwi," she replied, simply because her name was no secret in the human tongue.

The addict started as if stung, then began to laugh and cry at the same time. "It's you!" she gibbered. "You're the one!"

Lathwi scowled. Of course it was her. Who else could it be?

Margita was muttering to herself now. Eager to be rid of such an unsavoury creature, Lathwi gave her a shove toward the door. She staggered forward a few steps, then clanked to a stop. Lathwi shoved her again. There was a queer chirring in her ears now. The curra-chewer's mutterings had masked it at first, but now it was as loud as a field full of crickets. Her amulet began to pulse.

"Milord Jamus!" someone in the distance shouted. "Come quickly! Something queer's afoot!"

At the same time, there came a sound like breaking glass from the loft. Lathwi's amulet began to throb with urgency.

Liselle came bursting out of the water closet then. Her face was ashen. Flecks of vomit studded her chin. "Lathwi!" she croaked. "Shut her up! She's using unwarded magic!"

Lathwi's hands flew to Margita's throat. But before she had a chance to choke off her breath, the addict convulsed on her own and then swallowed her curra-stained tongue. Moments later, she was dead. Lathwi let go of the body, then turned to share her confusion with Liselle.

"I do not understand," she rumbled. "I did not take her life."

"My compulsion caught up with her," Liselle replied, and then tried to look brave as footsteps sounded overhead. "But not soon enough.

"She has let the enemy in."

CHAPTER 19

The naj was in position atop of Lathwi's roof—the moonless night cloaked its presence as well as any shadow. It was excited, impatient; as anxious as a pregnant bride. As it waited for the addict to take action, it reviewed its plans for the hundredth time.

Once inside the house, it would secure the talisman and subdue the sorceress—preferably in that order. Then, with both prizes in hand, it would return to Malcolm Blackheart's stronghold. That odious little stump of a man would have the other talismans out and ready for the ritual which would call the Dark One back to Her world. How convenient! For the naj meant to knock him unconscious and perform the rite itself—using his body instead of Lathwi's. It bared its teeth as it envisioned him writhing beneath the Dark One's weight; bit by awful bit, Her burgeoning presence would grind his essence to dust. What a satisfying revenge that would be: so ironic, so complete. And when The Daughter of Death was fully restored, the naj would celebrate by sacrificing Lathwi in a most slow and painful way.

An excited shiver rippled down its spine then. What was taking that curra-chewer so long?

As if in response to that thought, the wards beneath its feet began to buckle and warp. Long moments later, a fissure appeared, and the addict's sorcery started to spill into the night. The naj howled, signalling the other demons, then went diving through the sky-light which could no longer resist its might. A hard spray of glass crashed to the floor only to be pulverized beneath its weight.

Triumph coursed through the naj's veins like poison. It was in! Malcolm's scheme had worked. Now nothing could stop it from claiming its due! It grinned, then went hunting for the talisman. The attic was dark, but that was no hindrance; its nose was sharper than its eyes. Its search led it past a cot which it overturned, then over to a mound of fur. There, nestled among a diamond and some insignificant coins, was the object of its unholy desire. It scooped the talisman up with a swipe of its gnarled fist, then loosed a gleeful bellow.

Its thoughts turned to Lathwi then. It could sense her cowering somewhere downstairs; and the sickly sweet smell of her fear was as heady as a drink of fresh blood. It shifted into human guise, then leapt out of the loft. The room below was empty, so it stalked into the hallway.

"You have intruded," a voice said then. "Now you will answer for it."

Lathwi was standing at the mouth of the hall with Jamus' sword in hand. Her stance was perfect, her stare was lethal. She looked and felt as confident as a full-grown dragon-dam.

"I have seen how poorly you wield that thing," the demon jeered in reply. "It would be best if you put it down before you hurt yourself."

Lathwi did not say a word, but only watched and waited. The naj's fiery eyes flared with frustration at this tactic, then simmered into guileful slits.

"Look what I have," it said, offering her a glimpse of the talisman. "You cannot hope to overcome me now. If you give yourself up, I will spare you much pain."

Although incensed over the plundering of her scant nest, Lathwi remained true to Pawl's training and held her tongue. There would be plenty of time for words later on—after she had destroyed this impudent creature and recovered her stone.

Her silence maddened the demon, for it craved more than her death. It wanted to sink its teeth into the meat of her fear, then gnaw on the bones of her humiliation and despair. So it decided to show her what it really was.

As Lathwi stood on guard, her amulet began to throb. An instant later, the intruder's form began to shimmer and quake like viscous mud. Plump breasts became a solid span of scaly muscle. Dainty hands became taloned gnarls. A set of stubby wings appeared, then a vestigial tail. The eyes which glared at her were red as embers. A dragon's roar boiled out of her memory then. She hurled it at the creature like a curse.

Believing her unnerved at last, the naj charged, talons poised to rend. That was a mistake, for not only was Lathwi still in possession of her wits, she was also bristling with ancient hate. Nimble as a thought, she sidestepped the naj's headlong rush. As it went racing past her, she hacked at its scaly torso with all of her might.

Such a ferocious blow would've cleaved a man in two, but the naj was made of sterner stuff. It scurried out of range, then turned to face her again. The gaping wound in its side burned like a fire, but that was nothing compared to the pain it meant to give her. It feigned another unreasoning charge. As she went to slash it again, it pulled up short and punched her in the face. Rich, red blood spurted from her nose. The sword went flying from her hand. Before she had a chance to recover, it folded her into a suffocating embrace.

The ammoniac stink of the naj's wound revived Lathwi, as did the sudden pressure to her spine and ribs. She struggled wildly to free one or both of her arms, but only succeeded in depleting her already truncated supply of air. This krim was strong, terribly so; her newly healed ribs could not take too much more of its abuse. She strained downward, fishing for a claw. The tip of her middle finger brushed across the top of one, but she could not manage to squirm any closer to it. In the meantime, her vision turned red and began to blur. There was no more air in her lungs. Truly desperate now, she tried to summon her Will. But even as it flickered within her, the world winked out like a shooting star.

The sudden pliancy of Lathwi's body told the naj that it had won. It grinned, then began to gloat. An instant later, something pierced its vitals from behind. It let out a howl, then dumped Lathwi onto the floor and spun around to confront its new adversary. What the demon saw then sent its thoughts whirling into confusion. The woman was small and mouse-like, an insignificant mite. But while she seemed barely worth its notice at first glance, she proved exceptional at the second. For she was a sorceress! And one of considerable power! Had there been two of them all along?

The naj jettisoned its consternation with a snarl. One or two, it made no difference—both were its meat now. This newcomer was terrified; the air was rank with her fear. Even so sorely wounded, it could dispose of her before it returned to the catacombs with Lathwi. Better yet, it could bring her to The Blackheart in Lathwi's stead! That way, it could kill Lathwi right now; and now was better than later where she was concerned. Malcolm would not suspect the switch, and even if he did, the naj did not intend to let him live long enough to question it. It grinned, pleased with its plan, then started toward the woman. Words were pouring past her tremulous lips now. At first, it thought that she was begging it for mercy, but then the awful sounds of human sorcery burrowed their way into its awareness and her utterances suddenly became all too clear.

The Spell of Unmaking! How—?

"That's for Pieter," Liselle rasped, as the not-shadow's liquified flesh began to flow from its bones. Then she went to see how Lathwi had fared. The big woman's eyes were still closed, and she didn't seem to be breathing. Liselle went to look for a pulse only to have her wrist caught in a ferocious grip.

"Lathwi!" she yelped then. "Let go! It's me!"

Lathwi let go. Then, with a groan, she dragged herself into a sitting position. Her gaze wobbled around the room, then came to rest on Liselle.

"Where—?" she began.

"Over there," Liselle replied, pointing toward the naj's stinking remains. "You know what it was, don't you?"

"It was krim," Lathwi said, as foul a curse as she knew. Then, prompted by Liselle's uncomprehending scowl, she added, "They were called demons in your book of myths."

"But…that's not possible," Liselle stammered. "There hasn't been a demon on this world since the first dawn."

"Nevertheless, that was krim. My memories are true."

Liselle did not want to believe that assertion. Nor did she want to think about its implications. But like a rotting tooth or battered ribs, they compelled their own exploration. "No man could have brought a demon to this world on his own," she said, "not even The Rogue. And the only one who could've possibly helped him has been dead for ages!"

There was no doubt in Lathwi's mind as to whom that One might be. "Could it be that The Rogue has brought Galza back to life?"

Liselle shook her head. "It all boils down to a matter of power. And as mighty as The Rogue is, he still has limits to his strength. No one but the Dreamer Herself could bring Shadow back to life; and I have to believe that She wouldn't inflict that kind of nightmare on the world again."

"Then perhaps," Lathwi said, as casually as if she were discussing the weather, "Galza was never really entirely dead in the first place."

Liselle's thoughts became a gyre of disbelief. Demons were story-book creatures used to frighten naughty children back into their beds; The Dreamer's Daughter was a long-dead legend. She did not want to accept them as anything else—such a reality could be the ruin of the world.

Meanwhile, Lathwi struggled to her feet and went poking through the naj's fetid remains with the sword which Liselle had plunged into its back. The next time Liselle saw her, she had a ruddy stone in her hand.

"Krim took this from my nest," she said. "It seemed to think it was important. Why would it think that?"

"It must be the talisman that I heard the Rogue talking about," Liselle replied. "But it cannot be his, for it does not bear his essence, so I don't know why he wants it."

"A most unsavoury riddle," Lathwi rumbled then. "I know someone who might be able to answer it, though."

"Who?"

"My mother," she replied. "She was the one who had the stone before me. Maybe she will know why others are suddenly interested in it. Any why krim are roaming the world again."

"Let us go and see her then," Liselle said.

Lathwi scowled. Seeing Taziem was exactly what she had in mind. But it hadn't occurred to her to take Liselle with her. The sorceress was too soft and house-bound.

"My mother lives in the mountains," she told her. "It is not an easy journey, even for those who are used to life on the road. And I will be travelling hard."

"I understand," Liselle replied.

"If you come with me, you must keep up," Lathwi went on. "I will leave you behind before I let you slow me down."

"I will keep up," Liselle promised.

"I am leaving tonight," Lathwi said then.

"And I am going with you," Liselle replied. She would rather take her chances with Lathwi on the open road than be left behind in an unwarded house with who-knew-what snapping at her heels! "Just give me a little time so I can cover our tracks—"

Someone knocked at the door then. Liselle started like a spooked hare, then glanced around the room as if in search of a bolt-hole. Lathwi rumbled disapprovingly.

"Do you think krim have suddenly acquired manners?" she asked, and then went to see who it was.

As soon as she opened the door, Jamus came stumbling in. His face was flushed; his clothes, dishevelled. With a tired grunt, he kicked the door shut and then leaned against it as if he were in need of support.

"My men and I have spent the last twenty minutes fending off an attack," he told them. "They stuck to the shadows, so we couldn't see who they were, but they were savage bastards. They're gone now—I think—but I've sent for reinforcements just in case.

"How have—" He stopped, then sneezed. His harassed frown turned to one of revulsion. "What's that awful stink?" Before either of them could answer, he finally recognized the drying blood on Lathwi's face for what it was. "What went on here? Where's the addict?"

"She set off a compulsion that killed her," Liselle told him in a brittle monotone. "In the process, she collapsed my wards. Shortly thereafter, a demon broke into the house and tried to kill Lathwi."

"A demon?" Jamus scoffed. "Come on, Liselle, this is no time for jokes. There's no such thing."

"There is now. Don't ask me how such a evil has come to pass," she added, as he opened his mouth to do exactly that, "for I don't know and I don't have time to speculate. Lathwi and I are leaving Compara. Tonight."

"But why? Where will you go?"

"This business with The Rogue is far more serious than I had ever dreamed. I'm in over my head, I need information as well as help. And Lathwi knows somebody who might be able to provide me with both."

"Who?" he demanded, swivelling his scowl toward Lathwi.

"My mother," she replied.

Jamus puffed up like a threatened adder. A vein in his temple began to throb. "Liselle," he said, barely resisting the urge to shout, "that's ridiculous. You won't accomplish anything by chasing after wild geese. Stay here. My men and I can protect you—"

"Jamus!" she exclaimed, her voice cracking with stress. "Weren't you listening to me? I can't stay here! My wards are in a shambles and there are demons afoot. Moreover, my enemy may very well be in league with The Dreamer's Daughter. Perhaps I'm going on a wild goose hunt as you say, but right now, it's my only hope. If I don't find out what's going on, you may soon see a day when no one is safe. And that day, my dear, could last forever."

He did not try to digest everything she had said—too much of it strayed beyond the bounds of easy credibility. It was enough for him to know that she wanted to leave; and that he had no chance of changing her mind.

"All right then," he said. "I'm coming with you."

"No, you aren't," she replied, and then touched her hand to his lips to forestall another argument. "We need you here to camouflage our absence."

"Oh?" His tone was barbed with sarcasm. "And how am I supposed to do that?"

"Make it seem as if Lathwi's been seriously hurt. Have your physician visit the house at least once a day. Have him spread rumours about a mysterious attacker. At the same time, increase the number of patrols to the catacombs—with a bit of luck, The Rogue will think that the hive's been stirred up but not broken. Oh, and bury Margita's body in the basement. If the bastard can't find her, he'll have to wonder; and it's to our advantage to keep him guessing as long as possible."

"Anything else?" he asked.

His stropped tone brought a flush to her cheeks, but she went on nonetheless. "Yes. We need horses. Lathwi's bay is in the stable, but I'm afraid I'm going to have to borrow the other from you. Bring them here so we can ride out when your reinforcements do. In all the darkness and confusion, maybe no one will notice two extra riders."

"And what if I refuse to go along with this ruse?"

"One way or another, we're leaving tonight," she said. "How far we get before we're discovered could depend on you."

He swore, stricken to the core of his heart by that last guilt-laden nail. And although he'd shouldered more than his fair share of difficult decisions in his career, none of them had galled him as badly as the one he made now.

"I'll do it," he told her. Then, because he desperately needed to have the last word, he added, "But be warned, lady: when you return from this insane trip of yours, you and I are going to have a long talk about your headstrong ways."

"If we get back," Liselle countered, "I'll gladly listen to whatever you have to say. Until then, though, you'll have to suffer in silence.

"Now go. Please. The night grows no younger."

He stared at her for a long moment, then abruptly pulled her close and crushed his lips to hers. Then, before she had a chance to react, he turned on his heel and went rushing out of the house.

"Goodbye," she whispered, as the door swung shut. Eyes downcast, she then turned to Lathwi and said, "Meet me in the laboratory when you're done packing and I'll show you how to patch a ward. We won't have time to do a good job, but maybe The Rogue won't notice right away."

Lathwi shrugged, then headed for the loft to collect her few possessions. The length and breadth of Liselle's agenda for their leaving amazed her. All she had been meaning to do was walk out the door and never come back; in the end, it all boiled down to that one simple event anyway.

Humans, she thought then, and wondered what Taziem would think of them.

Later that night, Lathwi and Liselle rode out of Compara amidst a company of soldiers. Every mile or so, two of these riders peeled away from the pack and went their separate ways to confound any would-be followers, until finally, the escort was gone. The two women rode on and on without looking back.

Liselle was excited, but a little homesick as well. She was a city-dweller born and bred; these wild, open spaces did not reassure her like Compara did. It was not the sights and sounds and smells she missed; or her house and her things and all the comforts of home. It was the people, or rather their presence, the knowledge that she was surrounded at all times; insulated; secure. And there was one person she missed above all others. Jamus had not been a part of the escort tonight, and his absence panged her heart. She would take him to task for that when she returned. And then, at last, she would let him make it up to her.

The warmth of that thought pulled her deeper and deeper into a fuzzy grey netherworld. The next thing she knew, the sun was coming up and Lathwi was far, far ahead of her. She urged her sturdy grey mare after the stallion's dusty trail, but drew no closer. Finally, afraid of being abandoned, she shouted.

"Lathwi! Please! Wait up."

Lathwi reined her horse to a standstill then, but only grudgingly. Taziem's mountain was visible on the far horizon as a fang-like spire crowned with cloud, but between here and there lay this seemingly endless stretch of prairie; a swatch of rugged wasteland; and then the wooded foothills. It would take them fortnight to cover that much ground, longer if they dallied on the way. And there were krim in the world again!

"You must not shout at me like that again," she said, as Liselle came to a stop alongside her. "Everything with ears will know where we are."

"I'm sorry," Liselle replied. "I didn't think there was anything with ears out here." She ran a dusty hand along the frazzled rope of her braid. As she did so, she gave Lathwi a critical once-over. The right side of her face was a mottled bruise. The stiffness with which she sat in the saddle spoke of sore ribs. "Are we going to stop anytime soon?" she asked then. "You look as though you could use a rest."

"I am fine," Lathwi said, although that was stretching the truth as far as it would go. That krim had left her sore all over, and the re-warding ritual that she and Liselle had performed had left her fatigued as well. "We will ride until we find a suitable place to stop."

Then she urged the bay onward again and into a ruthless trot.

Somewhere around midday, they came upon a shady copse of cottonwood trees. Liselle didn't need to wonder if they were going to stop here. Lathwi was out of her saddle already and on her belly in front of the watering hole.

An instant after Liselle got down from the mare's back, she cramped from toe to crotch. She crumpled to the ground, then curled into a fetal knot and tried to will the pain out of her body. Minutes or hours later, Lathwi strode over and sat down beside her. Gently but firmly, she straightened one of the sorceress' pain-wracked legs and began to knead it.

"Pieter did this for me when I got the riding-sickness," she told her. "It did not feel good at the time, but it made it easier for me to get back into my saddle the next day. He made me swallow some kind of broth as well, but you will have to do without that."

Liselle rolled her eyes and groaned. She had never hurt this badly in so many places, and Lathwi's fingers felt like hot pincers to her tenderized flesh.

"Talk to me," she begged. "The sound of your voice will keep my mind from the pain."

Lathwi contemplated the request for a long moment, then rumbled as an idea struck her. "I will give you dragonkind's version of the last days of Everlight. Perhaps then you will understand my need for haste on this trip."

Then, without further preamble, she began the memory as she had gotten it from Taziem.

"It begins with an image of trees," she said. "Giant, broad-barrelled cloud-scrapers whose tops cannot be seen from the ground. These are dragon trees. Their dish-like crowns are our homes.

"We are a populous race, strong of limb and long-lived. We spend the majority of our lives hunting and playing above the treetops. We are not concerned with the passage of time or the doings of lesser creatures.

"One day, though, everything changes. At one moment, we are dancing across the sky; in the next, we are attacked by a host of shadow-black creatures whose like we have never seen. Smaller, slower, and less agile than dragons, they descend in packs—a score of them against one of us. Full-grown sires and dams with hides as tough as weathered stone are wrestled to the ground and savaged; tender-skinned younglings are torn apart while still in the air. Our fire does not damage them. Many of the young are lost before we finally drive these krim off.

"Afterward, angry sires go hunting for the reason behind the attack. When they return, it is with shocking news. For the first time ever, we have an enemy—an unnatural being of immense power. Krim call this being A'Gal-Zanna, which means 'Daughter of Death' in their tongue. We name Her Galza, the Dragonbane.

"She sends Her krim against us again. As we take to the sky to challenge them, they take refuge in the forest. Trees begin to burn then. Oily spirals of black-green smoke invade our nests. Clutches of newborn, still too young to fly, honk for help, but before their dams can swoop in and rescue them, the krim-set fires eat through the bottoms of their nests and send them plummeting toward the ground. We are outraged now, half-insane with grief and loss. We go hunting for the krim who laid waste to our young, and when we find them, we slay them with unprecedented cruelty. Then, still sick with hate and sorrow, we abandon the smoldering ruins of our ancestral home.

"We find refuge among the craggy peaks and valleys of a mountain range. The first of a new generation of dragons is born in cold, dark caves. But our humbling does not satisfy foul Galza. She wants us gone from the world. So she sends Her krim after us again. And again. We slay vast numbers of the creatures, but win only a series of brief reprieves.

"Then the day that we have been dreading comes. An army of krim appears on the horizon—a distant patch of blackness as massive as a thunderhead. Alarms are sounded, tanglemates are Called. By ones and twos, the last scraps of dragon-kind gather on a windswept mountain-top to watch and wait. No one suggests flight. We know we have no place left to go.

"As the horde advances, we spy an alien in its midst. It is two-legged like krim, with a swollen abdomen and shrivelled dugs. Its hide is coloured like corruption: jet-black marbled with obscene green. Wingless, it cannot ride the wind, so it grinds it beneath its spurred heels instead. A thought races from dragon to dragon: this must be Galza, come to watch the final slaughter. Our dread converts to rage.

"Brave-hearted Fevver bugles a challenge to Galza, then takes wing. But before he can get close enough to lay a claw on Her, the little red eye in the center of Her brow flashes. A streak of black lightning goes tearing across the sky, then buries itself in Fevver's chest. He bursts into umber flames and is consumed. As the wind herds his ashes back toward us, Galza shrieks with glee.

"A huge silver-backed dragon by the name of Oma answers that fell cry with one of her own, then vaults into the air. But she who has been Fevver's life-long mate does not fly at Galza. Instead, she launches into a dance of fury and grief. As she wings anguished patterns across the rust-coloured sky, she invokes great Names that no dragon has petitioned before or since.

"Galza's third eye erupts again. Oma does not see the bolt of corruption until it burrows into her chest. For one long heartbeat, she remains motionless, as if she is being held aloft by an invisible set of wings. Then she begins to fall—a bottom-first plummet that ends in a bone-shattering collision with the upper reaches of our mountain. An ominous rumbling fills the air then, and the ground beneath our feet begins to convulse. Plates of solid rock sprout fast-growing cracks, boulders go tumbling down the slope. When we take to the sky to escape the quaking, we see that the mountain-side is now growing a earth-encrusted bulge. Upward it swells, as if straining for the sky. Everything in its way is uprooted. Then, with one last violent tremor, its rubbled dome erupts, leaving a massive crater behind.

"From out of that crater emerges a silver-backed dragon. She is huge, an animated mountaintop; her body is made all of stone. At her glance, the Lesser Sun flares. A single beam of its ruddy light engulfs her. Heartbeats later, she begins to glow like mound of heated coals. As she basks, the first wave of krim close in on her. She stretches her neck toward them, then disgorges a stream of the Lesser Sun's fire. Krim fall from the sky as greasy ashes. We flock to this new Oma, eager to follow her into the fray, but she takes no notice of us. She is staring across the void which separates her from Galza. The Dragonbane responds with a roar of utter hatred.

"The battle is joined then: black lightning versus ruddy sun-fire. Time after time after time, the two forces collide over the void; and for a long while, one demolishes the other without gaining any ground. Hundreds of krim are consumed in this cross-fire; we dragons take refuge on the mountain's lee side. The earth shakes as if with ague. The air grows thick with resinous smoke.

"Then, without our noticing it at first, fortune shifts in the Stone Oma's favour. Her fiery exhalations are reaching further and further across the void now; and each one absorbs more of Galza's corruption than the last. Finally, realizing that Her cause is lost, The Dragonbane turns to flee. As She does so, the Stone Oma breaths two dazzling streams of power: the first catches Galza by the legs; the other encases Her in a fiery sphere of energy. Galza lavishes fury beyond measure upon Her peculiar cocoon, but She cannot breach its walls and so remains suspended over the world like a ferocious parasite caught in a giant's bladder.

"Oma rumbles then. It is a sound as deep as the earth's bowels. In response, the Lesser Sun flares to near-blinding brilliance and extrudes another tendril of intensified light. It streaks down from the sky and toward Galza's sphere, then in a flash, encapsules it. A second rumble boils from Oma's stone throat. Jagged bolts of ruddy lightning tear through Galza's body then; and as She writhes in apparent agony, Her obsidian spurs slough off one by one. Her ivory horn defects next, then Her golden hands. Finally, Her third eye lurches free of its socket. Galza howls, an impotent scream of rage and hatred. An instant later, Her head bursts into a miasma of shifting black mists; save for two laval eyes and a gaping maw, it is now featureless.

"Oma rumbles yet again. The sphere thickens, obscuring Galza's foul visage from sight, then flares to incandescence. For a long moment, it burns above the world like a miniature replica of the Lesser Sun. Then Oma unclenches her jaws and looses a last burst of sunfire. The ensuing explosion blinds us. The shockwaves which follow a moment later knock us into unconsciousness.

"When we awake again, Galza is gone. The only proof of Her erstwhile existence is the devastation that she has left behind. The Stone Oma is gone, too. All that remains of her is a crater full of glittering, blue-white pebbles. We keen our grief, mourning ourselves as well as Oma, for while Galza has been vanquished, it appears that Her malice has triumphed nonetheless. For the sky is black now. It is beautiful in a stark sort of way, but terrifying at the same time. Not even the wisest among us can imagine life in a world with no light or warmth.

"Yet even as we grieve, a faint smudge of violet appears in the sky. It is followed by glimmers of lavender and dusky rose, then streaks of red and gold. The Greater Sun comes up on the horizon then; it is still as bright as a dragon's eye. As its light burns the last of the darkness away, we roar for joy and relief, for our lives have been redeemed.

"That is the way dragons remember the end of the days of EverLight," Lathwi said then. "Our memories are true."

Liselle did not hear her. She was sound asleep and had been for some time now. Even so, Lathwi was glad that she'd reviewed that ancient memory, for it reinforced her decision to seek out Taziem. Her mother would know what was going on; the she-dragon was well on her way to knowing everything.

Her eyelids were heavy with fatigue now. She leaned up against the back of a tree to give them a rest. But only for a moment, she told herself. Only for a moment...

The stallion's nervous whickering dragged Lathwi back to consciousness. Ignoring the soreness in her ribs, she sprang to her feet and then had a look around the campsite. Nothing seemed amiss: the horses were still picketed among the trees, and Liselle was still fast asleep in the dirt. She was just about to blame the bay's fidgeting on a swarm of biting gnats when the sound of approaching hoofbeats caught her ear. She fingered the hilt of the sword that Jamus had given her, then hid herself behind a tree and waited for the intruder to show himself.

A tall buckskin with black stockings soon sauntered into view. Its rider was trim and well-formed, a leather-clad man with a deep tan and a long brown braid. Lathwi's jaw dropped as she caught sight of his face.

"Pawl!" she exclaimed, not loud but in a tone rich with surprise. "What are you doing here?"

"I followed you," he replied, and then slung himself out of his saddle. "Someone told me you might be in need of some help."

The unfamiliar voice rippled through the gauzy layers of Liselle's subconscious until it pinched a nerve. She shifted out of her fetal knot, then gasped as the hazy image of a man lodged in her brain. Her face was studded with clods of dirt and cottonwood litter; this gave her alarm a comical facade.

"Who are you?" she demanded. "Where's Lathwi?"

"I am right here," Lathwi replied, then strode over and sank into a squat beside her. "All is well for the moment."

"Who's that man? What's he doing here?"

"His name is Pawl," she said. "He's the swordmaster of Compara. He is here because someone told him to follow us."

Liselle rubbed the last vestiges of sleep from her eyes, then sized the stranger up. His face was rugged rather than handsome: a compelling blend of character, hardship and harsh weather. He carried himself with a soldier's self-assurance. The gleam in his eyes hinted at a potential for extremes.

"Who sent you?" she asked warily.

"Jamus," he replied.

"I'm afraid he misled you," she told him. "This isn't a military mission. One sword more or less isn't going to make much of a difference."

"I wouldn't be so sure about that," he said. "This part of the country is thick with outlaws. They wouldn't hesitate to attack two women, but they might think twice about attacking two women and a soldier. And if that's not enough of an incentive for you, then consider this: I can also hunt, keep watch, and scout a decent trail."

Liselle had to admit: his arguments were seductive. She had no desire to face a band of cut-throats on her own and no heart for hunting. As tempting as his offer was, though, she did not want to be the one to accept it. That would make her responsible for any grief that might befall him; and she had enough blood on her conscience already. So, craven that she was, she turned to Lathwi.

"He's your friend. What do you say?"

Unlike Liselle, Lathwi wasn't daunted by the prospect of bandits or blood. And as for a trail, one was as good as any other so long as it got her where she needed to go. Even so, Pawl's company was not a thing to be lightly refused—he was smart and cunning, a human of remarkably few words. And his skill with a sword was undeniable.

"So long as you can keep up," she decided aloud, "you can ride with us."

A corner of his mouth twitched, a flicker of amusement that then spread to his eyes.

"Fair enough," he said. "Now all you need to tell me is where we're going."

She led him to a space among the trees, then pointed to Taziem's imposing, dusk-mantled spire. As he took it in, he whistled through his teeth.

"You don't make anything easy, do you?"

Her only response was a shrug. It was, he thought, an exquisitely appropriate reply.

To Liselle's relief, they had a quick supper before they returned to the road. It was humble fare—sweet apples, dry journey bread and jerked venison—but it seemed like a feast to her. She ate with an appetite whetted by fresh air, sleep and exercise; and only a fear of seeming gluttonous prevented her from eating more. A short time later, though, she became glad of her restraint, for a full belly in the saddle was not nearly as restful as a full belly on the ground. She shifted and squirmed in search of an angle that would accommodate her supper as well as her stiffened limbs, then gave up and tried not to think about either.

They rode past dusk and into the night: a hard, wordless trek punctuated only by the drumming of their horses' hooves. Pawl was a natural in the saddle, as relaxed as a cavalryman; and while Lathwi lacked his easy style, she was more than his equal where endurance was concerned. Liselle felt like a bag of laundry by comparison—a bag with an aching back and sore thighs and a burgeoning need for sleep. Nevertheless, she kept up as best as she could; and in time, her horse's steady gait rocked her into a waking trance. It wasn't the same as being asleep, but it was better than nothing at all.

Dawn came and went. The new morning turned hot and dry. Pawl scrubbed a trickle of sweat from his brow, then scowled at the sun-washed foothills which mounded the horizon. They would not get that far today, perhaps not even tomorrow; and if they went on at this brutal pace, they might not get there at all. He reined his buckskin to a sudden halt. Lathwi and then Liselle pulled up alongside of him.

"What is wrong?" Lathwi demanded. Her frown was all for him.

"I think we ought to leave the road and head for yonder trees," he replied, pointing toward a distant strip of green. "We can sit out the hottest part of the day there, then start out fresh come sunset. With any luck, we'll flush something out for dinner along the way."

The thought of food made Lathwi's stomach growl, for she had declined Pawl's earlier offer of apples and bread, and so was quite hungry now. But hunger could be ignored, and after a while, it would fade away. She couldn't say the same about krim.

"I agree that it is time for us to leave the road," she told him. "But I see no need for stopping at those trees."

"Maybe you don't," Pawl retorted, "but your horse does. Look at him—he's winded and slick with sweat. If you don't give him a chance to rest, he'll collapse in this heat. Then you'll either have to wait for him to recover, or carry on by foot. Either way, you'll lose more time than you thought to gain."

Lathwi ran a hand along the stallion's sweaty neck, then frowned as she imagined this long and arduous journey without him. "Very well," she said then. "We will stop."

Liselle suppressed an urge to cheer. Pawl nodded his approval. Then, as they steered their mounts away from the road and into the tall grass, he parted with another bit of advice.

"It would be best to let the horses walk for a while. That way, their legs won't cramp up when we finally stop."

Lathwi did not object simply because they were going no further than those trees anyway. So they plodded across the grassy plain, slower than sloths. No one spoke. No one had anything to say. Then a pair of shadows raced overhead—too fast for clouds, and going against the wind as well. The bay snorted a warning, then laid his ears flat. The other horses began to prance nervously.

"What is it?" Pawl asked, as he fought his buckskin to a standstill.

"Dragons," Lathwi replied. Her head was slanted toward the sky. Her expression was a bittersweet mixture of longing and delight.

Liselle glanced toward the fringe of trees, then licked her lips. "Do you know them?" she whispered.

Lathwi silenced her with an upraised hand, then returned her attention to the airborne duo. They were long and gangly like overgrown lizards, and their wingspans were mere slivers compared to Shoq's. Their unembellished flight patterns told her that they were hunting; and their sudden change of course could only mean one thing.

"Well?" Liselle prompted. "Should we make a run for the trees?"

"No!" Lathwi snapped. "You must never turn your back to a hungry dragon."

"Then make them go away!"

"To do that, I would have to challenge both of them; and although they are still juveniles, they are still bigger than me. If I were to lose—"

"I'll help you," Pawl volunteered, and then flinched as a shadowy wingtip sliced across his face. "I have no desire to wind up in a dragon's belly."

"I do not want to hurt them if it can be avoided," she told him, though his courage impressed her. "Let us try to trick them instead."

"How?" Liselle asked, as she followed the now-circling dragons with her eyes.

"Dismount," Lathwi ordered. At the same time, she slung herself out of her saddle. When they hesitated to follow her example, she snapped, "Hurry! We do not have much time." An instant later, they were on the ground. "Now we need to make the horses lie down. Liselle, is there a spell that will put them to sleep?"

"That won't be necessary," Pawl said, and then grabbed his buckskin by the head. To the amazement of both women, he then toppled the beast with a single fluid move.

"Liselle, come over here," he called. As she scurried toward him, he added, "Lie down alongside of his neck. Use your weight to hold his head down. And cover his eyes with your hands."

Although the sorceress didn't think she would be able to hold something so big and powerful down against its will, she did as she was told without delay. When the buckskin made no move to escape, but merely rolled its eyes and trembled, she forgot her reservations and began to murmur reassuring noises into its ear. Meanwhile, Pawl hurried over to Lathwi and her mount. The bay bared his teeth as he came near, but received no exemption for the display—with a twist and a shove, Pawl brought him to the ground. As Lathwi scurried into position, he raced off to take care of Liselle's skittish mare. Then, from his patch of flattened grass, he called out.

"Now what?"

"Keep still," Lathwi told him. "I am going to make us disappear."

Liselle sucked in a scandalized breath. Lathwi couldn't work an illusion of that magnitude while they were this close to Compara—the echoes of her magic would reach The Rogue in no time and expose their charade! But even as she started to blurt that out, a belated realization shushed her: so long as Lathwi was wearing her amulet, she could work as much sorcery as she wished without drawing a stitch of unwanted attention. That fact might have rankled her at some other point in time, but now it raised nothing but the purest relief.

The dragons flying lower in the sky now. The larger one was a black and bronze calico; its companion had scars on its belly. Both had golden eyes and predatory grins. The notion of confronting them with a nothing but a sword made Pawl want to go bolting for the impossible safety of yonder trees. Yet despite the fear which they inspired in him, he couldn't help but admire their absolute grace and power and confidence.

If only they weren't so close!

He swallowed hard, then began an agonizingly slow reach for the hilt of his sword. As if in response to that motion, the calico dragon warbled an alarm. Its companion tilted its triangular head and hissed. They quit their deceptively lazy circling and came swooping out of the sky as if for the kill. But while they passed directly overhead, close enough to stir the grass with their tailwind, they did not seem to see them. One rumbled, the other honked. They doubled back for another pass, then abruptly veered off toward the clouds. Soon, they reverted to airborne specks.

Lathwi released the stallion then. He lunged in one direction, she rolled in the other and then bugled. What a grand trick that had been! She could hardly wait to try it on Shoq!

The absoluteness of her glee intrigued Pawl. Where was the relief, the taint of residual fear? Did she not realize that they'd all come within a hair of being dragon meat? He looked at Liselle then, but there was nothing puzzling about her expression: it was one of stunned redemption. He strode over to her with the mare in tow.

"What's with her?" he asked, as they exchanged reins.

Liselle twitched a commiserate half-smile at him, then replied, "This is her idea of fun."

That intrigued him, too.

CHAPTER 20

Malcolm was stunned, as bewildered as a drunk who's just woken up from a week-long bender to find his world in smoking ruins. Had he really been poised on the brink of his dearest dream just twelve short hours ago? It did not seem possible, yet the evidence was right here for all to see. His robe was clean—a gesture of ceremonial respect. And the focal point of that would-be ceremony still adorned the floor in front of him. It was unused; incomplete; a symbol of his failure.

He dragged his fingers through the sweaty tangles of his hair as if trawling for the strength to endure. Last night's fiasco had cost him an unparalleled opportunity, and a number of irreplaceable tools as well. The naj was gone, reportedly destroyed by catastrophic magic; and the nonborn which he had slated as its replacement was missing, too. In addition, one of the lesser demons had been hurt in the fight with Lathwi's guards, and the curra-chewer's whereabouts remained a nagging unknown. None of these details would have been noteworthy on its own, but together, they became the framework for Lathwi's second victory over him.

The bitch! He should be the king of the world by now.

His only consolation was based on a rumour; and the petty satisfaction which it sparked within him was accompanied by a sizzling dread. This rumour said that Lathwi had battled with an unknown intruder last night. It also said that she'd been grievously hurt.

He cursed the naj with heart-felt vigour. If it had not been dead already, he would've reduced it to a puddle himself for daring to harm the only person whom he desperately needed alive. Fool! He was almost glad that Lathwi had relieved it of its miserable life.

Almost.

He would've liked to have asked it a couple of questions now. Like: had it found the talisman? And: what did it look like? And: where in hell was it now? He also wanted to know what 'grievously' meant. The Dark One required an able body, not dying meat. If Lathwi couldn't satisfy that contingency, he'd have to go in search of a sorcerer who could. That hunt could take months, maybe even years. Such a long delay would earn him no favour with his impatient Mistress. Indeed, he'd be lucky to survive Her disappointment.

Rather than dwell on that awful possibility, he shunted his thoughts back to the more immediate matter of Lathwi. He needed to know how badly she was hurt. And he needed to know now. Rumours weren't dependable, for they swelled like greedy sponges as they skipped from one tongue to the next. And his drudges weren't completely reliable, either, for they lacked the wit or inclination to distinguish important details from happenstance. If he didn't ask them the right questions, he might well starve in the midst of plenty. The ideal solution would be for him to see how she was for himself, but the idea of making any kind of contact with such a powerful sorceress outside of his stronghold left a sour taste in his mouth.

If only there were some other way…

He clapped a clammy hand to his forehead then. What an idiot he was! Lathwi was wounded, her wards were in tatters, and the naj had given him a clear image of her. What was to stop him from translocating her out of her sick-bed and into yonder diagram? If she was damaged beyond use, he would put her out of her misery; if she was salvable, he would put her in stasis. A smile spread across his mouth like a crack in thin ice. This new plan of attack pleased him, for it made last night's disaster seem more like a setback than a true failure.

Eager to embark on this new course of action, he focussed on the thought-image that the naj had given him. But even as Lathwi's fierce countenance took shape in his mind, a psychic alarm disrupted it. He suppressed a spasm of annoyance, then stretched a finger of his Will toward his stronghold's warded entrance. It brushed against a demon's turbid mind. Malcolm considered sending it away until such time as he had finished his other business, but then decided to hear what his spy had to say.

The drudge came skulking into the chamber, then dropped to its knees in front of his throne and pressed its forehead to the floor. Malcolm didn't consider that a good sign.

"Did you find the talisman?" he asked.

"No, Master," it replied.

Although he had braced himself against such an answer, a sharp pang of disappointment tore through him nonetheless. Damn that woman! How could she have hidden the talisman so well? Could it be that she wasn't so terribly incapacitated after all?

"Tell me what the wags at the garrison are saying about Lathwi today," he commanded.

"Speculation is rampant, Master," it said, now daring to sneak glimpses of him. "One set of rumours forecasts a speedy recovery for her; the other reckons she's already dead."

His heart fluttered, a sickening feeling that threatened to spread throughout his guts. He suppressed an urge to snap to his feet and pace. "I see. And what's it like around her house—all quiet? Too quiet? Have people started to avoid the place?"

"No, Master. Everything is as it was before the attack, perhaps even livelier. The one called D'Arques has come and gone several times already.

An aged man who responds to the name of 'physician' travels with him. They converse in dour whispers and wear unwavering frowns."

"Have they removed any bodies from the house?"

"No, Master."

That bit of news encouraged him, but he did not dare to hope too much. "Did you or any of the others see any bodies when you searched the house for the talisman?"

The demon's gaze dropped to the floor again. Its nasal flap began to flutter like a leaf in a breeze. "We did not search the house, Master."

"What?" Outrage yanked him out of his chair. "How can this be? Did I not tell you to do so?"

"Yes, Master—"

"Fool! How did you expect to find the talisman without going through the house? Did you imagine that it would come flying into your imbecilic hands of its own accord?"

"We tried to do your bidding, Master," it told him, "but we could not enter the house. Every time we tried, her wards repelled us."

Malcolm snarled. "That house has no wards, demon. The addict shattered them last night."

"I know, I was there. But they have undergone repairs since then."

Overwhelmed by a whirlwind of implications, he sank back into his seat. Oh, but this Lathwi was a sly bitch, he mused to himself. Engaging the physician to lend credence to those manufactured rumours had been a brilliant ploy. He had been a breath away from believing that she was nearly dead. But not anymore! Those regenerated wards had given her away! Nobody with one foot in the grave could have maintained the power or concentration necessary to achieve such a feat.

So. Why would she want him to think that she was on her deathbed? To buy herself some time? That possibility didn't sit well with him. Lathwi was a smart woman, surely she knew that he would regard any sign of weakness as an invitation to attack…

The hair on his arms and nape prickled then. Of course! She wanted him to attack. More precisely, she wanted him to come bursting in on her off-guard and unprepared so she could pounce on him like a spider on a fly. He wouldn't have stood a chance.

"Tell me more of these rehabilitated wards," he said to the demon. "Are they as impregnable as ever?"

"No, Master," it replied. "They are imperfect now—a patchwork with many raw seams. I could not breach them, but someone of your immense power and cunning could."

"I see," he murmured, already envisioning a new avenue of attack. Bit by bit, he would pick at one of those seams until it sprung a leak.

Then, at an hour when she was least likely to be awake, he would slip his Will through that back door and translocate her. When she was safely imprisoned in stasis, he would collapse the rest of her wards and send the demons in for the talisman.

"You have done well," he said then, rewarding the demon with a rare bit of praise, "so you may feed before you return to your post."

"As you will, Master," it gurgled, and then went loping from the chamber.

Malcolm did not see it go; he was already beginning his surreptitious invasion.

It took him over thirty-six hours to compromise Lathwi's reconstituted wards. He laboured with consummate stealth and care—extruding his Will, then retracting it again, pausing only long enough to lavish a thin film of corrosive magic on the seam of his choosing. The repetitions involved left him increasingly fatigued. Tired or not, though, he remained as keen as a hound on a fox's trail. All he could think of was that glorious moment when his jaws would come shut around her neck.

Finally, his slow-acting malice ate a hole in the seam. A miasma of scents engulfed his spectral face then. The first whiff was intoxicating, the embodiment of triumph. The next was as sour as an old fart. These were residual odours, faint ghosts of days gone by. Where was the distinctive tang of living flesh?

Fighting back temblors of sudden alarm, he projected his senses through the gap and into the house. The bedrooms were deserted, as was the loft. The laboratory was lifeless, too. His hope flickered as he descended into the basement, but the cowering shadow that he had thought he had seen was in fact a shallow grave. He probed it with a thought only to encounter the moldering remains of the addict's aura. Good riddance to her, he thought, and went streaking back upstairs. There, he explored the pantry, the fireplace, even the odiferous gloom of the water closet. But even as he did so, he knew what he would find.

Nothing.

Lathwi was gone. So was the talisman.

An instant after he acknowledged those impossible facts, an insane, uncontainable fury erupted within him. He vomited a flood of psychic acid, then detonated it with his Will. As Lathwi's house began to fall, he catapulted himself back into his own sanctuary. There, he knotted his Will into a furious fist and then sent it screaming after an image of a blue-eyed bitch.

As dawn spilled over the still distant foothills, Lathwi shifted in her saddle, then stretched to pop the kinks in her spine. As she did so, an annoying buzz filled her ears. She shook her head, attempting to drive the unseen mosquito away, but it continued to plague her. An instant later, her amulet erupted—a breath-taking surge of power which coincided with a violent psychic blow. The impact jarred her from the bay's back and onto her own. She took no notice of her fall; every fibre of her being was already centered on the alien presence that was now in her head. Its Will was strong beyond belief. She could feel it dragging her toward a void from which there could be no return. She dug the heels of her own Will in and struggled to stay put.

Lathwi's sudden tumble to the ground shocked Liselle out of a meandering daydream. She scrambled down from her saddle with a dexterity born of fear, then raced to the big woman's side. Pawl was already there, cradling her head in his lap.

"What goes on here?" he demanded, in a voice edged with helplessness. "Does she have the falling-down sickness?"

For so it appeared. Every muscle in Lathwi's body was stretched taut, her brow was streaked with cold sweat. But the almost imperceptible haziness about her extremities told Liselle that this was far worse than any epileptic fit.

"She's being attacked by sorcery," she replied, fighting off the urge to panic. "The Rogue is trying to draw her back to Compara."

"What can I do to help her?"

"Just shut up and hang on to her!" Liselle snapped. "I need a moment to think!"

He wrapped his arms around Lathwi's rigid torso and then held her with all his might. She wasn't going anywhere—not not if he had anything to say about it.

Meanwhile, Liselle gathered up her powers. She couldn't think of a tried-and-true way out of this plight, but she did have an idea that stood a good chance of working if she could just get past Lathwi's amulet.

"Lathwi," she grated. "Can you hear me?"

Lathwi grunted, the only reply she could manage. Her Will was in a deadlock with The Rogue's, and she could not relax so much as a muscle without tipping the advantage to him.

"Do you remember what I taught you about mind links not so long ago?" Liselle asked then.

Again she grunted. That lesson had been one of the most traumatic experiences of her life. Until now.

"I hope so," Liselle went on, "because he made a serious mistake when he attacked you in this way. If you can hold on to him for just a moment, it may be that we can make him pay for his audacity."

The thought gave Lathwi a savage thrill. She would very much like to hurt the person who had stuck his fingers in her head. So all at once, she shifted tactics: instead of trying to drive The Rogue away, she concentrated on making him stay. His Will rippled with sudden alarm, then tried to break free. Both reactions fanned her excitement.

"I have him," she rasped.

Liselle was brimming with power now: a sorcerous cannonade. It was not the death curse she would have liked it to be, for she suspected that Lathwi's amulet would repel something that explicit, but with any luck, it would have the same effect.

"I'm going to feed you a mass of power," she told Lathwi. "Channel the whole lot into the link all at once. As soon as you do that, release The Rogue and hope for the worst."

Lathwi hissed. "Do it."

Liselle extended her Will then, meaning to create a link with Lathwi's amulet. It rebuffed her first advance, and the second one as well. She started to tremble from the pressure of holding so much power in. She approached again, this time projecting desperate good will. Lathwi's wards indented like a sheet of rubber, then abruptly yielded with a pop. Linked now, Liselle groaned like a woman in the last stages of labour and loosed her magical salvo.

As Lathwi strained to keep The Rogue's writhing Will in her death-grip, a pressurized hum intruded on her awareness. It grew louder and closer, then louder and closer still. She could see it with her mind's eye now; it was white-hot like a shooting star and bristling with power. She sent it down the imaginary alley which led to The Rogue's mind. His struggles to free himself turned frantic. Instinct told her she should let him go now, but she could not resist detaining him for a moment longer. She wanted to be sure he bore the full brunt Liselle's enmity.

The last impression she received was one of overwhelming pain. Not all of it was The Rogue's.

A gentle tapping against her cheeks jarred Lathwi out of a soft, comfy darkness. She peeked past one eyelid, then the other. All she could see was the half-blurred outline Pawl's head and the worried slants that were his eyes.

"What happened?" she asked. The question came out as a groan.

"You didn't let go of him fast enough," Liselle replied, in an equally croaky tone. "A bit of the backlash got you."

"I see." That must explain the headache, too.

"So," the sorceress said then. "Did we kill him?"

"I cannot say for certain," Lathwi replied, remembering a series of long, shivering screams that may or may not have been her own, "but I do not think so."

"Oh, well," Liselle said, too spent to be disappointed. "At least he'll think twice before poking his grubby fingers in your mind again." Then she turned her gaze to Pawl. "If you're smart, you'll get on your horse and high-tail it away from us. Once The Rogue recovers from his little shock, he's going to do everything possible to make our lives miserable."

"In that case," he said, with a peculiar glitter in his eyes, "we ought to be on our way again. This Rogue won't be able to plague us if he doesn't know where we are."

Liselle groaned: a pained, incredulous sound. "You want us to move? Pawl, you have no idea what you're asking! I'll be lucky if I can find the strength to keep my eyes open long enough to finish this conversation. Let's make camp here and call it a day."

For once, Lathwi was in complete agreement with the tiny sorceress. All she wanted to do was sleep.

"We can't camp here," Pawl informed them in a reasonable tone. "It's too exposed. If the sun didn't get us, a dragon would."

"I'd just as soon face an army of dragons as climb back into that damn saddle right now," Liselle told him.

"See that ridge?" He pointed to a distant outcropping of rocks. His reasonable tone suddenly had a ruthless edge to it. "That's where we're going to camp, even if I have to drag the two of you every step of the way. Now get moving."

He got up then and went to collect the horses. Neither Lathwi nor Liselle offered to help.

By the time they finally reached that distant ridge, the sun was already on the downside of its zenith. The two women rolled out of their saddles without a word, then curled up on the ground and fell immediately asleep. Had they been a pair of his recruits, Pawl would've rousted them from their rocky beds and made them attend to their animals, but as it was, he left them alone and did the job himself. Liselle's grey mare nuzzled him as if in thanks for the attention; the bay tried to bite him while his back was turned. He reviled the beast with a few colourful words, then cheerfully continued with his work. When he was done, he secured their perimeters and then finally settled down for a well-earned nap.

Some soldierly instinct woke him at dusk, but he did not try to rouse the women. They weren't going anywhere tonight. He didn't wholly understand what had transpired back there in the grass this morning, but he'd been on enough campaigns in his lifetime to recognize battle fatigue when he saw it. And both Lathwi and Liselle had it.

He fetched an apple and several twists of jerky from his saddlebags, then climbed to the top of the ridge. As he ate, he surveyed the world around him.

As it happened, the ridge was a natural boundary line. To the west of it spanned the grasslands, which were now cast in the ruby hues of sunset.

To the east lay a darkening maze of eroding plateaus, skeletal cousins of the foothills which loomed beyond. These defiles assumed an eerie beauty in the waning moments of twilight. Canyons traversed the crumbling moonstone bluffs like black-and-blue claw-marks; the riddled pinnacles which stood apart gleamed faintly violet. Nothing stirred, not even a breeze—it was as if the whole world was holding its breath. The effect was hypnotic, almost magical.

His reverie soured then. He did not want to think of magic—not now or ever again. But this was a futile wish. Every time he tried to dismiss such thoughts from his mind, they returned with greater force.

No sword, no matter how smartly wielded, could cleave a sorcerer's spell.

He'd been utterly useless during this morning's attack. The women on whom he had imposed himself in the name of their own protection had won the battle by themselves. He wondered if they laughed at his presumptions behind his back.

A flush burned its way up his neck as the imagined sound of Lathwi's disdain scoured his ears. For although he hadn't known her for any decent length of time, he held her opinions in high regard. Indeed, while he was closeted in the privacy of his own mind, he could strip away the last gauzy layers of ambiguity and acknowledge the naked truth.

She fascinated him.

There was a definite physical side to this fascination, for he could not look at her muscled body without wondering what she would feel like beneath him. But it was her other, less tangible qualities which appealed him most. He admired her independence and predatory grace; her odd but compelling sense of honour, and her unconditional confidence in herself. In another lifetime, she might have been his twin. In this one, she could easily be the mate for whom he had never dared to look.

But that was one secret he intended to keep strictly to himself. There was no time or place for romantic thoughts on this expedition. And furthermore, he wasn't at all sure that she shared his feelings. She respected him as a sword master, that much he knew, but beyond that, he had no idea as to what she thought of him, if indeed she thought of him at all. And as his granddam had once told him: it was better for a man to keep his mouth shut and seem like a fool than to open it and prove everyone's suspicions.

The homespun advice brought a smile to his lips; at the same time, it banished his restless ghosts. He scooted down from his rocky perch, then quietly returned to camp.

🐉

Liselle and Lathwi slept until noon, and even then, they were still too tired to travel. So they feasted on the hares which Pawl had trapped while they were sleeping and then went their separate ways for a nap.

Lathwi found a flat, sunny rock and began to bask in the warmth of a mid-summer day. Heat seeped into her veins, then baked her fatigue to a languid crisp. She dozed for a while, then drifted back into wakefulness and stretched—a sensuous tightening of muscles that went all through her body and into the tip of her imagined tail. Afterward, she rolled over and sunned her other side.

It felt good to be a dragon again.

Liselle would have argued against that sentiment. She hated this place with all of her city-bred might. The heat left her as limp as a week-old corsage; the countryside left her oppressed and restless. She shifted irritably, a futile search for comfort amongst a scrub oak's roots, then scowled at Lathwi for being able to relax in such an forbidding land. She ached for a soft bed and sugared tea, a warm hearth and a hot bath. It was going to take hours to scrub the ingrained reek of horses, dirt and sweat from her skin; and even longer to do her hair. Oh, what a pleasure it would be to be clean! And oh, what she wouldn't do to be rid of these nasty fleas!

She pinched one of the bloodsuckers from her shin, then tried to crush it into pulp. As she ground her fingers back and forth, the insect which she held between them became The Rogue. It was his fault that she was as tired as The Dreamer Herself; his fault that she slept on hard stone and bathed in sweat; and his fault that she could not hope for better, only worse until this journey was finally over. She was glad that she'd been given a chance to strike at him; and glad that she had taken it. Her only regret was that she had not been able to collapse the roof over his head and so squash him like the loathsome roach he was.

A pang of sorrow tweaked her then. At one point in her life, she would never have entertained such savage cravings; at another, they would have shocked and horrified her. Now they were commonplace, and no more disturbing than any other futile wish. She decided that she hated The Rogue for that, too.

"All right, miladies," Pawl said then, "you've loafed around long enough. Get up so we can get going. I want to be halfway through those defiles before it gets dark."

They travelled single-file, silent except for the thud of steel-shod hooves on sunbaked clay, and slower than a trio of slugs. Lathwi had wanted to go faster, but Paul persuaded her otherwise.

"This is brigand country," he'd told her, when she took him to task for the pace he had set. "And these canyons are a great place for an ambush. By proceeding cautiously, we'll minimize our chances of being bushwhacked. Not only that, we won't get lost as often."

Lathwi knew about ambushes now. She agreed to go slow.

As it happened, though, no one challenged them as they navigated that maze of convoluted straits, and no false path sprang up to lead them all astray. And so by moonrise, they were well into the defiles. Pawl offered the women a choice then: they could either camp in the cave that he had scouted out, or ride throughout the night. Liselle took one look at the dark, bat-infested hole among the rocks and decided that it was an excellent evening for riding. Lathwi did not even bother to look.

So they rode on.

At daybreak, the shallow gully of a canyon that they had been following emptied them into a vale. It must have been a mighty river's cradle at one time, for there was still a hint of fish in the air, but now it was a dry bed of water-rounded stones where nothing wanted to grow. The first true foothill stood on the far side of this wadi; and its lower slopes were shingled with boulders.

"We'll make camp there," Pawl said, pointing to the top of the hill. It seemed obscenely green compared to all that lay below it. "The horses won't be able to carry us through this rock-field, though, so we'll have to get down and walk."

Neither woman argued with him. Liselle was too tired to do so, and Lathwi was busy watching the sky.

Three days later, they were deep into the foothills. The terrain had changed along the way, becoming steppe-like at first, then wooded in spots and finally, heavily forested. At the moment, they were camped on a plateau amidst a pocket of shaggy pines. Liselle and Lathwi were still sleeping off the aftereffects of a hard night's ride; Pawl was already up and contemplating the next leg of their journey.

They were travelling strictly by night now. He was not happy about that. Hazards multiplied in the woods at night, as did the bloodsuckers; and it was harder to find and keep his bearings, too. But these were inconveniences, piddling complaints compared to the matter Lathwi had raised shortly after they had crested that first rocky foothill.

"From now on," she'd told him, "we would be wise to keep our movements as inconspicuous as possible."

"Why's that?" he had asked, suddenly and absurdly afraid that he might've done something to draw The Rogue's attention to her. "Can your enemy see us?"

"No, but passing dragons can. And many look upon these hills as a hunting grounds."

He hadn't asked how she knew such a thing and she hadn't volunteered the information, but he had gotten the impression that she knew what she was talking about and so began to plan accordingly.

And he had to admit: they were making good time. By his calculation, they were less than a week away from the base of Lathwi's mountain, and maybe ten days from the upper heights. This, he thought proudly, was no small accomplishment, for he knew by observation that neither woman could have gotten this far on her own. Lathwi would've gained more ground initially only to lose it as her horse and then her own self broke down in the wake of her single-minded obsession for haste. On the other hand, Liselle lacked faith in her ability to endure and wouldn't have pushed herself past the first obstacle that got in her way.

A sardonic half-smile tugged at his lips then. Now that he'd justified his worth to himself, he thought, it was time to do some honest work.

With an efficiency born of many years in the field, he packed up his saddlebags and loaded them onto the buckskin's back. Then he went in search of Lathwi. She wasn't easy to locate, for her mail blended in with the lengthening shadows, but eventually he found her curled up among the gnarled roots of an ancient pine. The air of utter serenity which she was exuding amazed him, for he had spent many a night on a forest floor and knew exactly how miserable a bed of roots could be. She was such a strange woman, he thought, as he ran his eyes up the length of her body: a compelling melange of contrasts. How could anybody with that many scars sleep so peacefully?

An impulse to lie down and take her into his arms skated through him then. He extended a leg and gently nudged her in the side instead.

As soon as he touched her, her eyelids rolled back; and he could tell by the clarity of the look which she then gave him that she'd been awake for quite some time. Delight blew through him like a sweet summer breeze. The big sneak! How many people had she spied on while pretending to be asleep? How many secrets had she glimpsed? That air of serenity was no contradiction; it was camouflage.

"I'm sorry to disturb you," he said then, "but I thought one of you ought to be awake while I'm off scouting tonight's trail."

"Why would you think that?" she asked.

"I came across the remnants of an old campfire and some charred sheep bones while I was hunting this afternoon. That could mean one of three things: peasants, thieves, or both."

"Peasants," she hissed, suddenly all venom and contempt. "If I see one poking its filthy nose around here, I will eat it."

"Sounds like a distinctly unpleasant experience for all concerned," he joked. "Let's hope you don't see anyone."

She did not respond. She was staring up at the sky now; and her expression had undergone a change. The vehemence was still there, but in an exalted form; its fierceness had given way to rapture. This sudden difference in her intrigued him. He strode off wondering if it was more camouflage.

The object which had Lathwi so enthralled was a dragon. It was so high in the sky, it was almost invisible, but even from this distance, she could tell that it was dancing. She wondered who it was and what Name it bore and who its mother was. She would've liked to have lured it closer for a better look, but only a fool distracted a dragon from its amusements to satisfy a whim. Besides, there were two jittery humans in the area.

The thought brought a faint impression of a smile to her lips. When it came to dragons, Liselle and Pawl were just as foolish as she was, if in the opposite way. Where she longed for a glimpse of one of her own, they praised their feckless Dreamer for an empty sky; and where she looked forward to the next sighting, they recalled the last one and swallowed hard. Silly people! She didn't begrudge them their fear—that was natural, a dragon's due—but they were going to have to come to grips with it sometime soon. Even at her best, Taziem had a low tolerance for weakness; and her mother was never at her best when she was pregnant. If they lost control while they were in the she-dragon's presence, she was apt to scorch them to cinders out of sheer testiness.

She hissed then. Neither Liselle nor Pawl deserved that sort of end. Perhaps it would be better for everybody if she left them both behind.

Although the notion had occurred to her more than once during the course of their journey, this was the first time she gave it serious consideration. And the more she thought about it, the more sense it made. She would be able to cover more ground faster without one or the other of them troubling her about things like food, sleep or dragons.

Suddenly decided, she sprang up from her nest of roots and padded over to the picket-line. As she saddled the bay, she snuck quick glimpses at Liselle. Curled up beneath her leaf-littered cloak, the still-slumbering sorceress looked like any other forest lump. That would keep her safe until Pawl's return.

She started on her way then, heading north to avoid the swordmaster and the argument he was sure to give her. Later on, when she was beyond his reach, she'd veer eastward again. Her thoughts raced ahead to Taziem's mountain then. But even as an image of that craggy spire formed in her head, a series of distant shouts dispersed it. She wheeled her horse around and to a standstill. A moment later, a frantic cry for help rang out.

Liselle!

Her first thought was of trickery. Pawl was cunning, he might use such a ploy to lure her back to camp. But the next scream convinced her otherwise. As clever as the swordmaster was, he couldn't make Liselle sound like that. The sorceress was truly scared. And Lathwi couldn't refuse the call of one who had been as a tanglemate to her.

She dug her heels into the bay's ribs and went charging back toward camp. Halfway there, she realized that the world had gone quiet except for the drumming of her horse's hooves. It was a lurking silence, like the calm before a tempest; and it was too late for the bay to become a part of it. She gave him a slap to keep him going, then pitched herself out of her saddle and tumbled to her feet. Then she eased her sword out of its scabbard and went prowling through the woods.

The spot where she had last seen Liselle was vacant when Lathwi got there. The surrounding ground bore a confusion of boot prints. Not peasants, she reasoned—those muck-dwellers were never so well shod. So her quarry must be thieves.

Just then, a twig snapped at her back.

In one fluid move, she whirled into a fighting stance. The helmed man who'd been stalking her froze for an instant, all but his rat-like eyes which swarmed up the length of her sword, over her body and into her face. When he came to the scars which bracketed her nose, he tipped his head back and loosed a hyena's laugh.

"The third time's a charm, bitch," he said then. "And you're due."

She looked past the metal veil then. What she saw there swept her back through time and into a darkened alleyway that stank of blood and sweat and souring meat. Her pain-spangled limbs were pinned to a wall; and a man with a broken nose was cutting into her face. A strange feeling ignited within her. Wilder than a proper grudge and virulent as plague, it urged her to throw the sword aside and to tear into his throat with her teeth. She fine-tuned her lethal pose instead.

An instant later, something hard rammed into the back of her skull and the world abruptly went black.

CHAPTER 21

Taziem waddled from one end of the chamber to the other, then lay herself down and rumbled irritably. Bloated to near incapacity by the clutch of younglings in her womb, and bored to within a membrane of madness, her thoughts were anything but motherly.

This was absolutely the last pregnancy she was going to suffer, she told herself, in a most vehement tone. No amount of pleasure could make up for an entire season of discomfort and inconvenience; and no dance was worth the side-splitting agony that was yet to come. Randy Bij would no doubt try to persuade her otherwise when the time finally came, but there was nothing he could say or do that would make her change her mind. Unless…

She shuddered at the erotic image which rippled across the skies of her mind then. That would do it, she admitted, and resolved to think of a way to counteract it.

But not now. She didn't want to think about such things while she was in this condition. Indeed, she did not want to think at all. She wanted to escape the mind-numbing boredom of these caves and roam the open skies, then bask in a sunlit meadow amidst the gleaming bones of a kill.

Hare-brained cravings. She wasn't even hungry. Yet. She shifted, searching for a position that would satisfy her vast and sensitive bulk. No matter which way she turned, though, some part of her complained. She roared, an eruption of petulant regrets. If only she had not sent Lathwi away!

An all-too-familiar rationale followed that lament. If she hadn't driven The Soft One away, Bij would've killed her to satisfy a morsel of his spite for mankind; or she herself would've eaten her during her post-coital feeding frenzy; or Lathwi would now be on the verge of acquiring a second set of tanglemates. None of these arguments were powerful enough to ease Taziem's restlessness today, though. The first two were academic. And as for the third, well, what was really so bad about that? It was true that no other dragon had more than a single set of tanglemates, but that was simply because no one had ever considered the possibility. Taziem was The Learned One. Her fortune demanded that she explore those paths which no other dragon thought to go.

And The Soft One was different.

By the she-dragon's reckoning, Lathwi was an adult now, and as full-grown as she was apt to get. There seemed little chance of her attracting a mate; and less chance still of her producing viable young. If she could not breed, the only way she could pass her experiences on to the next generation was through a second set of tanglemates. Those younglings would benefit from Lathwi's knowledge. And in the meantime, Taziem could put her quick mind and nimble fingers to good use.

The tip of her tail quivered. She was decided now: she would Call Lathwi. And when The Soft One got here, she would perceive the extent of her good fortune and be grateful.

Or would she?

Uninvited doubts swarmed into Taziem's mind like a crop of biting flies. Curious Lathwi would not accept her early repatriation without questions. She would press for details, poking and probing with badger-like persistence until she was sure she had all of the pertinent facts. And what was Taziem to tell her—that she had changed her mind? That would only prompt a 'why?', which would lead to others in turn. In the end, Taziem would have to concede that she had Called simply to assuage her own misery.

The she-dragon hissed, appalled by the enormity of the folly which self-indulgence had almost coaxed her to commit. Such a concession would be tantamount to admitting weakness; and that would encourage every caveless dragon in the country to come and challenge her. She'd rather endure a century of unrelenting hardship alone.

So be it, she thought then, capitulating to pride and pragmatism. She would let Lathwi be and undergo this last birthing alone.

But that didn't mean she had to be happy about it.

CHAPTER 22

Lathwi! Can you hear me? Please, please wake up."

The sounds were like the steady tap-tap-tappings of a woodpecker hunting for grubs in the trunk of a hardwood tree. Lathwi wanted them to go away so she could lapse back into a pain-free slumber, but they became louder and more persistent instead. Each new round nudged her closer to consciousness.

"Come on, Lathwi! Wake up! We're in trouble here."

She prised one eyelid open, then the other. The effort sent tiny brands of red lightning shooting through her head. She bit back a hiss and tried to focus on her surroundings, but all she could see was a fuzzy array of lumps and shadows. The nearest of these lumps reeked of human sweat and horses. She shifted toward it. In doing so, she discovered that her arms were tied behind her back. Her legs were bound as well.

The lump stirred then, becoming a pair of shoulders and a pale, bedraggled, heart-shaped face. "Lathwi? Praise The Dreamer! How are you feeling?"

Had she been compelled to reply, Lathwi would've had to admit that she did not feel very well at all. The insides of her head felt as if they were being spurred by each and every passing thought, and her stomach, although empty, was on the verge of revolt. But there was no compulsion on her to speak the truth here and now, so she kept it to herself and asked a question of her own.

"Where are we?"

"Shh! Not so loud," Liselle whispered, her eyes darting furtively toward the yellow outlines of a door. "We're in an abandoned shepherd's shack. As near as I can tell, it's east of yesterday's camp by a half-day's ride."

"How did we get here?"

"That's my fault," the sorceress confessed. "I woke up to the sound of horses running through the woods. I thought it was you or Pawl so I got up to see what was going on. But it wasn't you and it wasn't Pawl, it was a band of half-drunk brigands on their way home from a hunt. I couldn't hide, for they had already seen me, so I tried to run. One of the pigs rode me down. I cried out then, I couldn't stop myself. I'm so sorry, Lathwi. I didn't mean to land you in this mess."

Lathwi had no use for apologies and so did not bother to acknowledge this one. "Tell me more about these strangers."

The fine lines that webbed the corners of Liselle's eyes and mouth puckered. She peered into Lathwi's face for a long moment, then said, "I was going to ask you the same thing."

"Why would you do that?"

"Because some of them seemed to know you!" the sorceress exclaimed. "That one man in particular—you must know who I mean. He's taller than you, and as broad as an ox across the chest. He was wearing a helm that screened his face when you met, but even so, you couldn't have missed those fresh-healed burns or his broken nose—"

Lathwi went rigid as though scorpion-stung.

In the same instant, a long-buried memory lurched out of its grave and grabbed Liselle by the throat. Broken-Nose was Lathwi's name for the outlaw who had come so close to killing her back in Compara. Could he and the man in the helm be one and the same? She didn't want to believe it was true, but it made too much terrible sense to be otherwise.

"Oh, Lathwi! What have I done to you?"

Caught up in a cyclone of restored memories, Lathwi did not hear that devastated groan. Broken-Nose! How could she have forgotten that craven or his pack of jackals? Just like last time, they'd come at her from the rear! She glimpsed at her trussed-up body. Her sword was gone, as were her dragon claws. The pouch containing her stones and gold was missing, too. Miserable scavengers! They had picked her as clean as any carcass. Why had they not taken her life as well?

The answer came to her in the shape of a knife beneath her nose.

Outrage flared within her only to sputter immediately out again. She did not have the strength to maintain such intense feelings. Indeed, it suddenly seemed as if she had no strength at all.

"Lathwi?"

She lolled her head toward Liselle. Even in the shack's pervading gloom, there was no mistaking the worry in the tiny woman's eyes.

"What are we going to do?"

"I do not know," she replied, too tired to notice that she was slurring her words. As a random, almost whimsical afterthought, she added, "What has become of Pawl?"

"I've wondered the same thing myself," Liselle admitted. "He never came back from his scouting trip. Or if he did, I didn't see him." She gnawed on her lower lip as if it were a source of hope, then asked, "Do you think he could be looking for us?"

"Is possible. What you think will happen if he finds?"

"I'm sure he'll try to rescue us," Liselle replied.

Then reality passed its cruel hand before her eyes, and her visions of deliverance evaporated. Pawl was alone while the brigands numbered eight. Not even a swordmaster could be expected to overcome such unequal odds. And that was exactly what he would have to do, because neither she nor Lathwi were in any position to lend him any aid.

"So it's up to us to save ourselves," she murmured then. To her surprise, an idea came to her straightaway. "Lathwi! Do you still have your amulet?"

Lathwi started out of a drowse, then stared at Liselle through sunken, half-closed eyes. Her face was slack, void of expression; and shadows clung to her skin like bruises.

"What say?"

"Do you still have your amulet?"

There was a long pause, then a hiss which sounded like, "Yess."

"Good," Liselle said then, although her enthusiasm was tainted by sudden concern for Lathwi. "Because I've thought of a way out of this mess."

"How?"

"All you have to do is cast an illusion of invisibility over us. When this Broken-Nose comes to call and can't find us, he'll send his men off to search the area. While they're doing that, we'll stroll out of here and hide in the forest.

"What do you think? Shall we give it a try?"

A long moment passed in silence. Liselle was just about to repeat the proposal when Lathwi shook her head and mumbled something.

"What was that? I didn't hear you."

"Be too tired," Lathwi said, struggling to make herself clear. It was hard, so hard, like wading through a quagmire. "Head hurts. No can con-cen-trate. I sleep now. Tomorrow I try."

"No, Lathwi," Liselle insisted. "It has to be done now. Tomorrow may be too late!"

The prediction left no impression on Lathwi, for she was already sliding back into unconsciousness. And while Liselle tried everything short of shouting to rouse her again, it was to no avail.

Dread gnawed at her even as she gnawed at her lower lip. She didn't want to be anywhere near here when the Southerner came barging through that door. A man like that didn't need an excuse to be cruel, but he was sure to go to extremes with a woman who'd set his face on fire. And she was not so naive as to think that she'd be treated any better. She'd already been groped and pawed by most of her captors on the ride back to this place; and only a surprising command from Broken-Nose himself had postponed a multiple rape.

So she had a credible sense of how the near future would unfold. The question was: should she dare to escape it? She could cast that illusion of invisibility; to her, it would be as easy as breathing. And while moving her sleeping giant of a friend would be a more taxing feat, she could manage this, too. But should she? Using her power would be tantamount to writing HERE WE ARE across the sky. Then their one advantage over The Rogue would be gone. She frowned, trying to wring a decision out of herself. Who did she fear more: Broken-Nose or The Rogue? Who was more dangerous overall?

She could not decide, so she compromised instead. If their situation deteriorated to the point of life or death, she'd use her magic. Until then, she would wait.

And hope. And worry.

A loud bang jarred Liselle out of a fitful cat-nap. She started awake just as three pairs of weather beaten boots came striding into the shack. She shied toward the still sleeping Lathwi, but was not sure if this was an impulse to protect or be protected.

"How cozy," a fire-scarred man with blonde hair jeered. "If she's your one and only, you've just missed your chance to kiss her goodbye."

He hauled a knife out of its sheath then, and sank to a crouch in front of Lathwi. Liselle tensed, ready to unleash the deadliest curse in her repertoire, but held back when he only slashed the ties which bound Lathwi's legs.

"How 'bout you, pretty lady?" he asked then. "Would you like to feel my shaft between your legs?"

"Pig," she hissed.

He laughed, then sliced through her hobble and slung her to her feet. His comrades bounced her back and forth between them, manhandling her breasts and buttocks.

"Save some for me," the fire-scarred man quipped, and then booted Lathwi squarely in the ribs. "Wake up, bitch."

The blow knocked Lathwi to semi-consciousness. Her eyes opened. She could hear and taste and smell things, too. But her thoughts remained shrouded in a viscous fog. She was so incoherent, she didn't even wonder where she was or who these strange people were.

"Get up," a man snarled at her.

She wobbled to her feet. The sudden change in altitude touched off a new round of drumming in her head. She swayed, then stumbled. The man hit her for that.

"None of your tricks, you hear?" he growled.

She did not know what he meant.

A huge shadow occluded the doorway then. "Are we ready for our little picnic?" he asked.

"All set, Jarrad," Lathwi's captor replied.

"Good. Let's get these bitches moving then."

Jarrad's men herded Lathwi and Liselle out of the shack and onto an old goatherder's track that wove its way down the steep hillside and toward a distant plateau. Lathwi's guards watched her intently, but such wariness was unnecessary. She moved like a dream-walker, looking neither left nor right nor at the ground beneath her feet. She knew she was in trouble, but lacked the energy or motivation to act on her own behalf.

Three heads back, Liselle continued to gnaw on her now ragged lip. Lathwi's docility worried her. So did Jarrad's intentions. That shack had been secluded, an ideal spot for mayhem and murder. Why would he take his victims elsewhere? And what was this picnic he had mentioned? Once again, she wondered if this was the time to use her magic. Once again, she decided to wait. Lathwi was in no immediate danger yet. And there was still a chance that she'd snap out of her daze before they got to wherever it was that they were going.

A tree-root tripped her up then. Her fire-scarred guard saved her from a fall only to grope her breasts as he set her on her feet again. She banished the curse that came to mind, then shuddered as inspiration whispered in her ear: maybe she could turn this pig's lust to her own advantage. The thought of playing up to such a one nauseated her. Even so, the next time she stumbled, she allowed him to paw her before elbowing him away.

Eventually, the goat-track brought them into a stand of shaggy pines. A curious congregation of peasants was waiting there: six elderly men and one maiden. The child was clad in a bridal white robe and garlands; and as Liselle drew closer, it became obvious that she was weeping silent tears. Fingers of unease prickled down her back then, leaving a sticky trail of sweat behind.

"My," Jarrad said, as he circled the weeping girl, "what a tasty-looking young morsel. Whose daughter is she? Yours, Milk-Eye?"

Milk-Eye dismissed the question with an icy glare. His fellow elders developed a sudden fascination for the ground. Jarrad scorned their timidity with a laugh, then returned his leer to the girl.

"Strip off her garments," he said.

Baffled by this request, the graybeards stood as still as statues and gaped at him. He laughed again. "Dullards! Do as I say! She won't be needing those rags today. Can't you see? I've found another to take her place."

They glimpsed furtively at Liselle. She saw no pity in those looks, no regrets or chagrin, but only a houndish sort of relief. The sorceress averted her eyes as they undressed the girl, then tensed as a hand cupped her buttocks. Only a belated wave of restraint prevented her from invoking a fatal mistake.

"Very tasty indeed," Jarrad said, when the maiden stood naked before him. "I think we'll keep her for a while. Take her back to the shack and tie her up."

"Is that necessary?" one of Milk-Eye's stoop-shouldered confederates demanded, his voice quivering with indignation.

"I'll leave it up to you," Jarrad replied, flashing the peasant a nasty smile. "But if she's not where I want her to be when we get back, me and the lads will be by to visit your private stock of womenfolk shortly thereafter.

"Now go on and get out of here—the smell of pig-shit is starting to give me a headache."

Old Milk-Eye bristled as if with an itch to answer that insult with violence, but an instant later, he recovered his composure and spat at the ground instead. Then he seized the still-weeping woman-child by the wrist and stormed off toward the goat-track. As the other graybeards went scurrying after them, Broken-Nose laughed and flung obscene gestures at their backs.

"Men from the north are nothing but bearded women," he jeered. Then, shifting his gaze to Lathwi, he added, "And the women are nothing but boys with breasts. Right, bitch?"

Lathwi did not respond with so much as a batted eyelash. He shed his reptilian smile.

"Get that thing on her," he told his men then, pointing to the cast-off robe. "No, you dolt," he snapped, as someone started to fumble with the bindings around her wrists, "don't untie her. Just pull the damned thing over her head."

Lathwi's world suddenly went white. The change did not alarm her. Nor did the flurry of tugging that followed. She was still caught in a netherworld where urgency didn't exist.

"It won't fit," she heard someone say. "She's too big."

Broken-Nose swore, then drew his knife from its sheath. "Like this, you morons," he said, slashing here and there at the cloth. "Who cares if it's in tatters?" A moment later, he barked again. "Dev, get her tether."

With one last tug, colour returned Lathwi's world. Then a man who bore the touch of Fire on his cheeks looped a noose over her head.

"I hope you're still alive and squirming when he goes to swallow your heart," he snarled, as he yanked the knot tight.

That seemed a fine sentiment to Lathwi.

"And now the flowers," Jarrad commanded. "Maybe they'll make her look more appetizing."

His men sniggered, then began to pitch garlands around Lathwi's neck as if she were the stake in a ring-toss game. She did nothing to spoil their fun.

"Well, bitch," Broken-Nose said then, "it's time to put you out to pasture. When you're knee-deep in your own guts, think of me. I'll certainly be thinking of you."

He paused, clearly expecting some sort of response from her. When she failed to oblige him, he speared her with one last poisonous glance, then said, "Dev, Quinn, Crowley: take her into the meadow and stake her to a spot where she can be seen from all angles. Then take up your positions on the far side of the field and wait. Remember: no one attacks until I give the signal. Is that understood?"

The trio grunted. Then Dev grabbed the end of Lathwi's tether and started off. Lathwi followed, docile as a holiday lamb. Liselle tried to catch her eye as she passed, but was thwarted by the pair of men who flanked her. Helpless to do anything else, she watched in dismay as the group disappeared from sight.

"Hobbs, Reever," Broken-Nose continued, almost bubbling with good humour now, "you're to the east. Birk, you're with me to the west.

"And Marl, you're in charge of this little bitch. Take her down to the tree line, as close to the meadow as you can get. I want her on hand just in case that bastard turns its nose up at the piece of trash that's out there now."

Marl nodded, then gave Liselle an eager shove toward the meadow. She stumbled forward only to be jerked back again as Broken-Nose added, "Just one more thing, Marl."

"What's that, Jarrad?"

His helm-veiled eyes acquired a menacing slant. "You've ridden with me long enough to know that it's not a smart idea to act against my orders—especially over a bit of quim that you're going to have sooner or later anyway. So don't let me catch you trying to sneak a root when you should be watching for my signal."

"You won't," Marl assured him.

"Good," Jarrad said, and headed off into the trees.

"Bastard,"

Marl muttered then, and turned his suddenly smoldering gaze to Liselle. "One wrong word out of you, and I'll make you wish that you were the one staked out in yonder grass."

Liselle lowered her eyes, a gesture of submission. For now, it was all she could do.

"Hurry up, Dev," Quinn urged. "That thing will be here any moment now."

Dev gave the stake one last whack with his cudgel, then stepped back and tugged on Lathwi's tether. Sure that it was secure, he then turned to Lathwi. "If I see you messing with that stake in any way," he warned, "I'll come back and pound your brains into a pudding. I'm sure our maiden-slayer won't mind a meal that's already had the kick bashed out of it."

Lathwi didn't respond.

Dev grunted, a satisfied sound. Then he and Quinn took their leave of her.

As Lathwi stood there in the hot sun, her nose began to itch. It started out as a tiny quiver in her nasal passages, then intensified like poison ivy. She thoughtlessly tried to rub the itch out against the round of her shoulder, but wound up burying her face in the corona of flowers around her neck. Her eyes began to water; her sinuses began to run. Something within her cried out then: a scratch! A scratch! She needed a scratch.

And for that, she needed her hands.

So she tried to break free of the rawhide thongs which held her arms behind her. Her first attempts were failures: the leather was more than a match for brute strength. Then it occurred to her to scrape her bindings against the grain of her scales. It was slow, painstaking work, but the itch in her nose forbade her to stop. As she worked, she started to pace in unwitting circles. The tall, drying grass around her stake grew flatter with every lap.

From her vantage point among the trees, Liselle rejoiced to see Lathwi moving of her own volition at last. She didn't know why the big woman was thrashing a circle into the grass, but that didn't matter. Lathwi was up to something, she just had to be. And that meant that Liselle had to be ready when that something came to a head. So she shifted, seemingly in search of a more comfortable seat among the pine needles and gnarled roots. Her baggy trousers shifted, too, riding high up over one leg to expose the knee and more.

"What are we waiting here for?" she asked then, in what she hoped was a sulky tone.

The annoyance which flared in Marl's eyes hardened into a wicked gleam as his gaze slid down the length of her bared leg. "Haven't you guessed yet, pretty lady?" he asked then. "We're waiting for a dragon."

Even as her expression melted into an astonished blank, a riot of formerly unaccountable details tumbled into place. They were using Lathwi as bait to catch a dragon! The notion set her on the edge of hysterical laughter. Oh, the irony of it all! Then, remembering that she was their alternate lure, the joke suddenly soured. She shuddered, an unfeigned spasm, then focussed on Marl again.

"But dragons are so big," she said, her voice a helpless flutter. "So dangerous. We'll all be killed!"

"I won't let it hurt you," he told her, looking at more than her legs now. "Not if you promise to be nice to me."

Her heart flip-flopped, a cue as pointed as an elbow in the ribs. She smiled, projecting desires that had nothing to do with sex, then murmured, "I'll be nice to you." He raised a fire-scarred eyebrow. She pressed her luck. "I'll be nice to you right now if that's what you want."

He strained a breath through his teeth. His gaze darted westward and back again. Then he grabbed her by the hair and drew her into a rough embrace. She closed her eyes and tried to imagine Jamus in his stead, but the illusion crumbled even as she invoked it. This man's kisses were hard and mean; his hands raised welts instead of gooseflesh. Even so, she egged him on, for this was the only chance of escape she was likely to get.

"Untie my hands," she whispered. "Let me show you what I can do."

His expression went flat and cold then, like a mirror of Liselle's own transparency. She opened her mouth to deny the conclusions to which he had rightly leapt, but he shut her up with a slap to the face.

"You brainless bitch," he snarled then. "How stupid do you think I am? You're not going to need your hands for what I have in mind."

He cast her face-down in the dirt then and began to tear at her clothes. Two tugs later, her drawstring trousers were in a tangle around her ankles; and he had tufts of her sturdy one-piece undergarment in his fists. Liselle cried out: once as the fabric gave way, and again as Marl dug his fingernails into her hips. But while every nerve in her body screamed at her to avert what was coming next with sorcery, she tearfully refused. While Lathwi was alive, there was still a chance of them getting away without leaving any magical tracks. So she would pay the price for her ineptitude and endure what had to be endured.

Marl was fumbling with the strings of his own pants now. He grunted as they gave way, then seized Liselle's hips again and angled them to his liking. She closed her eyes, bracing for pain. He grunted again, then abruptly let go of her. An instant later, a horrid gurgling filled her ears. She didn't have to look to know what had happened—Jarrad had obviously caught his man in the act of disobeying orders. She tried to crawl away then, before the Southerner could murder her, too, but came nose-to-nose with a pair of leather boots. In spite of herself, she sobbed aloud.

"It's all right," a familiar voice assured her. "It's only me. Now get up and put yourself back together. Hurry. We haven't got much time."

With a snick, the bindings which held her arms parted. She fell over and onto her side then. In the next instant, she was back on her knees, retching bile. She heaved until her quivering stomach was empty, then dragged herself to her feet. Marl's corpse was sprawled across a pile of moldering leaves to her left. Its eyes were open, its pants were down, and its throat was professionally slit. She stared at it for a moment, waiting in vain to feel some sense of satisfaction, then turned her back on its unseeing gaze and got dressed.

She found Pawl down by the treeline. As she approached, he swivelled toward her and demanded, "Why have these bastards got Lathwi staked out like that?"

"They're using her as dragon-bait," she replied, and then grabbed his arm as he lurched toward the meadow. "Not so fast! At the moment, she's in far less danger out there than she would be here with us."

He broke her hold on him with an effortless twitch, then brought the full weight of his scowl to bear on her. "How do you figure that?"

"Lathwi was raised among dragons. She understands them. She understands their language, too."

"So?"

"So when her would-be dinner date finally shows itself, she'll introduce herself dragon-style."

Pawl was tired and his nerves were on edge—two days of skulking after outlaws could do that to a man. So he was not inclined to trust Lathwi's continued well-being to a dragon's willingness to be tamed.

"And what if this dragon doesn't care for her manners?"

"Then I'll translocate her out of there with my magic," Liselle told him. When he scowled, still radiating doubts, her patience snapped. "Do you think charging to her rescue here and now will accomplish anything? There are eight, no, seven armed men lurking throughout in these woods."

"Make that six," he corrected her. "I've surprised more than one louse this morning."

"Six or seven makes very little difference when there's still only one of you," she argued. "I won't be much help in a fight—the only blade I know how to use is a butter knife. And who knows about Lathwi? The last time I saw her, she was so dazed, she didn't know a sword from a lamb chop. The only definite ally you have at the moment is surprise. And if you don't use that to its full potential, you'll either be killed or captured. Is that what you want?

"Please, Pawl," she urged then, "Give my plan a chance. "If nothing else, that dragon will distract Broken-Nose and his men. While they're trying to kill it, you can close in and rescue Lathwi."

For a long moment, Pawl stared at her as if he doubted her sanity. Then he glanced toward the meadow one last time and ground his teeth.

"Very well," he rumbled, "I'll go along with it for now. But if I don't like the way it starts to look," he hastened to add, "I'll take matters into my own hands."

"Fair enough."

They hid themselves in the bushes then, to watch and to wait.

The furious itch in Lathwi's nose was long gone, but she didn't notice. She didn't notice the pain that was radiating out of her shoulders and into her spine, either. She was too intent on freeing her hands. As long as they were still tied behind her, she couldn't think of anything else.

Hands. Her hands. She had to have them back.

She didn't notice the great, barrel-chested shadow with the tapering ends circling over her head, either.

A savage thrill raked its fingernails down Jarrad's back as he watched the dragon circle the plateau. This was it, he gloated to himself. The northern bitch's hour was finally at hand. And she didn't even know it yet!

His gaze darted toward the meadow. She was still pacing round and round like an ox at a turnstile. It was, in truth, a most disappointing show. He'd wanted her to put up more of a fight, to bite and scratch and flail for her freedom like a trapped animal. Such a spectacle would've been an incidental salve to his still blistered pride.

But no matter, he reassured himself. That dragon would have her dancing soon enough.

He licked his lips, savouring the thought, then settled back to wait. As he watched the dragon circle overhead, his hand crept up to stroke the ruins of his face.

"There it is!" Liselle hissed, a whisper fringed with excitement and dread. Then, in spite of herself, she added, "Dreamer, look at the size of it!"

Pawl already knew how big this dragon was, for he'd been watching it ever since it had appeared as a glint in the sky. It was more than that now; much more. Its chest was as broad as an old oak tree.

"When is she going to stop that confounded pacing and do something?" he muttered. "That monster is only moments away from landing on her back."

"Patience," Liselle urged, in spite of the doubts that were starting to gnaw at her own gut. "For all we know, she could be doing exactly the right thing as far as that dragon is concerned."

He dismissed that possibility with a grunt, then emerged from his hiding place in the brush. "You stay here," he told her. "I'm going in for a closer look."

Shoq orbited the meadow, studying his would-be playmate. He knew this couldn't be Lathwi. He knew because she hadn't answered his last Call; and The Soft One would never do that unless she was gone from the world. Even so, he was excited. This imposter was different from the others he'd come across in this field. She had a peculiar sort of presence, and her circling seemed like a crude sort of dance. If she liked to dance, she might like to play games, too.

He slanted out of the sky then, a showy dip intended to catch her eye. She continued to plod along as if she had not seen him. Her aloofness offended him. Didn't she understand that he wanted her to quit that ugly dance and play with him? He doubled around for another pass—one which would make his wishes as clear as a mountain tarn. To his vast displeasure, she ignored him again.

So, he decided then. This one was no different from the others after all.

His upper lip curled back to bare a new set of desires. He folded his wings and went diving toward the ground.

Grass thrashed and crackled as he landed. She turned to face him then, but he did not want her attention anymore. He wanted her to run so he could chase her down and kill her and feed upon her sweet, warm carcass. She stayed where she was, though, and bared her teeth at him. This brazen grin created a strange fluttering in his head. It was a ticklish feeling, not entirely unpleasant, like a hatch of butterflies looking for a way out of his skull. On any other occasion, it would have intrigued him. But because he knew it was her trying to play some trick on him, it stoked his rage instead.

Shoq crouched, then charged forward, fully intending to rend her throat.

Lathwi could feel the rawhide thong's sinewy filaments slipping, then catching, then slipping again like desperate fingers clinging to the lip of a cliff. Very soon now, she would send them over the edge once and for all. Then, with her hands free, she'd think of something else to do.

The grasses to her rear hissed then. It was a ponderous noise, one that could not be ignored. She pivoted toward the sound, then froze again as the magnificent aspect of a dragon spanned into view. Within the span of a quickened heartbeat, she recognized it as Shoq.

She grinned at her tanglemate for an incredulous moment, soaking up details like a long-parched sponge: his marvellous size, his bone-ridged brow, the lustrous sheen of his scales. As familiar as he seemed, though, there was something unusual about him today. She could not decipher that odd, unfocused glint in his golden eyes. Out of reflex, she tried to touch his thoughts. But she was still groggy from that blow to her head, and only managed to skim the surface of his awareness.

His lip curled then. The tip of his tail went suddenly still. The next thing she knew, he was hurtling toward her. She strained at her bonds with a desperate strength. With a muffled pop, the last stubborn fibrils finally parted. Shoq was nearly upon her now. She didn't have enough time to slip her tether and run, or enough leeway to evade his charge; all she could do was stand her ground and wait for him to go for her throat. He did so with an almost hypnotic sort of grace, then honked like a witless juvenile as she boxed him soundly in the nose.

He reared back for a moment, an astonished pose, then sent her tumbling backward and onto the ground with a flick of his tail. As she rolled to a stop, his head came snaking toward her again. Daring all, Lathwi sat up and touched her nose to his.

"It is good to see you again, Shoq," she told him.

The thought was clumsy and unsubtle, but its flight was true. She sighed with relief as it slid into his mind, then wondered at the swirl of confusion and undragon-like hope that welled up in its wake.

"*Lathwi?*" His Voice was half-shy, half-suspicious. "*Is it really you?*"

"*Who were you expecting, you overgrown bladder of gas?*" She thumped the space between his eyes to quell any remaining doubts, then flashed another thought at him. "*Let me up.*"

"It is you!"

He loosed a joyous bugle, then nuzzled her to her feet. An instant later, he bowled her over and pounced. She wormed her way out of his playful embrace, but before she could tell him to quit his frisking, a human voice shouted out her name. Shoq pounced on her again as she rolled toward the sound, but not before she caught sight of Pawl charging across the field with a sword in hand.

Comprehension blew through her like a monsoon wind: Pawl thought Shoq was hurting her! The dragon-foolish human. Now he was the one in danger. Shoq was staring at him with angry amber eyes; and his tail was quivering with territorial rage. She scurried to her feet to warn the swordmaster away only to see a pack of less audacious men sneaking through the meadow. Recognition flared then, hand-in-hand with hate: Broken-Nose and his jackals were heading this way.

Shoq sucked in a mighty breath then. Lathwi knew what was going to happen next. She also knew that she could not prevent it.

"Pawl!" she bellowed. "Get down!"

The warning was still racing across the field when Shoq belched forth his column of fire. It surged through the air like a swarm of hungry orange light, its goal the spot where the swordmaster was standing. Without pausing to think about what she was doing, Lathwi diverted the stream with her Will. It veered away from Pawl, then abruptly sputtered and died—a victim of Shoq's surprise.

"*That never happened before,*" he told her, wide-eyed as a sun-dazzled youngling.

"*Do not be concerned,*" she replied, taking care to hide the spangles of her amusement. "*It is not likely to happen again today.*"

She glanced in Pawl's direction then, but Shoq's breath had ignited the tall dry grass and she could not see past the billowing smoke and flames. She shrugged, refusing to worry, then turned to survey the rest of the field. Broken-Nose and his pack were closing in on her and Shoq now. With a flicker of thought, she pointed them out to her tanglemate.

"Here are men who deserve your wrath," she said, letting him taste a measure of her hate. "Let us make them our prey today."

Shoq gathered himself into his most menacing pose and bugled. She was Lathwi, his soon-to-be Chosen. Her grudges were his grudges now.

His challenge was answered by an ear-splitting shriek—no human utterance, but an outcry which had not troubled the world since the end of EverLight. Three krim appeared in the sky then. Shoq roared again; his wings unfurled with a snap. Moments later, he was airborne. He might be confused about a lot of things, but when it came to krim, he knew exactly what to do.

Lathwi trumpeted as Shoq went tearing after the demons. She wanted to be up there, too—slashing and scratching and scrabbling for a toehold in their chitinous hides. But even her tanglemate started his attack in earnest, the crack of a twig behind her called Lathwi's attention back to earth. She swivelled toward the sound. Broken-Nose strode out of a smoky haze and into her circle of trampled grass.

"I'll grant you one thing," he said, as he levelled his sword at her. "You're the luckiest bitch that ever lived."

She eyed him coolly. He was wearing her girdle of claws crosswise over his chest like a bandolier; her knife sheathed in his boot; and her leather pouch on his belt. He grinned, obviously pleased that she had noticed these things.

"The gold's gone," he told her. "I gave it to the lads. But I kept everything else as a souvenir. I think I'll keep a lock of your hair as well."

He strode toward her then—a slow, sadistic march. She backed up, seeking the only advantage available to her at the moment. Misunderstanding her reason for retreating, he began to gloat.

"You can't run away from me this time."

She scorned the sloppy thought with a dragon's humourless smile. She did not need to run, not when Shoq's wildfire was raging all around them. It had avoided them thus far because it had better things to eat than trampled grass, but she knew its Name and meant to call it hither.

But not yet. This human had shown her how to be cruel. Now she wanted to show him how well she had learned. So she continued to back away, step by step. And step by step, he continued to advance. She came to the end of her tether. He came into striking range. As he raised his sword to cut her down, she roared her contempt and spoke Fire's Name.

An instant later, she was standing in the middle of an inferno.

Head-high spikes of blue-veined Fire jigged at her feet, an angry dance which berated her for calling it away from its glorious feast. The garlands and robe became a flurry of hot black ash. The rope around her neck began to sizzle. But as furious as it was, Fire did not forget who she was. Her skin reddened, but didn't blister. Her vision blurred, but didn't boil.

Broken-Nose was standing just beyond the wildfire's new edge now, and she could tell by the way he kept shifting back and forth on his heels that he was torn between his hate for her and a fear of being burned again. She bade Fire to fall back just far enough to offer him an undistorted view of her. Then, standing dragon-proud in scales blacker than soot, she dared him to come and get her.

His red-rimmed eyes narrowed. His sword began to tremor in his white-knuckled fist.

"You can't hide in there forever!" he howled.

"I am not hiding," she replied, in a voice as dry as the fire's. "I am here. I am unarmed. There is nothing to stop you from cutting me down." When he made no reply, she goaded him further. "Perhaps it will make you feel braver if I turn my back to you."

"Bitch!"

Almost in spite of himself, he lurched toward her. She reached out as if encouraging a child to walk. Bluish flames cascaded down her arms. "Come," she crooned at him. "The fire is hungry. And it likes the taste of your flesh. Come and let it feed on you."

A spasm of unreasoning fear contorted his sweat-slicked face. He jerked to a stop, then glanced all around him. His panic sheered off into wild relief as he spied a break in the fire.

"You and I are not finished yet," he rasped, as he went to make his escape. "I will have satisfaction from you."

Just then, a huge shadow came striding through that gap in the fire. Jarrad thought it was the dragon at first, but he soon realized that it was something far worse. It walked upright like a man, but was like no man he had ever seen: its shoulders were too broad; its hide, too thick. And its face was hideous. Paralysed by consternation, he could only gape as it came toward him; and by the time he finally remembered himself, it was too late. With one swipe of its gnarled paw, the thing clouted the sword from his hand; with the next, it hooked its talons through his mailshirt and into the bones of his chest. As he gabbled with pain and shock, it hoisted him into the smoky air, then sniffed him up and down with the two slimy slots that served as its nostrils.

"You have something that does not belong to you," it said then. "My Mistress wants it back."

Through a haze of agonized tears, Jarrad looked past the creature to Lathwi, who was still enclosed in a fiery cocoon. In a blood-thickened voice, he panted, "Who in hell are you?"

The demon eclipsed any answer she might have made with a swipe of its free hand. An instant later, Jarrad's guts hit the grass with a sickening splash. He screamed, then started to convulse. The demon scowled as if irked by his twitching, then casually tore the heart out of his chest.

Blood fountained. Jarrad slumped. The demon flung his still-spasming body out into the fire, then squatted down and began to strain its talons through the mess of trampled grass and gore. When it drew itself erect again, it had a dull red stone pinched between its fingers.

"I will be well rewarded for this!" it crowed, and then popped it into its maw.

"I think not, krim," Lathwi hissed. "That is my stone. I mean to have it back."

Its back stiffened as if with surprise. As it turned to confront her, the greedy gleam in its eyes grew brighter.

"You are Lathwi," it said. "You must come with me. If you submit willingly, I will deliver you to my master free of pain. If you resist—" It licked the rim of its mouth with its black, serpentine tongue. "—you will regret it, for I am only required to deliver you alive."

Lathwi snorted, scorning the ultimatum. No matter how small or soft, dragons did not submit to krim!

Once again, her hands strayed to her waist—a wishful reflex. Not that weapons were apt to do her much good, she thought, remembering her last encounter with krim. Despite the terrible wound that she'd dealt it, it had still nearly crushed the life out of her. Even so, she would rather have a sword than not right now.

As if to prove that wishes could come true, a glint of fire-chased steel caught her eye then: Broken-Nose's sword. She remembered now—the krim had knocked it from his hand. It was lying in a tuft of blackened grass now, well beyond casual reach, but close enough to engage her hopes. Maybe, if she pretended to bolt in one direction but then reversed course and made a dive for it…But no, that wouldn't work. Her arms were still rubbery, the rest of her was either stiff or sore, and she was tired all the way down to the bone. That krim would have her under its heel long before she ever reached the sword.

The demon was closing on her now. Hoping to stall its advance, she goaded the fire with a thought. As it flared up, hissing like a nest of coruscating snakes, she remembered another way of getting things from there to here, and lashed out with her Will. But krim wasn't distracted by her little trick. And when it saw Jarrad's sword careening through the air, it abandoned its game of cat-and-mouse and lunged. She scrambled to elude its grasp, In doing so, she lost contact with the sword. Her Will came back to her empty-handed; and the now furious demon did not give her a chance to try again.

"*Fool!*" it spat, as it seized her. "*You are my meat!*"

Truly desperate now, Lathwi invoked her last defence.

Liselle ran back and forth along the meadow's near edge, desperate for a glimpse of Pawl. The spot where she had last seen him was ablaze now, torched by a dragon's wrath. As she searched, she ranted to herself: she'd told him not to go out there. That dragon was Lathwi's friend, she had argued. Why else would Lathwi be so unconcerned by its approach?

But restlessness continued to fester within him; and by the time the dragon finally came to ground, his self-control was in rags. Its first pounce drew him into the grass. The second spurred him into a full-fledged charge. Now the whole meadow was on fire and he was nowhere to be seen.

The brush to her left crackled. She half-turned, ready with a tongue-lashing, only to see a pair of wild-eyed hares go plunging out of the smoke-filled field and into the woods. Her hopes faded, leaving her at a loss as to what she should do next. Should she look for Pawl? Or go to Lathwi? Which of them needed her more? She snorted then, mocking herself. Given her fighting skills, the best thing she could probably do for either of them was stay here and hide with the other bunnies.

A dragon's roar shook the air then. It was followed by a terrifying shriek. Liselle knew that sound, she had heard it before, but please, Dreamer, it couldn't be.

As if in response to this prayer, the canopy of treetops over her head shuddered. She backed away from the barrage of twigs and green leaves which came raining down on her only to freeze as a shadow swooped to the ground in front of her. It furled its leathery wings with a snap, then held her captive with its lidless gaze.

Now her worst fears were confirmed. Despite her costly policy of restraint, The Rogue had tracked them down!

Oddly enough, the demon seemed puzzled. It sniffed at her as if she were a piece of rotting meat, then frowned and sniffed again.

"You do not look like Lathwi," it rasped, more to itself than to her. "Yet you stink of magic. So you must be Lathwi after all." Having come to that plodding conclusion, it then ordered her to submit. "Do so willingly and I will spare you much pain."

"The lady does not submit to vermin," a familiar voice said then.

In the next moment, Pawl came striding out of nowhere to take a stand between Liselle and the demon. The left side of his jaw was pimpled with red blisters, and his leather jerkin was scorched, but he seemed to have escaped the dragon's fire unscathed elsewise. As glad as Liselle was to see him alive, though, she couldn't let him face this new and greater peril.

"Get out of here while you still can, Pawl," she said. "You have no idea what this thing can do."

That much was true. But Pawl knew a thing that needed killing when he saw it, so he answered Liselle's advice with some of his own.

"Stay behind me."

Even as he had ignored her, she now ignored him. Since the enemy already knew where they were, the use of her magic could not betray them. So she side-stepped her guardian and began the Spell of Unmaking. But the words were unwieldy, as slippery as eels, and even as she tried voice them, the demon lunged past Pawl and dealt her a blow to the mouth. She flew backward, then crash-landed on her back. A maelstrom of pain blew through her then. A moment later, she blacked out.

Although Pawl didn't react fast enough to stop the demon from hitting Liselle, he did manage to open its scaly hide to the bone with a double-fisted stroke of his sword. It howled with pain as foul-smelling ichor spurted from its wound, then spun around to backhand him. He ducked, then struck again—an upward thrust to the back of its thigh. Although this cut wasn't as deep as the first, his enemy retreated with a limp. Pawl followed, meaning to press his advantage, but before he could strike another blow, the demon unfurled its wings and vaulted toward the treetops.

An instant later, it came diving back at him, its talons poised to rend.

The manoeuvre took Pawl by surprise. In all of his long years of soldiering, he had never fought anything with wings. Nevertheless, he was a man who knew how to think on his feet; and so as the demon closed in on him, he stayed still. Then, at what seemed like the last moment, he tucked himself into a ball and tumbled away. But he misjudged its speed and reach, giving it too much credit on the first account and not enough on the other. As he started to roll out of his somersault, a pair of talons tore through his jerkin and into his back. He cried out, for the pain was immediate and intense. The demon doubled back to attack again. Although he fought it off, it left two more excruciating grooves in his back.

Pawl already knew he wouldn't be able stand against this thing much longer. He hurt too much; and the pain was eating away at his concentration. If he didn't find a way to cut it down in the next few minutes, he was one very dead man.

High above the trees, Shoq danced as he had never danced in his life. Ancient memories spurred him on. Through them, he knew where to strike, when to swerve, and how to keep his own soft spots safe. No instinct could've been that precise; no reflex, that sure. It was as if he had been fighting krim all of his life. Two of them had fled from him already. The third was in full flight after losing an eye to his claws and a crater-shaped hunk of one leg to his bite. As it struggled to outrace him, he circled around and broke one of its wings with a savage crack of his tail. For one moment, it remained aloft. Then gravity grabbed it by the ankles and started to drag it down.

As it fell, Shoq cruised along in its wake. He did not think it was likely to survive its landing, but he wanted to be sure. Besides, watching it fall was fun.

A thought slammed into his mind then. He veered out of his lazy spiral and into a rapid, headlong dive.

Liselle's eyelids shuttered open, exposing a world full of blurs. For one dizzy, pain-laced moment, she didn't know where she was. Then the scuffling of feet and a human groan refreshed her memory. She scrambled into a sitting position, then tried to look past the obscuring haze. The first thing she saw was Pawl falling to his knees. His back was an ugly network of deep, bleeding gashes. His head was bowed, as if no longer had the strength to hold it up.

Shock rolled through her in sickening waves, then arced into horror as she spied the demon. It was swooping down at Pawl like some grotesque bird of prey. Her immediate thought was to voice the spell that would save his life, but when she tried to open her mouth, an excruciating pain locked her jaw. But no amount of pain could've distracted her now—the demon was nearly on top of Pawl. She leapt to her feet and flapped her arms, a desperate attempt to redirect its attention. As she did so, Pawl suddenly thrust his sword into the air. The demon shrieked and tried to swerve away, but momentum carried it onto the blade and split it open from chest to crotch. It crashed to the ground then and began to flop around in a pool of its own severed intestine.

Pawl struggled to his feet, wincing as the interplay of muscles reopened the wounds on his back, then limped over to the flailing demon. His sword was still stuck in its bowels, so he unsheathed his hunting knife and plunged it through its skull. The demon twitched one last time, then began to melt like rancid lard. With a grimace of disgust, Pawl reclaimed his weapons and started to walk away.

Liselle followed. She wanted to congratulate him; thank him; grieve for his savaged back. But her jaw was broken and her tears were all dried up, so all she could do as was catch his hand and give it a feeble squeeze. He acknowledged the gesture with a phantom smile.

"Let's go and find Lathwi," he said.

They returned to the tree-line only to discover that the dragon's blaze was now a full-fledged wildfire. Pawl cursed, damning his luck and fate in general, then began to scan the smoke-filled meadow for human-sized shadows. As it happened, though, Liselle was the one who spotted Lathwi first. Relief surged through her veins only to clot in her heart. She gave Pawl's arm a sharp tug, then pointed frantically as he turned to frown at her. As he squinted in that direction, the cords in his neck went taut.

"Who's that with her?" he asked. "One of those Southern bastards?"

She shook her head, an emphatic refutation that left her eyes brimming with agonized tears. He understood her all too well.

"This is indeed an evil day," he murmured, in a tone as raw and bloody as his back. But while he dreaded the idea of facing another monster, especially under these conditions, he went striding into the meadow without another word.

An upwell of fire drove him back.

He swore, then tried a different route. Again, the fire barred his way. He retreated once more, then gathered up the shards of his courage for one last desperate dash. He should be able to get his sword to Lathwi before he was overcome by the heat, he told himself. And once she was armed—well, he had to believe it would make all the difference in the world. He sucked in a last breath of semi-fresh air only to expel it as a nasal sigh as Liselle stepped in front of him. Her face was too bruised and swollen to register any expression other than pain, but it was obvious by the angry lights in her eyes that she did not want him to do this. Yesterday, he would've been touched by her concern. But today, it was just one more obstacle for him to overcome.

"Get out of my way, Liselle," he told her, straining the words through gritted teeth. "Lathwi needs my help; and she needs it now."

She wanted to shout at him, to rage herself hoarse: how was his immolation supposed to help Lathwi best a demon? But she knew better than to try and talk by now—she had no time for more pain. And besides, it took more than angry words to sway rock-stubborn Pawl; it took viable alternatives.

And she believed she had one for him.

So she summoned a mote of Fire. It appeared in the flat of her palm, then danced along the length of her fingers. As it did so, it sang a happy song about all the tasty things it had eaten. Liselle asked it for help then: safe passage into the meadow for her and this man beside her. But while it was happy to help her who knew its Name, it was not so sure about that man-thing. He looked quite delicious. She asked again, bearing an image of Lathwi in mind this time. The mote leapt as if with joyful recognition, then granted Liselle's wish.

She grabbed Pawl by the hand then and started toward the meadow. Although he didn't understand what she was doing, he had seen the fire-bug in her hands and so resorted to trust.

Bright orange flames leapt up all around them then. But while they snapped at Pawl's heels and flirted with his face, they left his flesh unscathed. He marvelled at this, but only for a moment. For a dragon's shadow came hurtling out of the sky then. It passed directly over their heads, low enough to stir the fire with its wind, then disappeared behind a cloud of smoke.

"If nothing else," Pawl begged the Dreamer then, "please let it be the same one."

Through a haze of oxygen-starved tears, Lathwi watched as the krim's
fist came arcing toward her temple. There was no hope of escaping the
blow; the krim had her pinned to the ground and she was suffocating
beneath its weight. But even as she braced herself for the eruption of pain,
a triangular blur swooped in and turned the punch aside. The outlines of
an outstretched neck appeared next, then a colossal expanse of muscle and
scales. Krim disappeared then; and the angry lash of a dragon's tail went
streaming out of sight. Lathwi rolled over, meaning to climb to her feet,
but began to cough up clots of bile instead. Over the sound of her own
heaving, she heard the portentous thud of a dragon's landing and then a
furious scuffling. She turned toward the noise as soon as she was able to
stand.

It took her no time at all to spot Shoq. He was lying belly-down on the
ground little more than a dragon's length away, flailing both neck and tail
like a sire gone suddenly rogue. She tried to touch his thoughts, but was
driven back by a gyre of absolute pain. Comprehension slammed into her
like a demon's fist: that krim was still alive beneath him!

"Get off of it!" she shouted into his mind.

He ignored her.

Stupid dragon, she raged to herself. He knew as well as she did that that
was no good way to fight krim.

She started toward him, her thoughts as wild as slashing knives, then
suddenly remembered Broken-Nose's sword. With a facility born of pure
urgency, she translocated it out of the scorched grass and into her waiting
hand. Then, eager for a chance to wield it, she raced to her tanglemate's aid.

As she approached the still-writhing dragon, she flashed him another
thought: *Get up!* As stubborn as her, he refused. She hissed, venting
frustration as well as fury. Then, fully intending to knock some sense into
his thick skull, she raced past his scything tail and along the length of his
body. The bitter bouquet of dragon's blood grew thicker with each step;
and as she neared the hollow behind his forearm, the reason for that smell
became abundantly clear. That spot which she so loved to tickle was in
tatters now, ripped to shreds by a gnarled hand. As she watched, for a
moment too horrified to react, that same hand gouged at him again.

A murderous frenzy overcame Lathwi then. She hacked the hand off
and kicked it away, then went hunting for something else to punish.
She found a wingtip; two twitching toes; a tiny strip of hairy flesh. She
chopped at all of these with equal fanaticism—vicious, inelegant strokes
which mirrored her frame of mind.

Then Shoq began to move—a slow, lumbering progression which
gradually exposed the krim's mangled remains. Wanting to make sure that

it was thoroughly dead, she strode over and buried her sword in its skull. By chance, that thrust sprung its jaws; and as she stared at that pit of gold-coated teeth, she remembered the ruddy stone. She wanted it back—and not just because it was hers. Before she had the chance to probe the krim's remains, though, a dragon-thought slipped into her head.

"Lathwi."

Although the image was soft and blurry, its underlying need was clear. Forgetting all else, she went in search of Shoq.

To her relief, he had not gone very far. She vaulted over the thick whip of his motionless tail, ran past a hind leg whose claws were stained black with gore and then skidded to an appalled stop. Shoq was lying on his side now; and the damage that had been done to him was terrible to behold. His vulnerable underbelly was a network of canyons: great, gaping fissures which revealed muscle and bone; strips of perforated intestine; sections of his billowing lungs. There was also a mouth-sized hole at the base of his throat. Golden blood was oozing from these wounds in sickening profusion; as it pooled on the ground around him, it took on the aspect of honey.

She cried out, a roar of rage and protest. This should not have happened!

"Lathwi."

His Voice was weaker now, a mere shadow of thought. Her rage dissolved into dread. She ran to the place where he was resting his head, then dropped to her knees in front of him. His eyes were closed. The rims of his nostrils were a pasty shade of white. Up close, he smelled of brimstone and krim. In a Voice as gentle as a springtime rain, she Named him.

His outer eyelids rolled slowly back, but the membranous inners remained shut. These gave his stare a fey remoteness.

"*Is this another trick?*" he asked, flaring his nostrils as if for a scent. "*Or is it really you?*"

"It is me."

As a further reassurance, she framed his triangular head in her hands, then raised it and touched noses with him. His contented sigh tailed off into an unwholesome gurgle.

"*I do not understand,*" she told him then, a thought as painful as a bone-deep bruise. "*Why did you do this?*"

"*You Called,*" he replied. "*I came.*"

There was no reproach in the thought, no regrets; only a hint of surprise that he should have to explain such a simple thing to her. She smiled, sadly amused by his misconception, then dismissed the matter as he Voiced her Name again.

"I am here, Shoq."

He projected an image of a rapidly spreading emptiness at her, then plaintively said, "*I am hungry, Lathwi.*"

She was about to tease him—he was always hungry!—but suddenly his breathing stumbled to a standstill, and his head turned as heavy as stone. Wide-eyed with disbelief, she went plunging into his mind, but even as she did so, she knew what she would find.

Nothing.

For a long while afterward, she continued to cradle his head in her lap. She ached, oh, how she ached; and the abuse that she had endured over the past few days could not account for all of the pain. As she languished in its grip, an image unfolded before her eyes. In it, she and her tanglemate were soaring through the sky, both of them trumpeting with delight as he danced his pride to the world.

"Lathwi?"

For one incredulous moment, she thought it was Shoq—it would be just like him to play such a trick on her. Then the cruel hand of reality crumbled that hope. Her name had come to her as a sound, not an image, and dragons did not know the language of men.

She looked up to find Pawl and Liselle standing nearby. They looked haggard and hollow, like two spent husks waiting for a breeze to blow them away. Both of them bore the brutal mark of krim. Their presence came as a dull and not particularly welcome surprise.

"What do you want?" she asked.

"How are you?" Pawl asked, and then scowled as his gaze drifted from her to Shoq. He was, she noticed, positioned in a fighting stance. "Is it... Did it...?"

"He," she hissed, despising his misplaced concern, "not it."

Her agitation swelled beyond all restraint. She gently set Shoq's great head down on the ground, then thrust herself onto her feet and began to pace.

"His name was Shoq." She shouted his Name for all to hear; its power gladdened her ears. And because the human tongue garbled its meaning and beauty, she added, "Shoq the Playful, who danced the sky and teased the clouds. Shoq the Proud and Ever-Hungry. He was my tanglemate, a brother as you would say, and now he is gone from the world."

At that, Pawl lowered his eyes as well as his sword. A flush crept its way into his fire-kissed cheeks. "I'm sorry, Lathwi," he said then. "I didn't understand. Do you want us bury him?"

She scorned the offer with a hiss. "Dragons belong to the sky, not the earth."

"Then say your farewells and let us be gone," he urged. "Your human enemies have retreated for now, but they could come back at any time to collect their dead. I do not wish to meet them."

"I will leave when I am ready to leave," she told him, and then strode right past him as if he were not there.

Confused, hurt and angry, Pawl turned to Liselle for an explanation. As confounded as he was, she only shrugged and went trailing after Lathwi.

They followed her away from the dragon's hulking carcass and over to a circle of blackened grass. There, they watched in puzzled silence as she picked up a sword and began to poke at a demon's molten remains. Then she flicked a slime-coated stone from that mess and Pawl's resentment flared. A bauble? She was endangering their lives for a bauble? He would never have dreamed that she could be so mercenary.

Lathwi scrubbed the stone clean with dirt, then went to stash it in her pouch only to realize that she no longer had one. She hissed with annoyance, then turned to Liselle.

"Carry this," was all she said before she walked away.

Too tired and sore to take offense, Liselle wrapped the stone in a square of cloth that she tore from her sleeve and tucked it into her boot.

"Why?" Pawl asked her then.

All Liselle could do was shake her head.

Meanwhile, Lathwi returned to Shoq. She would've given a whole mountain of diamonds not to be standing here, caught up in memories that wouldn't let her go. But her tanglemate had come when she had Called. She could do no less for him.

"Now what?" Pawl muttered, when he saw where Lathwi had gotten to. His back throbbed, his arms were a useless blend of slush and lead, and he'd endured enough on this deceptive woman's behalf for one day.

But then he saw the fire.

A moment ago, it had been racing toward the meadow's far side. Now a sudden wind was driving it back this way. As it approached, its leading edge began to curve at both ends—as if it had a mind to embrace the dragon's body. Understanding came to the swordmaster then. He should've known that Lathwi wouldn't abandon a brother—not even one so unlikely as this dragon of hers—to the sun and scavengers. And he should've known that she could be more than she seemed, but never less.

Shoq's empty shell ignited with a brilliant white flash. Lathwi waited until the sharp smell of roasting dragon flesh invaded her nose, then turned on her heel and headed for the woods. She didn't look back to see if Pawl and Liselle were following.

CHAPTER 23

Although it was not by choice, Liselle was the first to awake. The agony that was radiating from her jaw had seeped into her dreams, poisoning her sleep as salt poisoned a well; and her subsequent tossing and turning had only made matters worse. Finally, her eyelids had fluttered open of their own accord.

She eased herself into a sitting position, then looked around for her companions. Lathwi was curled up beneath an old oak, seemingly no better or worse for yesterday's ordeal. Conversely, Pawl was sprawled face-down on the ground like a dead man. The gouges in his back leered at her: fat, lipless grins whose interiors were marbled with fresh blood, whitish sera and spring-green pus. Liselle didn't need a physician's training to recognize infection when she saw it, or to know that he was in dire need of hot poultices and clean bandages. Otherwise those wounds could go septic and corrupt his whole body.

Poor man.

Poor Liselle, too, she added, as the throbbing in her jaw reasserted itself.

She was thirsty now. Her throat felt like it was lined with powdered glass. She struggled to her feet, rolling her eyes as abused muscles complained, then went limping toward Pawl's saddlebags. His buckskin nickered as she approached. The space where their other two horses should have been was conspicuously empty. A knot formed in her belly.

What were they supposed to do now?

Getting the horses back from Jarrad's men was out of the question. It would take too much time to track that band of blackguards down for one thing; and for another, no one here except for maybe Lathwi was in any sort of shape for a bit of thievery, another fight, or—given their luck lately—some nasty combination therein. And they couldn't afford to risk Lathwi like that. Without her, there was no reason for them to be in these mountains.

She hoisted the water skin to her lips. Drinking was an awkward, painful process. More water dribbled down her chin than her throat. Between one sip and the next, she sat down in the dirt and tried to think of other options. But things did not look good. There was little chance of them getting replacement mounts in this sparsely populated land. Even if they did come across a village with horses to spare, they had nothing to offer in trade; and she knew better than to expect charity from a breed of people who sacrificed their daughters to mercenaries as part of a killing fee.

They'd have better success begging from the mountains themselves—their hearts were not as flinty.

So. Barring an act of providence, they were stuck with one horse. She supposed that they could take turns at riding double, but the going would be slow as well as awkward. They needed speed to outrace a demon's wings.

If only they had wings of their own...The wish sent a thrill coursing down her spine. Dreamer! Where was her mind? She could have wings if she wanted them. So could Lathwi.

Transformation. The ignorant called it shape-shifting, which was, at best, an inadequate description. Changing was a better term, but not quite right, either, for it implied a flexibility that didn't exist. No matter what it was called, though, transformation was the art of remaking reality. This was different from transmogrification, which could make a man look like a cow but never act or smell or think like one. A man transformed would be mooing for the milkmaid twice a day. And sooner or later, he'd forget he had ever done otherwise.

Therein lie the danger of this magic. The longer a person remained transformed, the more likely she was to assimilate her new shape's instincts. This wasn't necessarily a bad thing so long as she maintained a firm grip on her original awareness. But if she forgot herself for any prolonged length of time, she stood a good chance of spending the rest of her life as a beast.

She didn't see that happening to Lathwi, though. Lathwi was one of the most self-aware people in the world. The only problem was: how was she supposed to teach the big woman what she needed to know? She couldn't speak—just the thought of it brought tears to her eyes—and it would take far too long to write out every last detail in the dirt.

Just then, the buckskin nickered again. Liselle looked up from her thoughts to see Lathwi prowling toward her. She waved a welcome at her, then politely held out the water skin. Lathwi accepted it without a word, and when she had drunk her fill, she gave it back and turned to leave. Liselle grabbed her by the arm, a gentle bid for attention, then recoiled as Lathwi rounded on her with a snarl.

"What do you want?" she demanded.

Liselle gaped at her for a moment, at a loss as to what might've prompted such surliness. Then, because what she had to say couldn't wait, she scrawled a string of runes into the dirt.

Can you heal me?

The question provoked images of splints and bandages and a lard-faced physician with sour breath. Lathwi was proud to say, "No."

Are you sure? Liselle scribbled then.

You once cured the pain in my legs.

The assertion appalled Lathwi. She could not have such a power.

Otherwise, she might have been able to succour Shoq, seal his wounds before his life leaked into the ground.

"I cured you of riding sickness, nothing more," she told her. "This time you have a face full of broken bones."

Nevertheless, I want you to try.

"Why?" she demanded, temper flaring. She did not have the power to heal. Nor did she want it.

We need to talk.

Lathwi's irritation took a scornful turn. Talk, talk, talk—what was it about people that made them want to vomit up their petty thoughts all the time? Why couldn't they try to be more like dragons, whose silence was far more eloquent? She stared at Liselle, taking in details. The lower half of her face was a mass of turgid bruises. The swelling pressed her mouth into a thin, unmovable crack. In a spiteful sort of way, she was glad of the damage and its quiet guarantees.

"Why?" she demanded again.

Although annoyed and confounded by Lathwi's churliness, Liselle refused to be distracted. She took a deep breath to center herself, then plowed her next thought into the dirt.

Our horses are gone.

That seeming irrelevant took Lathwi by surprise. Since she never concerned herself with the bay's whereabouts until she was ready to ride, his absence had felt perfectly natural to her. But now that she thought about it, she realized that Liselle was correct. Her reasons for bringing the matter up, however, remained an annoying mystery.

"What do horses have to do with healing?" she asked.

The sorceress cleared her earthy slate with an impatient swipe of her hand, then wrote: How will we get to the mountain now?

"We still have feet," Lathwi told her haughtily. "It may be that we will walk."

Why walk when you could fly? Lathwi hissed. A moment ago, she had been ready to turn her back on this ridiculous conversation. Now she was hooked as thoroughly as a fish, and twice as aggravated about it.

"Enough of this riddling already," she grated. "Tell me plainly what flying and healing have in common."

Confident of her full attention at last, Liselle wrote: Transformation can give you wings. But if I cannot talk, I cannot teach you. So in order to fly, you must heal me.

A gust of longing blew through Lathwi as she viewed this message. If she had wings, she could fly away, so far and so fast that neither Liselle nor any other of her garrulous race could follow or find her. She'd be free then—free of their problems, free of their demands, and free of the clamour which defined their so-called civilization. But even as this sweet fantasy unfolded within her, cold logic denied it. She could fly to the end of the earth and back, wind-blasting the stink of mankind from her hide, but what good would that do her if Galza returned to the world? That one hated dragons first.

And one of Her krim had killed Shoq.

"Lie down and stay yourself still," she told Liselle then. "It may be that this will hurt. And I cannot promise success."

Liselle did as she was told. Lathwi folded into a squat beside her. They exchanged a look—green eyes gleaming with desperate hope, blue ones dark with complex regret. Then the sorceress nodded and squeezed her eyes shut, an invitation to begin.

Lathwi scowled, trying to rid herself of Shoq-images and a concomitant desire to fail. Regardless of her own needs or wishes, she had to believe this would work. She could do it, she had to; therefore, she would. Encouraged by this mantra, she reached out with both hands and began to knead Liselle's jaw.

The insides of Liselle's eyelids flared brilliant red at Lathwi's first touch, and a howl tunnelled its way up from her belly. She dug her fingers into the earth, then knotted them there, trying to anchor herself to the waking world. But the second touch sent every nerve in her brain into a frenzy, and the third plunged her into a void.

When she came to her senses again, she found everything as she had left it: sunlight was still filtering through the canopy of trees, the birds were still twittering their ritual songs, and Lathwi was still staring down at her with the same inscrutable look. She tried to say something then, but while the effort was less painful, it still failed.

"I feared it would be so," Lathwi said.

Disappointment spread through the sorceress like a crack in thin ice, then opened into a chasm that swallowed the last of her hopes. Suddenly, she was tired beyond all endurance: tired of hurting and hating and being afraid; of sleeping on rocks and eating dirt and failing at every turn. The biggest mistake of her life had been her decision to accompany Lathwi on this black, heart-breaking comedy of a quest. She should have remained in Compara and made her stand against The Rogue on familiar ground. She might not have been able to overcome him there, but neither would she have had to taste the bitter dregs of her own inadequacy time and time again.

"There is, however, another way that you might teach me what I need to know," Lathwi said then.

Liselle sat up and stared at her. There was no sign of mockery in her expression, and no belligerence, either. Her eyes were half-hooded; dragon shrewd. Although Liselle tried to deny it, fragile new hope stirred within her. It prompted her to scratch a question into the dirt.

How?

"Show me," Lathwi replied, perfectly dead-pan. "Let me look into your mind."

Her first impulse was to raise her psychic barriers and shout a refusal from the ramparts. But that was instinct, a knee-jerk reaction to the idea of giving somebody of Lathwi's power free access to her mind. From a strictly logical point of view, the proposal made perfect sense. So she lowered her defences, both mentally and physically, and gave her consent. Then she retreated deep within herself to prepare the way.

Lathwi was eager to begin. All she could think of was having her own wings at last. As soon as the sorceress shut her eyes, she extended her awareness. An instant later, she was floating in Liselle's mind. It was a noisy place, abuzz like a honeybee's hive. Out of curiosity, she isolated a single vibration from that multifarious hum. As she focussed on it, it shaped itself into a thought.

Pawl's wounds were starting to fester, he needed clean bandages and hot poultices soon...

She couldn't resist. She singled out another vibration, one with a slightly lower frequency. Prepare a pentagram and the vision-melange before swallowing the separation dust...

She absorbed the thought without pausing to digest its meaning, then reached for another. As she did so, something impinged on her awareness. Startled, her curiosity stalled. The touch came again, mild yet insistent. This time, Lathwi recognized the subtle pressure as Liselle's Will and allowed it shepherd her where it would. As she glided along through the hive, though, she triggered chords at random just to hear what they had to say.

...mix rye blight with a pinch of belladonna, then...

...Pieter! Sweet Dreamer! What had he done to deserve such a cruel, lonely death? Her fault, all her fault...

...The Spell of Unmaking was her only hope now. Turruc, abbraxxuman, surriqac...

Some thoughts whispered their secrets, others roared. Some seemed familiar, others were wholly new. Fascinated, Lathwi listened to them all.

The next nudge sent her bobbing into the heart of what seemed like a cumulus cloud. The hum was more intense here, momentous. Liselle's Will led her to a fat band of thoughts. As soon as she touched it, it began to sing.

...Transformation is the art of turning illusion into reality...

On and on the lesson went, a detailed recitation of fact and effect. Lathwi listened to every nuance, again and again and again until she was sure she knew everything there was to know about transformation. Then she set out to see what else she could learn.

A familiar touch urged her to withdraw. She did so, but slowly, sampling thought after thought as she went.

...that golden hair, those lake-blue eyes. And oh, what sweet lips he had. If only she dared to give in...

...the cardinal rule of ritual magic was strict attention to detail...

The touch came again—no gentle nudge this time, but an angry shove. She responded with a shove of her own and then greedily reached for the single most scintillating thought in the sorceress' head.

To her surprise, it proved to be Liselle's secret Name.

The first thing Pawl noticed when he came awake was that Lathwi and Liselle were both missing. Adrenaline incinerated the syrupy vestiges of sleep from his veins and jolted him to his feet. An instant later, pain shot down the length of his back: punishment for the spontaneity of his movements. As he suffered through this paroxysm, his panic gave way to reason. A demon would've murdered him in his sleep before taking the women; and bandits would have taken his horse as well. Since he was still alive and the buckskin was still picketed in the same spot, Lathwi and Liselle were probably somewhere nearby, too.

Nevertheless, he was not about to leave that to chance. As soon as the pain reached a tolerable level, he groped for his sword and went in search of the two women.

He found them over by his saddlebags. They were sitting side by side on the ground. Both appeared unnaturally tense. The expressions on their faces were strained and blank. He'd seen that look once before—when their enemy had been trying to take Lathwi away. The crazy bastard must be trying again! He slung his sword aside, then went rushing to Lathwi's side. Then, because he didn't know what else to do, he did exactly the same thing he'd done the last time. That is, he grabbed her by the waist and held fast.

"I'm here, Lathwi," he told her. "Tell me what to do!"

She shifted as if trying to shoulder off an other-worldly embrace. Encouraged by this show of resistance, he tightened his grip and hailed her again.

"Lathwi! What can I do?"

"You can stop shouting in my ear," she snarled then. A heartbeat later, she added, "You can also stop squeezing my ribs. They are sore enough already."

His jaw dropped. His fear for her spun into confusion. He released her as if she were a sack of snakes, then pushed himself onto his feet and stared at her. Her scowl was close to murderous. If she had been beset by The Rogue, he thought then, the poor bastard had surely lost again.

As soon as Pawl got out of her way, Lathwi got up, too. Her foul mood was back, resurrected by a blast of resentful steam. If the swordmaster hadn't interfered, she'd still be exploring the treasure trove that was Liselle's mind. As it so happened, though, her concentration had flickered when he seized her; and that lapse had allowed the sorceress to expel her.

A moment after Lathwi stood up, Liselle also climbed to her feet. She was livid, enraged by Lathwi's extracurricular plundering. How dare that big barbarian treat her mind like a sack of greasy sweet-meats! How dare she abuse her trust? She wanted to shout at the deceitful woman, to revile her for her thick-skinned greed. Denied that outlet, she slapped her across the face instead.

Lathwi hissed, despising the feeble blow. Pawl stepped between them before Liselle could strike again.

"Would one of you please tell me what's going on here?" he demanded. "I thought you were fending off another attack of magic, but obviously I was wrong."

Liselle loosed a bitter snort. Lathwi frowned as if offended by the sound, but then shrugged and said, "I needed some information. I was obliged to look into Liselle's mind to get it." Before Liselle had a chance to contest that flat and severely truncated explanation, she went on to say, "Now that I have that information, I must be on my way."

"I think it would be wiser to rest for a while longer," Pawl countered. "It's been a rough couple of days for all of us."

"If you wish to rest, do so," she said, confounding him with her persistent indifference. "I am leaving."

"Very well," he grumbled. "If you want to leave, we'll leave. Just give me a minute to saddle up."

"That will not be necessary," she said, and then started to turn away.

His confusion multiplied like fleas on a mongrel's back, then abruptly expanded into anger. He grabbed her by the arm as she tried to pass and bullied her around to face him. She hissed a warning at him, but he did not release her.

"We are not leaving that horse behind," he informed her through gritted teeth. "We can take turns riding if—"

"The horse is yours to do with as you please," she said. "Take him with you when you go."

His stomach knotted. The tips of his ears turned bright red. "If that means what I think it means—"

"It means you are not coming with me," she told him, in a tone as flat as a sledge-hammer's head.

"—then you had best change your plans," he concluded, flushed all over now. "Because no matter what you say, I'm going with you."

But Lathwi had no intention of saying any more—as far as she was concerned, there was nothing left to be said. So she shouldered him aside and began to walk away again. This time, Liselle stepped in front of her to bar the way. While the swelling about her mouth distorted her expression, there was no mistaking the fury in her eyes.

"I am leaving," Lathwi told her, countering that blaze with ice. "If you wish to come with me, come now."

Liselle did not budge. If she had her way—and she did mean to have it this time, regardless of the consequences—neither she nor Lathwi was going anywhere until Pawl knew why he was being left behind. He had suffered too much on their behalf to be so summarily dismissed. So she glared at Lathwi until she was sure she had her attention, then sank down and scratched out a message. You owe him an explanation.

When Lathwi narrowed her eyes, a prelude to refusal, she added: I can and will compel you to do this.

A fresh gust of resentment howled through Lathwi. Pawl was reasonably smart for a man; he ought to know without her telling him that their fortunes were now diverging. Talking wouldn't change that fact, only complicate it. But although she was tempted to leave them with that thought and nothing more, she did not because she had not forgotten how vicious Liselle could be when she was angry. Instead, she swivelled toward Pawl.

He stood stiff-backed and cock-jawed, his arms crossed like swords over the span of his chest. Anger jigged in his eyes as he stared at her, but it seemed to her like a dismal sort of dance, one which knew no hope. Something about that look triggered a notion not her own.

Pawl loves Lathwi, does she love him back?

The alien thought took her aback. Love? She recognized the word from Liselle's ridiculous book of doggerels, but she didn't understand such a concept or see how it might apply to her. She respected Pawl's talents, admired his character and mostly enjoyed his company. Was that love? She didn't know. Nor did she care at this point. So, for now, love would have to remain an empty word.

He was still staring at her with those desolate eyes, still waiting for answers that would do him no good. She ground her reluctance into a paste between her teeth, then bowed to Liselle's demand.

"Liselle and I are going to transform ourselves into creatures with wings," she told him. "Then we are going to fly from here to my mother's mountain."

"Transform me, too," he proposed, although the thought filled his stomach with butterflies.

"I would not be able to control you as you would need to be controlled while I myself am Changed," she said. "Without my guidance, you would forget yourself and fly away and spend the rest of your days as a beast."

"Then I'll follow you on the ground," he persisted. "My horse is well-rested, I'll keep up."

"For a while perhaps," she conceded. "But remember, we are bound for the top of my mother's mountain. What will you do when the slope gets too steep for your horse—attempt the incline on your own? I have lived on that mountain. Believe me when I tell you that it is not an easy climb."

He opened his mouth, no doubt ready to make an exception of himself, but she pressed on before he could voice it.

"There's the matter of krim to consider, too. What will you do if a pack of them catches up with you while you are on our trail? No krim will disregard a human who bears the mark of another krim; and I may very well be too far away to mount a timely rescue."

"What I'll do then," he grated in reply, "is buy you a little more time to escape."

She hissed, venting her exasperation. Pawl knew she was right—she could tell by his now permanent flush and the way he kept avoiding her eyes. So why was he being so stubborn? She cast a scathing look at Liselle for serving as futility's champion, then focussed on Pawl again. Ridiculous or not, she had committed herself to this argument. Therefore, she would finish it.

"Let us suppose that you do follow us," she said, pacing now to dispel her agitation, "and that you do manage to reach the top of my mother's mountain unscathed. What then, Pawl? My mother will not be pleased to find you in her caves."

"I'll try to stay out of her way," he commented, hoping to put her off with sarcasm.

Lathwi continued to pace back and forth in front of him. He got the feeling that he was being circled by some shadowy man-eater.

"You feared Shoq, who was half-grown and good-natured," she said, in a tone that was both roguish and matter-of-fact. "It would be smarter of you to fear my mother, who is neither of those things. She will probably suffer Liselle's presence because she's never met a sorceress before, but soldiers she has encountered in plenty over the years. No doubt, she has lined her belly with—"

"Enough!" he snapped, galled by her ability to terrorize him with his own fears. "You've made your point. I won't go anywhere near your mother or her blasted caves. I'll stand a watch somewhere nearby instead. And if any demons come, I'll hold them off until—"

"Until what?" She swerved out of the set course of her pacing to take a hair-raising stand at his back. "Until help arrives? How long do you think you could last against a pack of krim?"

"Long enough," he declared.

"Think again."

With that, she plunged her fingernails into the worst of his wounds. His shoulders flexed backward, his spine arched. Whatever else that he had been about to say sheered off into a full-fledged howl.

"Go home, Pawl," she told him then. "Take yourself back to Compara and teach your recruits how to fight against krim. They will have need of such knowledge if Galza has Her way."

Still struggling to contain the pain, Pawl conceded the argument with a nod. He'd been a fool to carry it this far, especially since he'd known how badly he was hurt all along. But pride had distorted his perceptions, inflated his sense of importance to blinding proportions. So beguiled, he had refused to believe that two untrained women could survive in these wild lands without him. Lathwi's brutal demonstration had punctured that delusion. And while his back still ached because of it, some part of him could not help but admire her style: if their situations had been reversed, he might have done the same thing.

Someone nudged him then. He looked up from his thoughts to find Liselle standing at his elbow. There was an apology in her eyes.

"It's all right," he told her. "I understand."

"That is good," Lathwi said, "for we must go. Taziem's mountain grows no nearer."

Without another word, she started to walk away. It was then that Pawl noticed that she was weaponless.

"Wait," he blurted. At the same time, he undid the ties which bound the sheath to his hunting knife to his thigh. "I want you to have this."

She eyed him suspiciously, then took the blade from his outstretched hand and unsheathed it. It was better balanced than her lost not-claw; its edge was keener, too. She didn't understand why he'd want to part with it. But as unaccustomed as she was to the giving of gifts, she was in no way adverse to receiving them—especially when they were as fine as this. She sheathed the knife with a flourish, then strapped it to her thigh. When it was securely in place, she looked up and favoured the swordmaster with a grin. Prompted by an old ghost, she then formally thanked him as well.

A surprised smile danced its way into Pawl's eyes. After all that had passed between them over the past few months, he had not been expecting something so uncommon as courtesy from her. It seemed to him like a most precious gift.

"You are most welcome," he replied solemnly, as if they were swapping vows instead of farewells. "And when next you come to Compara, look for me. I'll be looking for you."

Tempted to kiss her then, he turned to Liselle instead. "Hurry home," he bade her. "From what I understand, there's someone waiting for you as well."

Even as she blushed, she blessed him with a look. Then, while she still had his attention, she dropped into a crouch and wrote: Do not linger long in this place. The sound of my magic will attract unwanted attention.

"Many thanks for the advice," he said. "And since I've already had as much unwanted attention as I care to stomach, I'll leave as soon as I'm packed."

He glanced at Lathwi one last time, half-expecting her to say something more. When she did not, he nodded as if to assure her of his sincerity and then started back toward the camp. Halfway there, he turned to wave goodbye, but she was already gone.

It was something he would have done. And that made his sudden solitude easier to bear.

In the hot morning sunlight, the blackened meadow seemed to Liselle like a giant grave, hastily dug. She shuddered at the memories when came to her at the sight.

It had not taken them long to get here from the camp—indeed, the brevity of the trip both amazed and appalled her. Last night, the same trek had seemed to go on forever. Short walk or not, though, she was tired now—emotionally depleted as well as physically sapped. Far too much had happened this morning. She looked ahead to Lathwi, who wanted to Change in a wide, open space. Liselle had yet to forgive the big woman for plundering her thoughts; or for treating Pawl like a sack of old bait. Neither of them deserved that kind of treatment from her. They were her friends, dammit! They had feelings. Was there no such things among dragons? Lathwi came to a stop in a far corner of the meadow. She did not want to be here, did not want to view the ash heap of Shoq's remains, but she needed a place that would accommodate her magic and this was it. She reviewed the information that she'd picked from Liselle's mind, and then drilled herself on the particulars of the shape she intended to take. Then she turned to Liselle.

"Are you ready?" she asked.

Liselle shot her a weary look, but made no outright sign of denial. Lathwi chose to interpret this as an affirmative.

"Good," she said then. "You go first."

Resentment tried to bud within Liselle, but she squashed it like a roach. Regardless of Lathwi's pushiness, there was no denying the fact that the time for action had indeed come. That required a clear mind, one free of grudges both big and small. She took a deep breath to calm her thoughts, but only managed to trade one battery of worries for another. Transformation involved an extravagant expenditure of power. Unwarded, it would make more noise than a three-day festival.

And The Rogue had found them twice already.

Did she dare to take this step? It had seemed like the right thing to do when she had first conceived of it, but now she was no longer sure. What would happen if she simply went home with Pawl instead? Lathwi would go on to that mountain of hers, that much was certain, but what would The Rogue do? Her best guess was that he would continue to follow Lathwi—she was, after all, still the decoy. That might give Liselle enough time to return to Compara and rebuild her wards, maybe even surprise the bastard while he was looking the other way. But what about Lathwi in the interim? She wasn't a match for The Rogue, not even with all the extra arcana she'd purloined during her last mind-scry. And while there'd been many times when Liselle had cursed Lathwi for her overweening arrogance, she could not leave her at the mercy of so powerful an enemy. So, for better or worse, she had to dare this step—and any others which might span before her afterward.

Minutes passed. Lathwi waited in silence. She did not know why Liselle was taking so long to begin, but neither the delay nor the not-knowing troubled her. Now that she was on the verge of realizing her life-long ambition, she felt calm, almost detached. Returning to Taziem's mountain did not seem like the pinnacle of good fortune anymore, but rather a small stepping-stone along a more convoluted path. The realization was both heady and sobering.

All of a sudden, the ethereal sound of Liselle's magic sang out like distant windswept chimes. Her aura flared to visibility and then thickened into an opaque curtain. This curtain shimmered and quaked, rippled and shrank: a hypnotic series of fluid contortions. The carillon which accompanied it swelled beyond the meadow's capacity to contain it, then abruptly climaxed for all the world to hear. At that precise moment, the curtain dissolved into a shower of scintillating silver sparks.

In the mind-numbing silence that followed, Lathwi stared at the place where Liselle had stood. A white she-raven with eyes as green as sunlit leaves peered back at her. The bird flapped her wings, then cocked her head as if to hurry Lathwi along. She acknowledged this prompting with a nod, then took her own transformation in hand.

It began with an image in her head: big, bold, beloved. When it was as clear and true as she could make it, she drew it over her existing form like a blanket and called upon her power and her Will to stamp it in place. Pain erupted in her flesh and bones then—a terrible, stressed sort of ache, as if she were being drawn in all directions like a curing hide. Her balance shifted. So did her perceptions. The world was suddenly a whole muzzle's length away. Something hit her in the back then. Looping her head around, she saw that it was her tail: as fine a whip as Taziem's. And a pair of the most exquisite wings lie folded against her scaly sides!

Her cry of surprise and delight leapt from her throat as a full-fledged roar.

The outburst startled a nearby raven. It half-hopped, half-flapped out of range only to circle back and stare at her. An image surfaced in Lathwi's mind: it was of a tiny, heart-faced human. She remembered then. This was Trueheart, the sorceress who called herself Liselle. She acknowledged the not-bird with a rumble, then abruptly unfurled her new wings and launched herself into the sky. As the green world fell away, becoming an ocean of blue, an exhilaration whose like she had never known swelled within her. For the first time in her life, she was truly a dragon in flight; and for the moment, nothing else mattered or sufficed. She roared with pride and delight.

Behind her, Liselle followed in silence. Her thoughts were of exile and pursuit.

CHAPTER 24

Now confined to the rough-walled chamber which she used exclusively for birthing, Taziem was as restless and bored as only a dragon in the last days of pregnancy could be. Hungry dragons weren't the only ones who kept track of the time, she grumbled to herself. And anyone who said otherwise had never carried a clutch of younglings to term. As she brooded, echoes of an indistinct scrabbling caught her attention. She slanted her head toward the mouth of the chamber and listened intently. The clatter came again. This time, she recognized it as the sound of claws scraping across stone. Her outrage was instant. She roared a warning, then projected an image of teeth and dragon-fire after it.

"Who dares to trespass on my territory?"

Almost shyly, an image unfolded in her mind. It was soft and pink. The accompanying thought contained a Name: Lathwi.

For a long moment, Taziem could do nothing but wallow in her own astonishment. The Soft One was here! How could this be? She hissed then, venting resentment. No other dragon in the world would have defied Taziem's decree of exile. And no other dragon could have so sorely tempted her to reverse such an order. Indeed, she did not know which perturbed her more: Lathwi's audacity or her own self-centered ambivalence.

"*I did not Call you,*" she said then, a thought brimming with disapproval.

"Nevertheless, I have come," Lathwi replied. "These are strange times, Mother. I have brought troubling news."

That cryptic string of thoughts intrigued Taziem. Which was, she surmised, exactly what Lathwi had intended it to do. She rumbled, a sound of grudging admiration, then granted her permission to continue.

"I am listening."

"My tanglemate Shoq is dead."

Taziem received these tidings with the equivalent of a mental shrug. "*Stupid dragons die every day.*"

"Shoq was slain by krim."

A leering image of dragonkind's ancient enemy stole into Taziem's mind then. She tensed reflexively. Within her, the unborn dragonets stirred as if echoing her distress.

Strange times indeed, she grumbled to herself. Who else but long-gone Galza knew how to call krim to this world? Who else hated dragons that much? These questions could not wait for a more convenient time. Taziem wanted answers now.

"*Come to me,*" she told Lathwi, flashing her an image of the birthing chamber.

"There is something else you must know first," Lathwi thought in reply. "Tell me."

"I am not alone. My companion is not a dragon. Still, she knows things that may be of interest to you. I urge you to grant her an audience, too."

The she-dragon hissed, astonished anew by the extent of The Soft One's impertinence. Inviting a strange dragon here would have been bad enough; inviting a strange species simply was not done. Not even Bij himself would've dared to try her patience like this. But as much as she wanted to send Lathwi and this companion of hers a fiery sample of her displeasure, she did not because she wanted to know what they knew.

"Come," she thought then, an irritated command. "Bring your companion if you must. But do not tax me with any more of your tricks. I am in a foul enough mood already."

The soft scraping of feet across stone resumed. Taziem got ready for company.

As Lathwi lumbered down the tunnel, she revelled in those details which were to her the essence of home: the cool stone floor, worn smooth by centuries of dragon feet and tails; the glow of rocklight; the faintly sulphuric smell of dragon. She was tired from her headlong flight, but no amount of fatigue could have spoiled this moment for her. For better or worse, she was home.

The mouth of the birthing chamber loomed straight ahead. Lathwi paused so Liselle could catch up. A moment later, the she-raven appeared in the tunnel. Her wingstrokes were rapid and laboured, as if she were flying against a strong wind. As soon as she saw Lathwi, she went to ground. Lathwi pressed a thought into the not-bird's head, commanding her to stay put, then headed into the chamber. Liselle watched until the dragon was out of sight, then lapsed into an exhausted sleep.

The first and only thing Lathwi saw when she entered the room was Taziem. She was huge, a veritable mountain of flesh and black scales. The rocklight's faint glow framed her vast bulk like an unreadable aura. Although she was coiled around herself as if she had been sleeping, there was nothing drowsy about her. Her eyes were wide-open. The tip of her tail was twitching furiously.

"*Lathwi,*" she said then, a thought steeped in wonder. "*Are you truly as you appear to be?*"

"*For the time being,*" she replied, peeling her lips back to reveal a draconic grin. "*And for as long as I so desire.*"

Taziem's scrutiny turned critical. Her fosterling's colouration was a bit peculiar, she mused—all black except for her face which was ivory striped with ochre—but aside from that, her unlikely size and those remarkable blue eyes, she seemed no different from any other dragon.

What a fascinating riddle!

"The Change becomes you," she commented. "How was it accomplished?"

"It was done by sorcery," Lathwi told her, "which is an esoteric form of man-lore. My companion is a master of this lore. She has taught me many things."

A new kind of Lore? Taziem was tantalized. She wanted to know more—much more. But she did not want to appear too eager in Lathwi's eyes lest that give her clever daughter an undue advantage.

"*Where is this companion of yours now?*" she asked, an almost idle thought.

"I left her in the tunnel."

"Go and get her. I would see a master of man-lore with my own eyes."

Liselle's sleep was shattered by a gentle rumble. The raven-half of her awoke first; it then roused the woman-half with a blast of primal fear. Groggy and confused, her first impulse was to flee. Then she saw the white-faced dragon and changed her mind. For reasons she could almost but not quite explain, she knew this creature meant her no harm. The raven argued against that notion—nothing that big, with that many teeth could ever be trusted—but Liselle ignored its raucous squawking and looked to the dragon. When it gestured with a forearm, she somehow understood that she was to follow.

The dragon strolled into a spacious cavern, then curled up on the cool stone floor. She flapped past it in search of a suitable perch only to catch sight of a pair of eyes. They were yellow and slit-pupilled like a snake's, and the gleam in them was lethal. The woman in her froze then, paralysed with fear. The raven in her swooped in and seized control.

Now her only thought was of escape. She wheeled around, intending to sweep back into the tunnel, but the white-faced dragon was blocking the way so she veered toward the heights instead. She circled round and round, frantically searching for a glimpse of blue sky, until finally, exhausted but still afraid, she alit on a lofty jut. Chest heaving wildly to the beat of her heart, she then stared mindlessly down at the two dragons.

"You trifle with me at your peril," Taziem warned Lathwi then, ringing the thought with teeth. "Summon your companion now, and without further trickery. Otherwise, I will eat the both of you."

"*That is my companion,*" Lathwi replied sourly.

Taziem had to believe her, for dragons did not lie, but even so, she was incredulous. "*Your companion is a bird?*"

"For the moment. Her original shape is human."

"*How curious.*" She angled a deceptively casual eye at the raven, projecting reassuring thoughts. When it did not respond, she rumbled. "*Tell it to come down from there and Change. I will not be bombarded by bird droppings in my own caves.*"

"*What you ask is not as simple as it may sound,*" Lathwi told her, and then hastened to explain before the she-dragon could get upset again. "It would seem that my companion has forgotten her true self. And since she does not understand the language of dragons, I will have to Change my own self to refresh her memory."

"Is that difficult?"

"Not exceptionally so."

"Then do it."

"There is one other thing you must know first—my magic is silent, but Liselle's is not. If I succeed in convincing her to Change, she will make a noise which krim can hear. It may be that krim will then come here."

Taziem lapsed into a contemplative silence. The threat of krim was a most unpleasant complication. She could almost see them rampaging through her caves, fouling everything they touched. What were a few raven droppings by comparison? And there were her soon-to-be-born younglings to consider, too—she remembered very well what krim could do to the weak. But as provocative as these arguments were, they were not enough. Taziem wanted to meet a master of this remarkable human-lore, and see for herself what sort of creature she might be. This need for knowing was stronger than any maternal instinct, and more compelling than the notion of encountering krim. So she chose to satisfy her curiosity rather than common sense. But even as she did so, she hedged the decision with a invocation of long-unused Names.

"Do what needs to be done," she told Lathwi then. "If krim come, krim will suffer."

Lathwi savoured the feel of her dragon form for a wistful moment, then dismissed her regrets with a twitch of her wings and focussed on her original shape. It came surging back into being with breath-taking swiftness. That which had been long became short again; that which had never existed in the first place disappeared. All of a sudden, she was standing high up on a set of skinny legs and trying to look past a muzzle that was no longer there.

For the second time in a single day, Taziem doubted her senses. At one moment, she'd been looking at the new Lathwi; in the next, a shimmering blur. Now the Lathwi of yesterday was back, seemingly hatched from thin air. An excited quiver worked its way up the length of her tail. She could hardly wait to learn how this marvellous trick was done!

A sudden burst of raucous chatter ruptured the chamber's silence. It was coming from Lathwi, who was now gesturing at the raven.

"...come down and Change, Liselle," she was saying. "My mother wishes to look upon your true form. Have no fear, she will not eat you."

The she-raven stared down at the strange creature which had sprung up from the white-faced dragon's ashes. Its song was an ugly jumble of sour notes and croaks, but even so, it sounded vaguely familiar. Curious, she cocked her head and waited for it to sing again.

"Liselle!" Lathwi said then, her tone now burring with annoyance. "Fly down from there. My mother's patience is not without its limits."

The bird continued to stare down at her.

Lathwi hissed—once out of frustration, then again as she realized how foolish she was being. She did not need to threaten or coax the sorceress down from her perch, not when she possessed the means to compel her.

"TrueHeart," she said then, "by your secret Name, I bid you to remember yourself. TrueHeart, I bid you to answer my Call. Then, TrueHeart, I bid you to Change."

That one oft-repeated note dazzled the raven like a gold gaud. At the same time, it burned away the haze in which the woman had been lost. Liselle reasserted control then; and as she went gliding down from that ledge on the back of Lathwi's magic, she rejoiced. For not only was she herself again, she now knew her secret Name. She could feel its power thrumming within her, urging her to Change. She was happy to obey.

"*Your description was quite accurate*," Taziem commented, as she monitored this transformation. "*Her magic is noisy.*" Then, catching her first glimpse of Liselle's true form, she snorted. "*Another runt.*"

The first thing Liselle saw with her now human eyes was Lathwi's amused half-smile. She arched an eyebrow at the big woman, wanting to know what was so funny.

"My mother is dismayed by your size," Lathwi explained.

Liselle tensed. Distracted by her Name and the demands of transformation, she'd forgotten that she was in a dragon's den.

"Turn around," Lathwi told her then. "Taziem wishes to look upon your face."

Echoes of a raven's fear spurred her pulse to a gallop. In her mind, she knew the dragon didn't mean to harm her—if it had, it surely would've done so by now—but a part of her heart remained stolidly unconvinced.

"It is not wise to keep a dragon waiting," Lathwi said.

She turned slowly around only to be arrested by a pair of eyes. They were beautiful and cold, amber as a hunter's moon. The dagger-like pupils transfixed her twinned images. She couldn't move, not even to look away. She was mesmerized; elated; appalled.

Minutes or hours later, the she-dragon blinked and bared her teeth. Instinct urged Liselle to turn and bolt then, but she resisted the impulse for reasons that had more to do with weariness than bravery or pride. She was sick of running and being chased, of glancing over her shoulder after every other step. If the dragon wanted her, she could have her—but she would have to take her face-first. So she held her ground as well as Taziem's amber gaze.

"My mother commends you," Lathwi said at last, in a tone flecked with approval. "Few have withstood her scrutiny with such composure."

Stunned by such unexpected praise, Liselle continued to stare at the dragon. Taziem endured her wide-eyed gaze for a moment longer, then rumbled—a sound which Liselle perceived as a dismissal. Unable to express her newfound admiration in any other way, she dropped to one knee and bowed her head.

"What is she doing?" Taziem asked.

"Krim broke her jaw so she cannot talk," Lathwi replied. "Yet she wishes you to know that she is in awe of you."

"How quaint," the she-dragon remarked, more amused than flattered. "Does that also explain why she is now scratching at the floor?"

"This is called 'writing'," Lathwi told her. "It is a form of communication. Those scratches are an illustration of her thoughts."

Taziem's tail twitched. More secrets! How had she ever dared to call herself The Learned One when there was so much in the world that she still did not know?

"What thought has she depicted?" she demanded eagerly.

Lathwi squinted at the string of runes, then rumbled. *"She wants me to tell you why we have come."*

A sly glint stole into the she-dragon's eyes. "Tell her I will agree to listen only if she will agree to teach me how to interpret these scratches for myself some day."

She bit back an admiring grin, then translated Taziem's terms for Liselle. The sorceress scowled, then scribbled a caustic note. You two are obviously related. This time, Lathwi did not even try to hide her grin.

"What does she say?" Taziem asked.

"She accepts your offer."

"Then proceed with the telling. Start at the beginning and stop at the end."

Malcolm's stomach twisted itself into knots as he beheld the blackened meadow. Something momentous had happened here, something that had involved his fugitive sorceress—he knew because the air was still thick with residues of her sorcery. What he did not know was the specifics of that happening; and he would have no peace of mind until he did.

"Spread out," he said to his demons. "Search the woods for things that seem out of sorts, then report back to me."

As the duo hastened away, he set off toward the curious mound which occupied the center of the field. Every now and again, he stopped to dab the rheum from his eyes with a soft cloth. It wasn't a pleasant job, for even the slightest bit of pressure on his still swollen eyeballs felt like a hive of red-hot needles to his brain. But if he didn't wipe the ooze away, it clotted in his lashes and sealed his eyes shut. And prying them open again was agony compounded.

Nevertheless, he considered himself fortunate. A week ago, he had been utterly senseless, on the verge of filling his own grave.

And all because he had underestimated his quarry.

He still couldn't believe how foolish he had been. No sorcerer in his right mind would even dream of translocating somebody as powerful as Lathwi on the spur of a moment. But he had been furious, insanely so— his only thought had been to drag her back to Compara by the hair. And in his fury, he had forgotten how tired thirty-six hours of magic could leave a body. So he'd gone streaking across space and time only to be caught in the fist of her Will. If she'd counter-attacked with a proper death curse instead of that bitch-vicious burst of power, well—needless to say, they had both made mistakes that day.

Lost in thought, he didn't see the charred remains of a fallen tree until he stumbled into it. An instant later, his nose told him that it wasn't a tree at all, but a human body. His pulse quickened with suspense, then subsided again as he flipped the corpse over and onto its back. For while it had been badly burned, he could tell that it had once been a man. A soldier of some sort, he guessed, judging by the chain-mail helm. He searched the body then, hoping to uncover a clue as to what a warrior might have been doing in this fire-ravished field, but all he found was a terrible hole in its chest. No man-made weapon could've caused that kind of damage. That was pure demon work.

But why? Had Lathwi hired mercenaries for protection?

Once again, he berated himself for his stupidity. If he hadn't acted so recklessly, he could've accompanied that trio of demons to this place and watched as events unfolded. Then he wouldn't have had to waste all this time on guess-work and confusion.

He daubed at his eyes as if he were blotting away tears, then continued on toward the mound. There was a stink in the air now, one too familiar to ignore. It led him to a noxious pool of green-black slime. A corrosion-tipped sword lie next to it. Malcolm cursed this new and unwelcome discovery, but before he had a chance to consider its implications, a crunch sounded behind him. It was followed by a leathery rustle and then a series of footsteps.

"Well?" he rasped, as the demon came to a stop alongside of him. "What news have you?"

"There are dead in the woods, Master," it replied.

His stomach knotted again. The question which he had to ask next ate at his vocal cords like acid. "Is Lathwi among them?"

"No, Master," it told him, to his immense relief. "We found three humans—warriors, by their look—and two of my kind. I see you have found a third." It grinned then. "At least this one met with some success before its demise."

"What do you mean by that?"

"It possessed the talisman sometime not too long ago."

"Where is it now?" Malcolm demanded.

"I do not know."

"Who took it?"

"I cannot say. But since these remains reek of dragon gore, perhaps yonder dragon scavenged it."

With that, it pointed a gnarled finger at the mound.

Malcolm seized two fistfuls of his hair and pulled on them, reining in an urge to scream. First men, then demons and now dragons? What in hell had happened here? The more he learned, the less he understood! He limped his way over to the mound then. It was all cinders and fine ash. Hoping that the talisman was somewhere underneath that mess, Malcolm conjured a breeze. All he got for his efforts, though, was a face full of sulphur-laced dust.

As he struggled to rid his eyes of the dragon's remains, the second of his demons swooped out of the sky to take its place alongside of the first. Its ugly face was smeared with a dark, viscous fluid.

"What did you find?" Malcolm asked.

"One more body," it replied, "and two separate trails. The first belongs to a single rider heading west. The other belongs to a horde riding south."

"Any sign of the talisman or the sorceress?"

"No, Master."

He snarled an impotent curse, then turned his back on the demons for a moment of private contemplation.

Although it galled him to the marrow to admit it, he was stymied. There were too puzzles here, and too few clues. He believed that Lathwi was still alive and in possession of the talisman: no other possibility was acceptable. But where she was going and for what purpose remained two nagging unknowns. He could solve this conundrum for himself in time, but he did not want to cede her that much breathing room—not while she had that all-important talisman. He had to track her down as quickly as possible.

And that meant asking the Dark One for help.

He could not do that here and now, though. If he Called Her to this unwardable place merely to beg for directions, he stood very little chance of surviving Her resulting fury. So he would have to return to Compara, then set out anew once he had a fresh fix on Lathwi. He rued the amount of time he was going to lose in the interim (and the punishment he was bound to receive for his perceived incompetence), but there seemed to be no way of getting around it.

He wiped the rheum from his eyes again, then gestured at the nearest demon. It came over and lifted him into its arms with slavish care.

"Where do you wish to go?" it inquired.

"To Com—"

His ears began to ring, a tintinnabulation as sudden as it was faint. He concentrated on the sound, then laughed as its growing volume exonerated his imagination.

It was Lathwi.

And she had just made her last mistake.

"...so we transformed ourselves and flew from there to here," Lathwi concluded.

"*I have heard,*" Taziem said, her first thought since the start of the telling. "*Now I must think. Be still for a while.*"

Drained from the long and often awkward telling, Lathwi was only too happy to comply. She stretched the kinks out of her back, then glanced around as if to draw strength from her surrounds. The rocklight had faded to the merest suggestion of a glimmer hours ago, mirroring a sunset which none of them would've noticed otherwise. Since then, their only source of light had been the tiny mote of Fire which she had Called to illuminate Liselle's increasingly garbled script. It was by this faint radiance which she now beheld the sorceress. She was on the floor next to her, dozing in reluctant fits. Dark half-moons cradled her eyes; her jaw was a mottled bulge. As Lathwi watched, her head bobbed on its wobbly stem of a neck, then dropped to her chest. Lathwi reached over and eased her onto her backside. A moment later, she dismissed the mote of Fire and lay her own self down.

The sound of slow, steady breathing filled Taziem with a melange of regrets. There would be no sleep for her tonight. She had too much to contemplate; and not all of the problems up for review were Lathwi-made.

A contraction rippled down the length of her belly, more nauseating than painful for the moment. She had endured such spasms for hours now, at intervals far too regular for her to dismiss as gas or distress. This was the perversity of youth at work—they could always be expected to honk for attention at the most inconvenient times. But while she would have to give in to their urgings sooner or later, no dragon had ever said that it had to be sooner. Tonight, she would give this new brood their first lesson in patience.

Her thoughts turned from birthing to the bleaker matters that Lathwi had raised. One image in particular haunted the she-dragon. It was of a man-shaped, red-eyed ravener. This was Galza as her ancestors had known Her. And if Lathwi and her peculiar little companion were right, it was Galza as She hoped to be again.

A part of Taziem balked at the notion. Dragons believed that The Stone Oma had killed The Dragonbane—the memory was rooted in the first dawn of this long, one-starred age. Now, on the cusp of dawn so many centuries later, some puny human wanted her to believe that dragons had been wrong; that Galza had not been destroyed, merely exiled; and that some upstart lore-master named The Rogue was conniving for Her return. It would've been too much to swallow if Lathwi had not been here to lend her support to these claims.

But support them she had; and there was no arguing with her newfound memories of krim.

So, Taziem thought then. A human sorcerer was in league with The Dragonbane. It seemed reasonable to deduce that She needed him for a reason—most likely to bring Her back from wherever it was that The Stone Oma had sent Her. If She were back already, she'd have no need of anything. And krim would be far more plentiful. Her sides spasmed again, a more emphatic contraction this time. She endured the pain with a dragon's patience and then went back to her thoughts.

So. Galza needed a human to do something for Her; and it had to be more than just bring Her back because otherwise she would be here already. This, she deduced then, was where that talisman-thing came in. She called an image of Lathwi's stone to the forefront of her mind and pondered it for a long moment. Although it was not much to look at, Taziem had the feeling that she had seen it somewhere before now.

"Lathwi."

The summons erupted in Lathwi's mind like a thunderclap. Conditioned by a lifetime of such rude awakenings, she roused to semi-consciousness without resentment or regret.

"*I am here*," she replied, though the thought was framed by sleepy cobwebs.

The she-dragon projected an image of the stone at her. "*Where did you get this?*"

She considered a number of vague responses, then decided that she was too tired for anything other than the unadorned truth. "*I stole it from you on the day you sent me away.*"

The answer troubled the she-dragon, not because Lathwi had successfully thieved a stone from her hoard, but because it did not leave her satisfied. The stone may well have come from her cache, but where had it been before that? She knew, she could feel the answer lurking somewhere inside her.

So she began to comb the folds of her memory.

Hours passed as she conducted her search. An indistinct gleam crept into the chamber and then gradually grew brighter as rocklight began to warm to the new morning's arrival. She was deep into ancient memories now and on the verge of giving up. There was nothing here about a stone, nothing to justify her feelings. Despite her misgivings, though, she continued to look—further and further back. Then, half-hidden among those last, tragic days of EverLight, Taziem finally found a coincidence. It was protruding from a monstrosity's brow: a ruddy gleam that spouted black fire.

That was it then: the stone was Galza's third eye.

No wonder Her human ally was so anxious to possess it. Without it, She could never be whole. Without it, perhaps, She could never return.

An image of The Dragonbane wallowing in Her own impotent rage for all eternity expanded in Taziem's head. She rumbled to herself, savagely pleased by the thought, then bellowed as a surprise contraction strangled her pleasure. Distracted by her ruminations, she'd forgotten that she was on the verge of parturition. She'd also forgotten to maintain her repressive hold on that process. As a result, the luxury of control was now beyond her. Her insides spasmed again as if to emphasize that point. A moment later, a warm gush of fluids bathed the base of her tail. She roared again— no surprise this time, only pain.

The first roar wrenched Liselle halfway out of a deep, dreamless sleep. She bolted upright and glanced wildly about in search of raiders or leering demons, but all she saw was a terrible blur which then roared again. Too bewildered to do anything else, she covered her head with her arms and started to cry.

The sudden commotion roused Lathwi, too, but she awoke with her wits intact. And as soon as she saw the spreading puddle around Taziem's tail, she knew there was no cause for alarm.

"Calm yourself," she told Liselle. "My mother is giving birth, nothing more."

The sorceress did not seem to hear. She was shivering now as well as weeping, and there was a feverish look in her eyes. Lathwi frowned, disapproving of such foolishness, but then abruptly remembered her own first reaction to Taziem's birthing throes: she'd been terrified. Her frown assumed a more tolerant bend.

"*Lathwi.*" The thought was hazy, clouded by an overflow of pain.

"I am here," she replied. "What do you require?"

"The stone," Taziem huffed, doggedly trying to relay a night's worth of conclusions to her. The attempt was futile. Her concentration was in shreds. She had to content herself with a question instead. *"Where is it?"*

"Liselle has it," Lathwi told her.

Taziem turned her gaze to the trembling sorceress. The waves of warm-blooded fear that were radiating from her made the she-dragon's head swim. "She cannot stay here. Take her elsewhere."

"Shall I relieve her of the stone first?"

She considered the possibility for a sluggish moment, then decided that she did not want her brood to be born in the presence of such a baleful token.

"Let her keep it for now. But do take her elsewhere. Her mewling is most annoying."

"Do you wish me to stay with her?" Lathwi asked then, as casual as she could be.

Although her powers of perception were deteriorating at a rapid pace, Taziem knew what Lathwi was really asking. And while she had fully intended to expel her from the chamber at this point in time, instincts now argued otherwise. If Galza did manage to worm Her way back into this world, her newborns would need all of the advantages that Taziem could give them. And having clever Lathwi as a tanglemate would definitely be an advantage.

"That will not be necessary," she told her fosterling. "Once you have taken Liselle to a place of safety, you may return."

Then another contraction seized her and she forgot about everything but the pain.

Lathwi showed Liselle to a cozy little sleeping nook in the outer caves, but the now hollow-eyed sorceress refused to stay there. Taziem, it seemed, was making too much noise.

I'm sorry, she had scrawled in the dust, but as exhausted as I am, I just can't sleep through a dragon's roar. Isn't there some place I can go where I won't hear her?

Lathwi knew of a place like that: it had been one of her favourite spots as a youngling. So she led Liselle out of her mother's caves and then up a path that had been worn into the mountain's side by countless generations of nimble dragonets. It brought them to the top of an enormous, sun-washed boulder whose center was a bowl-shaped basin.

"Shoq and I used to come here to nap in the summer," she told Liselle. "It is very quiet."

It wasn't a spot that Liselle would've sought out on her own. They were very high up now, and the boulder jutted into blue sky on three sides.

Prompted by sheer human perversity, she peeked past her would-be cradle's rim. There was nothing there but sunlit space; and then, far, far below, a tree-line that looked like a hedge of pine-green quills. The sorceress shied back away from the edge, then flashed Lathwi a worried look.

"Do not worry," the big woman assured her. "It is safe. See? The basin is deep; you will not roll out. And it gets just the right amount of sunlight and shade."

Liselle sat down in the middle of the basin. It did not look so imposing from this angle; and as Lathwi had promised, it was neither too warm or too cool. Maybe this wasn't such a bad idea after all.

"Stay here," Lathwi said, as the sorceress curled into a ball. "Sleep as long as you wish. If I am not here when you awake, do not come looking for me. I will fetch you when the birthing is over."

Liselle nodded, then closed her eyes. A moment later, she was sound asleep.

The dragonets surged into the world in quick succession: first-born Masque, golden Eldazed, roly-poly Javvad, piebald Flap, greedy Pinch, and grey, undersized Quirk. There was at least one more on its way. Taziem knew because she was still wracked with contractions; and because afterbirth didn't have claws. She pushed at the mass in her birth canal with all of her might, as determined now to be done with this delivery as she had been to delay it earlier.

A triangular head surged past the opening at the base of her tail. It was followed by a stretch of neck, then a pair of flailing forearms which Lathwi gently seized. Working in tandem with the next contraction, she then hauled the neonate into the chamber. As it slid free of her body, Taziem roared with relief.

Exhausted from its ordeal, the dragonet lie on the floor and gasped for breath. Its tanglemates crowded in around it; all curious, and all eager for a taste of the neonate's still intact birth sac. Lathwi cut its umbilical cord with Pawl's knife. Pinch nabbed the tissue and ran away, with Masque and Eldazed in hot pursuit. The other dragonets began to scratch at the newborn's caul. Lathwi didn't try to stop them: these fetal membranes were the only nourishment they were likely to get until Taziem was ready to render that first all-important suck of mother's milk. And a newborn who didn't get any help with its sac stood a good chance of suffocating in it.

But that would never happen to any tanglemate of hers!

She peeled a strip of tissue away from its nostrils. As she gobbled it down, a thought popped into her head, as proud as it was infantile.

"Shygyre," it said. "My Name is Shygyre. I am hungry."

"Shygyre," she replied, filling its mind with her smile, "my Name is

Lathwi. If you are hungry, eat this." She gave it a piece of its caul. "It is not much, but the afterbirth will be here soon. After that, Taziem will give you a drink of milk. And after that, either she or I will go and get us all something good to eat."

"*And after that?*" Shygyre asked, excited by the series of images which she had presented to it.

Thinking of Galza and krim again, she replied, "*I do not know, Shygyre. I cannot see that far ahead.*"

Taziem roared again then, voicing another birthing pain. Shygyre struggled to its feet and began to introduce itself to its other tanglemates, who were intent on eating its sac. In the midst of all this chaos, Lathwi stood perfectly still and tried to forget what she knew.

But she was a dragon. And dragons couldn't forget.

CHAPTER 25

The mountain range was imposing—a desolate collection of windswept crags and spires. Malcolm had to admit: Lathwi had chosen her hiding place well. This was perhaps the last place he would've thought to look for a city-witch.

He was closing in on her now—the residues of her magic were like a fine wine in his veins. He couldn't wait to find the bitch and look upon her dismayed face. That moment would make up for all of his past failings with her, and indemnify all the delays and doubts and confusion.

And giving her to The Dark One would be nothing short of a heartfelt pleasure.

Even as he imagined that glorious moment, the demon who was carrying him chuffed and pointed toward a span of rock in the distance. Out of reflex, he squinted in that direction, but his rheumy eyes could not see past the jagged tip of its talon.

"Is it her?" he demanded.

"It is possible, Master," the demon replied. "She reeks of fresh-worked magic."

"Has she seen us?"

"No, Master. She appears to be sleeping. Or dead. I cannot tell from this distance."

His heart froze for an instant, then redoubled its pace. She couldn't be dead, not after all he'd gone through to find her.

"Take me to her. Quietly," he added with a feline grin. "I want this to be a surprise."

A shadow engulfed Liselle's sun-warm face. Registering the sudden chill in her dreams, she tried to shift away from it. As she did so, twin vises clamped themselves to her arms and wrenched her to her feet.

Her eyes snapped open, but refused to focus. All she could see was a big, black blur. A protest howled through her mind: no, Lathwi! Not yet! She needed to sleep a few hours more!

"Wake up, Sorceress," an unfamiliar voice crooned then. "Destiny awaits you."

Surprise and sudden fear tidal-waved through her head, leaving her vision clear. And what she now saw in front of her nearly shocked her senseless. The big, black blur that had her in its grip was not Lathwi, but a demon! The Spell of Unmaking rushed to the forefront of her mind, begging to be used, but the injury to her jaw would not permit it. So she tried to struggle for her freedom instead.

"I wouldn't do that if I were you."

That amiable-sounding advice raised every hair on her body, for it hadn't come from the demon. And if the demon wasn't the one doing the talking, she was quite possibly in worse trouble than she'd imagined. Playing for hope as well as time, she feigned resignation and let herself go limp in the demon's grasp.

"Much better," that friendly voice said then. "Now turn around. I wish to look upon the woman who has caused me so much grief."

In one fluid motion, too fast to counter or resist, the demon spun her around in a half-circle. The next thing she knew, she was face to face with a seemingly ordinary man. He was of average height, rail-thin but not starved, and clad in a filthy beggar's robe. His face was spare, a hard-weathered slab framed by hanks of scraggly blonde hair. His upper lip was cloven; his eyes were ugly, gummy slits.

"Admiring your handiwork?" he asked, mocking her with a brittle smile. "Savour the moment then, sorceress. It's all you have left."

The last of Liselle's hopes withered then. This was The Rogue, he who had terrorized her for so long. She yearned to wipe that grin from his face, to strike him down with a curse as black as his heart, but it was a futile wish. Her jaw was broken, and he was on guard. All she could do was glare.

"It's funny," he said then, giving his stubbled chin a thoughtful rub, "but I expected you to be bigger, blacker—sort of like Shyv here, only with blue eyes."

Suddenly, she was glad of her injuries. If she couldn't talk, she couldn't be compelled to spill any secrets.

Malcolm shrugged as if the discrepancy were of no real importance to him. But fortune had already forgiven him for a fair share of mistakes, and he did not intend to tempt its benevolence again. So he gathered up his Will. Then, with a sudden thrust, he tried to break into the vaults of Liselle's mind and make certain of her identity.

As debilitated as she was from pain, fatigue, hunger and fear, her defenses were not so easily breached. She repelled his probe with a resounding psychic slap.

Surprised and pained by the force of the blow, he cried aloud. Then a slow, predatory smile curved across his mouth. His doubts were dead—she was the one. He could not fail to recognize the power which had almost killed him. Now he only had one question left.

"The talisman," he said to Shyv. "Where is it?"

"She has it, Master," it replied. "It is somewhere on her person."

"Find it. And for our Mistress' sake, do no more damage to her flesh."

The demon began to paw at her, seizing great handfuls of her body and then pinching just hard enough to bring tears to her eyes. Waves of humiliation and bile lapped at her throat as it groped her breasts, buttocks and crotch, but she didn't truly despair until it tipped her onto her backside and began to tug at her boots. One came off, then the other.

"I have it!" the demon gurgled then.

"Give it here," The Rogue commanded, in a tone riddled with hunger.

The demon placed the dirty swatch of cloth in Malcolm's outstretched hand. A tingle of recognition coursed through him as he extracted a ruddy stone from its folds. This was it, he gloated then. He had all of the talismans now! From this moment on, he was the king of the world!

The Rogue's obvious euphoria filled Liselle with dread. So, she thought, he had his talisman. Now he would kill her as he had killed all the others before her. But if that was so, a troubled voice countered, why had he ordered the demon not to harm her? 'For their Mistress' sake,' he'd said. And that Mistress could only be Shadow.

Why would such a hateful spirit be concerned about the state of any body other than Her own?

The thought curled over and back on itself, revealing an evil underbelly. At that moment, the last bits of a terrible puzzle slid firmly into place. The witch's familiar had told her that The Rogue was searching for a body for his Mistress: not some necromantic corpse as Liselle had conjectured, but a living, breathing body which Shadow could occupy when She was returned to the world. A body accustomed to power.

Her body.

She could not allow such an occupation to take place. And there was only one way to stop it.

Inch by silent inch, she began sidling toward the rim of the boulder. Neither The Rogue nor his demon took any notice of her movements: they were still gloating over the talisman. She hated to leave that ill-omened stone in their possession, but there was no chance of her getting it out of their hands. All she could do was hope that Lathwi would come and reclaim it from them before they could do further harm.

Ah, Lathwi! If only she could warn her of what waited for her beyond her mother's caves! But no, she had no time. She had to do what must be done before The Rogue remembered her. So she summoned her courage and strength, and pitched herself off the mountain.

Wind whistled its Name in her ears as she fell. Another force knuckled the pit of her stomach. Below her, the trees reached up to receive her. She closed her eyes and beseeched The Dreamer to stop her now racing heart before she landed in their embrace.

An instant later, something slammed into her ribcage and drove the air from her lungs.

She tensed, anticipating the bone-shattering crash which must come next, then realized something was wrong. The thing that had struck her was wrapped around her waist now; and her heart was thrilling to an upward rush. Had Lathwi arranged a miracle? She dared a peek through her eyelashes only to have her hopes dashed. Once again, she was in a demon's clutches.

Disbelief became despair. She'd failed again. And now the world was going to die.

The demon brought her back to The Rogue. He was livid. His hands were bunched into fists. A convoluted vein bulged from his temple as if it were on the verge of bursting.

"You stupid bitch!" he raged, showering her face with a spray of furious spittle. "You crazy, stupid bitch!" Then he punched her squarely in the jaw. As she crumpled to the ground in a faint, he snarled, "Let's see you run away from that!"

He took a deep breath to still his trembling then. She must have guessed what he had in store for her, he supposed. And if he hadn't looked up from his thoughts just as she was casting herself off the cliff, she might well have succeeded in thwarting him once again. Which was just one more reason to get her back to Compara as quickly as possible.

"Do you and Qwrl need to feed before you can fly again?" he asked the demon. "Or can you go wait until we're back in the city?"

The demon shrugged its massive shoulders. "I am strong. I can wait."

This declaration sparked a pang of envy in Malcolm. He was still suffering from the aftereffects of Lathwi's magic. That, combined with the stresses of their breakneck hunt and the scare he had just been given, had him feeling like a rag that had been dragged across a washboard one too many times. Still, it was an exhaustion well worth enduring. The sooner he restored The Dark One to this world, the sooner She would give him strength beyond the scope of mortal reckoning. Then he'd never be tired again.

Just then, Qwrl appeared in the sky overhead. It had been standing watch on a nearby peak.

"What is it?" Malcolm demanded. "What's wrong?"

The demon pointed toward a speck on the eastern horizon. At first glance, Malcolm thought it was a bird. But no bird, no matter how big, would be visible from this distance. And if it wasn't a bird, it could only be—

"A dragon," he breathed.

The demons confirmed his guess with hair-raising growls. Then, forewarned by some sense that he did not possess, they turned toward the west and growled again. He wiped his eyes, then squinted in that direction.

Another speck appeared. It was larger than other one. He sputtered a curse, then kicked Liselle in the leg. This was her fault, it had to be.

"Is there any chance of getting past them without their noticing us?" he asked.

"No, Master," Shyv replied, and then bared its teeth in a daunting display of eagerness and hate. "Look to the east. The first has been joined by a third. Give us leave to tear them all from the sky."

He ground this unforeseen complication into an unsavoury paste between his teeth and then cringed in spite of himself. Those dragons were closing in fast, and he didn't want to be out here in the open when they arrived. His thoughts turned to a cave he had noticed earlier. It seemed as good a place as any to hole up until his demons chased those accursed lizards away.

Taziem turned to behold her new tangle. They were all muzzle-deep in rich, springy afterbirth now, all but Lathwi, who was watching the feed from a distance. Her strange blue eyes were bright with fresh pride. Her flat face was awash with nostalgia. The she-dragon offered her a thought.

"It is a satisfying sight, is it not?"

Lathwi agreed with a nod. "They will gladden the skies some day."

She settled back to resume her watch only to stiffen as echoes of a dragon's furious roar billowed into the chamber. The dragonets instinctively froze. Curiously, Taziem did not react.

"Do you know this dragon?" Lathwi asked her.

"He is Rue," she replied, a deadpan thought. *"He is my tanglemate."*

"Why has he come?"

"I Called him. I Called the rest of my tanglemates as well. All who are still alive will come."

Another roar rolled into the chamber. It was followed by an all-too-familiar shriek. Lathwi's alarm escalated.

"Krim!" she exclaimed, pounding the image into Taziem's head with no regard for subtlety or volume. *"Krim have found their way to this place!"*

"I am not so weary that I need to be told the obvious," came the she-dragon's testy reply. "If there were no krim, Rue would not be voicing challenge."

Without another thought, Lathwi unsheathed her hunting knife and started toward the tunnel. Taziem barred the way with her outstretched neck.

"It may be that krim will come this way," she said. "If they do, your new tanglemates will have more need of you than mine ever will."

"I left Liselle out on the sunning-spot," Lathwi told her, projecting an image of the boulder. "I must go and get her before krim take her away. If they get her, they get the stone as well."

What she did not say, not even to herself, was that the stone only accounted for only a portion of her concern.

"Wait," Taziem said, and turned her thoughts elsewhere. A moment later, her tired amber eyes focused on Lathwi again. "Rue has seen no humans, only two krim. And neither krim is bearing a burden. Liselle must have taken refuge in my outer caves."

"I have to be sure," Lathwi insisted.

"Cannot you use your magic to do that?"

Lathwi hissed, instantly irked with herself. Of course she could use her magic—it simply never occurred to her to do so when there were other, more familiar ways of achieving the same goal. She summoned her Will, then went feeling for Liselle's familiar presence. She found it in an outer cave, just as Taziem said she would. The impression she skimmed from the sorceress' surface thoughts was one of deep, pained sleep. She retracted her probe, then sheathed her knife.

"You were right," she told Taziem. Then, as another roar filtered into the room, she added, *"But it is hard to just sit here and wait."*

"That is what a patient dragon does best," Taziem replied.

But she, too, had a restless gleam in her eye.

As soon as Malcolm Blackheart caught his first close-up glimpse of a full-grown dragon, he knew he had seen the last of his minions. Those lizards were enormous, at least twice the size of that charred lump he'd come across in the meadow.

And they obviously knew how to fight demons.

He cursed this wretched turn of luck. With the demons gone, it would take him at least a month to get Lathwi back to his stronghold in Compara. And as long as that slippery bitch remained unsacrificed, he stood a chance of losing her. It was a terrible thought; intolerable. He could not let her get away again.

That was why he meant to give her to the Dark One now.

And why not, Malcolm mused, as he dragged the sorceress deeper into the cave. He had the talismans, he had the body. Surely his Mistress would overlook the absence of ceremonial robes. This place wasn't warded, true, but there was plenty of good stone to muffle the sound of his magic. And who here in these dragon-infested mountains had the power to hear him? The feckless Dreamer? He snorted. By the time that One bestirred Herself, if She ever did, the world would be a very different place.

The cave widened into a smooth-floored chamber. It had a smell like stale brimstone to it, but Malcolm did not care. The sorceress was heavy and his bad leg hurt, so he was going to work his magic here. He withdrew the talismans from their hiding place in his cloak, then arranged them on his victim's spread-eagle body: a spur for each heel; a fist for each hand; the ivory horn between her legs; and the ruddy stone between her eyes. Next, he sketched a hasty hexagon around her with a piece of charcoal. If he had been fed and well-rested, he would've raised a Sphere of protection then. But he was sore and tired and hungry, and bringing The Dark One back to this world was going to take every last drop of power he had. So he skipped the warding and instead started the most dreadful ritual any man had ever attempted.

All was quiet in the birthing chamber now. The newborns were grooming themselves. Lathwi was listening for the sound of krim.

"How goes the fight?" she asked Taziem.

"It is over," the she-dragon replied, a thought tinged with grim satisfaction. "There were only two krim. One is destroyed, the other has fled. My tanglemates are hunting it down."

"How did they fare?" Lathwi asked then, recalling Shoq's savaged underbelly.

"Two krim are no match for three full-grown dragonsires. They are all well. You may—"

A sharp, discordant whine cut Taziem off. Lathwi bolted upright, immediately alarmed. The last time she'd heard that buzz, The Rogue had been trying to translocate her. She knew she wasn't his target today, for her amulet wasn't reacting. But if it wasn't her, it had to be Liselle.

"What is that annoying noise?" Taziem demanded.

"*Sorcery,*" she replied, and then sent her Will streaking toward the outer caves. This time, she sensed two presences. One was still unconscious. The other was radiating terrible power. She knew then that the worst had come to pass.

Her defiant hiss startled the dragonets. They projected infantile concern at her, but their tiny Voices were drowned out by the buzzing of The Rogue's fell magic. She unsheathed her knife again.

"What transpires?" Taziem demanded then.

"The Rogue is here," Lathwi replied, filling the thought with faceless menace. "He is working some sort of sorcery on Liselle. I must stop him before he finishes his spell."

With a sudden heave that sent her younglings scrambling, Taziem stood up. *"Wait here. I will investigate."*

Lathwi's agitation soared to new heights, carrying her beyond the boundaries of propriety. *"No! You cannot—you do not understand—"*

Taziem silenced her with a look of hauteur and disdain. "This is my territory. Any who dare to trespass upon it must answer to me."

"But he is a sorcerer! He is—"

Taziem rumbled, warning Lathwi against further argument. *"He is an intruder. Soon he will be dragon meat."*

The she-dragon went streaming out of the chamber then—a departure as quick as it was silent. Lathwi stayed behind with her tanglemates. But she wasn't at all happy about it.

🐉

A distant whirring, like that of a field of dissonant cicadas, ate its way through the shocked strata of Liselle's mind and then bit into a deeply buried nerve. It screamed a warning: something was wrong.

Her brain did not want to function on more than a basal level: breathe in, breathe out, sleep until the hurting went away. But the offended nerve would not fall silent; and its wailing soon set off a chain-reaction. Layer by reluctant layer, her awareness began to knit itself.

Something was wrong. Something about the whirring. She had heard it before. Somewhere…

🐉

Malcolm was done with the preliminary phases of the rite now. He could feel The Dark One looming close, struggling to catch and hold his sorcerous hand so he might pull Her out of exile and back into Her rightful domain. He took a moment to rest, for he was pushing himself far beyond the limits of his strength. As he breathed the chamber's stale air, an ominous rumble filled his ears.

His heart began pumping double-time.

He held himself as still as a statue and slowly strained his eyes toward the sound. At first he saw nothing but filmy darkness, but then two amber eyes winked into view. The cold intelligence he saw in them chilled him to the bone.

Another rumble shivered through the chamber. Then the darkness parted, revealing a mouthful of ivory daggers. He swallowed hard, fighting panic, and started to mutter under his breath.

🐉

So, Taziem thought, as she spied on the intruder. This was the human who connived on Galza's behalf. He was a puny thing; filthy, too. She was not impressed.

At her contemptuous rumble, he went as still as a fawn caught in an open field. An instant later, the smell of his fear fouled her nostrils. It was the stink of a man who had just outlived good fortune. She rumbled again and bared her teeth, encouraging him to run. He started to gibber instead. That buzzing noise returned then, but she barely noticed it: she was getting ready to attack. Although she rarely killed for reasons other than hunger, she was looking forward to doing so now.

She began to close in on him then, only to discover that she couldn't

330

move. This wasn't some sort of weakness brought on by birthing: she could have delivered fifty younglings and still been strong enough to come and go as she pleased. No, something else was doing this to her, something more sinister than fatigue. And judging from the grin that was now curving across her would-be quarry's mouth, that something had sprung from him. She understood what Lathwi had been trying to tell her now. She also had some idea as to what she would be made to forfeit in return for this newfound comprehension. Stupid dragons died every day—Taziem had never dreamed that the adage might someday apply to her.

She sent a thought fletched with warning flying back toward the birthing chamber. Then she watched on in novel helplessness as The Rogue returned his attention to Liselle.

Liselle's thoughts were eddying now—a chaotic gyre of memories, confusion and fear.

There was something wrong…

…Jamus. Sweet, handsome Jamus. No man had ever made her heart sing so…

…She was a bird, fluttering panicked circles around a dark cave, then a two-legged woman sleeping on a sunny rock. A shadow eclipsed her dreams, then…

…everybody called her Liselle, but Her secret Name was TrueHeart…

What was that infernal buzzing?

The answer spun free of the whirlpool, then erupted like fireworks at a festival: sorcery in progress!

All of a sudden, she remembered everything: herself in a demon's grasp; The Rogue's feline leer; a thwarted attempt at self-sacrifice; and that awful blow to her jaw. She couldn't tell how long she'd been knocked unconscious, but that wasn't important. It was enough for her to know that she was in The Rogue's custody, and that he was trying to work some terrible spell on her. She could feel it bearing down on her now—a cold, malignant force whose core was unmitigated rot. This could only be Shadow coming home at last.

She had to do something!

Please, Dreamer! she prayed. Let her do this one thing right.

Then she rallied her Will.

It came to her with a passionate flash, then snapped the magical fetters that had shackled her to The Rogue's diagram. In the next instant, she was on her feet and staring into her enemy's entranced face. An impossible strength was upon her now—a strength born of righteousness rather than hate. In the Names of all she loved, she moulded this newfound potency into a miniature sun and cast it at Malcolm's unguarded mind.

Almost done, Malcolm urged himself as he chanted. Five more words, and all would be done. As close to the end as he was, though, he couldn't force himself to go any faster. The invocation had turned his throat to raw meat; its empowering had left him dizzy and weak. He was sweating profusely—an outpouring that chilled his skin and burned his rheum-clotted eyes.

Nevertheless, he persevered—syllable after slippery, pain-wracked syllable. One word hobbled past his lips, then another. As he fought to articulate the third, a sound like windswept chimes impinged on his awareness. Then a fleeting clatter boxed his ears, and a blur sprang up before his eyes. Before he could react, before he could truly understand what was going on, a white-hot comet came streaking into his mind. It threw him backward through the room and into solid stone. He slid down that wall like a broken egg, then puddled to a stop on his butt. The force within him began to corrode his wits.

A terrible presence bespoke him then: it was so strong, and so close, it sounded as if it were shouting in his ear. *Finish the invocation*, it urged. *Speak the last three words.* Elsewise, he would not survive.

Devastated as he was, Malcolm was still a strong-willed man. And life was a powerful incentive. He defied the power that was destroying him and doggedly coughed up a last series of ragged syllables.

Drained to the point of stupefaction, it took Liselle a moment to hear the burr of The Rogue's magic; and another to recognize it for what it was. Only then did she realize that she was still standing within the hexagon; and only then did she try to escape. But by then, it was already too late. A shaft of icy malice plunged deep into her brain, chilling her to the core. It was accompanied by a stab of severe pleasure and a thought not her own.

"Free at last!"

The shock of being so intimately violated by so evil an essence left Liselle sober and fighting-mad. She raised her Will like a battle-standard, but Shadow only mocked her.

"You, a mere mortal, would dare to contest A'Gal-Zanna's Will? Fool! Be content with a speedy death!"

The Dark One's essence began to swell—a cold, creeping expansion that ground everything in its way to dust. Liselle resisted this icy invasion with all her passionate might; and for what could have been minutes or hours, she held Shadow at bay. Then The Dreamer's daughter started to bear down on her in earnest. One by one, Liselle's memories began to crumble. There went her mother: a fleeting, faded image. The house in Compara disappeared, too. Yet even as she was being whittled away, she continued to resist. Instead of mourning the parts of her that had been swept away, she stubbornly clung to all she had left.

She was Liselle. This was her body, her life, her world.

Dreamer, please help her!

A'Gal-Zanna continued to expand. But the going was much too slow for Her liking. She wanted to have this body all to Herself—now! She seized control over Her host's eyes, then searched the area for The Blackheart. He was leaning against a wall, twitching like a freshly hooked fish. By affinity or chance, he looked up then and met Her gaze. But Her would-be high priest was beyond easy repair now, so when he raised his hand, begging Her aid, She coldly looked the other way.

It was then that A'Gal-Zanna noticed the dragon lurking in the shadows. Her initial spurt of alarm sheered off into poisonous delight as She realized that it was spellbound. A gift from The Blackheart, She concluded. Amused by so quaint a gesture, She started to spare him another look.

A flaxen gleam distracted Her. She glanced after it, then thrilled to Herself as She spotted a tiny golden fist. It was lying on the ground just beyond the diagram's border. The other talismans were nearby, too, scattered like so many seeds from an exploding milkweed pod. She guessed what must have happened then: Her host had overcome her binding spells, then cast off the talismans and cursed The Blackheart before he could complete the invocation. What a pity he had been so careless at the very end.

A'Gal-Zanna laughed then, because She had no pity. Then She tried to collect her talismans.

Liselle's memories continued to disintegrate. There went Pieter—a foxy blur. Then a blonde man with tender eyes and a silly hat disappeared with her heart in his hands. She was down to the bare bones of her existence now—a creature with no recollections of the past or hope for the future—but she still had her Name, Will-power, and a single-minded desire to thwart that cancerous presence in her head. So when it tried to reach for those things on the floor, she dedicated herself to keeping stone-still.

A'Gal-Zanna raged at the woman's stubbornness. Did she not understand that her struggles were futile? Or had humans changed that much in Her absence?

"Go back to that not-place from whence You came, Galza," a Voice told her then. "You will find more welcome there than here. As she resists You, so shall we all."

A'Gal-Zanna cranked her host's unwilling head toward the she-dragon. "Your welcome means nothing to Me," She sneered, lacing the thought with acid. "You parasites have feasted on The Dung Queen's bowels long

333

enough. It is my turn, my time now."

A tall, scarred woman clad in black scales stepped past the bespelled dragon then. A swarm of dragon-sprats followed her.

"Liselle," the woman said, "I Name you TrueHeart; and by your Name, I bid you to hear me."

Although A'Gal-Zanna tried to stop her, Liselle stared at the woman and wondered. She looked familiar, achingly so. But she had no recollection of her.

"TrueHeart, can you defeat the presence within you?" Liselle continued to stare at the stranger and wonder. Defeat the presence? Why did she ask? What did she know? Was such a thing possible?

These questions troubled The Dark One, too. She sifted through Her host's ruined memory in search of clues, but like Her host, found only powdered rubble. Threatened now as well as annoyed, She strove to complete Her expansion with all Her preternatural strength.

The pressure became too much for Liselle; the stubborn core of her essence began to swirl away. Unable to deny or delay her impending extinction any longer, she used the last of her crumbling Will to answer the woman who knew her Name. She twisted her head left, then right; and then fell utterly still.

Lathwi understood.

"Now!" she urged her tanglemates.

The dragonets surged toward the diagram, slipping and sliding and honking with surprise as the smooth stone floor played havoc with their still blunt claws.

A'Gal-Zanna laughed: a fell sound rendered more dreadful by the injury to Her jaw. That black-clad woman must be mad! As limited as Her powers were at the moment, She could easily repel a gaggle of squawking newborns. And once She retrieved Her talismans, She would slaughter everyone in sight.

What a delicious way to celebrate Her return!

But the dragonets did not attack Galza like She thought they would. They went for the scattered talismans. A calico seized Her third eye in its jaws, the grey one nabbed a spur. A'Gal-Zanna swept them away with Her Will, but all except one cinnamon-coloured runt got back up and charged again. Intent on beating the little marauders to the rest of Her talismans, A'Gal-Zanna sank to Her knees.

Lathwi let Pawl's hunting knife fly then. Guided by her indomitable Will, it plunged into Galza's left eye and buried itself to the hilt.

Disbelief chasmed across the face that had once belonged to Liselle. Then her jaw fell open and a sound boiled forth: no human cry, but an ear-splitting howl of frustration, rage and perpetual hate. An instant later, the already dead body pitched backward and onto the floor. As skull-bones cracked, the scream subsided; and a stunned silence overcame Taziem's caves.

334

CHAPTER 26

Lathwi stared at Liselle's corpse, half-expecting it to get *up* again. When it remained motionless, she expelled the breath that she'd been holding and bowed her head. A thought came to her then, honey-thick with disapproval.

"You should not have risked the younglings. Shygyre is gone." The ache in her heart swelled to dragon-sized dimensions, but she did not wish to appear weak in Taziem's eyes, so she flashed her the mental equivalent of a shrug. *"If I had not risked them, they would all be gone now. You know as well as I do that Galza had to be killed."*

"You could have tried to kill Her before the younglings charged," Taziem countered.

Lathwi turned around to confront her mother. There were angry lights in the she-dragon's eyes, but hints of curiosity as well. Such was the way with Taziem.

"I only had one knife," she explained, "so I needed to be sure that Galza was thoroughly distracted before I threw it. Otherwise, She would have seen it coming and turned it aside with Her Will."

"Furthermore," she added, deciding to be totally honest, "I wanted to be sure that Liselle was truly gone. It was bad enough that Galza possessed her in life. She did not deserve to be possessed beyond life as well."

Taziem rumbled, then flashed Lathwi a stylized image of the heart-faced sorceress. *"She fought very hard to thwart Galza's minion. She will be remembered."*

The statement both surprised and pleased Lathwi. To be remembered by dragons was to be remembered forever. It was a most exceptional honour for a human.

"This position is beginning to grow tiresome," Taziem complained then. "How much longer am I going to be made to keep it?"

Lathwi looked at the she-dragon with a sorceress' eye, then suffered a bittersweet pang. Liselle had cast a spell like this on her once—back when Lathwi was first learning about sorcery and Wills. The remedy was transparent: remove the illusion. Lathwi did so with a bit of unnecessary flair. Taziem stepped out of her rigid pose with a grateful hiss, then turned to eye the man who had cursed her with it in the first place.

The Rogue was ringed by curious dragonets now. His eyes were unfocused, his chin was slick with drool. He whimpered when Masque poked him with a claw, but did not try to escape.

"What shall we do with him?" Taziem wondered.

Lathwi strode over to the magic-ravaged sorcerer, then grabbed him by the hair and yanked his head up so she could look past his oozing eyes and into the cesspool of his mind. This harsh treatment provoked a childish whine from him, but nothing more.

"He has lost his powers and his reason," she said, as she examined him, "but his primal instincts remain intact. And he can still feel pain." An instant later, she added, "Now I know what to do with him."

She hauled him onto his feet, then leaned in close and whispered in his ear. He gasped. His unseeing eyes widened with fear. Then he shoved her aside and went bolting out of the chamber as fast as his blighted leg would carry him. As the darkness swallowed him up, Taziem loosed an angry hiss.

"What have you done?"

"I gave him control over his limbs, then told him to run for his life."

"Why?"

Lathwi grinned, a sanguine curve of the mouth. "How old does a dragon have to be to learn how to hunt?"

Taziem bared her teeth. A terrible gleam danced its way into her eyes. She rumbled, bidding her younglings to attend her. Six heads popped up and swivelled her way.

"There is food loose in the caves," she informed them, making her imagery explicit. "If you can find it, you can eat it."

An excited squawking broke out among the younglings. A moment later, they all went stampeding after The Rogue.

As the last eager tail disappeared from the room, Lathwi strode over to Liselle's body to get her knife. It was then that she noticed that her ruddy stone and the other talismans were gone.

"Do you know what happened to Galza's tokens?" she asked Taziem, trying hard not to betray her alarm. *"Of course,"* the she-dragon replied, a smug thought which implied that Lathwi ought to know, too. *"The younglings ate them."*

"All of them?"

"Every last one. Why? Did you want them for yourself?"

"No," Lathwi replied, an emphatic denial. "I only wanted to make sure they did not get away from us. They have caused enough grief."

"They will cause no more," Taziem assured her. "Nothing can survive a dragon's digestive tract—not bones or gold or even Oma-stones."

A series of melting screams came roiling into the outer caverns then. The she-dragon rumbled, approving the sounds, but Lathwi did not appear to hear them. She was staring at Liselle's corpse again; and her expression was as guarded as her thoughts.

"What will you do with her?" Taziem asked.

"There is one in Compara who would have been her Chosen. I will take her to him so he may at last take care of her."

"Where will you go after that?"

Lathwi did not answer. Her form was shimmering like a moonlit lake, growing longer and denser and hard to behold. An excited shiver worked its way up from the tip of Taziem's tail; and by the time it reached her wings, she was staring at a white-faced dragon with blue eyes.

"You must come back and teach me how to do that some day," she said, thinking of all the tricks she could then play on Bij.

"I will," Lathwi told her. *"Some day."* Then, with a gentleness that she had seldom shown the living woman, she picked Liselle's body up and carried it out to the landing. As she unfurled her wings, she glanced at Taziem one last time.

"You know my Name," she said.

"And you know mine."

The blue-eyed dragon launched herself into the sky then. As she winged her way toward the horizon, her mother watched on in amazement and marvelled at fortune's peculiar ways.